The Stranger at the Palazzo d'Oro

BOOKS BY PAUL THEROUX

FICTION

Waldo
Fong and the Indians
Girls at Play
Murder in Mount Holly
Jungle Lovers
Sinning with Annie
Saint Jack
The Black House
The Family Arsenal
The Consul's File
A Christmas Card
Picture Palace
London Snow
World's End
The Mosquito Coast
The London Embassy
Half Moon Street
O-Zone
My Secret History
Chicago Loop
Millroy the Magician
My Other Life

Kowloon Tong
Hotel Honolulu
The Stranger at the Palazzo d'Oro

CRITICISM

V. S. Naipaul

NONFICTION

The Great Railway Bazaar
The Old Patagonian Express
The Kingdom by the Sea
Sailing Through China
Sunrise with Seamonsters
The Imperial Way
Riding the Iron Rooster
To the Ends of the Earth
The Happy Isles of Oceania
The Pillars of Hercules
Sir Vidia's Shadow
Fresh Air Fiend
Dark Star Safari

The Stranger
at the
Palazzo d'Oro

....

AND OTHER STORIES

....

Paul Theroux

HOUGHTON MIFFLIN COMPANY

BOSTON • NEW YORK

2004

For information about permission to reproduce selections from
this book, write to Permissions, Houghton Mifflin Company,
215 Park Avenue South, New York, New York 10003.

Visit our Web site: www.houghtonmifflinbooks.com.

Library of Congress Cataloging-in-Publication Data
Theroux, Paul.
The stranger at the Palazzo d'Oro and
other stories / Paul Theroux.
p. cm.
The stranger at the Palazzo d'Oro — A Judas
memoir — Pup tent — Seeing Truman — Scouting for
boys — An African story — Disheveled nymphs.
ISBN 0-618-26515-5
I. Title.
PS3570.H4S77 2004
813'.54 — dc21   2003050893

Printed in the United States of America

Book design by Robert Overholtzer

MP 10 9 8 7 6 5 4 3 2 1

Portions of this book have previously
appeared, in different form, in *Granta*.

April is the cruellest month, breeding
Lilacs out of the dead land, mixing
Memory and desire, stirring
Dull roots with spring rain.

—T. S. ELIOT, *The Waste Land*

Contents

The Stranger
at the
Palazzo d'Oro

I

THIS IS my only story. Now that I am sixty I can tell it. Years ago, when Taormina was a village most travelers avoided in the summer, because of the heat, I sought it out, to feel the heat. Heat was everything in the poem "Snake," that D. H. Lawrence wrote in Taormina. Great names and associations also mattered to me, which was another reason, lingering in the steep town of old stone and fresh flowers, I stopped by the Palazzo d'Oro, loving that name too. Beyond the gilded cast-iron faces on the spiked gateway to the terrace, I saw a handsome couple, a golden-haired woman and a beaky-faced man, dressed in loose white clothes enjoying a big Italian lunch. I imagined being seated at that table. I thought, I want your life — the sort of envious wish I was too young to know was like asking for my undoing.

I always excused my waywardness by saying that I was poor and so was forced into this or that course of action. The truth was that I enjoyed taking risks. I should have been ashamed. It was not that I behaved badly, rather that I was secretive and seldom straight. I was creative in my lies. Saying I was poor was one of them.

The world knows me as a hero. My paintings are like good deeds, the pictorial record of my lifetime of travel, the nearest thing to the pharaonic "profession of sinlessness" — the negative confession: all my arduous journeys, the discoveries I made my own, the arrivals I turned into triumphs. At a time when celebrated painters stayed home and splashed paint or used slide rules, or glued feathers and broken pots to canvases, painted stripes and circles and whole large monochromes, I was in distant lands painting portraits of people in their landscapes — ornery people, kind people, all of them native, none of them posing. I have had my detractors, professional critics mostly, who carped about the explicitness of my line, my clear figures, their sideways glances, but I believe that what rankles are my other figures, the profits I have made. Yet my patrons and collectors have defied the belittlers and chosen to travel with me through my pictures, my exotic views, the many series available in signed lithographs, *Pictures of India, Pictures of China, Pictures of Africa* — not single pictures but narratives.

When I am disparaged for painting "accessible" pictures I say that my strength is storytelling. What I have never said is that the most resourceful storytellers are the ones who avoid a particular story, the only story the teller has; the very avoidance of it is the reason for the other, wilder tales. The source of fantastic narratives is often this secret, the fantasist using a concealment to hint at the truth, but always skirting the fundamental story. Or the stories may not be bizarre, but numerous and various, for the same reason. This is one ritual of creation. As I say, this is my only story.

Such a traveler as I was could easily have found a way to return to Taormina, but I steered clear of the place, even when I was traveling in Sicily. I resisted, yet I knew that the time would come, when I was myself turning sixty. Not old — though everyone else seemed to think so.

At fifty, I had painted a birthday self-portrait of my watchful face, and the subtle suggestion of the haunted eyes only made people praise it for seeming beatific. Ten years passed. But sixty was not an occasion for that sort of self-portrait. I needed to travel, and in the same spirit as before, for in travel I became someone else — in this case, in my birthday month, the person I had once been, a boy of twenty-one, in the hot summer of 1962, when I found myself in Sicily, being rebuffed by a girl I liked, Fabiola, a principessa. "It means nothing here!"

The title meant something to me, though. I had followed her to Palermo from Falconara and Urbino — more lovely names — but she was home in Sicily and it was forbidden in those days for her to be seen with me unless we were engaged, or nearly so. She had to be my *fidanzata*, I had to tell her I loved her, otherwise she was a slut, she said. Maybe she suspected I was not very serious, just a brash, too young American (Fabiola was twenty-three) searching for the Italy of Fellini and Antonioni, hungry for experience. I told her I was an existentialist — it was a popular word in the Italy of 1962 — because it was a convenient way of avoiding responsibility. I was intense, impatient, game, and wary of being trapped. These qualities made me a loner. Fabiola wanted romance, she wanted me to adore her. *Love me,* was the appeal in her eyes, *love me and I will give you what you want,* but to me love was surrender, love was death. In those days I swore I would not utter the word.

And then I had my life, forty years more, the ones that matter most: the years of family and struggle, love and acclaim, but with enough disillusionment and loss to show there would be worse to come in the tapering off nearer my death.

In Sicily again, a man of sixty, I retraced my steps, avoided the good hotels, looked for traces of my earlier self. Palermo was a more Americanized place these days, and freer — women using cell phones, men in blue jeans, even the nuns looked somewhat

secular in their dowdy dresses. I called Fabiola, but she was unknown at the only address I had for her and she was not in the
phone book. I prowled and looked for the past and found very
little that related to the frugal boy I had been, moving lightly
through Sicily.

I took the train to Messina, changed for the express to Catania,
got off at Taormina-Giardini, climbed the hill, as I had done
many years before, glad for this chance to test my memory,
sketching in my head, mumbling as I do when I want to remember.

Hotels stand up better than restaurants. The Palazzo d'Oro on
the Via Roma was surrounded by newer and fixed-up places yet
it had aged well. I was relieved to see that I could happily stay
there again, to recall the old days, and do some serious sketching, and write my story — making this visit a significant occasion, or, more than that, a kind of ceremony, a ritual to mark the
passing of all those years.

Walking by the pool, a new pool, I saw a girl of no more
than seventeen, with short untidy sun-struck hair, sprawled on a
striped chaise longue. She was topless, small breasts with no
weight in them. Her legs were open, her hands behind her head,
a Balthus fantasy but only for seconds, for she crossed her legs,
yanked on her knees, rolled over, plucked at her gold bikini bottom like a sprite, half innocent half wicked, or else just a bored
teenager. I was tormented. Because she did not see me I stared,
and could not take my eyes off her — breasts so small and firm,
nipples so pale they made her seem chaste.

I was led past her by a room boy in a robe and a white skull-
cap — Arab, a *Moro* in the Palazzo d'Oro.

The young sunbathing girl reached for a glass of pink liquid
and drank. I watched her drinking, loving the motion of her
neck muscles working in a pulsating way, her throat filling as she

swallowed. I imagined that she was looking at me over the rim of her glass.

In 1962, on my way from the Via Fontana Vecchia, where Lawrence had lived and — I guessed — written his lovely poem of sorrow and self-accusation, I had lingered by the wall of this palazzo. I was struck by the name, the images of the gilded faces, and, still looking around, the sight of the man and woman at lunch. I had wanted to stay but had no money for anything except one of those very dirty places on the road below the town, between the public beach and the railroad track. I was hot and tired, having traveled third class on the train, a slow train, and at just this time of year, in the heat.

In those days I traveled with one change of clothes. I wore a seersucker jacket over a T-shirt, and a pair of jeans. My bag was so small I didn't look like a traveler but rather like a student on his way from school with books and papers. With so little to carry it was easy for me to explore and make sudden decisions: to stay, to move on, to kill time at the beach, to hitchhike, or to sleep third class on the night train to save money. It was not until nightfall that I would decide where to stay, and now it was hardly midmorning in Taormina. I imagined writing someone — perhaps the Principessa, Fabiola — a letter on the headed notepaper of the Palazzo d'Oro. I saw a sheet of it on a menu posted near the terrace — the two gilded Moorish faces, and palm trees, a glimpse of Africa in Sicily.

From my room, I saw my younger self entering the hotel, crossing the hot terrace, passing the wall of yellow glazed tiles, ordering a cup of coffee and asking for a glass of water, pretending to be poised.

And where that half-naked teenager lay on the chaise longue there had been an awning — few people sunbathed in Sicily then

— and under it the couple near the pool wall, like lovers, wearing identical Panama hats, the woman in white, and wearing lovely lacy gloves, intent in conversation, no one else around.

From a distance — and I had been a little bleary-eyed from my sleepless night — the golden-haired woman looked young and attractive — mid-thirties, maybe — and the man seemed more attentive than a husband. I took them to be lovers for the way he beseeched her, imploring her, looking helpless, the way Fabiola beseeched me. The meal set up in front of them looked delicious — the sorts of salads and antipasti served at lunch in the Italian summer, yellow tomatoes, red lettuce, sliced meat, lobster tails, prawns, olives and pickles, artichokes and palm hearts, fruit drinks in tall glasses, and this lovely day, the blue sea in the distance, a rising trickle of gray smoke from Etna, and the squat thick-walled palazzo. The two people looked magical in their white hats under the big green awning.

Thinking again, *I want your life,* I envied them with an envy I could taste on the roof of my mouth, something unfamiliar and corrosive. They had no idea how lucky they were, and I tried to imagine displacing them, being at their table myself this fine Sicilian noon, eating lunch, with nothing else to do, with a room in this amazingly named hotel. My curiosity made me bold. I got up and strolled nearer to them as I made sketches of the glazed plates and the flower vines on the wall and the beautiful blue sea beyond the tops of the poplars and cypresses. Often bystanders said to me, "Let's see," asking to look at my sketches.

The couple said nothing and, closer to them, I realized that only the sea was real.

The sun's glare had been kind to the woman, had smoothed and simplified her features. I could see from her lips that she was older than I had guessed, a tight white fish face and bleached-blond hair, a very skinny figure — a girl's stick figure, somewhat starved. But I was still intrigued by her hat and her sunglasses and her strawlike hair and her gloves of lace. The man was scribbling on a pad, the meal was untouched and probably inedible.

I was on the point of walking back to my table when the man said hello and beckoned. The way he crooked his finger, and his intonation, told me he was foreign, not Italian.

"We want to see your sketches," he said.

Just as I had guessed, yet I hesitated.

"You'll have to show us, you know," he said with the sort of confidence I associated with wealthy people. "There is no one else here."

In the moment of saying okay I was betrayed by my first feeling, my sense of *I want your life*. I had seen these people as lovers enjoying a romantic lunch. I could not have been more mistaken. I knew at once that I was wrong and it seemed to me that I would have to pay for this envious feeling of finding them attractive and wishing to displace them and wanting what they had. I approached their table feeling disappointed and yet compelled to follow through, for I had nowhere else to go.

"Have you just come to Taormina?"

"I've been here awhile," I said, being evasive. "In town doing some drawings and a little literary research. D. H. Lawrence lived up the road in the Via Fontana Vecchia in the 1920s."

Ten minutes at Lawrence's house, looking for a water trough to sketch. I could not tell them the truth, or give anything away: the hard seats of third class, the long walk up the hill, the stink of cigarettes called Stop, were just too awful.

"His wife was German," the woman said in a correcting tone. "Thomas Mann was also here."

The statement, and her accent, told me she was German, but she said nothing else. The man, who was swarthy and yet fine-featured, with a thin face and a beaky nose, did the rest of the talking, praising my sketches and asking questions. I answered him untruthfully to put myself in a good light.

I had been wrong about their ages. A twenty-one-year-old knows nothing of time and cannot assign anyone an age — thirty-eight is old, forty is hopeless, fifty is ancient, and anyone older than that is invisible. Desirable and ugly are the only criteria. The German woman was not ugly, but in attempting to appear young she seemed faintly doll-like and trifled with.

Yet they were obviously rich, and the rich to me then were like the mythical El Dorado: a race of golden giants, powerful in every way, even physically superior, protected, able to buy anything, confident, speaking a special language and, from their towering position in their palaces, regarding only each other. It was painful for me to think about the couple in this way. I tried to forget how limited my choices were. And how, if I were to succeed in life, I would have to penetrate that palace and inhabit it — not lay siege to its fortifications but insinuate myself, creep in through a mouse hole, use the postern.

The woman seemed to be smiling to herself and presenting her profile to me, her chin slightly lifted on a lacy finger of her gloved hand.

"We were just talking about opera, what a shame it is that the Teatro Greco here has no production," the man said.

This was a helpful cue. I had no material resources but I was well read, I spoke Italian, and in my determined self-educating mission I had tried to know as much as possible about opera.

I said, "I've just seen a new production of *Otello* in Urbino."

"The common people love Mr. Green," the woman said.

"Not Verdi's *Otello*," I said.

This seemed to perplex them, which pleased and emboldened me.

"Rossini's *Otello*. They did the version with the happy ending."

"French opera is more to my taste," the man said.

"I wish Bizet had succeeded with *Salammbô*."

"There is no *Salammbô*," the woman said, a querulous tone of literal-minded contradiction pinching her face.

"He never finished it. Flaubert wouldn't let him."

Was what I was saying true? Anyway they believed it. They were listening closely to my cleverness. Instead of dealing with Wagner or Verdi, whom they would have known well, I made myself seem intelligent by mentioning obscure works. We would take the others for granted — though I knew very little, just the records, not the performances. Removing the great works from the discussion deflected their scrutiny. I was young but rich in ruses.

"I get tickets for Glyndebourne every year."

Saying this, the woman revealed that the man was neither husband nor lover. Otherwise she would have said "we." The man was a flunky or a friend.

"We have very good opera where I come from. In Boston. And at Tanglewood, in Lenox."

"I have heard so," the man said.

This was to impress them with the fact that they were dealing with a bright and cultivated person.

"You're right — it's a shame they don't use the Greek theater here for operas."

"Well, they do of course," the man said.

Fearing that I had revealed my ignorance, I risked another generalization and said, "I mean, this summer," and the man nodded, and I knew I was flying blind.

"The seats are so hard," the woman said. "I refuse to sit on marble stone. I want a soft chair in a balcony!"

Spoiled bitch, you're supposed to think, but I admired her for her forthrightness and for being uncompromising. No Greek ruins for me, forget the ancient stone benches of Siracusa and Taormina.

We talked some more — trivialities about the heat, the blinding brightness of noon, the wildflowers, the emptiness, the absence of visitors.

"It is why I come," the woman said.

Again that "I" told me she was in charge and the man a mere accessory.

"Have you had lunch?" the man said with a gesture that took in all the plates of food. "You are welcome to help yourself."

I was ravenous yet I said, "No, thank you." I was too proud to accept, and anyway, by my seeming restrained and polite they would be reassured and would respect me more.

"You will forgive us?" the man said, and picked at some salad. The woman, still with her gloves on, and using a silver tool, pierced olives from a dish of antipasto and nibbled them.

"Such a pleasure to talk with you," I said, and excused myself. I went back to my table, my empty coffee cup, and opened my sketchbook again and indulged myself in shading a sketch I had done.

The couple conferred some more. Then the woman got up slowly and, in a stately way, for her white dress was long and lovely, she left the terrace, shimmering in the dazzling light. The man paid the check — the Italian business, the saucer, the folded bill, the back and forth, and more talk with the waiter. When the waiter left, saucer of money in hand, the man came to my table.

He looked at me intently and then smiled in a familiar way, as though he knew me well.

"I have arranged for you to stay here," he said. "I was once a student" — I had started a polite protest — "no, no. It will be pleasant to have you as a neighbor. We will talk."

He had read me perfectly.

2

So, within an hour of happening past the Palazzo d'Oro, I was installed in a room with a view of the sea, seated on my own balcony, in a monogrammed bathrobe, eating a chicken sandwich, clinking the ice in my Campari and soda, the breeze on my face. I had been transformed: magic.

"This is my guest," the man had said — I still did not know his name — and he asked for my passport, which he glanced at. "Mr. Mariner requires a double room with a view of *il vulcano*. Put it on my bill."

A moment later he gave me his name but in an offhand way: "You can call me Harry" — as though the name was fictitious; and it was. His name was Haroun.

When I tried to thank him he put a fingertip to his lips and then wagged the finger sternly. There was no mistaking this gesture. He made this admonishing finger seem a very serious instrument, if not a weapon.

"This can be our secret," he said. "Not a word to the Gräfin."

That gave me pause, yet I had no choice but to agree, for I had accepted the free room. To ease my conscience, I told myself that if I wished I could leave at any time, as impulsively as I had come; could skip out and be gone, as I had left Fabiola, the Principessa. Even so, I felt that in acquiring the room I had been triumphant, it was a windfall, and there was a hint of mystery about Haroun that I liked, a conspiratorial tone that was comic and pleasing. And Gräfin? I supposed Gräfin was the woman.

"Not a word to anyone," I said.

"The Gräfin is not my Gräfin, as you probably think, but she is a very dear friend. I have known her for years — we have been absolutely everywhere together."

This was in my room — he had followed me there with the

room boy — not a *Moro*, then, but a square-shouldered Sicilian boy, and Haroun was sort of eyeing the boy as he spoke to me, sizing him up as the boy bent and stretched, putting my bag on a small table and adjusting the fastenings of the shutters.

"Look at the skin these people have!"

He pinched the boy's cheek and arm, like someone choosing cloth for a suit. The boy, preoccupied with the shutters, smirked and allowed it.

"Never touch their women," Haroun said. "That is the iron rule in Sicily. They will kill you. But their boys — look what skin!"

Now it seemed to me that the boy knew he was being admired, and he stepped away from Haroun and said, "*Bacio la mano*" — I kiss your hand — and somewhat giddy with this byplay, Haroun snatched the boy's hand and pressed some folded money into it.

"*Ciao, bello,*" Haroun said to the boy, smiling as he watched him leave my room and shut the door.

Alone with Haroun I felt more uncomfortable than I had when the boy was there — the compromising sense that it was not my room, that in accepting it I had accepted this small, dark, smiling man who I felt was about to importune me. But from what he said next I realized that his smile meant he was remembering something with pleasure. Sometimes people smile to show you they are remembering something happy in their past.

"The Gräfin is such a dear friend," he said. "And we have our secrets too."

Something in the way he spoke made me think the woman was giving him money.

"She is a fantastic person," he said. "Wonderful. Generous."

Then I was sure of it.

"And she is very sensitive." The way he stood in the room, lingering and looking around, conveyed the impression that the room was his — and of course it was. "All her noble qualities have given her a great soul and a fantastic capacity for friendship. I think somehow you guessed that about her."

I had guessed that she was a rich, difficult woman who was not interested in anyone but herself, yet I smiled at Haroun and agreed that she was a sensitive person with a great soul. In this room I felt I had to agree, but agreeing was easy — this was small talk, or so I thought.

"I can see that you understand things quickly," he said. "I admire you Americans, just showing up in a strange place with your passport in your pocket and a little valise. Fantastic."

He saw everything. He made me shy.

"Probably you want to rest," he said. "We usually have a drink on the terrace at seven. This is a lovely place. I think you will enjoy it. *Ciao* for now."

Was that an invitation? I didn't know, but it did seem to me that I was part of a larger arrangement that at the moment I could only guess at. After he left I ordered the sandwich and the Campari and soda and tried not to ponder what the larger arrangement was. I told myself: I can leave tomorrow, just as I came, on the train to Messina. Being hard up in Italy didn't frighten me — people were friendly, strangers could be hospitable, I spoke Italian, I was personable — well, this hotel room was proof of that.

I guessed that something was expected of me. I did not know what, but something.

Because I had not been specifically invited, I did not appear on the terrace until nearly eight o'clock. The woman Haroun called Gräfin was holding a glass of wine and looking at the lights on the distant sea — fishing boats — and Haroun raised his hand in an effortless beckoning gesture that had a definite meaning: the languid summons of a person who is used to being obeyed. The woman herself, her head turned to the bobbing lights, seemed uninterested in me.

"Look, Gräfin, our friend the American."

I was convinced now that he was a man of calculation. *This can be our secret* and *We usually have a drink on the terrace at seven.* I was glad I saw this conspiratorial gleam in his eye, for it made me wary enough to listen for meanings and look for motives.

I joined them. Gräfin — a name I first heard as "Griffin" — still showed no interest in me. She sipped her wine, she might have been a little drunk — the way drunks can seem to concentrate hard when they are just tipsy and slow, with a glazed furrow-browed stare. I studied her smooth cheeks. She was German, he was not. She looked like a ruined and resurrected queen — someone who had suffered an illness that had left a mark on her beauty, not disfiguring it but somehow fixing it, aging it.

We talked. Haroun asked me questions which, I felt sure, were intended to impress Gräfin, or any listener — sort of interviewed me in a friendly appreciative way, to show me at my best, to establish that I had been an art teacher at the selective school inside the ducal palace at Urbino, that I was traveling alone through Sicily, that I was never without my sketchbook, which was a visual diary of my trip, that I was knowledgeable about artists and books — "Raphael was born in Urbino, he says."

"I know that," Gräfin said. She always spoke with a lifted chin, into the distance, never faced the listener, never faced the speaker for that matter. "I prefer Tiziano."

"Would that be Titian?"

She didn't answer. "I have one, like so, not large." But her slender measuring hands made it seem large. "However, yes, it is a Tiziano."

"You bought it yourself?"

"It has been in my family."

"And your Dürer," Haroun said.

"Many Dürer," Gräfin said.

"I'd hate to think what those would have cost," I said, and as soon as the words were out of my mouth I regretted them for their vulgarity.

"Not much," Gräfin said. She was addressing a large glazed salver hooked to the brick wall of the terrace. "Very little, in fact. Just pennies."

"How is that possible?"

"We bought them from the artist."

I saw Albrecht Dürer putting some dark tarnished pfennigs into a leather coin purse and touching his forelock in gratitude as he handed over a sheaf of etchings to one of Gräfin's big patronizing ancestors.

Gräfin had a brusque uninterested way of speaking — but saying something like We bought them from the artist was a put-down she relished. She never asked questions. She seemed impossible, spoiled, egotistical, yet strong; in a word, she was the embodiment of my notion of wealth. I did not dislike her, I was fascinated by her pale skin and soft flesh in this sunny place, by her full breasts and pinched doll's face and bleached hair and plump disapproving lips, even by her posture — always facing away from me. I saw her as incurious and something of a challenge.

"I am hungry," she said to Haroun. "Will you call the boy?"

This was also interesting, the fact that she spoke to him in English when I was present. When they were alone, I was sure they spoke German. The English was for my benefit — I didn't speak a word of German. But why this unusual politeness, or at least deference, to me?

Haroun snapped his fingers. The waiter appeared with two menus. Gräfin opened hers and studied it.

Holding his menu open but looking at me, Haroun said, "Have you seen the olive groves?"

I said no, feeling that it was expected of me, to give him a chance to describe them.

"They are quite magnificent," he said, as I had expected. "We are driving out tomorrow to look at one near Sperlinga. You know Sperlinga? No? Perhaps you would like to accompany us?"

"Morning or afternoon?" I didn't care one way or the other, but I did not want to seem tame.

"It must be morning. Afternoons here are for the siesta," he said.

"I'd love to go with you."

"We leave at eight."

"I want the fish," Gräfin said. "Grilled. Tell them no sauce. Small salad. No dressing."

She snapped her menu shut. So, in that way, I was informed that I was not a dinner guest. But once again I saw how, in the manner of trying to appear offhand, Haroun was manipulating the situation. Gräfin was indifferent, though, or at least made a show of indifference. She did not look up as I excused myself and left. My audience was over. I had been summoned, I had been dismissed.

I walked through the upper town, from the Piazza Vittorio Emanuele down the Corso Umberto Primo, where most of the shops and bars were, the ones that catered to foreigners.

Down an alleyway I found a bar where some older Sicilians sat and smoked, listening to a soccer match being loudly broadcast on a radio. It reminded me of a religious ritual, the way they were seated around the radio with its glowing dial. I sat near them, ordered a bottle of beer and a panino, and I stewed, resenting the fact that my little discussion had taken place at Haroun and Gräfin's table, and that I had been sent away. My frugal meal was proof that I had very little money and because of that was at the beck and call of these people. So what, I told myself; I could leave at any time: just board the train at the foot of the hill and head east, where life was cheap and cheerful. And somewhere in Palermo, Fabiola was yearning for my love.

Haroun was in the lobby the next day before eight. Gräfin was already in the car. These people were prompt. I imagined that their wealth would have made them more casual. Haroun greeted me and directed me to the front seat, where I would sit next to the driver. This made me feel like an employee, one of Gräfin's staff. But Haroun, too, seemed like an employee.

We drove through Taormina and down the hill, took a right on the main road, and then another right after a short time, heading upward on a narrow road into the island.

"Bustano," Haroun said. Then he conversed with the driver in a language that was not Italian — and not any language I recognized.

Haroun laughed in an explosive way, obviously delighted by something the driver had said.

"He said it will take more than one hour," Haroun said. "Because, he says, this is a *macchina* and not a flying carpet."

"What is that language?"

"Arabic. He is originally from Tunisia."

"The *Moro* of the Palazzo d'Oro."

"Exactly."

"How do you know Arabic?"

Gräfin said, "Harry knows everything. I am lost without this man."

"I can speak English. I can write English," Haroun said. "I can write on a 'piss' of paper. I can write on a 'shit' of paper." He made a child's impish face, tightening his cheeks to give himself dimples. He tapped his head. *"Ho imparato Italiano in una settimana. Tutto qui in mio culo."*

"Now he is being silly."

"Where did you learn Arabic?"

"Baghdad," he said. "But we didn't speak it at home. We spoke English, of course."

"You're Iraqi?"

He winced at my abrupt way of nailing him down, and rather defensively he said, "Chaldean. Very old faith. Nestorian. Even my name, you see. And my people . . ."

"He is German," Gräfin said, and patted his knee as though soothing a child. "He is now one of us. A wicked German."

Iraq then was an exotic country which had recently overthrown its king and massacred his whole family, but Baghdad a rich cosmopolitan city, colorful and busy, full of banks and socialites, not the bomb crater it is now.

"Ask him anything." Gräfin's hand still rested on Haroun's knee. She was looking out the window at a village we were passing, near Randazzo, on the mountain road, a cluster of cracked farmhouses, one with black lettering that had faded but was readable on the side, a pronouncement in Italian.

I pointed to the lettering. "What does that say?"

Without hesitating, Haroun said, "'Do not forget that my' — genitori is 'parents' — 'were farmers and peasants.' It was put there long ago."

"Who said it? Why is it there?"

I had been through this in another village with Fabiola; she had sheepishly explained these old Sicilian slogans.

"Mussolini said this. It is from the war."

"You see?" Gräfin said with a mother's pride, and for the first time showed an interest, turning to read the peeling slogan on the cracked stucco wall of the ancient farmhouse. She turned to me and said, "It is so charming how they leave the words there!"

"Fascisti," Haroun said.

"Even fascisti can be sentimental," Gräfin said.

"What's the capital of Bali?" I asked Haroun, to change the subject.

"Denpasar," he said. He folded his arms and challenged me with a smile.

I was thinking how, when fluent foreigners uttered the name of a known place, they left the lilt of their suppressed accent on it.

"I sailed there once on my boat," Gräfin said.

"Your famous boat," Haroun said.

"My famous boat."

"But that's a long way," I said.

"Not long. I flew to Singapore and joined the boat. We sailed to Surabaja. Then I went by road to Bali. I stayed some nights with a member of royalty at his palace. Djorkoda Agung — *agung* is prince. He lives in Ubud, very beautiful village of arts, and of course very dirty. The people dance for me and they make for me a" — she searched for a word, she mumbled it in German, Haroun supplied the translation — "yes, they make for me a cremation. Dancing. Music. Spicy food served on banana leafs. Like a festival. We sail to Singapore and I fly home. Not a long trip but a nice one. I love the dancing. *Ketjak!* The Monkey Dance!"

That was the most she had said since the moment I met her. It was not exactly self-revelation, but it was something — something, though, that did not invite comment or further questions. It was a weird explanation, a sort of truncated traveler's tale. She was so wealthy she was not obliged to supply colorful detail. I wanted to ask her about the cremation — I wanted to joke about it: So they killed and burned someone in your honor? — but irony is lost on Germans.

"No more questions, Haroun," I said. "You know everything."

"Where is the olives?" Gräfin asked.

We were passing a settlement signposted *Nicosia*.

"Just ahead, beyond Sperlinga." There was something anxious in Haroun's helpfulness that suggested he was afraid of her. He said, "Bustano — that is not Italian. It is from Arabic. *Bustan* is 'garden.' Caltanissetta, near here, has a place Gibil Habib. From Arabic, Gebel Gabib, because it is a hill."

"But where is the olives?" Gräfin asked again, in the impatient and unreasonable tone of a child.

The olives was what she called the place, but Bustano was not a village, it was an estate, outside the pretty town of Sperlinga — many acres, a whole valley of neat symmetrical rows of ancient olive trees, and at the end of a long driveway a magnificent villa, like a manor house, three stories of crusty stucco with a red tiled roof, and balconies, and an enormous portico under which we drove and parked.

A man appeared — not the squat stout Sicilian farmer I was used to but a tall elegant-looking man in a soft yellow sweater and light-colored slacks and sunglasses. His dark skin was emphasized by his white hair, and there were wisps of it like wings above his ears. He greeted us, and though I spoke to him in Italian — and he deftly complimented me — Gräfin and Haroun spoke to him in French, to which he replied in fluent French. I smiled and nodded and stepped aside. I understood a little of what they said, but my study of Italian had driven the French I knew out of my head. I could hear what was being suggested. The Italian olive baron was urging us in French to come inside and look around and to relax.

I said in Italian, "I need to walk a little after that long ride."

"Yes, you are welcome," the man said in English, which disconcerted me. "Over there is a little pond, with ducks. And many flowers for you. *Bellina.*"

Haroun said he would come with me. We walked to the ornamental lily pond. Haroun picked a flower and held it to his nose.

I said, "He's right. It is *bellina.*"

Haroun shrugged. "The flowers, yes. But the trees. The frantoio. The storage and cellars." He crumpled his face, which meant, *I am not impressed.* "It is not great quality. Toscano is better. But this villa is charming — very comfortable. And the Gräfin wants it. She likes the business." He made a gesture of uncorking a bottle and pouring. "'This is my olive oil. I grow it. I press it. You eat it' — she is a romantic, you see?"

He had a way, in speaking of Gräfin, of being able to turn his criticism into a compliment, which made me admire him for his loyalty.

I plucked the petals from the flower I was holding and said in a stilted way — I had been practicing the speech: "This is nice, very pleasant. And you have been very kind to me. But — forgive me if I'm wrong — I feel you expect something from me. That you are arranging something. That you want me for some purpose. Tell me."

I was glad we were outside, alone. I would never have been able to say this back in Taormina, at the palazzo, where he had made me a guest. This setting, the olive groves, made me confident.

Haroun looked away. "See how they dig and scratch the roots to fertilize the tree. Some of these trees are hundreds of years old. Maybe here in Norman times." He walked ahead of me, and he glanced back at the villa in which Gräfin had vanished with the elegant olive man.

"What is it?" I asked.

"You are very intelligent," he said. "I like that. Very quick. Bold, too, I can say."

Two things struck me about this speech. The first was that he wasn't telling me what he really felt — that my intelligence made him uneasy. Second, even then I knew that when someone complimented me in that way, he was about to ask a favor.

As a way of defying him, and taking a gratuitous risk, I told him this.

"You are my guest, so you should be a little more polite to

me," he said, laughing in a peculiar mirthless way to show me he was offended.

So I knew then that what I had said was true and that his reply was a reprimand. Given the fact that I had accepted his hospitality, I should have felt put in my place, but I resisted, wishing to feel free to say anything I liked.

He said, "What do you think of the Gräfin?"

"I don't know anything about her."

"Exactly. You are right," he said. "She is a great mystery. That is why I love her." He came closer to me. I seldom noticed anything more about Haroun than his beaky nose, yet his nose was so big and expressive it was all I needed to notice. "But when you see the Gräfin, what do you feel?"

What did this man want? I said, "I feel curious. I feel she is very nice."

"She is fantastic," he said, another reprimand. "She has everything. But do you believe me when I say to you she is lonely?"

"I believe you."

"Because you are intelligent. You can see."

"But you're her friend. So how can she be lonely?"

"That's the mystery, you see," Haroun said. "I am her friend, yes. I am also her doctor. I qualified in Baghdad, I studied more in Beirut. I went to Germany for further study. I did my residence in Freiburg. And I stayed there. The Gräfin became my patient."

We had begun to kick through the avenues between the rows of olive trees. Men were trimming the trees, lopping branches, fussing with ladders and buckets.

"A doctor can be friendly with a patient, but not intimate," he said. "So we travel, and I take care of her. But it ends there."

"What a shame," I said, hoping for more.

"But you see, even if I were not her doctor I could not help her," he said. He was looking away. "I am of a different disposition." His gaze fell upon a strapping bare-chested man with a pruning hook, and Haroun glanced back as we walked on, seeming to hold a conversation with his eyes alone, the bare-chested man, too, responding with a subtly animated and replying gaze.

"What a shame."

"It is how God made me."

"I think you want me to be her friend."

"More than friend, maybe."

"I see."

As though he too had been practicing sentences, he said, "I desire you to woo her."

The expression made me smile.

"Do you find her attractive?"

I had to admit that I did. She was pretty in a brittle old-fashioned way. She was chic, she was demanding. Yes, she was much older than me — I could not tell how much; thirty-five, perhaps — and I was twenty-one. But strangely, her age did not prejudice me against her. I was attracted to her for it, for the oddness of it. She was certainly unlike any woman I had ever met — in fact, she was a woman; I did not know any women. I had only slept with girls, the nubile, pleading, marriage-minded girls like Fabiola. What did a woman want? Not marriage. Perhaps a woman of such experience as Gräfin wanted everything but marriage, and that included debauchery, and that I craved.

"But she's not interested in me."

"Because she doesn't know you," Haroun said, and I hated him for agreeing with me.

We walked some more, Haroun steering our course toward more young men trimming the thick twisted olive trees.

"Another question," he said. "Do you find Taormina to your taste?"

"Oh, yes."

The prompt way I answered showed that I had been a little reluctant in replying to his first question — the one about her. My sudden eagerness about Taormina made him laugh.

"What is it about Taormina?" he asked.

"Taormina has existed continuously for over two thousand years and has always been beautiful. People have gone there for its beauty — great people, famous people. I want to be one of them."

"You ask me what I want," Haroun said. "I want you to be content in Taormina. I want my friend to be content. I think you can find contentment together."

I saw exactly what he meant: he was, in a word, pimping for Gräfin. Well, I was not shocked. I was pleased. I was even flattered. I liked the obliqueness that had characterized the beginning — his getting me a room at the Palazzo d'Oro. And I liked the fact that he was petitioning me, soliciting my help in performing a certain specific task, as in a fairy tale's plot. I liked his asking me to do him this favor; for his strange request gave me some power.

"You will be my guest," he said.

His way of saying that he would support me at the hotel for this romance.

"And the guest of the Gräfin too."

"What a funny name," I said.

He half smiled with a distinct alertness, as though divining through a slip I had made that I was not so bright as I appeared.

"Not a name. Her name is Sabine, but I would never call her that."

"Why not?"

He looked a little shocked, and he stiffened and said, "Because she is the Gräfin. It is her title. You would say Countess."

"From her family?"

"From her husband. The Graf."

With that revelation I was dazzled, I was lost. But before I could reply, there was a scurrying sound on the road — a boy summoning us to the house.

"If the answer is no, you must leave tomorrow," Haroun said in a very businesslike way, as though trying to conclude a difficult sale, and he started toward the house where the olive man and the Gräfin stood waiting for us.

3

The day dawned fine and clear, another Sicilian day of high skies and golden heat, and I loved everything I saw and smelled — the prickly aroma of pine needles and hot bricks, the whiff of salt water from the blue sea, the cool air on my shaded balcony, my freshly laundered clothes, the new espadrilles I had bought in town, my breakfast of fruit and coffee, my feet outstretched on the chaise longue. I was reading *Il Gattopardo*, a novel — written by a Sicilian prince — recently published, which Fabiola had given to me so that I would be encouraged to improve my Italian. I read it slowly, using a dictionary with a sort of stealth, as though not wanting to admit I needed help. I had it in mind to visit the villa mentioned in the novel, Donnafugata, another beautiful name to drop. Donnafugata was in Agrigento province, in the village of Santa Margherita di Belice. I would go on a sketching tour, doing the settings of the novel, and I even imagined buying a special sketchbook, titled "Donnafugata," and filling it with this dramatic topography. In that moment on my balcony, which was full of promise and fragrant with the Taormina morning, I loved my life.

After breakfast I walked downstairs to the terrace, where I knew the two of them would be.

"Good morning," Haroun said.

"Hello," I said with as much friendliness as I could muster, trying to look at the Gräfin's face, which of course was turned aside. She was idly examining her gloves, twisting the lacy fingers to give them a tight fit.

"You mentioned something about leaving Taormina," Haroun said.

"I changed my mind. I think I will stay awhile."

Haroun smiled, exhaled, and looked away. The Gräfin turned her big blue eyes on me with curiosity, but again peering as though she hardly knew me.

"Contessa," I said.

She shrugged and lifted her gloved hand again, a fan of fingers that held her attention. And while she was preoccupied I imagined kissing her, holding her head, sucking slowly on her lips, slipping my hands beneath her dress and stroking her body.

Yes, I was staying. I excused myself by claiming I was poor; not ruthless but desperate. This excuse made me untruthful, it made me willing.

Haroun had given me the impression that the Gräfin was lonely and desperate. But in spite of that epiphany on my balcony, I was myself lonely, and I was probably feeling more desperation than she had ever known.

To succeed with her I had to convince myself that I desired her. I had to make her desire me. I did desire her, yet I could see that she was not particularly interested in me. She was vain, she seemed shallow, even her most offhand remarks sounded boastful, she was certainly aloof — now I knew why: not just money, she was an aristocrat.

Gräfin was a title, not a name. I had just found out her name, but I did not know her well enough to use it when speaking to her. I was still wondering whether to address her by her formal distancing title, for it was impossible for me to use her title without feeling submissive, even groveling.

Lonely? I did not think so, nor did it seem that she needed me.

There is wealth that makes people restless and impatient and showy — American wealth, on the whole. But the Gräfin was European. Her wealth had made her passive and presumptuous and oblique, indolent, just a spender, and as a countess she seemed to me regal now, queenly, superior-seeming, slow and somewhat delicate, even fragile.

I found it hard to get her attention. That morning, pleased by my announcing that I would be staying, Haroun began to devise ways of giving me access to the Gräfin. To me, his ruses were transparent; but she was so bored and inattentive she did not seem to suspect a thing. At the beginning Haroun developed a stomach upset; later that morning he disclosed his infirmity in a solemn, self-mocking way.

"Africa is taking its revenge upon my entrails."

"What are you talking about?" the Gräfin demanded, without seeming to care about Haroun's reply.

Another obvious trait of very rich European aristocrats was their literal-mindedness, I felt: you didn't become wealthy by being witty and alliterative, or hyperbolic like Haroun. He was the Gräfin's retainer, a sort of lap dog and flunky, roles I was rehearsing for myself.

"Africa?" I said.

"*Africa comincia a Napoli,*" he said.

"What revenge?" the Gräfin asked.

"The Visigoths came here, as you know, and they engaged in systematic plunder, raping and pillaging. And I am being blamed for these misfortunes."

"How can that be so? You are Arab."

Haroun's toothy smile was a keen expression of pain. But gallantly he said, "Not an Arab, my dear, but a Christian. Chaldean. From Baghdad. We spoke English at home. My father was a distinguished merchant. He had powerful friends."

"You are not white. You are *semitisch*. Arab-speaking."

"You are speaking English, dear Gräfin, but are you an Englishwoman?"

She said to me, "He makes me tired with his arguments, but he is my doctor, so I must listen."

"I am a witch doctor," Haroun said.

"Idiot!" the Gräfin said. She hated this sort of facetiousness.

Haroun said sadly, "I am not well."

The Gräfin gave him a querying stare, as though he was a clock face showing the wrong time.

"What will I do now?" she said, twisting her gloved hands in impatience. "This cannot be so."

"I will take some medicine."

"You really are saying you are sick?" The Gräfin was indignant. "How can the doctor be sick?"

Tapping his tummy through his shirt buttons, Haroun said, "I shall improve very soon."

"What about today?"

Still, she clung to him. Hearing this exchange, I got a distinct sense of witnessing a father and daughter at odds — an indulgent father, a spoiled daughter. This did not put me off or intimidate me, nor did it diminish the desire I had for her. If she had been highly intelligent and subtle, I would have been more wary, but her diabolical girlishness was something I felt I could deal with. Besides, her air of spiteful superiority was like a goad to me; I found something stimulating in it, a kind of spirit. I saw the Countess on a stallion, galloping through gold shafts of light, smacking the big excited beast with a riding crop and digging her heels into his sweaty flanks.

"I must go to my room," Haroun said.

"You cannot leave me alone."

"Gräfin, you are not alone."

All this time they were speaking English for my benefit in this stilted way, yet the Gräfin refused to acknowledge my presence. When they were alone — I knew this from my approaches to their terrace table — they spoke German.

"Would you be so kind?" Haroun said to me. "The Gräfin will need some things from the town. A particular shop near the station."

"Mazzarò?"

"Yes, down there."

"What things?"

The Gräfin behaved as though the question was inappropriate. She pouted and looked annoyed. In her role of little helpless girl she refused to make things easier by naming the things she wanted.

"Cosmetics, newspapers, some chocolate, a fruit drink, bottled."

"Maybe the hotel could send someone."

"You see?" the Gräfin said to Haroun. "He does not want to help."

"I do want to help," I said.

"The boys at the hotel are careless. They hold the chocolate all wrong. They melt it in their hot hands. How can I eat it?"

Whatever else I did, I would not bring the Countess melted chocolate.

Haroun said, "You will assist?"

"Of course," I said. "I'll go right away. But I will need a list. I mean, what kind of fruit drink?"

Haroun took out a prescription pad and wrote the shopping list on it while the Gräfin looked away, seemingly preoccupied — with what? I could not imagine what was in this woman's mind. She was like another species: I did not discern a single thing we had in common. The paradox was that this sense of difference made me desire her, but not in a way I had ever felt toward a woman. Though I did not fully formulate the thought at the time, I wanted to dominate her, and I saw that our difference gave me an advantage. It was true that I knew nothing of aristocracy, but I was astute enough to understand that she knew absolutely nothing of me or my background. I also guessed that her wealth had made her complacent and unsuspicious — Haroun ran all her errands, like this one he was foisting onto me.

The shopping list, which I came to see as a young girl's ritual list, was very specific: mascara, a copy of today's *Bild Zeitung*, a large bar of Toblerone ("no nuts"), and Orangina — three small bottles. She believed that the Orangina served at the Palazzo d'Oro was adulterated: her general belief was that Italians were cheats and dolts. She said that she liked Taormina because it was not popular with Italians.

I was given a string bag and directions to the lower town, Mazzarò, at the seaside — twenty minutes down, forty minutes up. I enjoyed the walk, for it reminded me of my freedom, reminded me especially that there was an adjacent world to the one in which I lived more or less like a house pet, with the same advantages and disadvantages: I was well fed and well housed but I had a master and a mistress jerking at my leash.

"This should cover it," Haroun said, handing me a sheaf of new, inky ten-thousand-lire notes. The Gräfin turned away as she always did when someone produced money, or a bill to pay.

I loved walking down the Via Pirandello into Mazzarò, by the shore below the cliffs of Taormina. The settlement was hardly more than a village and still inhabited by many fishermen. I drank an espresso at the local café, exchanged pleasantries with the owner, caught the eye of the pretty girl wiping the tables, and then set off to do the Gräfin's shopping, a task so simple as to seem unnecessary — but perhaps I was being tested? I didn't care. The weather was perfect, late August, and the life I had begun to live there was a variation of much of what I had seen in Italian movies.

In those black-and-white neo-realist movies, a solitary fellow, bright but hard up, encounters some bored wealthy people on the shores of the Mediterranean and is ambiguously adopted — the hitchhiker, the chance meeting, the stranger at the party, the wanderer. What seemed like random and apparently meaningless events were full of tension and complexity and were part of a larger design, which, as the movie advanced, became apparent. The arrangement was not American — it was European, dissolute, heavily textured, unmistakably vicious, with shocking plot twists — Fellini, Antonioni, De Sica, Rossellini. The films featured hot days, long nights, strangers, whispers, risks, excesses, and they were all tantalizingly vague. Even then I thought of these years as the era of the chance encounter. The foreign hitchhiker was picked up by the wealthy jaded Italians and from that moment his life was changed.

I had been rehearsing this sort of meeting ever since arriving in Italy. And here at last I had been chosen to play the part and was living it. I told myself: Sometimes life is like that — you fantasize so intensely that when the opportunity presents itself you know exactly what to do, repeating moves you have practiced in your head.

Haroun had given me more money than I needed for the items on the Gräfin's shopping list. Obviously he meant me to keep the change — and there was so much of it that I felt secure: money in my pocket, a lovely place to stay, all my meals paid for, and a mission — the easiest part of all, so I thought — becoming the Gräfin's lover.

That first morning of shopping I walked around Mazzarò, went to the station and watched trains arrive and depart (German girl backpackers got off, looking innocent), talked with some fishermen who had just returned with their catch, smoked some of my Stop cigarettes, and sketched on my pocket pad — the salt-white house fronts, the diving swallows, the slender shadow of a church spire like the hand of a clock, the blue sea of Odysseus and Circe, and the thought: Character is plot, incident is meaning, my Italy is an erotic painting — and I even saw the painting in its gilded frame, with a title something like *The Golden Age* or *The Stranger at the Palazzo d'Oro,* as detailed and suggestive as a Whistler, a baroque terrace on a hot day, a man directing a young virile boy to a drawing room where an older woman, golden-haired like a countess in a Grimm story and dressed in white (lingerie that resembled an elegant gown), looked at her reflection and his approach in a mirror.

Pleased with myself — I had never been happier; then, such happiness was my sense of being a man — I walked up the hill to Taormina and the palazzo.

The Gräfin was at her usual place on the terrace, staring at the sea. Her big black sunglasses made her seem not just mysterious but unknowable. Without turning, but she must have heard me place the string bag beside her chair, she spoke — the bug-eyed glasses seemed to give her an insect's voice.

"You are late."

I smirked at the back of her head and murmured, hoping that she would interpret this ambiguous noise as an apology, though it was intended as nothing of the kind. And then I saw that she had been watching me the entire time in a mirror, just as I had imagined in my large dramatic painting.

When she turned, the large collar of her loose dress slipped sideways and exposed the lovely smooth snout of a breast with its dark spongy nipple. She cupped it, caressed it rather, with her black gloved hand, but did not tuck it away. She touched it with a kind of admiration. She did not look down, though she watched my hot eyes.

"I will take an Orangina."

I lifted out a bottle and, gripping it by its potbelly, held it out to her.

"How can I drink it unless it is opened?"

I had been struck dumb by the sight of her soft plump breast in the palm of her black glove and the nipple between her lacy fingers. Not able to see her eyes because of her dense sunglasses, I could not read her expression, but it was pretty plain that she was teasing me.

A waiter had to be found, a bottle opener, a glass, a napkin, and then the presentation. By then her breast was back beneath her dress. She muttered that the glass should be served on a saucer. She took the glass without thanking me and I felt that Haroun — not I — was being mocked, and felt a stab of pity for the man.

"Let me feel the chocolate."

I had made a point of keeping the Toblerone bar out of the sun. She slipped it from its wrapper and poked it with her finger. Satisfied that it was not soft, she grunted. Then she took the newspaper and glanced at it.

"All bad news," she said with relish, and began to read.

"If there is anything else I can do for you" — and here I stepped in front of her and looked into her dark glasses, seeking her eyes — "just let me know."

Her handbag, a Sicilian raffia handbag, was in her lap. She rummaged in it, making its weave lisp and creak, and took out some large serious-looking bank notes — German — that reminded me of engraved war bonds, and without paying much attention to them, not counting them, just crumpling them and pinching them as she had the chocolate, she handed them over. Her gloved hand returned to her dress, to her loose collar, and she stroked her throat, and kept stroking to where her breast bulged, a narcissistic gesture that was also a languid form of autoeroticism.

Putting the money in my pocket, I said, "Anything you like?"

She said, "Yes," and made me alert, and then, "Tell Harry to get well."

I waited in my room, blackening a page of my sketchbook. I could only doodle; I could not read or write, knowing I might be interrupted. Yet I was not summoned again that day. I walked in the town. I swam in the pool. I emptied my pockets and counted the money they had given me, both Italian money and deutsche-marks — about forty dollars, which seemed to me quite a lot for a day's work.

At sunset I saw her again. She wore a dress I got to know well, a sort of silken crocheted gown which reached almost to her ankles and ought to have seemed rather chaste for the complete way it covered her, except that it had a loose open weave and through the interstices I could see her body, which was as white as her white dress, her skin more silken. As she approached me on the terrace, the sunset behind her, her thinly veiled nakedness made me swallow and clutch at my knees like an oaf.

She sat opposite me and said, "I will have champagne. A half bottle of the Mercier."

I felt distinctly that I was her servant. I relayed her request to the waiter, and watched her drink. She did not share. I ordered myself a glass of wine. She ate some of the chocolate. She said that she would not have anything more to eat and, grumbling about Haroun, she rose to go.

"Are you going out?"

"No. *Ich muss pinkeln.*"

I stared at her.

"I must pass water."

Later, walking down the corridor near her room, I thought I heard her laughing. No, she was sobbing. Hold on, she was laughing. God, I had no idea. That was my first day of wooing her.

The next three days were the same — the same shopping, the same waiting, the same snubs, even the same startling glimpses she gave me of her body; yet I was sure she was not teasing me. She did not expose herself because she was a flirt but rather for the opposite reason, because she was indifferent. And her aloofness was more erotic to me, because it made me a voyeur. The shame was mine.

"I am so hot," she said one afternoon, seated by the wall of fragrant flowers and vines, and she lifted the hem of her dress to her thighs, baring her legs, and I felt a catch in my throat and struggled to breathe and I could not turn away from the sight of loose panties of delicate black lace which matched her gloves.

The fact that she wore gloves was itself erotic to me — I kept seeing her stroking her bare breast with her gloved hand; and how could she have known that the way she licked her lips and drank thirstily also aroused me, that I loved watching her swallow, the strange snakelike movements of the muscles in her neck and her active throat.

In my running errands for the Gräfin, returning with the items, and hovering, and repeating "Anything else I can do?" (a question which irritated her), I kept my eyes upon her body — the smooth skin of her cheeks, her lovely lips which pursed into little pleats when she looked at the newspaper, her sharp nose and dark nostrils, her thick unnatural strawlike hair, her skinny legs, her bony feet in those Sicilian sandals. I imagined licking and nibbling her body, which was for me a sort of visual foreplay, saw myself cupping her bare breasts, each one filling my hand, and sucking on them and holding her spongy nipples lightly in my teeth. I would be hovering next to her and fantasizing about pulling out my cock, grasping her head and parting her lips and pressing it on her face and, as it thickened, helping it into her mouth. But I did nothing; I watched her, I was polite — too polite for her. Once she let the paper slip, and when I grabbed at it I brushed her arm and she recoiled and said, "Please" — meaning, "Don't touch me!"

She would sit with one finger in her mouth, looking cross, and although her sucking on this gloved finger was also erotic to me, it was just another way for her to express her impatience.

"He is a doctor! How can a doctor be sick?"

Haroun remained in his room all this time. I was certain he was faking his stomach upset, but he was resolute in sticking to his story. I told the Gräfin that he was probably improving and that we would see him any day now.

"He doesn't care about me," she said.

"He does," I said. "And I do too."

She frowned, looking insulted and intruded upon.

"How do you feel?"

"Not well," she said, still sounding insulted. As though it was none of my business. She was eating chocolate, kissing dabs of it from her lacy fingertips — and it all looked like fellating foreplay to my eager eyes.

"Maybe I can help."

She raised her head and looked at me as if I had just dropped from the sky. She said, "What could you do?"

Even though she was wearing sunglasses I could tell from the curl of her lips that she was scowling.

"Anything you suggest."

She went a bit limp just then, indicating a pause with her whole body, and her silence roused me. I was standing next to her, my tense cock level with her face. Still she did not say anything. Could she smell my desire?

She looked away and said in a little-girl voice, "Haroun brings me presents. You don't bring me presents. You don't care."

I was not insulted. I was fascinated: I fantasized that she was a small girl urging me to corrupt her. I was willing, the thought would not leave me, and I was now pretty sure that she knew what she was doing to me.

The next day, dipping into the stash of money she had given me, I bought her a bunch of flowers from the flower seller — another pretty girl — at her stall on the Corso.

"They will die unless they are put into water," the Gräfin said.

But she was pleased, I could tell, the little girl's satisfaction was as expressive as the little girl's tyranny. In the following days I brought her a pot of honey, a lump of dense amber, a chunk of lapis lazuli, a length of lace (the black intricate sort that matched her gloves and panties), a small nervous bird in a wicker cage the shape of an onion. I used the money she had given me, for there was always a wad of lire left over, but so twisted from the way she crumpled and handled it, the notes had taken on the appearance of a leafy vegetable — wilted kale, dying lettuce.

By now Haroun had emerged from his seclusion, frowning and clutching his stomach. "This is bad. When I have such an illness of the bowels it is like giving birth" — he made a face and grunted with pain — "to monsters." Then he seemed to forget his ailment and he said, "You are succeeding?"

"Of course."

The higher pitch in my voice was my inability to disguise my forcing a reply. Yet, even though I felt I was getting nowhere, it amused me to think that my efforts to woo this difficult woman were my bread and butter. Always I saw myself in a complex picture — these days it was like a full-page woodcut from a book of folktales.

The next day the Gray Dwarf went to the Wanderer's room and beckoned to him, and conducted him to a stone tablet on which was inscribed the task that had to be performed if the palace was to be released from enchantment.

I was the Wanderer of the tale, dressed in my newly bought tunic, on the parapet of the palace, perplexed because the task I had been given was to woo the Countess, who looked haughty framed in the boudoir window of her palatial tower; and if I failed, I would be banished from the palace. This was not fanciful, it was the literal truth, for I was a young wanderer, she was a countess, and the Palazzo d'Oro had once been the palace of a principessa.

If he did not succeed, he would be banished forever.

Haroun vanished again, groaning, and on the night of his disappearance, the Gräfin said she was hungry, which was her oblique way of telling me that I would be joining her at dinner. We drank wine together in silence on the terrace. As usual, I sat fantasizing, imagining myself licking her cleavage, fondling her, and in one mood dominating her and in another being her sex slave as she led me naked to her bedroom, ordering me around like a dog. I was tipsy when the food was served and I flirted with her, none of it verbal but rather a sort of overfamiliar manner of gesturing and facial expressions, behaving like a much loved and trusted waiter, which seemed the only relationship that worked with her.

She was wearing the dress I liked the most, the white crocheted one, all loops and holes and peekaboo, loose on her slender figure, her shoulder bare, her long collar affording glimpses of her breasts, which slipped against her dress as she leaned and moved, and now and then a nipple would catch and gape through a loop. Something sparkled in her hair, a small tiara, and tight around her neck was a ribbon of black velvet stitched with pearls, which she wore like a dog collar. She had applied her reddest lipstick, with a gleaming redness that made her lips swell, and in the candlelight of the Palazzo d'Oro she was beautiful to me, just like the vision of the Countess in the folktale that I was illustrating in my mind.

I desired her, I ravished her with my eyes, I gaped and I swallowed. But even as I was staring at her in this way, enjoying a fantasy of her sitting on me, demanding that I lick her, she began complaining about Haroun, and a hard and ugly expression surfaced on her features, defined by shadows.

I said, to divert her, "How about joining the natives in the *passeggiata?*"

On Saturday nights, the locals in Taormina paraded, chattering, along the Corso from the church of Santa Caterina down to the Duomo: men with men, women with women, children playing, groups of boys eyeing groups of girls. It was like a tribal rite, and sometimes foreign visitors like us, couples usually, tagged along for the fun, for it was a great noisy pleasurable parade.

"What a vulgar idea," the Gräfin said. "I would never do that."

"But I would protect you." I was still a little drunk.

She touched her fingers to her nose. She sniffed. She said, "I will go to my room."

This sounded like an invitation. I walked with her to the second floor, loving each step, following slightly behind her, anticipating what was to come, wishing with all my heart that I could cup her buttocks in my hands. I imagined that I could feel the heat of her body, the warmth of her bare skin, through the perforations in her crocheted dress.

At her room, she opened the door; in a distant second room I saw her bed, a frilly coverlet, some fur slippers. She turned briefly and said, "Good night."

I was tall enough to be able to look down into the collar of her dress and see each of her breasts, swinging slightly as she turned and then trembling as though eager to be touched.

I leaned and put my face near hers, to kiss her. Swiftly, she pushed me with her hands and made as if to bat me on my head. I jerked backward, noticing that she had exposed her breasts even more in that lunging motion.

"What do you think you are doing?" she said through gritted teeth.

Although she had only grazed me, I reacted as though I had been slapped in the face. I was so embarrassed I was off balance. I tried to explain. She rejected me, rejected my explanation. She entered her room — fled into it — and shut the door hard.

A foot-shuffle down the hall told me that someone had heard, and that bothered me more than anything.

The next day she was at breakfast as usual, looking composed, even refreshed; no sign of distress.

I said, "I am very sorry about last night."

Just a slight flash of her eyebrows indicated she had heard me, but there was nothing else, and not a word.

I said, "I'm afraid I was a little drunk."

For a moment I thought she was going to cry. Her skin wrinkled around her eyes, her mouth quivered, and she struggled with it, the effort showing on the thin pale skin of her face, and as she fought it her eyes glistened. Then the emotion passed, and though she did not say anything I knew she was angry — because of what I had tried to do, or because of my lame apology, I did not know, but I saw that afterward she turned to stone. Except for our chewing, breakfast was silent, and it was all so painful I finally crept away, feeling like the dog I was.

Haroun recovered that day. He looked brighter, he offered to run the errands, taking a taxi to the shops below in Mazzarò. He spent the day with the Gräfin and by afternoon he looked harassed and impatient. I began to surmise that in his absence he had been enjoying a dalliance with one of the boys on the staff, that he resented having to reappear for duty with the Gräfin. They spoke German that day. I was excluded, and it seemed to me that not I but Haroun was being given an ultimatum.

That night, exactly a week after I had arrived in Taormina, Haroun said, "The Gräfin is very unhappy. You must go."

"I did my best," I said.

He shook his head. He said, "No. I have failed."

It amazed me that he did not offer me any blame. He reproached himself. He sucked on his cigarette and spat out the smoke, looking rueful, hardly taking any notice of me, and not mentioning the fact that he had been paying my hotel room and all my expenses for a week, enriching me.

"She does not think she is beautiful," Haroun said.

That was not at all the impression I had. The Gräfin seemed impossibly vain about her beauty, and I knew from the casual way she moved her body and exposed herself that she was utterly unselfconscious, which was the ultimate sexuality: no matter how many clothes she wore, she was at heart a nudist.

"She is lovely," I said.

"You think so?" He looked into my face as though testing it for truthfulness.

"Yes, I do."

"She doesn't agree. She is not convinced."

Haroun stared in silence at the stars and dropped his gaze to where they sparkled on the sea.

"A lovely face," I said. "Like a Madonna."

This was a bit excessive, but what did it matter? I was on my way out. Why not leave them smiling? But Haroun liked what I said, and nodded heavily, looking moved.

"If you truly think so, you must find a way of convincing her. I will give you some days. Otherwise you must go."

4

That was my challenge: the strange task assigned by the Gray Dwarf to the Wanderer in the folktale, the young man on the parapet of the palace. The Countess was still in her tower, facing her looking glass — and in my version of this scene she had a mirrored glimpse of the young man on the balcony above her, as well as of her pretty face.

I had to succeed or else I would be banished. That was the narrative. But there was something beneath it. I had not been lying to Haroun in praising the Gräfin. I thought she was beautiful, I knew she was wealthy, she seemed like a sorceress, I desired her. I wanted badly to make love to this seemingly unattainable woman, who did nothing but insult me and reject my advances.

I did not want to think that I was in a trap. But a week in that great hotel, a week of luxury, had spoiled me — "corrupted" is too big a word; I was softened. I had become accustomed to the sweet life that, up to then, I had known only in Italian films. I was habituated to luxury, the easiest habit to acquire, like a taste for candy or for lying in a hammock, like being on a fine yacht and saying, "I don't want to get off — sail on!"

In this mood I had fantasies of inviting Fabiola, the Principessa, down to the palazzo and dazzling her with my new clothes (gift of the Gräfin) and my new friends, my vastly improved circumstances, my money. She would have been impressed, but not enough. She had a title but no money. She would have been pleased for me in her generous way, and then she would have begged me to tell her I loved her, implored me to utter the word. After that soft pitiful pleading, she would have raged at my selfishness, saying as she had said before, "This is meaningless. You will just leave me. I will be so sad!"

That cured me of wanting Fabiola to visit Taormina.

As for me, I was not ready to leave. I had begun to love waking to each hot day in the comfort of the palazzo; I had even begun to enjoy the challenge of the Gräfin, seeing myself as the youth being tested by the lovely Countess and her riddling adviser in the palace; I was enacting the struggle in the folk story. I was the young Wanderer in the woodcut, an evocative figure, black and pivotal, wearing a half-smile and looking jaunty, poised between success and failure.

I did not take her rejection personally. It was for me to solve the riddle, to find a way to make love to her. The oddest part was that I suspected that Fabiola was a virgin — and I could have had her merely by speaking the formula "I love you." The Gräfin, I gathered, had been married twice, had had many lovers, she constantly alluded to intrigues and liaisons in far-off places — and I could get nowhere with her. But the Gräfin's obstinacy did not turn me off; it made me calculating and desirous.

Haroun, confused by my lack of progress, was by turns abusive and encouraging.

Abusive: "How can you take my money and do nothing? You are selfish, in love with yourself. You pretend to be one of the elite, but I know you to be a poor American student. Oh, yes, maybe intelligent and you will amount to something, or maybe you will be like this always — taking money to look pretty, and lying to people and misleading them."

He went on in this vein but I just stared at him. He had a strong Iraqi accent overlaid by certain German mispronunciations. I found it hard to take any abuse seriously when it was spoken in such a heavy, unconvincing accent, since it all sounded faked or approximated.

"I could cut you off today and you would have to depart on a train traveling in the third-class carriage with all those dirty people, those stinking men and thieving boys, and you wouldn't think so much of yourself then!"

Stinking men and thieving boys were the object of his desire, and so this was a rather ambiguous threat.

I could bring you down, he was saying. But he was wrong, for I had arrived in Taormina with nothing and it made no difference to me if I left the same way. I could not be reduced, for I came from nowhere. I was strengthened by that thought. Having nothing to lose, I felt indestructible.

Haroun was not always so abusive. He could be the opposite, praising, highly pleased.

On one of these occasions we were on the stage of the Teatro Greco, the dramatic outdoor theater, the ancient setting within sight of Etna and the sea. In the purest gold there are many russet shades, among them the pink of the rosiest flesh, which is also the golden pink of sunset flames. From the direction we were facing it would have been easy to mistake the sunset for an eruption of the volcano, and even for the heat of a woman's glowing body. Clapping his hands he said, "You say she is beautiful. I did not command you to say that, correct? You say her face is like a Madonna — your own word. I am happy! This is very positive. It means you believe it. I did not tell you what to say."

I liked him in this encouraging mood, because he was so lively and joyous himself — inexplicable to me, but pleasant to hear someone so attached to his friend that he glowed when she was praised.

"You thought these thoughts yourself, from your own heart and brain. It is what I always hope — that people will make up their own minds and go forward."

I thanked him for understanding me.

"But the Gräfin does not understand," he said. "You are not so convincing to this wise woman."

"I'll try again."

He said, "People's lives are much the same. The rich envy the poor. The poor envy the rich. People with great riches are afraid of losing what they have. Famous people fear falling into obscurity. Beautiful women are fearful. Everyone in the world has the same fears."

Was it the setting, this Greek theater, that inspired this speech? He was strutting on the cracked marble of the ancient stage and striking poses. What he said made no sense to me, and I was on the point of arguing with him when he spoke again.

"Of growing old and ugly. Of dying."

I almost laughed at this, because I saw those fears as so distant for me here in Taormina, where I seemed just born and almost immortal. I wondered if he and the Gräfin had returned to Taormina to ease their fears.

The Gräfin was inert. Did she know that she was the subject of our strolls around the town, our whispered discussions among the ancient ruins of Taormina? But why should she care? She was above all this, she was powerful, she was resistant. Someone with little or no desire seemed very strong to me. It was hard to influence such a person. The Gräfin's rejection of me was a sign of her strength.

In the second week I saw this wooing of the Gräfin, this ritual courtship, as a battle of wills. I also believed that I was strong — at least wanted to believe it: Haroun had said what I felt deep in my heart. And for all their power, wealthy people always, I thought, had an inner weakness, which was their need to be wealthy, their fear of poverty. I had no such fear. What confused me was that I suspected them to be undeserving — lucky rather than accomplished. That luck had given them privileges, but left them with a fear of losing their luck. They were no better than me, but they were on top. I knew I was anyone's equal, even the Gräfin's. But I told myself that I lacked funds.

Even then, dazzled as I was, I felt resentful toward the people of power who had not created their own wealth. They were children of privilege. I consoled myself with the belief that privilege made them weak, and I had proof of it, for my short time in Taormina had weakened me.

The Gräfin was a countess by an accident of fate. She was someone's daughter, someone's lover, someone's ex-wife, just a lucky egg. She had done nothing in her life except be decorative. Her life was devoted to her appearance — being beautiful, nothing else. Yet what seemed shallow, her impossible vanity — her wish to be pretty, nothing else — attracted me. She was completely self-regarding, she existed to be looked at. She was utterly selfish; her narcissism made me desire her.

I wanted, in my passion for her, to discover her weakness and to awaken passion and desire in her. I feared that there might be none, that she was too powerful in other ways for these emotions. So far, I had failed to awaken even mild interest; so far, she had not asked me a single question — did not know who I was or where I came from.

I made no active attempt to woo her now. My one pass at her had been a humiliation for us both. But neither was I submissive. I continued to buy the German newspaper and the other trivial items from Mazzarò, I flunkied for her, watching her closely. I did not volunteer any information, did not allude to anything in my own life, nor did I ask her any questions. I imitated her; I put on a mask of indifference.

My coolness worked, or seemed to. I sometimes found her staring at me, silently quizzing me. But when I turned to meet her gaze she glanced away, pretending not to care.

Late one afternoon in the large crowded Piazzale Nove Aprile, some street urchins, Gypsy children perhaps, began pestering us, asking for money, tugging our clothes — the Gräfin hated to be touched. When I told them to go away, they began making obscene remarks, really vulgar ones, variations of "Go fuck your mother." I took this to be commonplace obscenity, but then it struck me that they might be commenting on the difference in our ages, the Gräfin's and mine, for she was noticeably older. That angered me and I chased them away, kicking one of the boys so hard he shouted in pain and called out, saying that I had assaulted him.

"*Di chi è la colpa?*" a shopkeeper jeered — So whose fault is that?

"Haroun never treats them that way," the Gräfin said. "I think he's a bit afraid of them."

That sounded like praise. We walked some more; still she was inscrutable behind her dark glasses.

"Or maybe he likes them too much."

Recalling their obscenities, I said, "I hate them."

She gasped in agreement, a kind of wicked thrill. "Yes."

So that was a point in my favor, my harrying the ragged children. I earned more points not long after that. The Gräfin was confounded and angered by anything mechanical. She saw such objects as enemies, they made her fearful. Breakdowns, even the chance of one, horrified her. She was very timid in the real world of delays and reverses — things she had no control over, which produced anxiety and discomfort.

We had gone back to Bustano, the olive estate, one day. She said, "Harry says he cannot accompany me, so you must come" — one of her usual graceless invitations. As she had hired a driver, I sat next to him, the Gräfin having the entire back seat to herself. We traveled in silence and I missed Haroun now. I looked for anything familiar: the village of Randazzo, the signs of old earthquake damage, the Mussolini slogan.

At Bustano we were greeted by the owner and some servants. I was not invited into the villa, though the owner (yellow shirt, pale slacks, sunglasses), with gestures of helplessness and fatalism, indicated that if it had been up to him I would have been welcome. I trembled to think what he made of me, in my white slacks and white espadrilles, my striped jersey, my new blue yachting cap. She had bought me the cap on the day of the pestering children.

"The cap now, the yacht later," she had said, and what she intended as humor sounded like mockery to me.

On the way back to Taormina, at dusk, nowhere near any village, on a mountain road beyond Troina, the car stalled at a stop sign — just faltered, chugged and coughed to a stop, like a death from black lung.

"This is impossible!" The Gräfin was angry. She repeated the sentence, sounding uncertain. She said it again, sounding fearful.

The driver fuddled with the key — the ignition key! — and stamped on the gas and hit the steering wheel with the flat of his hand. He knew absolutely nothing. He was a villager, he had grown up among animals, not machines. He treated the car as though it was an ox dawdling in its yoke, or a willful shivering dray horse. His Sicilian instinct was to whip and punch the car.

I told the Gräfin this, hoping to impress her, but she was too fearful to listen.

The car had faltered before this. When we had set out from Taormina it had been slow in starting up, and sometimes died while idling. I suspected a weak battery, perhaps a bad connection on the terminal. The engine was good enough. The car was an Alfa-Romeo TI.

"What is your name?"

"Fulvio, sir."

"Open the hood, Fulvio."

"Yes, sir."

The Gräfin said, "What do you know about these things?"

"It's a good car, the Alfa TI. You know what TI stands for?"

"Of course not."

"*Tritolo incluso.* Bomb included. *Tritolo* is TNT."

That was the joke in Palermo that year, where the Mafiosi

were blowing each other up in touring cars like this. The Gräfin did not find this the least bit funny. In fact, she was annoyed by it. "What can you possibly do?" she said, a sort of belittling challenge.

I said, "It's almost dark. We're not going anywhere. The only other living things here are goats." I could hear their clinking bells. "What do you think I should do?"

This little speech, so theatrical in its rhetoric and unnecessary detail, served to make her more afraid, which was my intention. But fear also made her nervously bossy, and she began to bully Fulvio in German-accented Italian.

"*C'era d'aspettarsela,*" he said, meaning, We should have expected this.

I said to the Gräfin, "He doesn't seem to care very much."

"We must go now to the d'Oro," she said. "I have had so much to drink. *Ich muss mal.* I must pass water."

The idea of relieving herself anywhere except in her suite at the palazzo being out of the question made me smile.

"I have pain here. *Ich muss pinkeln,*" she said, touching herself unambiguously, and I stopped smiling. "Maybe we need *benzina.*"

"We've got *benzina.*" I looked under the hood in the last of the daylight. Although the Alfa was fairly new, the engine was greasy and looked uncared-for. The battery appeared serviceable yet the terminals were gummed up with that bluey-green mold, as lovely and delicate as coral froth, that accumulates on copper wires. I could see that the clamps were loose and sticky with the same froth. This bad connection could have accounted for the faltering start. I easily twisted one terminal and lifted it off, and I guessed that it was overlaid with scum, a sort of metallic spittle.

Flicking the wire onto the terminal produced a strong audible spark. It might be just this simple, I thought. I had dealt with enough cheap old cars to reach this conclusion. A more expensive car would have baffled me, but this was Sicily, and although this was an Alfa-Romeo it held the same battery as a Fiat or an old Ford.

The Gräfin got out, and from her stamping and hand-wringing I could tell that she was bursting for a pee — or a *pinkel,* as she kept calling it in a little girl's voice. She berated the driver. I took pleasure in showing her the large greasy engine, of which she knew nothing.

I made an elaborate business of pretending to fuss and fix the engine, tweaking wires, testing wing nuts, tapping the caps on the spark plugs, all the while hoping it was just the battery. Fulvio stood just behind me, sighing, muttering *"Mannaggiai morti tui!"* — Damn your dead ancestors!

With a broken knife blade I found in a toolbox in the trunk — Fulvio seemed surprised there was a toolbox at all — I scraped the terminals clean, shaving the lead to rid it of scum. I did the same to the clamps.

Fulvio looked hopeful, though it was now fully dark, the goat bells clanking in the deep gully beside the road, the hooves scrabbling on the stony hillside.

The Gräfin said, "What shall we do? It's all his fault." She turned to Fulvio and said, *"Cretino!* Can't you learn how to fix the car?"

"I am a driver, not a mechanic," Fulvio said, and made a gesture with his hand and his fingers that can only have meant: This is irrelevant.

"You could try — you could learn," the Gräfin said.

With another rapid hand gesture, Fulvio said, "If you are born round, you cannot die square."

"This guy is useless," I said, laughing at his Sicilian folk wisdom.

"This guy is useless," she repeated, using my words approvingly. But she was still twitching, needing urgently to pee, clutching her sunglasses as though to ease her need.

"Don't worry. I'll get you back there. You'll be fine, Gräfin."

For the first time, I used her title. She looked at me with a kind of promise, a kind of pleading.

She was now a small girl. I was her father. I scraped away at the terminal for a while longer. Then I tightened the nuts on the clamp — just fuss and delay, for at last I was in control.

"Get out," I said to Fulvio, a little louder than I should have, but I wanted the Gräfin to hear.

I ostentatiously took the ignition key and sat in the driver's seat. Seeing the Gräfin beating her feet beside the car, I said, "Sit here," and indicated the passenger seat. Getting in awkwardly, made fragile by her fullness, she looked more than ever like a little girl.

I turned the key, pumped the gas, got the engine to chug, and then it roared.

"Ai!" The Gräfin clapped. "Hurry."

"Get in the back seat, Fulvio," I said.

So we drove back to Taormina sitting side by side, the Gräfin and I, Fulvio muttering *"Mannaggia"* in the back seat.

The Gräfin said, "I can hold it. *Ich muss dringend pinkeln.* I need to pass water but I like the feeling. The pressure makes a nice feeling. Hee-hee!"

She was five or six again, a *pinkel* on her mind, with her daddy in the car on the road heading home, but I was still thinking, What?

"I don't want to make an accident!"

We were going up the steep hairpin curves of the Via Pirandello to the town. She had never seemed so frail and small and helpless, so lost in the world. Gratitude did not come naturally to her, yet I could sense something like an admission of her dependency in her respectful way of addressing me.

She said, "I give you the key. You run and open the door to my suite — you are faster than me. Also, I think I can't open the door."

She was a bit breathless and almost hysterical in the same girlish way.

"This is so funny. The chauffeur is sitting in the back!"

At the hotel, she pressed the key into my hand. I hurried through the palazzo and into her suite, racing ahead of her, opened the door and switched on the lights. The suite was beautiful, smelling of floor wax and fresh flowers.

I was in the hall, turning on the light in the toilet stall when she pushed past me, flung the door open and ducked into the toilet, lifted her skirt and lowered herself. Not quite sitting, and canted slightly forward, she pissed loudly into the shallow ceramic bowl, sighing, straining, her face shining with pleasure, while I stood gaping, too fascinated to move. I thought that if I ducked aside and hid my face, she would be embarrassed. As it was, she seemed triumphant, like a suddenly spattering fountain.

I had heard of people so used to having servants that they walked around naked in front of them, got the servants to dress them, treated them as though they were blind, obedient, without emotion. But this was different. The Gräfin was engaged in an intimate, deeply satisfying act, and, still crouched there, she groaned with satisfaction. Then she straightened and slowly, fastidiously wiped herself with tissue, pulled the chain, rearranged her dress, and stepped into the hall where I stood, glowing from the sight of her.

"That was great," she said in a hearty way, and kissed me. "Now, you go," and she flicked the dampness from her fingers at me, but playfully.

I was not disgusted. I thought, Germans! The breakdown, this simple inconvenience, was our adventure. I told her that I liked her courage. I used this trivial event to apotheosize her. And she saw the day as a triumph with a terrific ending, the payoff that farce in her suite.

She told Haroun: "We were left by the side of the road. The driver was an idiot. *Ich musste pinkeln.* We could have died!"

As a result of this successful day, we spent more time together, and on better terms than before. She seemed much happier and more trusting. I began to dislike her, first in an irritated way and then with a deep loathing.

Haroun said to me confidentially, "Yet you have not succeeded."

I wondered whether I ever would. I wondered now whether I wanted to. I still saw her in the bright light of the narrow stall of her toilet, smiling, pissing, utterly human and helpless and happy, less like a countess on her throne than a small girl on her potty, crying, Look at me! Look what I'm doing!

Then, a few days after *Yet you have not succeeded,* we were sitting on the terrace.

Haroun said, "Now I go."

The Gräfin said nothing. Last week she would have said, "What about me?" or "Why so early?"

I said, "That smell, is it jasmine?"

"*Gelsomino,*" she said, teaching me the word.

I used the perfume to lead her into the garden, where the fragrance was stronger. She picked a blossom, sniffed it, inhaled the aroma. I sidled up to her and touched her. She was so slender, and there was so little of her — small bones and tender muscles that were wisps of warm flesh — she seemed brittle and insubstantial. I always thought of the Gräfin as breakable. I tried to hold her.

"*Nein,*" she said, startled into her own language.

I was thinking, If this doesn't work I am done for. I did not want to leave Taormina, yet leaving was the only alternative, the consequence of my failure. This was my last hope, and I truly hated her for making me do this.

I said, "The first time I saw you I wanted to kiss you."

"You're drunk," she said.

"No. Listen. You have the face of a Madonna. Kissing it is wrong. I want to worship it."

"How stupid," she said, but even saying that, she was thinking — I knew her well — not about my words but about her face.

"Please let me," I said, grappling with her a little, and also glancing around the garden to make sure that we were alone, that we were not being observed.

She did not say anything yet she was definitely resisting; she had a body like a sapling, skinny but strong. I got my mouth close to her ear. I breathed a little and my breath was hot as it returned to me from the closeness of her head. I was at the edge, I knew that; I had to fling myself off.

I said, "I love you," and as I said it the wind left me, and I went weak, as though I had said something wicked, or worse, uttered a curse — as though I had stabbed her in the heart and then stabbed myself. And that was how she reacted, too, for she began to cry, and she held me, and sobbed, and was a little girl again.

"Help me," she said. Her small voice in the twilight.

5

Then silence, and darkness fell; the darkness suited the silence.

In the long night that followed her surrendering words everything changed, and there were no more words, there was no language at all, hardly anything audible except a murmur in the silence — a sigh lengthening in desire. We communicated by touch, flesh was everything, and as though in mimicry of language, we used our mouths, our lips, our teeth, kissing, licking.

My mouth was all over her body, hers on mine. After days of starvation we were devouring each other in the dark.

We had stepped into her room and shut the door. I expected her to turn on the light but she didn't. At first I could not see her at all and seemed to be nowhere near her. I smelled the lily aroma of her perfume. I heard her moving on the far side of the room, the chafing of her lovely stockings — black, I knew — and from the kissing sound, a silk thigh slipping against another silk thigh, I knew she had taken her dress off. I headed toward the silken sound and realized she was in another room, the door open. We were in her large suite whose floor plan I did not yet understand. But I got to know it well; we were to spend hours of the night on that floor. I got to know all the carpets and all the sharp edges of furniture, the tables, the obstacles, the sliding oblongs of moonlight.

More distinct sounds: the familiar one of a cork being popped out of a champagne bottle, of glass flutes being chinked on a marble-topped table, and for a moment I thought, She will need a light. But when I heard the explosive release of the cork I knew she was able to manage in the dark. And now I could make out her profile in the darkness, for there was no real darkness in Taormina. The word "chiaroscuro" said it all — she was a clear shadow, a fragrant presence. I smelled her, I heard her, then I saw her, luminous and tinged blue in the Sicilian moonlight, as though glowing, radioactive.

But even then, especially then, in her suite, hearing the champagne cork, dazed by the crushed lilies of her perfume which was powerful in the dark, and reflecting on her admitting me at last to her room — her mirrored boudoir I had glimpsed from the distant front door, her bed with its frilly coverlet, her fur slippers, her silks like perfect skin, her kissing me with her famished mouth — even then I felt it might all be a trick. She might be teasing me, tantalizing me as she had before.

I was reminded of the many times she had exposed herself to me, shown me her breasts, opened her legs casually, held her gloved hands seductively between her legs. The worst for me, the cruelest of her teasing — if it *was* teasing and not indifference that I took for sensuality — was when she sat next to me and leaned over, placing her thin hand straight down on my stiffening penis, first exploring it and then using it like a handle to steady herself, while she said in a lecturing tone, "I am sorry, I hardly know you. I cannot imagine what you want from me. You seem to be a very presumptuous young man. Where did you get these ideas? It is so hard for me to say 'you.' I should be addressing you as *Sie*, not *du* — 'you' is just useless . . ."

She had used the flat of her hand to press down harder, and then I felt her warm palm and active fingers. Lecturing me with her voice but keeping her fascinated hand against my hard-on — that was the worst time. A woman who would do that would do anything. I did not assume because we were licking each other and kissing in the suite that we would become lovers. I was bracing myself for another reversal, more frustration.

That was why, when I said I loved her, I did so with hatred. Even pressed against her parted thighs I felt great hostility. As I spoke into her ear I was possessed by an impulse to bite it, and saying "I love you," I felt a strong desire to hit her. I spoke the endearments through gritted teeth, trembling, feeling violent, wishing to push her to the floor and shove her legs apart.

I think she knew this. She was trembling, fearful, cowering. She knew how much I resented the way she had treated me, how I disliked her most for making me say this, like the young peasant boy in my folktale woodcut who was forced to endure humiliation to obtain a favor from the Countess. And so the desperate Wanderer kneels and utters the forbidden formula and at that moment he is consumed by a fury of loathing, hating himself, hating the noblewoman who has put him in this position.

The instant I gave in and told the Gräfin finally that I loved her, I wanted to force her to the floor and fondle her until she begged me to stop. I actually still felt a strong sexual desire, but it was sullen and violent and not so much sex as a visceral wish to assault her. I felt the stirrings of what it meant to be a rapist — despising her as I spread her legs, and in my hatred and humiliation, on top at last. Not sex at all but penetrating her roughly, using my prick like a weapon in a vicious attack. Now I could not kiss her without enjoying a resentful fantasy of biting her, tearing at her lips with my teeth.

I tried to calm myself. I was almost fainting with frustration. She was pressed against me and, as I was preparing myself for rejection, I felt myself losing control.

She moved away from me, and though there was no direct light I could see by the glow from the town and the luminosity of the moon and stars that she was pouring champagne into glasses that made the rising wine into music, a note increasing in pitch as the liquid filled the narrow flutes.

In that somber starry light her lips were black, her skin was greenish, her golden hair was blue. She was a specter handing me a wine glass and still she wore her lace gloves. I drank and touched her hand and was surprised by the warmth of the lace, how her flesh had heated her gloves, and when I reached to touch her breasts I was surprised by the way in which her body had heated her silk chemise, her gown, her sleeves.

After all this she was still clothed. That had added to my sense of ambiguity — so strange, all those clothes in the semidarkness of her suite. I wondered if she was serious and sexual, and when I put my hands on her breasts and held their softness, the stems of her nipples hardening against my thumbs, I felt that she was on the point of rejecting me.

So I could not disguise my hostility. I gripped her tighter, and roughly, like snatching the arm of an unruly child, like a furious parent intending the gesture to hurt as well as restrain. I did this almost unconsciously, unaware of how angry I was until my fingers sank into the flesh of her upper arm where I fingered helpless softness, no muscle at all, finding the weak woman beneath the skin. Something in that softness roused me — I had never touched more appealing skin or such yielding flesh. It seemed to me so tender that I could eat it, chew on her edible arm — I felt like biting her, or at the very least holding on as though grasping a piece of delicious meat. I could not stop myself. I was on the verge of gathering her whole slim body tightly in my hand and raising her to my mouth — all my frustration and arousal concentrated in this one gesture, this revealing touch. As I had snatched her arm, I had become a rapist, an animal, a cannibal.

Did she smell this bloodthirstiness on me? She took a step forward and kissed me. I was surprised but not calmed — surprised because she was fiercer than me. She chewed softly on my lips, and still I held on, remembering again how she had rejected me before, saying no and holding my erection. I felt sure this might end that way too, that I would be sent off, sobbing with lust.

I pushed her away, my hand against her face, my palm jammed against her big wet mouth — and she kissed my hand, licked it like a frantic puppy, and as she struggled to clutch at me I tried to keep her back, to give myself space to slap her.

To show her that I was in control, I held her off with one hand and took an insolent sip of champagne with the other.

The struggle was mute: she said nothing, only sighed. I was afraid of startling the hotel staff: I said nothing. But when I relaxed my grip a little she went a bit limp and was less amorous, and so I grasped her more tightly and began to understand that my rough handling of her aroused her.

It was not in my nature to be rough. My experience until then had been with willing and eager girls. But this was a complex woman and she had made me angry. Of course I did not hit her — I couldn't — but I was furiously aroused with a kind of passion that was as urgent and blind as anger. The moonlit room and the shadows and her clothes maddened me more.

I fumbled and found her breasts again, loving the weight of them, loving their softness; they were full and heavy and now her nipples were hard. I lowered my head and licked and sucked them and could not restrain myself from nibbling them, and when I did she took her breasts with her gloved hands and lifted them into my face, sighing with pleasure as she touched herself.

My mind was still set against her — untrusting. At any moment I felt she would reject me. Yes, even as she was pushing her warm breasts against my mouth I suspected she was just perverse enough to stop herself cold and send me away, saying, "That's enough for you! What more do you want!"

And though she didn't, though she was compliant, more than compliant — active and eager — I was using more strength than was necessary, sensing somehow that I needed to overpower her. I thrust her backward, could not reach the bed, got her to the floor, and hiked up her clothes — silks, straps, garters, stockings, ribbons, all the underpinnings of the old-fashioned feminine Europe, a wilderness of lush lingerie and lace. I was surprised and obstructed by her large elaborate panties, and when I found I could not remove them, could not disentangle them from the silken underpinnings, I parted the lacy crotch of these panties, felt with my fingers the wet mouth and lips of her cunt, and drove my purple cock forward. It was then I knew she could not stop me, though I still gripped her arms and pumped, and each time I thrust she moaned like someone being stabbed to death.

I must not let her stop me, I felt, but the feeling was more intense than the words: I had animal hunger and this was the nearest thing to rape that I had ever known, because I still felt that although she would never succeed, she might try to stop me. She moaned but it was not protest; she writhed but it was not resistance. She wanted more.

The darkness was dazzling. I was convinced of her hunger now, for she reached down and gripped me with her gloved hand and squeezed her lacy fingers on my rigid cock. I felt the ribs and stitching on my hot skin, her whole glove encircling the stalk of my erection and tugging it, planting it deeper into her body. When I came, with a scream that tore through my guts, falling across her body, tangled in her clothes, she let out a little disappointed "Ach" that died away, scraping into silence.

The first word spoken in the darkness was my whisper: "Sorry."

She put her face against the side of my head. Her breath was so hot it scorched my ear. She said, "I want more," and in the darkness and in her hunger she had never sounded more Germanic. I made a picture in my mind: a forest demon demanding blood.

But I had nothing more to give her. She clung to me for a while, saying nothing, and when, sighing, she let go, I knew she was telling me to leave.

The next day, golden in the golden sunlight, under the brim of her big Panama hat, she was in charge again, sulky and spiteful, perhaps slightly worse than usual, as though tormenting me in revenge for having surrendered to me.

"That is not what I asked for," she said when I brought her the Campari and soda she had requested.

Haroun was there and heard this obstinacy. He smiled — he seemed to understand what lay behind her imperiousness.

"I said Punt e Mes. I never drink Campari at this hour."

A lie.

"And do stop staring at me. You are making me feel there is something wrong. Get the drink and go."

That hot day, the day in Taormina after we had made love in her room at the Palazzo d'Oro, was the worst, the most miserable, I had so far spent in her company. She was a shrew to me — demanding, insulting, unreasonable, reminiscing about ex-husbands and former lovers, mentioning large sums of money and her extensive travels, treating me as though I was another species — reminding me that I was an American, a mere boy, with no money except what she gave me, who could be sent away at any moment. But she was not a glamorous German countess speaking in this way; she seemed to me like a dreadful child.

I said, "What sort of childhood did you have?"

"How dare you ask me that!"

That was the daylight. In the evening, at dinner, she was calmer, as always studying her face in the dining room mirror, though pretending not to. She wore a small white Chanel (so she told me) hat with a little wisp of a veil and matching gloves of lace.

After dinner, Haroun sipped his coffee and said, "I must go and attend to a little business."

"Is that your name for it?" the Gräfin said, making an actressy gesture, holding her gloved hand against her cheek, her fingers delicately splayed in support.

Haroun smiled, he smoked, he knew he would be granted permission to go but that he would have to endure some teasing beforehand. He knew — and now I did too — that the Gräfin had to have her way.

"I do not want to think about your little business. Please take your little business somewhere else."

"Gräfin — of course, Gräfin."

She said, "Sometimes people speak words in an opera, and they are perfect, and there is a big pause. And the aria begins with those words, the people singing them in an aria. This aria begins, 'Little business' — wonderful. *Kleines Geschäft.*"

"Yes, Gräfin. Thank you, Gräfin."

She said to me, "Are you interested in Harry's little business?"

She was inviting me to mock him. I pitied him and tried to be gentle, saying, "Not exactly."

"Go on, then, Harry. Go and play." She twitched her veil as though shutting him out.

Alone with her, I did not know what to say. I finished my glass of wine feeling that I was at the center of a great silent void, like a boy in a bubble. She pushed her glass toward me almost contemptuously, as though reluctant to satisfy my gluttony. I finished it, saying nothing, but feeling that it might help to be a bit drunk because I did not know what to do next.

I finally said, "What is it about Harry that you don't like?"

She made just the slightest facial tic, using the tip of her nose and her upper lip, like a handsome animal reacting to a buzzing insect.

"That he's queer?" I said.

"What is queer?"

"That he's a sodomite."

She smiled and said, "The one thing I understand."

"Sure," I said, and she knew I doubted her.

Leaning forward, her warm champagne breath on my face, she said with a satisfaction like appetite, "I am a sodomite."

No words were available to me then, and with my mind a blank, I touched her hand, which was hot and eager.

She said — wicked child — "I don't like that jacket. You always wear that jacket. It's too dark."

"You bought it for me." Or rather, Haroun bought it for me, with the Gräfin's money. Haroun had loved fussing with the tailor in a small street behind the Naumachia, discussing textures of velvet.

"I suppose I'll have to buy you another."

"Good idea," I said, telling myself that I was humoring her and not being insulted.

"Tomorrow we will go to the tailor. I want you to wear a light-colored jacket, one that will look well with my dresses. This one is wrong. It attracts attention."

A child's demands are often meaningless, *pay attention to me* their only motive — even then, at twenty-one, I knew that, perhaps better than she.

"I suppose you want my key," she said.

The thought had not occurred to me. I had to think hard in my drunken slowness to reason what she was talking about. *Key?* I thought, and smiled, and she smiled back. *What key?*

Instead of replying — what was I to say? — I put my hand out. She pouted, putting on a sulky malicious face, and smacked the key into my palm. There were bite marks, hers, on the meat of my palm, the dark roulettes of her teeth.

In her suite that second night I was more confident. I knew what she wanted, I understood her contradictions, I was more polite, kissed her more gently, held her in my arms and delighted in the darkness, loving the feel of her clothes and the skin beneath them, and sometimes slipping my fingers through a placket and not knowing which was silk and which was skin, for both were warm to my touch.

I took my time, to give myself a chance to adjust to seeing in the dark, and when she began to glow slightly — as a darkened room grows warmer and emits a sort of frosty light — I could pick out her shape and soon the texture of her clothes: the loose dress of white loops, the velvet collar and the white shoes with such high heels she was nearly as tall as I was. The Chanel hat with the little veil she had worn at dinner she kept on, and the gloves. All in white tonight — I saw her easily.

"What do you want?"

"How can you ask me that?" Her tone was sharp.

We kissed. My hands roved delicately over her clothes.

"I have everything. How dare you ask me that?"

She pushed me aside, surprising me. I was offended and annoyed, and in a quick reflex I snatched at her wrist and held on, too tight, although it had not been my intention. She did not resist. Before I could let go, she went limp and dropped to her knees, her hat and veil brushing my shirt front and down my trousers, and I was thinking what a stiff skewering hat pin must have held it in place that it could rub me like that without moving.

I had not released her wrist, and the texture of her lace gloves gave me a better grip than if I had held her bare hands. I guided her fingers to the bulge in my trousers and rubbed them against me. Before I realized it — she was that adroit — she had unzipped me with her free hand and in the next moment she had me in her mouth. That heat, that busy tongue, and the fingers of her gloves on the shaft of my cock, the lacy fretwork of her fingertips stroking my hardness, as I held her head, her hat, her veil, my hands tightening on all this brocade. The harder I held her head, the more eagerly she sucked me and stroked me with her gloved hands, chafing me with the white lace. I came, sooner than I wanted, spurting in a succession of involuntary jerks, stabbing at her mouth and face and spattering creamy mucus on her veil and face and lacy fingers.

Seeing what I had done to her pretty gloves and her veil, I began to apologize in the shallow staticky tone of a man who has just had an orgasm. She was not listening, she was licking her gloves and her veil like a little girl licking the last sweet drops of syrup from her fingers.

I had hardly touched her, yet that was enough.

That she was cruel and fickle the following day made me

smile at the sight of her play-acting, for now she was predictable. And I even knew the reason: she intended to enrage me so that later, in her room, I would dominate her and treat as my slave. It was role-playing, it was harmless, it was perfect. I was not enraged, I was aroused; if she could pretend to be cruel during the day, I could imitate that cruelty at night — it was easy to make my passion into fury.

The softness of her skin in the dark, far softer-seeming because of the dark, was irresistible. And the aroma of her lily-fragrant perfume, mingled with the cat smell of her steaming cunt, made me salivate and pant like a lion, my nose tormented by damp feline fur and hot blood. Still I could not tell where her soft skin ended and her silk began, and the complexity of her vaginal lips was like another elaborate silken garment she had put on for me to stroke. I adored the gleam of her body in the light from the Taormina street lamps and the blistered moon.

But she preferred darkness to light, the floor to the bed, silence to words, my roughness to my gentleness, clothes to nakedness; preferred serving me to my making love to her. She knelt and worshiped my cock with her mouth and her gloved hands, and she cried out louder than I did when I came, spattering her face as she licked. One of those times when she was done with me I knelt myself and touched her between her legs, and she was so wet with desire my fingers sank into her, and as they slipped between the hot flesh folds into her enlarged hole it was as though they were being swallowed.

After her daytime sulks, her fickleness, her trickery, her cruel remarks and her imperious bearing, her contradictions, her outright insults, turning away from me to show me an uplifted profile of contempt and indifference, she liked nothing better, as darkness fell, than to be led to her suite and commanded to kneel before me; and for me to take my cock out and demand that she suck me off. And often when I was done she still had not had enough, and I watched from above as she went on sucking and gulping.

The strings and muscles in her neck, the pulsing of her throat, the motions of swallowing — I could see it all, as fascinated by her neck and throat as I had been weeks ago when she had turned away and drunk the wine to snub me. I loved to watch her swallowing, and there was no prettier sight than her subtle gulps, the active gullet, like a thirsty cannibal drinking her victim drop by drop.

So we lived on in the Palazzo d'Oro, and we flourished in Taormina, and the summer days went by, seeming to grow hotter as the nights grew cooler, and I kept wondering how far she wanted me to go with her, for I was, even after ten days or so, still learning. The Gräfin was my earliest lesson on the topic that every woman is different.

Nothing in my sexual experience had prepared me for this woman, and while she seemed positively to glow with health and strength, I was showing signs of physical strain. Her appetite was far greater than mine.

The season in Taormina was ending, the few summer guests leaving, the larger autumn crowd of older visitors about to arrive — so the manager of the palazzo said: English people, *gli Inglesi*.

"The *partita* is coming in a few days," the Gräfin said, and I knew she had been there before, that the party was an annual event, one of the other rituals in the routine of the Palazzo d'Oro.

When the day came, the long-term guests were present and they were gaped at by the people who were staying for just a few days or a week. This was an intimate occasion, like a family affair, welcoming some people, excluding others. Each group was seated at its usual table, though out of politeness — for we in the palazzo were a little family — other male guests danced with the Gräfin.

She wore a gown I had never seen before, and a tiara, and her jewels, and gloves, black ones that reached almost to her elbows, and stiletto heels, her hair in ringlets. She had lovely long legs, slender and straight. She was naturally glamorous and had never looked more chic.

"She is so happy," Haroun said with a grateful glance at me, but he looked even happier. He beamed at her while I marveled at how I had seen this perfect body attending to me, completely at my service, those beautiful legs bent and kneeling, that serene face eating me.

The Gräfin refused to dance with me, and I knew better than to dance with anyone else. She danced spiritedly with an Italian man ("He is a principe," Haroun said) and more sedately with an elderly German, who always sat alone at another table, often eyeing the Gräfin, especially when I was with her.

"Who is he?"

Haroun just smiled.

"Tell me, Harry."

"Too much to tell," Haroun said, making a complex gesture of helplessness with his whole body — eyes, mouth, fingers, shoulders. "He owns a *fabbrica*."

"What kind of factory?"

With the same helpless gesture, he said, "Many."

She danced with the swarthy overdressed man at the next table (*"Greco"*). She even danced — arms raised in teasing delicacy, a kind of puppeteering — with a woman, who was dressed severely in a suit. She held the woman's hands in the air and twirled her gently, glancing at my reflection in the mirror from time to time: our eyes met, she scowled with pleasure.

Near the end of the party the staff thanked her — effusive

Italian gratitude you knew you had to pay for: the wine stew-
ard with his absurd chain and key and *cavatappi*, the fat sweaty-
faced waiter, the pretty boy from the bar, the lurking *Moro*. She
tipped them, fluttering Italian money at them, and they laughed
and snatched at it like monkeys. The young scullery maid approached, about eighteen, very pretty. Gräfin pinched her cheek
and kissed her passionately on the lips and then curtsied, the
Countess making a low bow to the maidservant while the embarrassed girl clutched the money that had been passed to her.
This business with the girl was one of the most sexually arousing
scenes I had ever witnessed.

The Gräfin had the money, I had none. I was properly emascu-
lated, and even while I was watching this spectacle the woman in
the suit elbowed past me, hoping for another dance with the
Gräfin.

The Gräfin turned to me, looking insolent, nostrils like a
horse, and Haroun, seeing her sneering, seemed to take this as a
signal to leave.

"A little business for Harry," she said. "And what about you?"

I was so angry I was on the point of leaving altogether, except
that by now I recognized this as an established ritual.

I said, "We have some unfinished business."

When I stepped forward, she leaned back, looking anxious.

I put my face against the bright ringlets and found her ear and
said, "Go to your room and wait for me."

She left the party hurriedly, eagerly, and seeing her, the
woman in the suit snarled in my direction as I followed. I locked
the Gräfin's door as I shut it behind me. She was on her knees,
still elegantly clothed in her gown and tiara, facing away from
me, the spikes of her shoes protruding backward, the remote
and icy woman now cowering. I knelt, I gathered her skirts and
petticoats and lifted, and I held her, hipbone in each hand.

"*Hund! Hund!*" she cried. "Dog! Dog!"

6

"You have succeeded brilliantly," Haroun said. "You remind me of myself, you are so genius."

"Thanks, Harry."

"And yet you are not smiling! You should be so happy."

I was embarrassed to be praised for what I had done — especially to be praised by Haroun; and I seriously wondered whether it was I who had succeeded or the Gräfin.

"Thank you," he said, locking on my eyes and thumping his heart with his right fist in a matey Middle Eastern gesture of sincerity. I took this to mean that he was grateful for my liberating him — he was free to wander the streets, and his evenings were his own, for the Gräfin was my concern now.

She was willing, submissive, sexual — more than I had ever known in my life. I would have felt like a rapist had the Gräfin not also been so enthusiastic. Her full-throated gusto for submission aroused me, and after her surrender I was excited whenever she turned to me with a speculative "got anything for me?" smile, or tapped the back of my hand with Germanic insistence. From her I discovered how pathologically impatient the very rich could be. When she wanted something, she was fussed and furious until she got it, and she often touched me as though poking a Start button.

Muttering the slushy word *Schlüssel* — she mouthed German words all the time; I was beginning to learn some — she slid her key to me, and I preceded her to her suite. Always at dusk, often by candlelight, she remained dressed, or at least half dressed, showing her silken underclothes, the lingerie with its tiny ribbons and bands of lace, the pale colors, pinks and lavender, the flesh tones of her trimmed slip. Her shoes were spectacular and she never removed them, and so she always kept her silk stockings on, and the associated tangle of belts and garters, fasteners and straps, more beautiful for their clumsy complexity and more sensual than nakedness.

Her clothes were part of the attraction, for they emphasized her slim body by giving it teasing highlights. At the end of our lovemaking her clothes were disheveled and damp, twisted on her in a way that made her look lovely and wrecked, and I stood over her, triumphant. But she was not wrecked, I was not triumphant: she was made whole, and I was helpless.

She was physically much stronger than I had guessed. Often, when I had finished, she would say, "I want you again — take me now," and of course it was impossible for me to proceed. Perhaps she said that knowing that I could not perform at that moment. Was this her way of reminding me that she was in charge? She could be demanding. In my adolescence I had fantasized that this might be pleasant. It was more trying than I had ever guessed, for after the beginning, she was the one who initiated sex, not me. She sent for me, she sought me out, she poked me with her button-pressing finger and smiled wickedly. And because of the peculiar arrangement — she, not Haroun, was paying for my room — I had to be on call.

"Where were you?" she would say.

"Here I am."

"But I wanted you one hour ago."

Put in the wrong like that, I had to be more obedient, and when I was, only then would she submit — the logic was predictably perverse. She was able to exhaust me by being submissive, because in her pretense of submission, her hoarse barking eroticism, was a kind of dominance: I was serving her, not the other way around. She got on all fours and went woof-woof, but really she was the mistress mimicking a dog: I was the kept pet who had been commanded to hump her. She had always been the mistress; she had turned me into a dog. And when I was not a big jowly hound humping her from behind, I was her obedient lap dog.

Her appetite and her persistence made her seem much younger — younger than me, stronger, more sexual, greedier, more childish, more perverse, less inhibited, almost uncontrollable. I did not dread her beckoning, but after the first week I admitted to myself that my mood seldom matched hers. That was inconvenient, yet I could not make excuses: I belonged to her.

All we shared was sex. I liked that but I wanted more. These days we seldom talked, we never had a conversation. She was not a reader, not a sightseer, not the slightest bit animated by the Italians, whom she despised as cheats and monkeys (*Äffchen*, another of her German words that I learned).

"I like Taormina because there are so few Italians here" was her repeated pronouncement.

She was purely a sensualist and she demanded that I be the same — but how could I? Sensuality was almost impossible to fake, and so I was always struggling to satisfy her. We were reduced to two creatures groping in the dark. A few weeks before, in those awkward yet instructive days of visiting the olive estate, and shopping for clothes, and the three of us dining together — when Haroun was still one of us — we enjoyed many conversations. We talked about travel, politics, music, food — that is, her travel, her politics, the music she liked, the food she preferred. But however self-centered at least it was an attempt at polite discourse, and it helped me understand her a little. Now days were passed in silence, in the weird woolly humidity of sexual anticipation. I was bored, she was impatient, and we were distant all day until nightfall, when we resumed grappling, and by then I might have pinned her to the floor and be throttling her as she cried out, *Hoont! Hoont!*

"I love you" was never spoken again. And so after our initial familiarity began to wane, I knew her less and less, for sex had turned her into a stranger.

She signaled obscurely with her head — her blond ringlets danced at her ears; she gestured with one finger rather than her whole hand; she had a way of using her lips — everting them — which meant "Now." She wasn't initiating sex, she was testing my obedience, giving an order, saying "Come," and I had no choice but to obey, doglike, and go to my mistress, who was swishing her tail, for when she walked, her whole body in motion repeated, "Follow me," especially her bobbing beckoning buttocks.

"Ach!" she would say after we finished, her characteristic post-coital mutter, which was as close as she ever got to forming a word at those times. "Ach" had three syllables, sometimes more. Looking broken and thrown down on the carpet, her lipstick so smeared she had a clown's mouth, her hair and clothes tangled, satisfied in her ruin — more than satisfied, triumphant.

The resentment that built up in me during the day — a furious feeling that she seemed deliberately to provoke — I unleashed on her at night as soon as the door to her suite was locked and bolted. The double lock was necessary.

One night, early on in our lovemaking, she was loudly groaning and I was butting her hard with my hips. There was a knock at the door and a voice of worried, querying concern.

"Contessa . . ."

The Gräfin instantly ceased her pleading moans and through gritted teeth cried, *"Via!"* — Go away!

And almost without a transition we continued, all her bravado gone, for while outside the room she was an insulting countess, inside she was a cowering peasant girl, kneeling before me and pleading, imploring my hardened cock, holding it with her gloved hands, and caressing it with her lips and tongue with murmurs of satisfaction.

When she wanted something particular, she asked for it obliquely, using the childish method of paradoxical injunction — the way a panting bright-eyed child says, "Better not chase me! Better not tickle me!"

Only the Gräfin's suggestions were much more specific: "Whatever you do, I beg you, don't open the drawer of my dresser and find the dog collar and the leash. If you do, I will have to wear it and you will treat me like a dog and force me to lick you and get me on my hands and knees and take me from behind like a mastiff . . ."

She scattered rugs and pillows and blankets on the floor to protect her knees, for the Gräfin's preferred position was on all fours, facing the sofa, near enough to rest her head on it, to howl into the cushions and muffle the cries she knew would startle the palazzo's staff again.

Sometimes she rolled over, the way a dog does to have its belly tickled, only she would raise her legs and, pretending to cover herself, claw at the lacy crotch of her panties and protest insincerely, saying *"Nein."*

Licking her, humping her, nuzzling her back, buttock-sniffing like a spaniel, I was the dog — and a fierce one, too, for the way she treated me all day. I was the badly whipped and hectored hound that turned on its mistress, but in this case it was just what she wanted.

I did not naturally resist, I had lost the will, but instead I strayed, I procrastinated, absented myself, became scarce, wandered the side streets of Taormina, and generally avoided her during the day, as though not wanting to be reminded of my obligations. Haroun was never around. I guessed he had found a friend. I was the Gräfin's companion now.

In that week of resentment, my third in Taormina, I began to avoid her more and more, as I attempted to initiate another life in the town, parallel to the one I led at the Palazzo d'Oro. I became friendly with some of the shopkeepers, knew them by their first names, chitchatted with them about the weather, the local soccer team, a boxing match that was about to take place in Palermo. When I mentioned America they said, "Jack Kennedy!" but were otherwise circumspect. They had guessed that I was a German, and while they were friendly I realized they were being polite, for they disliked Germans. But they made an exception for visitors who stayed in Taormina and spent money and handed out tips and, in the Italian way, said they disliked "the other ones — not these."

All my clothes were from the men's boutique on the Viale Nolfi, a small street off the Corso. The Gräfin and Haroun had bought me clothes in the Teutonic style — the pointed shoes, the short sports jacket, the narrow trousers, the turtleneck, the mesh shirt, the silk suit — the sort of stylish clothes an idle, self-conscious German wore on vacation. They were so stylish as to be almost formal: the light suit was easily soiled, the shoes had thin soles and were wrong for the cobblestones of Taormina, the turtleneck was too tight, the trousers too close-fitting. I was a dandy — out of character for me, I felt, but it was her desire, German pride mostly, that I should look rich and respectable, in her fashion. And clothing me was another way of making me hers. I had barely realized how I looked until I tried to talk with Italians, most of whom benignly forgave me for being foppish and prosperous.

Waiters in Taormina, however, loved such people as I seemed, for we lingered, we smoked, we had nothing to do, we spent money and humored them and tipped them. One day at the Mocambo, where I had begun to take refuge from the Gräfin — but I went there mainly because the waiters knew me by name — I was addressed by a young woman in Italian. I took her to be a student, maybe French — she had an accent — definitely a traveler: she was dressed like a hiker and carried a sun-faded bag and a map. She wore a headscarf which in its simplicity gave her a wholesome peasant look that was also chic. As she spoke, a waiter wandered over to listen.

"*Scusi, signore, cerchiamo una pensione qui non più caro,*" she said. She was looking for a place to stay that was not too expensive.

"*Benvenuto, signorina. Vieni a casa mia. C'è libero,*" the waiter, Mario, said, urging her to come to his house because it was free.

"Nothing is free," she said in English, and was so assertive and indignant Mario walked away laughing.

I said, "But everything is expensive in Taormina. How long are you planning to stay?"

She said, "I want to see the Teatro Greco. The Duomo. Lawrence's house."

I said, "Lawrence lived in the Via Fontana Vecchia. 'A snake came to my water-trough / On a hot, hot day, and I in pyjamas for the heat, / To drink there . . .'"

"I like how he seemed 'a king in exile, uncrowned in the underworld,'" she said. "By the way, your English is excellent."

"It sure oughtta be."

She laughed and said, "Where in the States are you from?"

"Long story."

"I'm at Wellesley, but I am from New York."

"City?"

"Upstate."

"I just graduated from Amherst."

"I know lots of Amherst guys," she said, and sat down and named a few, names I recognized but none I knew well. "How long have you been in Taormina?"

"A few weeks." I did not want to admit that it was almost four, because I felt I had been so idle. "I came to see the Lawrence house too."

"I love that poem."

"English major?"

"Art history. I've been living in Florence — junior year abroad program. I'm just traveling. I thought I would look around here and then go to Siracusa."

"I've been meaning to go there."

"Two weeks here and you haven't got there yet! What's the attraction in Taormina?"

"Long story," I said. *"La dolce vita."*

She said, "Men are so lucky. If I just hang around an Italian town looking at buildings for my project, everyone takes me for a whore. That waiter was pretty typical. That's why I have to keep on the move."

"Maybe I could come with you to Siracusa."

"That's just what *they* say!"

"I mean, to protect you — to run interference."

"Maybe we can talk about it," she said nicely.

She took off her sunglasses, seeming to peel them in one motion from her eyes, which were gray, and she took off her headscarf and shook the dust from it as her hair tumbled to her shoulders. Her hair was streaked by the sunlight and she was slim and a bit damp from her exertion: she had been walking.

I loved her looks and her air of spontaneity and self-reliance, but just as much I loved the fact that we spoke the same language. I had gotten so used to talking with waiters in Italian and with the Gräfin and Haroun in basic English — slowly and always finishing my sentences — that I had almost forgotten the pleasure and directness of talking with another American. Meeting this woman was like meeting my sister — someone from my own family — and I was reminded of who I really was.

She said, "I thought you might be a German. Those shoes. That jacket. It's the look. Fashion is one of my interests. Usually I can spot an American a mile off. You had me fooled. I think that's pretty good."

The Gräfin and Haroun had turned me into a German. I liked the concealment even if I was not keen on the identity.

"I've got some German friends here."

"Italians can't stand the *Tedeschi*."

She spoke knowingly, sure of herself, which irritated me, because although it was true that Italians disliked Germans, they didn't hate them, they were too self-possessed to hate anyone — they were guided by village prejudices and village wisdom. Instead of telling her this I asked her what her name was — it was Myra Messersmith — and bought her a cup of coffee.

"Gilford Mariner. Please call me Gil."

And we talked in that familiar, self-conscious way of isolated Americans abroad. It was not until I began to talk, unburdening myself, that I realized how many complaints I had. We swapped grievances, another habit of American expatriates, complained about the irregular hours of bars and banks and shops, the uncertainty of museum hours, the watchfulness of men, the nosiness of women, the way Italians littered their landscape, the loudness of motor scooters, the tiny cars, the long meals, the irritable bus conductors, the slowness of service, the persecution of animals, the adoration of babies, the tedium of Sundays, the peculiarities of academic life, the pedantry of teachers, the smugness of priests.

"People with a simple BA degree call themselves *dottore*."

"Priests leer at my boobs and imply that they can personally get me into Heaven."

"Everyone smokes — even me!"

So we talked and compared notes and it seemed we agreed on most things.

She said after a while, "How much does your hotel cost?"

Her question took me by surprise and embarrassed me. I didn't have an answer. I said, stalling, "It depends on how long you stay."

"I'd like to stay a few days and then maybe we could go to Siracusa."

"It's really not far. We could get there in a few hours — maybe a day trip from here."

Already we were talking as though we were going together. It excited me to think that I would be leaving Taormina with this pretty girl who already was such pleasant company, a comforting prospect that eased my mind.

"I don't blame you for staying here. It's so beautiful. I guess that's Etna."

The shapely volcano emitted a trickle of smoke that rose in a ragged vertical rope, like a dark vine climbing into the windless air.

"That thing could blow at any moment."

Myra laughed and clutched her throat and said, "I love melodrama. Oh, right, I can see the red-hot lava pouring down the side and endangering our lives."

"I'd lead you to safety — into the catacombs of the Duomo."

"That sounds exciting, Gil."

This confident teasing was a sort of flirting and already I was saying "we." She liked me, I could tell; she didn't fear me. She was glad to have met me, she would test me a little more, and I would pass, and we would become traveling companions, cozier than ever, rubbing along through Sicily.

While I was talking to Myra Messersmith this way, needling her gently, she became interested in something behind me and stopped listening to me. Her eyes were fixed on a moving object and she seemed to grow warier, her face darkening a bit, almost alarmed, and then she jerked her head back, startled. At that instant I felt a sharp poke against my shoulder and the harsh whisper, "Come wiz me."

"What was that all about?" Myra said.

I had turned to see the Gräfin walking away.

"Long story." The Gräfin had never come to the Mocambo before.

"That's the third time you've said that."

"Everything's a long story to me. I'm an existentialist."

But Myra did not smile. She was thinking hard. Women know other women, because unlike men they are not beguiled by appearances: they know exactly what lies behind any feminine surface. Myra's alertness, the single woman's scrutiny, something new to me, amazed me with its accuracy in processing details and giving them significance — finding clues, searching for dangers, all in aid, I guessed, of choosing a mate. Men were casual, women so cautious. Even from this swift glimpse of the Gräfin, Myra knew me much better.

"Her heels are amazing. What's with those gloves? The hat's Chanel, and so is the dress. I bet she gets her hair done every day. The dress is raw silk — you can tell by the way it drapes. Did you see the gold threads? That's real gold. It's from Thailand."

I took Myra's interest for curiosity, a way of telling me that she understood fashion; and I was startled to see her rising from the café table. There was a cloud on her face, a sort of resignation and quiet anger that might have been rueful. I saw that in that moment of witnessing the Gräfin poke me, Myra had written me off as someone she could not rely on. She had summed up the situation before I said a word.

"I'm going to Siracusa."

"Why?" I said, sounding lame.

"It's not far — you said so yourself."

"I thought we were going together."

She said in a warning tone, "You're keeping your friend waiting, Gilford."

She had indeed written me off. She knew everything, it all

fitted, my clothes, my presumption, my vagueness, "Long story," the sudden appearance and unequivocal demand of the Gräfin. "These Germans really overdress. Especially the older ones," she said, and turned and passed the waiter, leaving a thousand-lire note on his saucer for the coffee and the tip: pride.

I felt like a small boy exposed in a needless insulting lie, who would never be trusted again.

"See ya."

Her false bonhomie gave her a sort of pathos, but she seemed brave as she crossed the Piazzale Nove Aprile with her bag in one hand and her map in the other. She walked purposefully but she was weary and burdened and so she was a little lopsided; but she was free. She was the person I had once been, before I had met the Gräfin. I could not bear to watch her go.

The Gräfin was on the terrace of the palazzo when I got back. The waiter stood beside her holding a bottle of wine. I sat down. He poured me a glass.

"Drink, drink," the Gräfin said.

I did so, and my anger flattened the taste of the wine, soured it in my mouth. I watched the shadows rise up the walls of the terrace, saw the last of the daylight slip from the roof tiles. I said nothing, only drank. When the waiter approached — and now I was self-conscious: what did he make of me? — and lit our candle, the Gräfin stroked the inside of her handbag and found her key, which she handed to me.

In her suite, I locked the door and shot the bolt. I drew out my leather belt with a sliding sound as it rasped through the trouser loops, lifting it as though unsheathing a sword.

"No," the Gräfin said with what seemed like real fear.

I prepared to tie her wrists with the belt and she relaxed a little — she had thought I was going to beat her.

In a calm voice she said, "There are silk scarves in the drawer of my dresser. Use them — they won't leave marks on my skin."

She extended her arms so that her wrists were near each bed-post and she lay while I bound her with scarves. She slipped one leg over the other, looking crucified.

"Please, whatever you do, be gentle. Don't rape me — don't humiliate me."

Not desire, nor even lust, but anger kept me there, forcing her legs apart, fumbling with her clothes. In my determination to have my way I did not even reflect on her desire but was single-minded, thrusting myself into her. Only when I was done did I realize that her sighs were sighs of pleasure. She had exhausted me again.

"We rest now." Her voice came out of the darkness, waking me. "Zen we eat."

Meeting Myra had retuned my ear: I heard the Gräfin's German accent as never before.

Over dinner, the Gräfin said, "Who was zat silly girl?"

"American."

"What shoes she had. Her blouse so dirty. And did you see her fingernails? She could at least brush her hair. Of course, American."

7

I could not escape without encouragement. My inspiration was Myra Messersmith disgustedly turning away from me to pick herself up and swinging her bag and, without looking back, walking away across the piazza, into the Via Roma. The Gräfin's contempt for Myra's clothes made me remember everything she wore, from the white blouse and headscarf to her blue jeans and hiking shoes. She was my example. And she might still be in Siracusa.

We had a great deal in common, Myra and I, but I knew that she was the stronger, and that it would help me to spend a few days with her. Just the half hour I had spent with her at the Mocambo had lifted my spirits and shown me who I really was, an opportunistic American who was out of his depth here, being used by Haroun and the Gräfin. In a flash, Myra saw me with some accuracy as an idle parasite who needed the patronage of a rich woman, I wanted to disprove that. I was twenty-one, still a student, who until meeting these people had been traveling light, passing through Italy making sketches. Well, not many sketches lately. I had done hardly any, as though I feared incriminating myself, or feared having to face the person I had become, a flunky in the Gräfin's entourage.

And what images would I have recorded in my sketchbook? A howling woman in twisted underclothes. A doglike woman on all fours, buttocks upraised. A woman — I now saw — addicted to rituals: a certain time of day, a particular sequence of sexual gropings, always in the same room on the same carpet on the same portion of the floor. All of this was shocking, for sex was the last thing I wanted to depict. Sex was a secret; sexual portraiture was the stuff of lawsuits. This was 1962: the topic was forbidden. You could buy "Snake," but *Lady Chatterley's Lover* was still a scandal. The Gräfin's suite was another country, without a language, without literature, almost without human speech, with no words for its rituals; where it was always night.

I woke as always in the daylight of my own room — the Gräfin insisted on sleeping alone — and felt preoccupied, with an excited edge to my determination, my hands shaking slightly as I drank my coffee like a farewell toast. To steel my resolve I did not talk to anyone; I needed to concentrate. I dressed, took all the cash I had, and hurried out of the Palazzo d'Oro and through the town, my head down, moving like a phantom.

A beautiful September day, fragrant with the sweet decay of dying leaves and wilting flowers; most of the summer people had gone. I had been in Taormina long enough to notice a distinct change in the weather — the intense heat and humidity were over, days were sunny and nights were cool, and the smell of ripeness, of yellow leaves and fruit pulp, and a dustiness of threshing in the air from the wheat harvest.

Halfway down the hill I hailed a taxi, and at the station I found that a train was due soon. I calculated that I could be in Siracusa by midafternoon, still lunchtime in Sicily, and I might find Myra. I also knew that the very impulse to look for her would liberate me.

A voice croaking from the strain of urgency called my name and I saw Haroun crossing the road toward the station platform where I stood. He was puffing a cigarette, looking terribly pale and rumpled, as though he had been casually assaulted — roughed up, warned rather than mugged. But he smiled, it had been pleasure, he was dissolute, careless, happy, like a child playing in mud.

"What are you doing?"

"Waiting for the train."

"No, no — the Gräfin must not be left."

He had read my intention exactly: he saw my wish to flee on my face and in my posture, like an ape poised to leap from a branch, an alertness in my neck.

"I can do anything I like," I said, and I remembered how at one time he had the choice of letting me stay or sending me away. Now the choice was mine. "I am going to Siracusa."

"Too far, too far," he said.

His sudden distress made me laugh — just a snort, but unambiguous, defiant. I said, "I need a vacation," though what I wanted was to leave for good. I had lost all my willpower in Taormina. I had become the lap dog of the Gräfin, who now seemed to me a woman of enormous strength and appetite. I needed to get away from her. I did not want to be possessed.

Haroun said, "There is a lovely beach across the road. Would you like to see it? *Bello* Golfo di Naxos."

"The train is coming pretty soon."

"Better we sit and talk on the beach," he said. He touched my arm and made a hook of his finger and hung on. "There is something I must tell you."

"Tell me now."

"A secret," he said.

"I know about you, Harry. It's pretty obvious."

"It is the Gräfin."

A stirring on the platform, a vibration on the tracks, a grinding down the line, all the sounds of an approaching but unseen train kept me from answering. I shrugged instead.

"It will astonish you," he said.

That tempted me. I took nothing for granted — one of the lessons of Taormina and the enchanted castle of the Palazzo d'Oro was that the unexpected happened.

Yet when the train drew in I got on, because that was my plan and I did not want to be dissuaded from it. Only when the doors closed did I see that Haroun had followed me into the train, and he sat beside me, looking reckless, still imploring me to listen.

"You take the train but the Gräfin can offer you her car!"

"That's why I am taking the train."

He threw up his hands, a theatrical gesture.

"So what's the secret?"

The train had started to race, to clatter, to offer up glimpses of the gulf and the seaside villas. The very sound of the speeding wheels excited me: I was going away — as I had come, with nothing but a little bag.

"She is very happy," Haroun said, sitting sideways, his hand clutching his jaw, speaking confidentially. "As you know, I am her doctor. So I also am very happy."

"Because she's healthy?"

The thought of Italian graduates with first degrees in something like language studies calling themselves *dottore* made me smile again.

"I have known the Gräfin a long time," Haroun said. "I have never seen her so happy."

"Really?" She didn't seem so happy to me.

"Happiness is different according to your age. And is relative. She was desolate before. She was suicidal." He looked out the window at the sight of a Vespa being steered by a young man, with an old woman in black sitting sidesaddle on the rear seat. "How does she seem to you?"

"Fine."

At twenty-one I did not look closely at anyone's mood. A person might seem sad, but it did not occur to me that she might be "desolate."

"I mean physically."

"She's pretty strong," I said. Her mantra was *More!*

"As you are."

"She's stronger than me in some ways."

"Good skin?"

"Like silk."

"Muscle tonus?"

I said, "Harry, what is this all about?"

"About the Gräfin. My patient. Your lover."

Instead of answering, I looked around to see whether anyone in the carriage had reacted to those last two words.

"You are beautiful together," he said.

"What are you trying to tell me?"

He sucked smoke from his cigarette and made a face. "It is hard. I don't want to shock you."

That I liked very much. Certain statements, when I heard them spoken like that — in a speeding train, under the blue sky — made me think: This is real life, this is my life, this is drama, this will be the source of my work, and moreover, now I have the images for it in the words. *I don't want to shock you* pleased me and made me patient.

I wanted to be shocked, I deserved it, I saw it as my right, not a gift but something I had earned.

Haroun flipped the cigarette butt out the window and lit another. He said, "When the Gräfin first came to me she was in great distress. She felt her life was troubled, she hated herself, she actually spoke of suicide."

"She certainly isn't that way now."

"I am speaking of many years ago."

"How many?"

He raised his eyebrows in an oddly comic way. The noise of the train, this public place, made him exaggerate his expressions. "Quite a few years now."

Quite a few seemed too many, and so I said, "How old is she?"

Haroun smiled and set his face at me: Was this his secret? He said, "Old enough to worry about her looks."

I laughed, since "worry" was not a word I associated with the Gräfin at all. She was supremely confident and imperious as she demanded *More!*

"I have been looking after her all this time. Many years."

"You're a psychiatrist?"

"My field of medicine is reconstructive surgery."

"Did the Gräfin have some sort of accident?"

"Growing old is worse than any accident," he said. "Old age can make you a monster."

"So you're a plastic surgeon?"

"I hate the American expression."

"It is true, though."

"It is imprecise, like 'cosmetic surgery.'"

"You give people face-lifts. You fix their big ears."

He waved his hands at these words as they came out of my

mouth. He said, "Much more than that. You are talking about surfaces. I go deeper."

"How deep?"

He loved this question. He said with a suitable facial expression — solemn, priestlike, unctuous, straining to be heard over the banging wheels — "To the very heart and soul."

"What did you do to the Gräfin?"

As though expecting the question, he raised his head, tipping his chin up defiantly, not answering for a while, but when he spoke it was like boasting.

"It would be easier to tell you what I did not do."

"Like what?"

"There is little that one can do with the hands except remove liver spots and age blotches. And the skin becomes slack."

"The Gräfin wears gloves," I said.

Haroun nodded a bit too vigorously, liking the attention I was giving him. I was happy to grant it: I was heading for Siracusa and the fugitive Myra. Yet he had said enough to make me curious about the Gräfin.

"Tell me her age."

"Golden age." He hadn't hesitated.

"What does that mean?"

"You too. Golden age."

At his most playful, Haroun was at his most irritating.

"How old is she?" I said in a sharp voice.

The clatter of the steel wheels on the steel rails was in great contrast to the peaceful sea and sky. Now Haroun looked coy and unhelpful.

"You will never guess."

"It doesn't matter. I am leaving," I said. "So, what — thirty-five, thirty-eight?"

"I love you for saying that."

"Forty-something?"

"I want to kiss you."

"Fifty?"

"No!" he said in a child's screech.

I could not imagine her being fifty, and so anything older than that was not an age at all, and sixty, to my young mind, was a sort of death, the end of a life, something unthinkable. Yet I spoke the absurd number.

Haroun stared, he said nothing; and his absence of expression was the most expressive he had been.

"Sixty?" I said.

"Golden age! Isn't she lovely? She is my masterpiece. And you are the proof I have succeeded."

The train clatter penetrated my body and nauseated me, and the carriage swayed, too, and the motion and noise intensified my sense of shock, for he had been right: the secret was shocking. I was disgusted and ashamed, as though I had broken a taboo. Perhaps I really had, for my mother was hardly fifty. I tried to summon up the Gräfin's face by looking out the window of the train, but all I saw was my own face and the cracked and elderly façades of the villas by the shore. What had seemed to me a ridiculous melodrama of greed and innocence and opportunism now seemed serious and portentous. The strangest thing to me was that someone else had been the object of my desire, not the young Gräfin but the elderly woman inside her.

"Why are you telling me this?"

"So that you will understand how important you are. I need you to be kind. She is not the woman you think she is."

As I had thought, there was a stranger inside her. But I also felt more powerful knowing this. I had learned her secret — I had something on her. Knowing her secret gave me power over her. I need not fear her anymore.

Haroun said, "And I want you to know who I am, too. You

think I just hang around this rich woman. But I tell you she would be nothing without me."

"She would still be a countess."

"She would be a monster."

He was too proud of the transformation of his surgery to keep it a secret. He wanted to impress me, but his boasting backfired. From that moment on the train, swinging down the coast, I saw the Gräfin as a desperate old woman, a crone, a witch, but a helpless witch. I knew that I had to go back and confront her — that, knowing her secret, I could not continue to Siracusa.

At Catania I got off and walked across the platform, Haroun following me, pleased with himself. We waited for the next train back to Taormina. *Addio,* Myra.

8

Rain had fallen on the town, washing its face. The piazza gleamed in the lamplight, the drenched leaves drooped and some that had lain plastered to the night streets were being lifted and peeled by a breeze funneling between the old stone walls. But there was something ghostly in the clean streets, for the lamplight illuminated their emptiness and made them seem abandoned and shadow-haunted.

Or was the feeling in me? I had given up on this ancient town, so luxurious on the lumpy mountainside, famous for its seasonal snobs, all its serious cracks hidden in layers of brittle stucco and whitewash, spruced up for sybarites and seducers, like an old whore winking from beneath a shadowy hat, not an Italian whore but rather some trespassing alien who refuses to go away.

"So lovely in the night, this town," Haroun said, contradicting everything in my mind.

The Palazzo d'Oro was in darkness. I knew I did not belong

there, so why had I come back tonight? The odd pointless trip to Catania, halfway to Siracusa, was characteristic of my time in Sicily — going nowhere. But I told myself that it had been a necessary trip: I had learned the Gräfin's secret. Sixty? The number made me feel ill, and reminded me of a morning in Palermo when I had been eating a meat pie, enjoying it, and Fabiola had laughed and said, "You like cat meat?"

The shutters were closed and latched on the Gräfin's windows. She was asleep, an old woman who had gone to bed early.

"Let us take some *tisana,*" Haroun said. He snapped his fingers. "Boy!"

The sleepy doorman stood, leaning from fatigue, and smiled — the staff knew Haroun too well to take his demanding tone seriously. Haroun repeated the order several times before the man brought us the chamomile tea, and to show his displeasure he grumbled an obscure epithet and set the teapot and cups down hard on the marble-topped table, to demonstrate his objection. I liked the man for not being intimidated.

"The Gräfin got the procedure early, while her skin was still elastic," Haroun said, picking up the thread of disclosure from the train. He had not stopped thinking about it, nor had I. "This is why she is so lovely. She didn't wait, she wasn't falling apart, it wasn't a rescue operation."

Yet that was just how she seemed to me: a corpse with a girl's skin stretched over it. Before, I had seen only the skin. Now all I could think of were her old bones and her weak flesh and her brittle yellow skull.

"I am the originator of this procedure. I take a fold of skin and lift, like so," Haroun said, raising and folding the edge of the table napkin. He tightened it and made it flat. "I stitch behind the ears. I tuck. I conceal. Like quilting. *Ecco fatto!*"

Conjuring with busy fingers, Haroun made the napkin small and smooth and gave its blankness a blind stare.

"I am so clever," Haroun said. "I could have made her a virgin. I was this close."

He measured with his thumb and forefinger, and seeing the expression on my face he began to laugh. I was thinking, You like cat meat?

I went to the Gräfin's door, and before knocking I looked right and left down the corridors where I had once detected the self-conscious shuffle of a stranger's footsteps. Seeing no one, I rapped on the door, and almost at once I heard her response, like a plea. And still with the door shut I heard, "Who is it?"

"It's me."

"Where have you been?" she said, dragging open the door and pulling me into the darkness.

She smelled of sleep and starch and perfume, and in her reaching out there was a flourishing of lacy sleeves. I hugged her and felt beneath her nightgown the frail old bones. But when she tried to kiss me I averted my head.

"I have been waiting," she said in a whiny voice as we moved deeper into her suite. "Why are you punishing me?"

She sank to her knees and dragged me down to the carpet and embraced me. In that embrace was all her eagerness and in that same embrace she felt my leaden reluctance. I was inert, like clay, heavy and unwilling.

"What is it?"

She was suspicious, defensive — she knew in those seconds that I was not interested. I was capable of guile, but desire was one feeling I could not fake. The darkness, her touch, revealed everything to her.

Pushing me away she said, "Why did you come here?"

I was not sure why I had come back — perhaps to verify that she was indeed sixty, and now I was convinced of it. She was aged, feeble, uncertain, clumsy, as older people seem to someone quite young — and to the young the old give off an unlucky smell of weakness, which is like a whiff of death. The Gräfin seemed more fragile than ever. I was filled with sorrow and disgust, a sadness born of pity. She seemed at last powerless, and not just powerless but a wisp of humanity, like someone dying.

"I'm sorry," I said.

That made her angry.

"Harry told you!" she said, poking me with her hand as she shouted. "He is a fool."

"How do you know?"

"Your disgust. Your confidence. The way you are touching me, as though I am a crème chantilly. I can't stand it. You are trying to look inside me. You're like him."

"Harry?"

"He is like a tailor. Always looking at stitches and lining. So proud of his stitches."

I wanted to tell her that for Haroun she was a masterpiece — his masterpiece. He had needed me to prove it, and with just a little encouragement I had done so.

"You were attracted to me," the Gräfin said. "You believed I was young. You sucked these breasts." She snatched my hand, and without gloves her hand felt reptilian. She used my hand to touch her, and jammed my fingers against her. "You entered me here."

Her frankness made me ashamed of myself.

"You desired this body," she said. "That was all that mattered."

I wondered whether she was saying "I don't need you anymore." This was sounding like a postmortem and I loathed it.

"Harry has a story, but so do I," she said. "He does not know my story."

There are deliberate postures people sometimes assume for long stories. An alteration in the Gräfin's voice told me that she was reclining, and staring hard through the darkness I could see that her head was thrown back, revealing her white throat, the gleam on her neck. She seemed braced to speak. I prepared myself for a long story.

"I have been here before," she went on. "I was your age, perhaps a bit younger. I came to Taormina with my friend Helga. We met a man — a very nice Englishman. I had an affair with him — one week. I liked making him happy, and of course he was very happy. He was sixty years of age."

"Is there more?"

She straightened her neck and faced me, saying nothing, meaning: That's all. So it wasn't such a long story, but it meant a great deal to me.

I said, "What happened to him?"

"He wrote me passionate letters for a while. He was *innamorato*."

The nice word was one I knew from Fabiola: more than enamored — smitten.

"This was — what? The twenties?"

I took her shrug to mean yes. She hated my asking her to look back, she loathed acknowledging the passing of time, and as a result she had no past. I knew very little about her, and nothing at all about her earlier life. I took for granted that she had led a charmed life, and yet if she had, wouldn't she have wanted to savor it?

She said, "It doesn't seem so long ago. Taormina gets more crowded but it doesn't change."

"D. H. Lawrence was around here then."

"You mentioned him the first time we met," the Gräfin said. "Yes. I met him. He was a nervous, irritable young man, and sick. His wife — I spoke to her, in German of course. He didn't like it that I talked to her like this. And I think he was scandalized that I was going about with a man of sixty."

I wanted to believe that the time she had spent with Lawrence was a link to me, too. But she didn't linger over the memory of Lawrence, she had something else on her mind.

"The man, my English lover, didn't like Lawrence or Frieda. He didn't even like Taormina."

"What was he doing here?"

Now that my eyes were accustomed to the dark, I could see her smile. "That's the interesting part," she said. "I wanted you to ask."

She left me hanging for a moment, and I thought how this evening was different from any other we had spent together. The others had been shadowy, wordless, passionate; this was serene and conversational. She was smiling again. Was this a long story after all?

"He told me that when he was young, forty years earlier, he had come here — he had met an aristocrat and had a *carezza*." At first it touched me that she knew such affectionate words, and then it occurred to me that she had learned them as endearments from her Italian lovers. "The aristocrat had been sixty. That's why the Englishman had chosen me."

And that was why she had chosen *me*, because of that incident forty years earlier, in 1880. I said, "Was he famous?"

"He was very rich."

It seemed odd to me that she, a German countess, would mention this detail of the man's wealth, but I let it pass.

"He was so rich I wanted his life."

For a moment, repeating her words in my mind, I could not speak. I knew exactly what she meant, but again I wondered why a German countess would think that, unless he was a giant. So I asked her, "What was his name?"

"Who remembers names? You will forget my name."

"But I'm like you — as you were then."

"No," she said with a ferocity that surprised me. "How dare

you say that to me!" But she seemed to regret that in losing her composure she had given something away, and her tone changed as she said grandly, "It was just an affair. It meant very little to me. It meant a great deal to him."

"So you came here to find out how it feels to be sixty and be desired."

"Sixty is not old," the Gräfin said. "Anyway, in my heart, and between my legs, I am not sixty, you know that. I think I am making you blush."

The blood rising in shame and embarrassment heated my reddening face and I could feel the heat on my hands when I covered my face.

"It was like something you might buy that you enjoy for a while and then you grow tired of," the Gräfin said. "Like a dream, sex with you in my room. I think it made me a bit strange, but now I am back to normal. You won't believe me, but it helped me to see you with that young girl."

"You were jealous," I said.

"No. I saw how foolish you were. How little you know of yourself. That your whole life is ahead of you."

A suspicion that I was being rejected made me want her again. Hearing her dismiss my ardor toward the girl aroused me. I desired the Gräfin again, with a lust that parched my mouth and made my tongue swollen. I remembered how she had pretended to be my dog, how she had groveled on all fours and howled like a bitch, and we had possessed each other completely; she had been ravenous and reckless. And now, in the neat nightgown, in the darkness of her suite, she seemed to me like a white witch.

I touched her arm. With a kind of distaste she removed my hand and sat up and looked away.

"I know what your life will be," she said. "You will be very successful in whatever you choose to do. You have ambition and you are ashamed of your past. Because of that you are ruthless. You will take risks. You have no family name — you have everything to gain. You have sexual energy. That always makes me think of men who want power."

"I don't want power."

"I know what you want. You are too young to know anything. You will get everything you want. You will be rich. Money matters to you — I know that. Do you think I haven't counted every mark I have given you? You'd be surprised if you knew the total amount. I am a bit surprised myself."

"Look, I never asked you for money," I said. But she was right: she had given me a lot of cash.

"You don't know what will happen to you," she said, "but I know. You are ambitious, certainly."

I said, "Staying at this hotel in Taormina, doing nothing for a whole month, doesn't seem very ambitious to me."

"It is the height of ambition," she said, laughing at what she took to be my self-deception. "In the future you will be well known, maybe famous. You will travel. You will accumulate wealth. You will have many admirers. What I am saying is that you will succeed brilliantly in whatever you choose to do. I can see this" — she began to falter and frown — "I can see it clearly."

A note of cynicism entered her prophecy. She had become somewhat sour and seemed to resent me in advance, to dislike me for the man she said I would become. She had begun to envy the success she predicted for me, seeing me as unworthy of it.

"You will work hard, of course. But other people will work much harder and not achieve your success. Still, you will want to be expert about everything — you will be preoccupied with your life and your struggle."

I was laughing softly and insincerely at the portrait she was painting of my future self, this odd conflicted public figure.

"But you will never talk about me, or how you fucked a sixty-year-old woman, who told your fortune and then rejected you."

That stopped me; already I was self-conscious and silent.
"You will not know me until forty years pass," she said. "By
then I will have been dead a long time."

From that moment I was powerless, in her power. It was as
though she had given birth to me and was abandoning me to the
world; and she could see what I could not.

She said, "If this were a novel, it would demand a tragic ending. I would kill myself, or you would do something foolish. But
it isn't a novel. Life goes on. Yes, I am humiliated, but I have a
life, and the will to live it is very strong. I am a stranger to you.
You will not know me until you are my age."

That was our last night together. I left her and went to my
own room and slept as though in a haunted house, woken repeatedly by violent and mocking dreams that I could not remember. The Gräfin looked rested when I saw her in the morning. She was walking on the terrace with the old lame man I had
seen from time to time in Taormina, who sometimes conversed
with the Gräfin in German. They were holding an animated conversation today; at least the old man was smiling — limping, and
grinning each time he limped.

"He's happy," I said to the Gräfin.

"Happy to be going home at last," the old man said, surprising me by speaking English. I was abashed that I had not addressed him directly. It had not occurred to me that he could
speak English.

"No more of Taormina," the Gräfin said.

She was wearing another white dress and her wide-brimmed
white hat, but even so, I could see her face plainly and she looked
the same as always. I had expected her to seem much older. Perhaps the man's seeming so decrepit made her appear girlish and
spry in comparison. But no: she was a beauty, she had no age,
though last night in the dark she had seemed very old. She ignored me but was attentive to the man, who had kissed her

slowly on each cheek and was limping away, saluting behind him
— not looking — as he left.

"Is he all right?"

"He was a soldier. He was injured in the war. Passchendaele."

"The First World War!"

"He was an officer."

"I can see it in his posture," I said. "The Kaiser came here to
Taormina with the royal party in 1905. Do you remember that?"

"How would I remember that? I was four."

"Where were you then?"

A look of stubbornness surfaced on her face, hardening her
eyes, stiffening her lips. "I was a little animal then, like all children."

To help her I said, "I have the idea that you grew up in a magnificent castle."

"I don't remember," the Gräfin said.

Her expression gave nothing away: her face was like marble —
as lovely, as pale, as hard, as cold. I wanted to know more. The
enduring mystery for me was her real identity. Who was she,
where had she come from?

"What is there to remember?"

Didn't remember her childhood? I said, "Taormina was Kes-
selring's headquarters during the Second World War."

"Yes. Lots of Germans here then."

"Tell me about Hitler."

"Always the American question," the Gräfin said. She lifted
her hat so that I could see her face better and she stared at me
with her blue eyes and said, "He was a monster, with little education, but he had some greatness."

"You met him?"

"On a formal occasion. I was married to an officer," she said.
Then eagerly, with a kind of passion, she said, "The Führer had

beautiful hands. A woman's hands. No one will ever tell you that. When I saw them I looked at my own hands. So that gives you some idea."

"Tell me more. Where did you live?"

"So many places. But in the war, in Berlin." She sighed and said, "I hate having conversations. Especially this one." Her face was still smooth impassive marble. "Your planes bombed my city."

"We never talked about these things before," I said. "You know so much."

"Of course," she said. "Because I have lived."

She walked away in the direction the old man had taken.

I spent the day packing, knowing that I was going to leave — this time not to Siracusa but more directly homeward, to start my life.

The next time I saw her — I was leaving the Palazzo d'Oro, Haroun was bidding me goodbye — the Gräfin's back was turned. She was a stranger once more, just another German in Taormina, talking intimately to the old German soldier.

"Who is he?"

Haroun said, "He is the Graf, of course."

9

I had just come to that last episode of revelation and was writing, "And this, my only story," when the bare-breasted girl wearing only a shiny gold bikini bottom moved toward me, obliquely, like a cat, and stood between me and the sun without casting a shadow, for it was noon. She said, "So you're a writer."

All this time, on my return to Taormina, as I had been writing this story by the pool, the young girl was watching me, and her nipples too seemed to stare, goggling pop-eyed at me. When I looked at her she smiled. At a certain age, sixty for sure, it is impossible for a man to tell whether a young woman's friendliness is flirting. She flutters her eyelashes, she twitches her bum. Is this sexual frankness or is she just being sweet to me? If you don't know, you're old; and if you accept that such warmth is not sexual, you are too old.

So you're a writer. I knew at once that she was simple. It was not a question but a strangely phrased demand, because English was not her usual language. I was woken from my meditation and in a self-conscious reflex I denied it, as though I had been doing something wicked.

That made her laugh — there was simplicity in her laugh as well. The sun was so bright I could not see her properly through the glare. She was a black blob hovering in front of me, bare tits and swinging hair — Slavic, not Italian, blond, small head, small chin, vaguely Asiatic eyes and cheeks, fox-faced. I had seen her all week with a deeply tanned man I took to be her husband.

"You are writing. You must be a writer." A very simple soul, trying to initiate a conversation.

The novelty of my clipboard, my big pad, my leather folder of loose sheets, so much scribbling did not interest her. It was a talking point, a way of introducing herself.

"I have been watching you."

And I had been watching her. Now and then in this story, at a loss for an image, I had used her. I had borrowed one of her gowns. I had used her see-through crocheted dress. Her wide-brimmed hat. Her tight bikini bottom had supplied me with a certain quality of gold. I had used the curve of her hip to describe the Gräfin's; the damp ringlets, the hint of weight in the rounded underside of her breasts, the hollow of her inner thighs. I had sketched these in this narrative. And her neck: I had closely watched her holding a glass to her lips and drinking, loving the way she swallowed, the way her neck muscles tensed, the beautiful pulsing throat, like a snake swallowing a frog.

She had chosen an awkward moment to interrupt me. I was not sure whether my memory was exhausted and I was faltering — my pen poised above the pad as I thought, And then —

And then the young bare-breasted girl blocked the sun and eclipsed my story.

"I wish I could write. My life has been incredible."

"Have a seat," I said.

I turned the pages over so that she would not see my handwriting, as I usually hid my pad from people who tried to peer at my sketching. And I told myself that I could not go any further today — or perhaps at all. What was left? Glimpses of myself on the road. The train to Messina. The night train to Palermo. A third-class berth next to seven Lebanese men on a Greek liner. The cold ocean crossing to New York. And then forty years more: my life.

"What do you do then, for a job?"

"I am a painter."

"You can paint me."

Her lovely body rose and arched and seemed to present itself to me. She knew she was beautiful, that her breasts looked edible. She had tiny hands and feet, a child's fingers, and sun-brightened down on her back, a little pelt of gold fuzz on her lower spine.

"You are American."

"Yes."

"I would love to go to America."

She reached into her cloth shoulder bag and showed me a CD player and a disk: Gloria Estefan.

"Where are you from?"

"Ex-Yugoslavia," she said. "I came here with a friend. You have seen him? He had to leave. Business." She shook her hair to fix it. "I like Taormina. Not many Italians. Where in America you live? New York? I know lots of people there."

Everything she said sounded like either a lie or a half-truth. She didn't seem to care whether I believed her. And she hardly listened to me, as though she assumed I might be lying to her too, for when I said, "I live part-time in New York. I have a studio in —" she interrupted.

"New York is incredible," she said. "You know Belgrade?"

"No."

"Incredible energy. But your planes, they bomb my city."

What she said shocked me — I had written those same words earlier that day. She took my bewilderment for sympathy.

"All the bridges, they break them. Because of Milosevic."

"What do you think of him?"

"A strong man and maybe a monster," she said, and smiled. "I like strong men."

Her cell phone sounded, played two bars of "When the Saints Go Marching In," which she killed by flipping open the receiver. She peered at the caller's number, then turned to me again.

"I see you all the time alone." She had forgotten Milosevic and the bombing. "I think to myself, He is writing a long love letter to his wife."

"No wife."

"Girlfriend, maybe."

"No girlfriend," I said. "Only you."

She liked that, an eagerness charged her body. "Yes. I your girlfriend. Nice." She touched my leg, grazed it with her small fingers. "You paint picture of me in New York City."

"Or here."

The waiter in the Moroccan robes who always avoided me, seeing me at work, now approached and asked if we would like to drink anything.

"I drink grappa," she said with a kind of bravado to the boy.

"That's rocket fuel," I said when her grappa was brought with my glass of wine.

"What do you mean?"

I explained the lame joke, and we toasted each other, and only then did I remember to ask her name.

"Silvina," she said, and drank the grappa in two swallows.

Because I was so distracted by her neck I did not look into her eyes for a moment, but when I did I saw they were watery and drowned-looking, she was already tipsy, she did not say anything, just smiled, looked at my shoes, my watch, my briefcase.

"You travel all over, I think," she said, inventing my life in her mind, imagining — what? "Like a bird. Free."

"An old bird," I said, to test her reaction.

"Not old," Silvina said, still looking me over, as though wishing to drink me and make herself drunker. "You like your life."

"Yes."

"I want your life."

I was at a loss for words, and had to remind myself that this was the young girl I had seen all week and not spoken to. Had she really just said those words to me?

"Another grappa," she said to the attentive waiter.

"How about dinner?" I said. "We could go to the Timeo."

Silvina did not reply until the waiter returned with her glass of grappa. She sipped at it, then tossed it down her throat, gagging slightly from its stinging fire.

"Timeo is the most expensive in Taormina. For the two of us, maybe three hundred American dollars."

"Maybe."

Her eyes were weakly gleaming, glazed with grappa, as she said, "So we go there and eat, and we come back here, and you will say, 'Please fuck me.'"

I tried not to seem astonished.

She was not smiling when she added, "So maybe just give me the three hundred and you can fuck me now."

I felt a sort of discouraged relief, as when an appalling secret is revealed, a person is caught in a lie. And my mind went back to my story, to the Gräfin, her dignity, her recklessness, and at last her coldness.

"Maybe we can discuss it," I said. I put my papers away, packed my notes, my pad, my pen, hefted my briefcase, and started away. Silvina followed me to my room.

"You want a massage?" she said, tweaking the bows on her bikini bottom and letting the tiny garment drop to the floor, the gold bikini bottom that had mimicked and masked the black patch of pubic hair. She picked it up like a monkey seizing a big leaf, with a movement of her foot and a scissoring of two toes.

I had no desire, and yet I wanted her to stay. I felt nothing, I felt sixty. But I knew, as the Gräfin knew, that she would do anything I suggested, anything at all. This knowledge, the anything, made me reticent.

"Let me make a picture of you."

The last of the daylight slipped across her body as she sidled next to the window, the golden and pink sunset, as though a fire was burning on the sea, blazing on her skin.

I sketched her slowly. I loved her small head and straight legs, her boyish buttocks. The sunset gilded her expression, made it ambiguous, something like a scowl. She touched herself between her legs. "You are arousing me."

"You are my model. You must not move."

"Not done yet?" she said a moment later. "This takes longer than sex!"

"That's the fun of it," I said, sketching her sneering lips.

"It will cost you more."

"Money, money," I said, and I thought: Hungry little whorelet.

"I need the money," she said. "Not now, but when I am old I will need it."

"What will you do with it?"

"Buy what I want."

"Maybe come back here to Taormina when you're sixty and find a man," I said, glad that she had relaxed, because the sketch was not done.

"First marry a rich man. Live my life. Then, afterwards, come here and find a young man. A *stallone.* Give him money," she said. She reflected on this. "Nothing is wrong with buying sex. It is a tragedy if you want it and have no money to buy it."

I said, "You don't need my life. You'll be all right. You are willing to take risks."

I talked, I sketched. She was too impatient to be useful, but that did not matter anymore. I knew who she was: my picture was precise.

She still believed that she was pleasing me. I spared her the truth. That I knew she was repelled by me and I by her. That she would never remember this. That I knew she was eager to get away. Nor did I want her to stay. I too needed to leave Taormina and would never go back.

At last my sketch was done. Silvina took the money and peered at the picture, frowning.

"It is all wrong," she said. "Why you give me a hat? Why you make my hands with gloves? Why you dress me with this horrible old dress? You are laughing at me. And you make me look like an animal."

"Like a Gräfin," I said. "A contessa."

"A monkey."

She tucked the money into the front of her bikini, where it made another bulge. When she left my room, a whore in a hurry, I knew everything, and especially that the Gräfin had spared me her past. Long ago, I thought that in knowing the secret of the Gräfin's age I would be stronger than she. But the secret was elsewhere. It was about being a stranger and having no past, the sense of shame that impels people to succeed. She had come from nowhere, which was why she had seen me so clearly, as I had seen Silvina. At sixty, I now knew, you have no secrets, nor does anyone else.

A Judas Memoir

I. Holy Week

I WAS GOING NOWHERE alone up the wet Medford street through slashes of drizzle pretending my footsteps in puddles proved I was braving a storm. The rain was personal, falling especially on my head, testing my willpower. Then I saw the girl hurrying ahead of me. Her jacket was drenched in patches, her soaked skirt flapping against her legs, and a swag of slip, satiny, pink-edged, with a ribbon of lace drooping beneath the hem. She was there for a reason, I felt: because I was there, braving the rain. She turned at the sound of my puddle-slapping steps, her face pale and small. She seemed to study me with her narrowing lips. So I dogged her in the rain, following that hanging scrap of slip.

She went into St. Ray's, I entered just after her, and the heavy iron-studded church door banged shut behind us. We were both in a shadow that smelled of hot wax and candle smoke and damp wool and a residue of incense, all the stinks of veneration. But there was candle shine on the girl's pretty face.

The holy water was tepid from all the dipped fingers, and dripping from my fingertips to my palm I smelled its stagnation as I crossed myself. The church was clammier and cooler than outside, dank with sweaty varnish and dying flowers. Though the church was large, entering it on this dark day was like going downstairs into a damp cellar.

When I had turned to dip my fingers into the holy water font I lost the girl. I took a seat at the far end of a rear pew, under a stained-glass window — Satan in a lower panel, his green face and veined crushed batwings and snakelike tail, his body twisted on the downward-thrusting spear blade of a glowing Saint Michael. The Last Supper, in an upper panel, showed thirteen Apostles at the long table, one with rusty hair and no halo — Judas looking guilty.

The colored windowpanes trapped the light and prevented it from entering the church. As my eyes grew accustomed to the darkness I saw that the girl in the wet jacket was in the pew in front of me, kneeling, her head bowed, and as she prayed and relaxed she lowered her small shapeless bottom onto her heels. I sat behind her and looked at her narrow shoulders, her skinny neck, her wet shoes — pigeon-toed behind the kneeler, and the scrap of satin, her smooth lace-trimmed slip, the more alluring for being mud-spattered.

Above the altar the candle flickered in the red chimney of the lamp on the long black chain: the red light meant that Christ was present as a consecrated host in the tabernacle, the gilded cupboard-shaped box in the center of the altar. A statue of Christ stood at the side of the altar, his robe parted, his right hand indicating his torn-open gown and his blood-drenched heart in flames.

The candles on the altar, the paschal candle, and the red-tinted sanctuary light were nothing compared to the heat from the sloping rack of vigil lights that blazed in front of the small side altar near me, the wicks standing in pools of liquefied wax, a bank of fluttering flames. A woman in a black coat lit a fresh one with a taper, then inserted a coin with a clink into the coin box, and she knelt and prayed.

As I knelt to get a better look at the girl, she sat back in her pew, her hair near my nose. She slipped her wet jacket off and a warm sweet soap smell crept over my face. I remained a moment, sniffing, and then sat and looked at the tiny buttons down the back of her blouse, one of them undone, showing in the parentheses of her parted blouse the fastening of the back strap of her bra. That she wore a bra at all seemed to me a miracle.

Feeling hot-faced at the sight of her bra strap in the church, I turned away and saw that I was sitting under the Eleventh Station, Jesus Is Nailed to the Cross, the soldiers banging the nails through Jesus' hands and feet with mallets while Jesus lay on the wooden cross, glaring at his persecutors.

"This is the ninth day of the Novena and the beginning of Holy Week," the priest said. It was Father Staley. "Scaly" Staley, we called him, because of his hands. "Those of you who have completed the Novena will be rewarded with sanctifying grace. Please follow the service on the pamphlet provided in the pew. Let us pray."

While he prayed aloud I looked at the Novena booklet, flipping through it until I came to the section of testimonials.

I was operating a machine at my place of work, watching the belts and wheels. Without any warning a wheel worked loose, the machine broke apart and scattered chunks of metal in every direction. Although I was not quick enough to get myself out of the way, I was completely unharmed. None of the pieces hit me and just one of them could have seriously harmed me or even killed me. I believe I was spared due to the divine intercession of Our Lord and Savior Jesus Christ, whom I had prayed to in the course of a recent Novena.

Father Staley was clearing his throat in the pulpit. He gargled and said, "This is a special week in the church calendar. We know it is a special week when we look at the Gospel of John and read the words of Christ. 'Did I not choose you, the Twelve, and one of you is a devil.'"

The big sleeve of his vestments crackled against the microphone as he paused to let this sink in.

"One of you is a devil," he said again. He nodded at us and dabbed at his mouth with his floppy sleeve.

Satan was grinning in the stained-glass window, his green face, his broken wings, his shiny thrashing tail.

"Who is that devil?" the priest asked. "The devil is you, if you betray Christ by committing sin."

Satan was grinning in the window because he was being speared, because he was in pain, because in stained-glass windows only the devils grinned. Grinning was a sign of wickedness.

"Later, John says, 'And when he had dipped the sop, he gave it to Judas Iscariot, the son of Simon. And after the sop Satan entered into him.'"

I could tell from the way his lips smacked that Father Staley wanted us to remember the word "sop."

"What is a sop?" he asked, and nodded and paused. I looked at The Last Supper for a clue. "It is something you eat. They were at the Last Supper, eating. Judas was eating with the Apostles. But Satan entered into him." The priest lifted the Bible and the lacy cuff of his big sleeve swung as he said, "'Then Jesus unto him said, "That thou doest, do quickly."'"

In the long silence that followed, Satan hovered over me and tried to enter me and make me look at the girl's gray bra strap.

Father Staley shouted from the pulpit, "'That thou doest, do quickly!' Betray me, but make it quick!"

This sharp cry of condemnation made the girl in front of me jerk her head back, and after that a shiver passed through her body. I became conscious that I was watching her and I shut my eyes.

Father Staley said, "Unless you are in a state of grace the devil is inside you, blackening your soul. You are Judas, betraying Jesus. You are a Roman soldier hammering a nail into our Lord's hands!"

And yet even then I did not believe the devil was inside me; I believed that if I struggled and prayed there, and let the girl leave the church alone, I could enter a state of grace.

2

I went to sleep that night, and woke the next day, with the same thought, not any words but a clear picture of the pretty girl with the wet jacket and the drooping slip. I remembered that grayish lacy slip swinging below the hem of her dress before I remembered her face, her green eyes, her nervous lips and skinny fingers. I wanted to see her again.

"Where are you going?" my mother asked as I headed outside.

"The Stations."

She was pleased and surprised, she looked at me in a kindly way, she said, "Don't forget to bring something for the collection."

I found some change on a saucer in my room that I had been saving to buy some ammo for my air rifle. I took a nickel, but hesitated. When I saw my face in my mirror I felt ashamed and pocketed the quarter.

The afternoon was bright and cool because of yesterday's rain; the sky was clear, the clouds bulky and white and tumbling overhead; the streets were dry but the gutters were still moist and muddy. At the corner of Webster and Fulton I saw John Burkell coming toward me, biting his necktie. He seemed glad to see me. He took his tie out of his mouth and jingled some coins in his pocket.

"Want to go to a show?"

"I'm going to church."

"You don't have to."

He meant it wasn't a sin not to go today.

"My mother's making me. The Stations."

"There's a pisser Abbott and Costello movie at the Square Theater."

"I'm going to be late."

Burkell didn't say anything. He just put the end of his tie back into his mouth and walked toward Medford Square.

The Stations of the Cross service was at four, and it was ten to four by the time I got to the Fellsway, where black cars were speeding past. I ran across one lane and onto the center of the island toward the trolley tracks. A sudden clanging of the bell of an approaching trolley made me jump, and the thing screeched past me on the metal rails as I imagined myself run down and smashed under the iron wheels.

That thought of dying was worse because I had not seen the pretty girl, and somehow I expected to, as I had the day before, at the Novena. On the area of the sidewalk where I had followed her in the rain I saw four big boys and a small one sauntering along in my direction.

Strange boys approaching on the sidewalk in a certain careless way always made me nervous, because they were bolder in a group. For a moment I wished I had gone with Burkell, but then it was too late to think anything at all because the boys were blocking the sidewalk and wouldn't let me pass.

I stepped off the sidewalk into the gutter and hurried onward with my head down.

"Want a fight?"

I said nothing.

"Get him, Angie."

One of them tried to snatch my arm.

"He's smaller than you and you're scared."

"Let go," I said, and hated the tremor of fear in my voice.

"Chickenshit. Hit him, Angie."

I winced and kept walking. I knew nothing crueler or more vicious and unforgiving than ugly hard-faced boys like these daring me to fight. One put his leg in front of me while another pushed me. I tripped and fell flat but scrambled to my feet and tried to get away.

"Fairy!"

Before I could move on, a boy I couldn't see punched my upper arm, then knocked me on the head. I was breathless and terrified.

"Asshole!"

I staggered along the gutter, splashing into a puddle left over from yesterday, and soaked my shoes, the water chilling my socks and feet. The boys laughed, and one of them threw a muddy stick at my arm.

My feet squelched, and what was worse was that one foot was wetter than the other and made a noise as I ran. I knew I was late for church, but at least I had a place to run to. I saw St. Ray's ahead as a refuge and was glad for my decision to go.

Easing the big door open, holding it ajar and hoping no one would see me, I slid through the narrow crack into the darkness of the church.

"Shame on you!"

With this hiss, which startled me, a hand snatched my ear and I saw the angry face of a nun — pale skin and a half-plucked mustache and a black hood like a villain, no lips and crooked teeth and a bristly chin. She twisted my ear and then punched my arm, harder than the attacking boy had done.

"It's a sin to be late," she said in a harsh sour breath. "It's an insult to Jesus."

I was startled and felt helpless again. Nuns were hardly human, bearded women, like demons, somehow incomplete, hidden beneath black gowns and starched collars. I could not imagine what their bodies might look like when I considered their scary faces and claw-shaped hands.

She had punched my coat where the boy's muddy stick had whacked me.

"You're filthy. Your shoes are soaked." She held on to my arm. "This is the house of our Lord and Savior!"

She twisted my arm and pushed me so hard I scuffed my feet for balance, and some people in the last pew turned to see what the fuss was about. I ducked down the side aisle and into the nearest pew to get away from the nun, and as I knelt I heard the chanting of the congregation and the loud "Amen!"

"Sixth Station," Father Staley said aloud, and raised his eyes to the image on a pillar. He stood there, an altar boy on either side of him, each one carrying a lighted candle. The priest went on announcing: "Veronica Wipes the Face of Jesus."

Palm fronds were folded behind the carved wood image that showed Veronica's cloth imprinted with the face of Jesus, the hanging cloth like a mirror, another miracle.

"Veronica in her mercy was guided by the angels," the priest said, "although there were devils all around."

Knowing human cruelty — boys who looked for fights, nuns who pinched me and tried to frighten me with threats, and other human scares — made it hard for me to believe in the devil. Human wickedness worried me and made me want to be alone, or else to find a friend.

She was not in church. I squinted into the dim light that was dulled by the soupy color of the stained-glass windows. I thought I saw her at the Tenth Station, Jesus Is Stripped of His Garments, but it was someone else, a bigger neater girl and not as pretty. I knew that in looking for the skinny girl I appeared attentive and pious, my face forward. I watched for her and heard Father Staley's shoe leather squeak. I watched for her and heard the chinking of coins in the collection basket. I dropped the nickel in and kept my quarter.

Father Staley had left the last Station, fourteen, Jesus Is Placed in the Sepulchre. He turned to face the people in the pews and said, "Confession will be heard tomorrow. You must be in a state of grace or else you can't perform your Easter duty."

As he spoke I saw the girl on the far side of the church — her lovely face — under the Eighth Station, The Women of Jerusalem Weep Over Jesus. I turned to get a better look and my arm went numb as though I had been bitten — it was the nun, bug-eyed in fury, pinching me.

"Kneel down!"

"I want ejaculations from you," she said in my ear. "Jesus, Mary, and Joseph, forgive me!"

"Jesus, Mary, and Joseph, forgive me."

"Five hundred times."

I knelt with my head down reciting them, and when I was done the church was empty, the girl gone. But it wasn't only punishment; we were promised that each ejaculation knocked one day off the time we would spend in Purgatory.

3

I still had no idea who she was, but after two days I had a better notion of what she looked like, her thin face and green eyes, the way her clothes hung straight down on her, her thin neck and narrow shoulders and bony legs, her limp skirt and the way her slip drooped beneath it, different clothes on different days but the same torn slip. She was like a certain kind of skinny doll.

I did not want to talk to her — didn't have the courage, had nothing to say. I just wanted a chance to stare at her. So outside the church on Wednesday afternoon I waited by the grotto, a statue of the Virgin Mary balanced on a ball, and standing there I realized for the first time that the ball was the earth and her bare feet were crushing a snake.

Earlier in the year we had had a special ceremony and a sermon on this spot, consecrating the statue, the pastor explaining the Assumption, that when the Virgin Mary died she rose to Heaven.

"The Blessed Virgin was not buried, her body did not decay, she was assumed into Heaven, body and soul, because she was the mother of God, the second Eve. This is Our Lady's year, the Marian Year."

I kept hearing the expression "Marian Year" and I knew it had something to do with Mary, but what was I supposed to do? It did not seem so odd to me that she had uprisen, flown to Heaven on rooster tails of flame: it was shown in all the pictures, even the oldest ones.

But now that the pastor kept insisting that Mary was assumed into Heaven, that this was official doctrine, saying "It's true," I started to think that it might not be true. Looking at the stone statue, the big hard folds of the Virgin's blue cloak and her heavy body, I tried to imagine her rising from the ground, over the tops of the telephone poles and past the trees in Hickey Park, into the glowing clouds, the whole grotto, scallop shell and planet earth and all, shooting like a rocket ship upward on a plume of smoke.

Then, staring past the Virgin, I saw the skinny girl hurrying along the sidewalk alone, wearing the jacket she had worn to the Novena — it had dried out — but a blue skirt, the same shoes, falling-down socks, and the scrap of drooping slip. Her tangled hair made her seem nervous and unhappy, as though someone was chasing her.

The devil was always after us, the priests said. Maybe she

was being dogged by the devil, walking lopsided, one shoulder higher than the other.

She turned to climb the church stairs, and I followed her, keeping my distance, waiting a few seconds after the big door closed on her before opening it again. The bad light blinded me as I entered, I stumbled in the shadows, and I paused behind a pillar until I could see clearly.

Two confessionals were in use. In the pews near them people were waiting, some of them kneeling, some sitting, waiting their turn to tell their sins.

The skinny girl was walking slowly up the center aisle trying to decide where to go. We knew that in confession some priests were stern and some friendly. I had no idea which priests were in the confessionals, but I knew where to go when the girl chose. I wanted to be near her but not next to her. Her confessional had two compartments for people to confess. The girl was in the line that fed into the right-hand side, and so I sat two pews behind her, in the line for the left-hand compartment, five people ahead of me, five ahead of her. She knelt and prayed.

Above her was a stained-glass window — Saint Rose of Lima, first saint in the Americas, from a rich family; but, the nuns told us, she decided to serve God. The next window showed Saint Theresa of Ávila. She was famous for having a vision of Hell, another nun's story: a tiny room made of white-hot metal in which she could neither stand nor sit, flames on the walls, where you burned for eternity.

Every time I saw Saint Theresa's odd comical headpiece and pleated cloak I was reminded of this hot room in Hell.

That was why we were going to confession. If you were not in a state of grace, with a stainless soul, you went to Hell when you died and you stayed in the flames forever.

Saint Francis, in another window, was a relief to me, the way the birds fluttered around his head — he spoke to birds, they talked back to him. On his hands were wounds, the stigmata. The cuts did not surprise me. If you were very holy, God made your hands and feet bleed, the way Jesus had bled during the crucifixion. I saw the wounds as a Jesus-like achievement, not something that was painful but a sort of reward, a bloody badge, and the proof of holiness.

People left the confessional with their heads down, and other people entered, looking anxious. We slid along the pews, awaiting our turn. Each time the priest began to hear someone's confession a window inside was jiggled open, like a kitchen cabinet. Then the priest pronounced a blessing, and when the confession was done he shut the slider with a smack and opened the one on the other side.

The girl was kneeling, praying. I tried to pray, but above my head the stained-glass window showed Saint Michael spearing the devil, his snaky tail whipped to one side. The windows were full of snakes. Saint Patrick holding a staff was casting wiggly snakes out of Ireland, and the Virgin in her window was squashing a squirming snake with her bare feet.

I looked from one snake to another, marveling at how fat and healthy they seemed. These evil things were the only images in the windows that were full of life, even struggling to survive as they were, and the saints were overcolored, with big sleeves and fat faces and dead eyes, and halos like gold donuts.

Thup-thrip, the jiggling slider closed on one side of the confession box, and *thrip-thup,* opened on the other. The girl was gone from the pew in front, so I assumed she was inside the confessional and perhaps the mumble I heard was hers. Since I knew the confession formula, I could follow the high points of what she was saying. Beneath the loose curtain I could see her scuffed shoes and falling-down socks.

"Bless me, Father, for I have sinned." After a pause, a breath, she continued. "It has been blee weeks since my last confession. Blee blee fault blee times. Blee my mother blee."

Hearing her say the word "sinned" made me eager and hot, and there was more.

"Blee blee blee impure thoughts blee times."

Lifting my hands to my face and blinding myself I saw in my dark damp palms someone new, not a pale skinny girl but someone friskier and fleshier, who committed sins and suffered guilt; someone like me.

"Blaw blew blee occasion of sin?" the priest asked.

"Yes, Father."

"Blah blay else?"

"No, Father."

"Blay blee Hail Marys and blaw Our Fathers and a good Act of Contrition."

"Oh, my God, I am heartily sorry for having offended thee," she replied. "I detest all my sins because I dread the loss of Heaven and the pains of Hell."

As she gulped and recited in a quavering voice I realized that I was in love with her — hearing her confession, her uncertain and guilty voice, her pathetic expressions of sorrow, a tone that said: I am sorry but I know I will sin more and I will have to come back here and confess my sins all over again.

Thup-thrip. Then she was pushing the limp brown confessional curtain aside and ducking out, and as she did, heading for the altar, her hands clasped, her head lowered, her eyes were on me, and she looked happy.

Instead of going into the confessional I slid out of the pew and followed her to the altar rail. I knelt beside her. The heat of the vigil lights, the flickering bank of candle flames, the smell of scorched wax, the warmth of the altar, and the sooty lingering whiff of incense. She was mumbling prayers, her forehead rest-ing on the altar rail. I watched her out of one eye, but when I turned away and pretended to pray she got up and left the church.

So only then did I go to confession, and now I had a descriptive phrase for my sins: impure thoughts.

4

"What happened yesterday?" Father Staley asked from the pulpit on Holy Thursday, and he waited a while, too long, and I was worried, because I was thinking about yesterday. Finally he said, "Judas was plotting to betray Jesus yesterday. What happens today?" The priest leaned forward and spoke angrily. "Today, Judas betrays Our Lord."

Father Staley was speaking directly to me. I could not look at him.

"And so Christ's message on Holy Thursday," he said, and he raised a flopping sleeve and shook his white finger at me, "Christ's message on Holy Thursday is, prepare to suffer."

She was sitting in front of me. I thought she had seen me on the way in. She had seemed to hurry ahead. How I loved her. Who was she?

"Tomorrow is Good Friday. Christ knew that he was going to be crucified. He knew that nails would be driven into his hands — big spikes, like the ones carpenters use. Driven into his feet. And a crown of thorns. Not the sort of thorns you see on rose bushes. These are big thorns — inch or so — you find them in the Holy Land. They didn't set the crown of thorns on his head like a hat — they jammed it down so the thorns pierced his flesh. Drove the thorns into the bone of his skull!"

Father Staley waited a little, picking at the dead skin on his fingers.

"He knew this was going to happen. He had been told. It was

written in the Scriptures. Holy Thursday, when Christ was betrayed by Judas, he knew he was going to suffer and die. 'That thou doest, do quickly!'"

She was listening with her head and shoulders, a stiff attentive posture, her hair out of place. I loved her loose hair, her untidy clothes, her twisted collar — one side up, the other down, the smudge on her upper arm where she had brushed the church door perhaps.

Something also told me — the way she sat at a slight angle — that she was aware that I was behind her. If she had turned just a fraction more she could have seen me. Though I was listening to the priest, I was watching her the whole time.

"The example of Christ's suffering has inspired many people to suffer themselves — to become better Christians. Maria Goretti was just a poor pious girl in a small Italian village. She was twelve years old. She did not know that Christ had chosen her. What was the choice he offered? It was to give way to the devil or to die. The devil lived in the village. His name was Alessandro Serenelli."

I almost laughed out loud when I heard this funny name, especially the "nelly." I looked down smiling at the floor of the church and did not look up again until I had swallowed the smile.

"Serenelli watched Maria Goretti. He followed her. Wherever Maria Goretti went, Serenelli also went. But his heart was filled with impure thoughts. Serenelli stared at Maria Goretti's innocent body. He stared at her modest clothes. Maria was never alone — Serenelli was always behind her, watching her with his lustful eyes. Waiting for his chance."

I picked up a hymnbook and leafed through it to take my eyes off the skinny girl in front of me. I felt the priest was warning her about me — she was Maria, I was Serenelli. I wanted it to be a love story, with a happy ending, but I was nervous: in church I never heard love stories, and there were no happy endings.

"Serenelli followed Maria even into the church. He watched her praying. But instead of admiring Maria for her faith, Serenelli harbored impure thoughts. Imagine! In church, this devil was sinning in his heart!"

I tried to read a hymn, I put my fingers on it.

"Serenelli sat in the church and watched the poor girl praying. Wicked thoughts kept him watching. He couldn't take his eyes away from her."

My eyes were so dazzled with fear for Maria and swallowed laughter I could not make out the words of the hymn.

"The devil was inside Serenelli."

The name Serenelli made me think of a small fat man with a big nose and black mustache and flat feet, a clown in a brown suit with spaghetti stains on his necktie and a smelly cigar in one hand.

"He followed Maria to her home. She took a shortcut through some woods. The pure innocent soul did not know that this demon was watching her. And when he got a chance he grabbed her and demanded that she commit a sin of impurity."

Until that point the whole story made sense to me — I could see each separate word as a vivid detail. But "sin of impurity" baffled me. I saw Maria, I saw Serenelli — Serenelli was me. But what did he want? Whatever it was, the sin was so enormous that she would be damned if she did what Serenelli wanted her to do — which was what?

"Maria said that she would never give in to him. She would not commit a sin."

But in this description — Maria in the woods, talking back to Serenelli — I began to suspect that she was tempted. That the sin attracted her. That she needed to pray, because part of her wanted to give in to Serenelli. In my mind the sin was something to do with kissing her, hugging her, touching her — Serenelli slobbering over her, still holding his smelly stogie in one hand

and squeezing Maria Goretti's cheek with the other. I smiled because I saw this clearly — the fat hairy man, the brown suit, the
skinny little girl in her ragged skirt and muddy shoes; the woods;
the shadows, the puddles, the lighted windows in the girl's distant house.

"When she refused, he stabbed her. Still she prayed to God for
strength. Serenelli stabbed her again and again. Even after she
fell to the ground this devil stabbed her."

I was so horrified I let the hymnbook slip to the floor. I saw
the knife plunging into Maria Goretti's body. I saw Serenelli
transformed from a guinea wop like Chicky DePalma's father,
with a mustache and cigar, into a devil with crazy eyes and a
bloody dagger. Maria was like the girl sitting hunched and attentive in front of me, so small in my imagining that it seemed especially cruel to stab her more than once. And so thin that I imagined the knife going in one side and the blade point sticking out
the other, each thrust of the knife making two wounds, blood
spurting out.

"All told, Serenelli stabbed Maria Goretti fourteen times."

I wanted Father Staley to stop using the name Serenelli, because it was still hard for me to picture a devil named Serenelli.

"As she was dying, her last words were merciful — forgiving
her killer. 'I want him to be with me in Paradise!' Christ on the
cross turned aside and said the same thing to the good thief.
That is why she is going to be canonized in a few months. She
will be a saint! Christ provided the example for Maria Goretti.
But who provided the example for Serenelli? It was Judas, the sinner, who betrayed Our Lord and Savior. Let us pray."

I knelt and prayed but all I saw was the skinny girl in front of
me, and wherever I saw bare skin I saw bleeding stab wounds.

More priests appeared in purple albs and frilly smocks at the
altar, and the service continued with chanting and incense and
foot-washing and the raising of a monstrance, a big spangled tro-

phy with the host inside a round glass door, and the whole gold thing shaped like a blazing sun.

But I sat and stared at the girl's shoulders and head, and I tried to sniff at her hair when she sat back in the pew. When the service ended I watched her leave. She did so in a hurry, not looking at me, which I felt was her way of noticing me.

5

Good Friday was a holy day of obligation: it was a sin not to attend church. I knew I would run into my friends. The week had developed slowly for me, the progress at church had allowed me to be near the pretty girl I devoured with my eyes from behind, the girl who, to my confusion, to my guilty flustered pleasure, had confessed to "impure thoughts."

John Burkell was sitting on the church steps chewing his tie. When he saw me he started complaining about the length of the service.

"This thing is going to last a year."

He was snapping a stiff card the size of a playing card.

"What's that?"

He handed it over. One side showed Jesus rising to a multicolored Heaven, and under a prayer was a small cellophane window with a cloth dot, the size of a dot that a paper punch made.

"Part of the Holy Shroud," Burkell said.

But I read, *Fragment of a piece of linen that has touched the Holy Shroud,* and pointed this out to Burkell.

"Same thing," he said.

As we were talking, Chicky DePalma walked over, his footsteps making clicking sounds from the metal taps on his heels, clickety-click, like a tap dancer.

"That's *gatz*," Chicky said. "Look at this."

He took out a small card with a similar cellophane window, but this one showed a dark chip of wood.

"Piece of the True Cross."

It looked like the sort of splinter that you tweezed out of your finger after you'd been fooling in woodworking class.

Burkell said, "My old man says they've found enough pieces of the True Cross to rebuild the Italian navy."

"What's that supposed to mean?" Chicky asked.

But I was laughing, imagining a whole harbor of bobbing ships, all of them made of tiny dark splinters.

"Your old man's a Protestant," Chicky said. "What does he know?"

Burkell went silent and chewed his necktie.

"They got a mixed marriage," Chicky said to me, and made an Italian gesture of emphasis, flipping the fingers of one hand.

"My folks aren't the only ones," Burkell said in a small beaten voice — he was embarrassed at having to admit that one of his parents was a Protestant — that is, damned to Hell for all eternity. He was watching the steps, his face tight with shame, looking at the people going in to the Good Friday service. "Her parents got one, too."

The pale skinny girl had just walked by.

"Her father's a Jew. Her mother's Catholic. That's worse. Jews are Christ killers."

I controlled myself and said, "What's her name?"

"Evelyn Frisch. She goes to the Swan School. Her sister's a tramp. She lives down near you, off Hickey Park."

I had never seen her. I said so.

Burkell said, "Because of her folks, the mixed marriage. She only started to come here a few months ago."

The fact that she had chosen to come to church alone, to attend Holy Week services, made her seem virtuous. She was always on her own. She got down on her bony knees and prayed. But I hoped that she was also showing up partly to be near me, to let me see her, as part of a flirtation.

In church we could be near, we could stare at each other, examine each other's clothes, study each other's face and body. At school this was impossible — someone would notice us and start teasing. And anyway, Evelyn Frisch did not go to my school. But in church, in the candlelight, in the mottled shadows of the stained-glass windows, it was possible for me to gaze at her for a long time and satisfy myself — and today, Good Friday, more than ever, for the slip that had been just peeping out last Monday at the Novena was now sagging lower, giving me a glimpse of satin and lace flopping against her leg as she mounted the stairs to St. Ray's.

"How did you know her sister's a tramp?" Chicky said.

Burkell said, "She's a pig. Vinny Grasso saw her making out with a tenth-grader at the drive-in."

A sharp voice startled us: "Why are you hanging around here? Get inside."

With a frown on her bristly face, a nun loomed over us like a bat in her black cloak.

"It's disrespectful to loiter here. This is the house of our Lord and Savior. Get a move on!"

As we started to go in, slightly hunched for fear she might hit us, she snatched at me, got a grip on my arm, and pulled me aside. Chicky and Burkell hurried ahead.

"I saw you yesterday," the nun said. "You were smiling."

That was true — I was sitting in the pew, smiling at the sound of the name Serenelli. But how had she seen me?

She pinched my chin and said, "Do you think there's something humorous about immorality?"

"No, Sister."

"Do you think that mortal sin is something to smile about?"

"No, Sister."

"Are you going into church to mock Jesus today?"

"No, Sister."

"And betray our Lord, like Judas?"

"No, Sister."

"Do you know what happened to Judas?"

"He went to Hell, Sister."

"He took a halter and hanged himself by the neck," the nun said. "And then he went to Hell, because he was a sinner. Do you know what Hell is?"

"Yes, Sister."

"Hell means you never see the face of Christ."

That did not seem so bad to me — in fact, I was relieved when she said it. She still had a grip on my chin. "I'm going to be watching you. I know your parents. If I see any mockery I'm going to tell them."

She pinched my chin one last time and pushed me so hard I stumbled on the granite step and almost fell. As I got my balance and looked back I saw her crooked lips and bristly cheeks.

Chicky and Burkell were waiting for me inside the door by the holy water font. We dunked our fingers and blessed ourselves and went up the aisle, sitting together, far behind Evelyn Frisch. When the praying Father Staley said the word "chrism" Burkell muttered it and had a laughing fit, covering his mouth.

Saint Theresa, Saint Patrick, Saint Michael, and Saint Rose of Lima looked down on us, and so did the nun. Chicky picked his nose and flicked a piece of snot into the aisle, and the nun hauled him out of the pew, gripping his head. A little later, Burkell folded the Easter Message into a paper plane and kept it on his lap, and he was next to go. Then I was alone, hungry from having fasted, no breakfast, no lunch, and straining to see Evelyn Frisch.

Good Friday was a terrible holy day. The service lasted three hours — each time I thought it was over there was a new prayer, more kneeling, another procession, an upraised ciborium, and a louder chant. The day commemorated the arrest of Jesus, his denunciation by Pilate, his robe stripped from him, the whipping, the jamming onto his head of the crown of thorns. He was given a heavy wooden cross to carry. He was spat upon by the same people who had welcomed him on Palm Sunday.

"And he was brought to Golgotha, which means the Place of the Skull," Father Staley was reading. And he described the rusty nails, the hammering, the bleeding, the cross raised up with Christ slumping upon it.

"*Eli, Eli, lama sabachthani* — Lord, Lord, why hast thou forsaken me?" — Father Staley was still reading.

Christ asked for a drink of water. A Roman soldier dipped some bread in vinegar and hoisted it on his spear to torment him. Another soldier stabbed Christ in the side to make sure he was dead, and later Christ was taken down from the cross by Mary and some others, and he lay dead and bleeding on their laps.

The service continued, recalling blood and pain, death and darkness, "Free Barabbas," the Jews saying "Crucify him! He is not our king. Our king is Caesar!," the rusty nails, the suffering of Jesus, "the passion and death," the Good Thief, the Bad Thief, the storm, the earthquake, the suicide of Judas. Much worse for me was that I was sitting at the back of the church, too far from Evelyn Frisch for me to see her. But at least I knew her name.

6

Kneeling alone in church on Holy Saturday in a thinner crowd than yesterday — today was not a holy day of obligation — I was not watching the altar. My gaze was fixed on Evelyn Frisch, now in the pew just in front of me. She had entered the church after me, she had chosen to sit where I could see her. She knew what was in my head: that I had come there to worship her.

I stared at her neck, her tangled hair, her limp jacket, her droopy slip. She was kneeling, and so I knelt. I was praying to her; I hoped she was praying to me.

The priest appeared with two altar boys hurrying beside him. He busied himself at the altar, muttering in Latin, the boys replying. He opened and closed the tabernacle, he fussed with the chalice, he smoothed the linen napkins. At the consecration one boy shook the hand bells and Father Staley shuffled the host and snapped it apart with his scaly fingers and said, *"Hoc est enim corpus meum,"* and I thought, This is my body, Evelyn.

The host was not bread anymore; it had been transformed into the body of Christ, as the wine sloshing in the chalice had been made into blood. Father Staley was leaning on the altar, his elbows on the marble, eating and drinking, chewing body, swallowing blood. I knew what was happening, I had half believed it because there was nothing else to believe. But now I believed in Evelyn Frisch, body and soul.

The way she knelt and prayed in a posture of struggle seemed to show that she was trying to believe, praying for strength. I was also kneeling, but I was not praying anymore, I was thinking: It is so hard to believe in God, and harder still to love him, or Christ the criticizer. It was so easy to love this skinny girl, who was full of life and yet frail, dressed poorly, probably in hand-me-downs, and yet her clothes attracted me. And half Jewish was alluring too; she was odd, exotic, didn't really belong here, and although she had never looked directly at me, she knew exactly where I was. We were together in church, worshiping together, worshiping each other, amid the watery flicker of lighted candles.

"On this Easter vigil, the burial of Jesus, we light a candle to signify Christ's passing from death to life," Father Staley was saying in his sermon. "God is love, and if your soul is pure, you too can have eternal life."

The candle flames were a nice part of the ritual that day, the warmth, the fire, the light, the dripping wax on the knob of the candle stump. And as I knelt she sat back in the pew and her head was against my face, her sweet soapy hair-smell in my nose and mouth.

I did not want eternal life. I had no idea what the words meant. What I wanted most of all was this, an hour in church with Evelyn Frisch, even if it meant I had to betray Jesus and be a sinner. She was love.

7

On Easter Sunday at eight o'clock Mass she glowed in a pink and white dress, wearing cream-colored gloves and a white hat with a gauzy veil over her face and the same scuffed shoes and falling-down socks. We were in the same pew, about ten feet apart — three people between us — but still I could see just beneath the hem of her Easter dress the same scrap of lace-trimmed slip like a lovely sin.

The day was warm and the sun so bright even the stained-glass windows poured bars of reddish light into the church.

People sang, their voices raised, their prayers flying up to Heaven.

I murmured earnestly but I knew that my prayers were not rising. I was glancing at Evelyn Frisch and not at the altar, imploring her, so that she would be kind to me, so that she would want me. I venerated her, I prayed to her, and all that I wanted from life was that she, or someone just like her, would want me.

I was frightened at the thought of seeing her outside, and perhaps having to speak to her, in the larger harsher world of light and air. I understood Judas — why he was tempted, why he gave in, why he was lost long before he betrayed Christ.

After the service, people left quickly, noticing each other's new clothes. I waited, I looked around, and seeing that the church was empty except for us, I slid a few feet toward Evelyn Frisch. She slid toward me until we were close enough to touch — her thigh against mine. I let my hand stray until I could take hold of hers. I asked a question with my shy fingers, and she answered with her hot damp fingers, and we sat there a long time, holding hands and not looking up.

II. Pup Tent

T O   C O N S O L E   M Y S E L F   at night when I was small, I used to prop up my blanket in bed, pretending I was in a tent in the wilderness. I crouched inside with a flashlight, reading. Only then could I get to sleep. I was nine, then ten. I dreamed mainly of monsters, lumpy potato men or wild children with bucketlike skulls, a huge particular woman in a cone bra, and bunny-faced girls in snug panties. I was naked and fleeing in all my dreams. Maybe it was the books I read — *Trap Lines North, Campcraft,* horror comics. I wanted to sleep outside the house. I thought: I'll camp in the yard first, and later I will go to the ends of the earth.

My parents were confused by my books and hated the horror comics. "Those things belong in the trash. Why don't you read *Penrod and Sam?*" I was so closely peered at I couldn't think straight. "Get a haircut!" "Wash your hands!" "Elbows off the table!" I felt lightheaded and helpless, like the tickle that teases your scalp the second before your hat blows off. Ever since Louie was born I had wanted to leave, and I was saving up for the journey. My books were my banks: I hid dollar bills, some between the pages of *Rich Cargoes,* some in *Treasure Island.* Eight dollars toward the voyage. I never bought anything new, always looked for bargains.

The confidence of my parents' friends made me gape. The loud woman who said "Is this thing an ashtray?" as she mashed a cigarette butt into a good saucer. I had no obvious confidence, only shyness. I sensed I was a sneak, but sneaking gave me some of the freedom I needed. The aromas of perfume and cigarette smoke, the sight of red lipstick on that cigarette butt, aroused me, but nothing aroused me more than being outside the house alone.

One of my pleasures was to take the electric car, the ten-cent trolley, to Boston and walk past the wharves, the ship chandlers and outfitters and nautical supply stores, that lined the ocean side of Atlantic Avenue. The wind off the harbor had the smell of kelp and the sea. In the window of Bliss Marine was an old diver's suit — a brass-domed helmet with a round goggling face of glass and breathing tubes, canvas arms and legs, heavy boots, and a belt of lead weights. The stores that attracted me most sold army surplus from the war. The war had been over for only five years and much of the equipment was new-looking — C rations you could eat, unused ammo boxes, polished leather belts, smooth helmets, gleaming bayonets.

Seeing these objects convinced me I could defend myself in battle, travel a great distance, survive hardships, endure severe heat or cold, even gunfire and enemies. I could live life in a foxhole or in the north woods.

They were piled on counters — tin mess kits, canteens, water bags, rucksacks, web belts, pistol holsters, flares, traps, goggles, field jackets and ponchos — all of them very cheap and most of them stenciled *US Army*. Gas masks too, and sterno stoves, German helmets looking wicked with upturned edges, sleeping bags, combat boots, jackknives, hatchets, khaki metal flashlights with dents in them. The things that interested me most were faded, scuffed, beaten up, "war-torn." I looked for traces of blood on the bayonets.

"This has seen some action," the salesman would say, turning over a holster or a worn canteen, and I could imagine gunfire, a muddy trench, Nazis, General Tojo's buckteeth. Most of all I imagined survival, making it through a dark night, watching the sun come up, being alone and self-reliant, like a fur trapper or a Canadian Mountie or a GI. I was a woodsman, alone in the forest, living in a tent.

Of all the tents, the cheapest and best was the pup tent. This was a model of simplicity that matched the lines of a church roof, steeply angled, with a ridge and guy ropes, supported by two poles and a clutch of tent stakes. A fly of two flaps was the door. Army surplus, ten dollars.

At Raymond's (motto: "Where U Bot the Hat") on Washington Street, pup tents cost more because they were new and oily, smelling of fresh waterproofing. Not having the stink and scuff of battle on them, they seemed less reliable to me.

The pup tent I saw as my own space, a little Eden where I could do as I pleased, a way of leaving home and being safe. The tent was just my size and seemed a familiar extension of my upraised blanket in bed, where I lay and read *Trap Lines North* with an army surplus flashlight. When I had had enough of a fur trapper in snowy Canada, snaring foxes and muskrats, and skinning and curing the pelts, I read the horror comics: *Tales of Terror* and *Weird Fantasy.* I needed a place to hide my books, to hide myself, a place to dream.

I mentally rehearsed the buying of the pup tent, and when I had the full ten dollars I took the trolley to Sullivan Square and the El to North Station and walked to Atlantic Avenue. I was fretful, anxious at the thought of being alone and having to hand over money to a clerk. The process of taking possession of a purchase made me fearful of being mocked or cheated.

The pup tents, rolled up, poles inside, were stacked like little logs. I chose one that was tightly rolled and carried it in both arms to the cash register.

"What can I do you for?" the clerk said to me. This was the sort of banter I feared.

I showed him the bundle.

"That'll be ten simoleons."

I handed over the money. I didn't answer or make eye contact, just held on to the pup tent and thought: When I get home and set it up and crawl inside, I will be safe.

Walking home from the electric car stop on the Fellsway, just past Hickey Park, I approached Evelyn Frisch playing hopscotch alone in front of her house, tossing a pebble onto a square, clapping her hands. When she saw me she held the ankle of one leg from behind and balanced on the other leg. Then she hopped toward me on the chalked squares as her short skirt jumped above her pink panties, five hops and she was in front of me, in white socks and buckled shoes, tugging down her short skirt.

She squinted and said, "What's that for?"

"Sleeping out."

"Want some fudge?"

I shook my head and walked on.

"You got a hole in your fence," she said.

She was twisting and screwing up her face at me when I looked back.

At home I took the tent into the back yard, unrolled it, and pitched it as far as I could from the house, banging in the stakes and tightening the guy ropes. I crawled inside and lay down with my hands under my head and thought, Paradise!

That night while I sat at the dinner table my father seemed surprised and annoyed. He was not eating; he was shaving. He shaved twice a day, morning and evening. He kept his razor and strop by a mirror in the kitchen, where he shaved — no one asked why — every evening before his bath. He held one soapy cheek tight with a finger and jerked the blade of his straight razor at the window. He said, "The hell's that all about?"

"Pup tent."

He scraped at his face. "Thinks money grows on trees."

"I saved up for it."

"A fool and his money are soon parted."

"I got it cheap on Atlantic Ave."

"Get what you pay for. Bet you dollars to donuts it falls apart."

My mother said, "Andy, your dinner's getting cold."

I clawed at my mashed potatoes with the turned-over tines of my fork while my father wiped the suds from his ears and sat down.

"Can I sleep out?"

"Pup tent is a peck of trouble," my father said. He snatched at my fingers. "You could grow vegetables under those nails."

The next day I put down a ground cloth, a rubber sheet from Louie's cot, and stocked my tent with a flashlight and a canteen of water and *Trap Lines North, Campcraft,* and the horror comics.

The horror comics I hid from my parents; they said they were violent and disgusting. I liked the comics because they were violent and disgusting. The women shown in them wore tight blouses and short skirts and had big red lips and were terrorized. Now and then they were dismembered, chopped into pieces and put into bloodstained bags, but only if they were cruel. Horror stories always had a moral. Good people were never killed in them, but guilty ones were always beheaded or devoured by ghouls or choked — blue tongues out, bloodshot eyes popping, neck squeezed small.

One hot afternoon in the summer of my pup tent I was reading *Tales of Terror,* two separate stories intertwined. In one a shapely blonde in a skimpy bathing suit was always lying in the sun, trying to darken her tan; in the other a pale-skinned brunette spent the day applying cosmetics, trying to devise ways to stay youthful. Their husbands were tormented by their vanity, one wife wasting time in the sun, the other wasting money on skin creams. By coincidence, in the middle of the story, both men met on the beach, just bumped into each other. "Sorry!" "Excuse me!" They did not realize how their lives were similar: henpecked by vain, demanding wives. One man was an electrician, the other man a chemist. This meeting was brief, a chance encounter before the stories diverged again, a detail of storytelling that impressed me.

Not long after, unable to stand the nagging, the men snapped. The electrician tied his wife to a table and burned her black, toasting her to death under the glare of a hundred sunlamps. She lay naked and scorched, her skin peeling.

You got your wish! Now you're nice and brown!

In another part of the same city, the crazed chemist had prepared a huge vat of clear molten plastic. He shoved his wife into it, drowning her and sealing her in the goop as it solidified. She was fixed in the posture of thrashing, her legs apart, her mouth choked open.

You said you never wanted to grow old. Now you'll be young forever!

The justice of it, the morality of it, the desperate husbands pushed over the edge; but I stared at the women's bodies, their tortured corpses, still beautiful in tight bathing suits.

"Andy?"

Evelyn's voice on top of the pictures made me flustered. I shut the comic book.

"Brought you some fudge."

She stuck her arm through the tent flap, with a small brown paper bag, three squares of flat crumbly fudge.

"How did you get over here?"

"Through the hole in your fence."

After she went away I heard her talking to herself, something she wanted me to hear, but it was only a meaningless murmur to me. Later I saw the missing pickets.

The next day just before dark she came again, saying, "Anybody home?"

"I don't want any fudge."

"Didn't bring you any." She put her face through the parted flap of the pup tent. "Can I come in?"

She was on her hands and knees in the grass, her face forward, her hair damp, and dampness on her face.

"I guess so."

She duck-walked into the tent, knelt for a moment, then sat down on the ground sheet, her pleated skirt riding up her thighs. She smelled of soap and bubble gum. She wore her hair in braids, a ribbon at each end, and twirled one braid with a stubby finger. With her other hand she gave me a wrapped piece of Dubble Bubble.

Chewing the gum and unfolding and smoothing the small wax-paper rectangle of jokes that was wrapped with the gum, I pretended to read it. But all the while I was glancing at her skirt and her legs, her pretty lips, her smooth cheeks, her small shoes and white socks.

She was daintily dressed and so clean, with a slight film of sweat on her face from the summer heat. Her blouse and the socks were pure white, and there were a few crumbs of dirt on her knees.

I was lying on my side and was both eager and fearful of her lying next to me.

"What's that supposed to be for?"

She meant the army flashlight. "So I can read after dark."

"My mother hates comic books," she said, seeing the *Tales of Terror* I had tried to hide.

I liked looking at her legs when she was turned aside, the way her little skirt was creeping up her thighs as she squirmed, interested in something else. Every time she shifted I saw her pink panties, the edge of them, trimmed with white lace, tight against her skin.

"Other books, too." I showed her *Trap Lines North* and watched her fingers as she turned some pages. Her small nails were painted with pink polish.

"No pictures in this one."

I took the book from her and showed her a one-page photograph of a stack of muskrat pelts, and another of a cabin in the snow.

"It's about fur trappers. And Mounties."

She had picked up the horror comic and was leafing through it, looking disgusted. "That's wicked."

A woman was being strangled by a crazy-eyed man. The woman's arms were flailing, her mouth wide open, her tongue sticking out, her eyes bulging, her legs apart, her blouse torn.

"She kills him with a hatchet on the next page."

"You can even see her bra," Evelyn said. The word, and the casual way she dropped it, excited me. She smiled at me and said, "I have to go to the bathroom."

I stared at her tongue lolling between her lips.

"Just tinkle."

She got onto her hands and knees and turned away from me. I watched her bottom twitch as she wriggled out of the pup tent. She hurried away through the space in the fence with the missing pickets.

I was glad she was gone, so that I could think hard in the darkness about what she had boldly said. I wanted to remember and repeat her exact words, and see her face, her lips, the way she had smiled saying them. Then I switched on my flashlight and tried to read *Campcraft,* but I kept hearing Evelyn, *Just tinkle,* and seeing her face.

That night at dinner I said, "Can I sleep out?"

"Something wrong with this hotel?" my father said, still eating. "You got a nice bedroom. Your mother works hard to keep it clean. Now pass the mouseturd. And get a haircut — you look like a girl."

"I know she —"

"Don't refer to your mother as 'she,'" he said. "So this hotel isn't good enough for you?"

"Louie snores."

Louie was three, a little kid, and my sharing the bedroom with him made me feel like a little kid, too.

"Quit your bellyaching."

That night, like every other night, I made a tent of my blanket and read *Campcraft* with my flashlight. How to purify water, how to cook wild plants, how to notch trees in the wilderness so that I would never get lost when I was out trapping animals, how to tie a sheepshank, how to tramp in snowshoes, how to read a compass and orient a map, how to smoke venison, how to identify poison sumac. I wished for a gun.

And the next day, like every other day, I lay in my pup tent that was pitched in the far corner of the yard, near the part of the fence with the missing pickets, and I read comic books.

I was in my tent reading *Weird Fantasy* — another bad marriage, another henpecked husband and cruel wife with a beautiful body. He stabbed her during an argument and dismembered her, cutting her into chunks, wrapping each piece in paper and taping it, and putting the whole pile of little parcels into his refrigerator. Then he was called away.

His poor relatives, stuck for a place to stay, used his house one weekend and raided his freezer. You saw them feasting as the phone rang. *We ran out of food! Hope you don't mind our eating that meat in the freezer!* You saw the man in the last panel holding the phone, his cheeks blown out, saying *Yech*.

"Andy?"

I stuffed the comic under the ground sheet.

"Can I come in?"

I was lying on the lump in the ground sheet as Evelyn Frisch crawled in on all fours, biting her tongue from the effort and pushing at her skirt. When she lay down I sat up, squirming, so that we wouldn't touch.

"So what's up?"

"Nothing."

She pretended to yawn and said, "I'm going to take a nap."

Holding her hands together across her white blouse, she closed her eyes, faking sleep, while I watched the way the pleated hem of her skirt was rucked against her thigh. I wanted it to twitch higher, to get a glimpse of her panties.

"I might not be able to stay too long," she said, but kept her eyes closed.

"How come?"

"I might have to go to the bathroom."

I did not recognize my pinched and strangled voice as I said, "Maybe you could do it here, behind the tent."

She sniffed and said, "If you promise not to look."

"I promise."

Sitting up and snatching at her skirt, she got onto her hands and knees again and poised herself like a monkey and scuttled out of the tent. When I stuck my head out I could not see her, but when I looked behind the tent she was squatting, her panties stretched across her knees.

"You promised not to look," she said in a grunting voice.

So I lay and listened to the low notes of dribbling music, her spattered leaking onto dry leaves, not a stream but a songlike sound I had never heard before in my life, which bewitched and aroused me.

"Bye."

She went into the half-dark of dusk, and I was glad she was

gone. Alone, I could think about her, what she had said, what she had done. She came the next day. I was happy when Evelyn Frisch visited, and I liked it when she left. The same things happened: the same words, even "Don't look," as if she had not said them before, though the second time, when I lay in the tent listening, she said "I'm tinkling" just before the patter and dribble came.

No one else knew our secret. Yet for me something had changed. At first I had needed only the pup tent, and I had been free and happy; but Evelyn Frisch had taken an interest. Her visits had been an intrusion. Then I had counted on seeing her. I wanted her to slip through the gap in the fence and visit me in the pup tent. I wanted her to tease me. I began to think that I would never be a fur trapper or a Mountie.

Now, in the tent I saw as my freedom, I lay feeling restless, waiting for Evelyn to show up, wanting to be near her, afraid to touch her.

Still I dreamed of sleeping out, of staying in my pup tent all night, not coming in: living in it as comfortably as I did under my blanket in bed.

"Louie keeps coughing."

But it was worse than that. I hated sleeping in the same room with him.

"Your poor little brother's got a cold and you don't even care."

"I do care, but his coughing wakes me up."

"He can't help it," my father said, shaving at the kitchen sink, scraping the razor down one cheek, filling the blade with whisker-flecked foam.

"I wouldn't hear him if I slept outside."

"Red sky in the morning, sailors take warning." My father wiped the blade of his razor and said, "It's going to rain to beat the band. You'd come into the house as soon as it got dark."

It was a dare, I could see, my father swiping at his face with the razor and chuckling. I pretended to be unsure, so that he would feel confident in his bullying me.

He said, "Then you'll appreciate what we do for you," seeing my sleeping out in the pup tent as a sort of punishment.

"Tonight?"

"It's a school night."

The following weekend I slept out. It was harder than I had expected: the ground was stony and flat under my back, and after a few hours the air was cold, the dew settled on the tent cloth and wetted it and made it sag, and I could hear the wind.

I lay in the stifling dampness of dusk, the stones pressing into my back through the wadded ground sheet, my head against a knotted bath towel, the oily smell of the pup tent's canvas in my nose. I was tempted to crawl out and hurry into the house. But I held on, I stopped smelling the smells, I stopped feeling the discomfort of folds and stones, and I slept. Around midnight, the rain came down, pattering on the pup tent, dribbling down the canvas, puddling on the ground, a pleasant water song that made me drowse in the humid interior of the tent. When I woke in the darkness, feeling heavy against the ground, I smiled and turned over and scratched and slept like a dog until sunup.

"Look who's here," my father said that first morning at breakfast. He was at the sink, stropping his razor, working the blade on the leather, a white beard of soap foam on his face. His voice was rueful. He began to scrape at the foam, holding his razor with his fingertips like a musical instrument. His voice was toneless, for he was shaving and tight-faced. "Wash your hands."

He knew that he had lost me, that I had another life. I liked the pup tent best when it truly sheltered me and looked used, when birds shat on it, streaks of green-flecked white, when neighborhood cats were baffled and repelled, when it was scattered with twiglets from the overhead trees, with blown leaves from the Frisches' poplars, when it shed rain, when it concealed me. I was free there.

Evelyn Frisch came back, always in her short skirt and tidy socks, half pleading to be let in, half mocking when I hesitated, offering me fudge or bull's-eyes, penny candy she'd bought at the corner store.

No one saw her come. No one saw her leave. We were hidden in the pup tent.

"My mother would kill me if she knew I was here. Wouldn't yours?"

I hadn't thought of it, I never thought of such things here.

But we did nothing except sit, or lie down — not touching; marveling at our boldness, being in this place apart.

"I've got new panties," she said one day, and lifted her skirt. I was stirred by the sight but pretended not to be. Clasping her close, they were purple, trimmed with white lacy tape.

"I have to tinkle," she said another day, and I was flushed and went breathless as she slipped out of the tent, and I listened, pretending to read *Weird Fantasy*, wondering at the word "ghouls."

One night a week, usually Saturday, I slept in my pup tent, my father sitting in the house listening to the radio, looking defeated. Most afternoons I spent there, and when my mother yelled at me I fled there. I was safe, I was alone except for those times when Evelyn Frisch showed up, I was still too young to take the pup tent into the woods, where I sometimes hiked.

Hurrying out of the tent one evening, I had left my flashlight behind, switched on, and when I looked back I could see the pup tent glow, a magic place suspended in the dusk, a shining refuge, a small sheltered island of light.

Anything I read there I remembered. Ideas I had there stayed in my memory. Food tasted better in the tent. I brought oranges, bread and baloney, Drake's cakes and Hoodsies. I ate out of my army mess kit, I drank water out of my army canteen, and the battle-dented canteen made the water taste of struggle. Evelyn Frisch joined me, bringing slices of Velveeta cheese and chocolate milk in a small waxy carton. We sat cross-legged, keeping our knees from touching, our heads brushing the canvas.

"I'm not even supposed to be here," Evelyn said one late-summer evening, licking her fingers. "I'm supposed to be home, taking a nap."

She was a year younger than me, but even so — a nap?

She said, "If you eat a lot of trashy food does your mother give you an Ex-Lax to get rid of it?"

"Nope."

"Mine does. Or an enema."

"Does it work?"

"Yup."

She was lying confidently on her back, her hands behind her head, a slash of light across her body from the crack in the tent fly, not the sun but lamps shining from the back windows of my house.

"I'm taking my nap here."

I wanted to object but I couldn't find the words.

"Like my new panties?"

White ones, with a pattern of tiny rosebuds, and pink trim of silken ribbon, small tight bows on the sides, the smug bulges of her bum and a wrinkle-smile between her legs.

"Don't you want a nap, too?"

I lay down beside her, being careful not to brush her with my arm. There was less room in the pup tent with two of us inside. I liked her there, and I liked lying next to her, my hand near the pink bows on her panties; and I wanted her to go away and leave me alone in my pup tent.

"Andy?"

"Yuh?"

"I have to tinkle."

I went anxious and damp-faced and mute. She said nothing more. She duck-walked through the tent flap and I heard her moving in the bushes, not talking but somehow fussing audibly.

Finally she said, "If only I could just see something."

I took my army flashlight and crept out and shone it at her.

"Not in my face, silly. Shine it down there."

She snapped the elastic of her panties with her thumbs and pushed them down, stretching them between her knees, and in the same movement squatted, sitting on her heels, while I lighted her white legs and the smooth white smile between her legs.

The day had grown dark and we crouched like conspirators in the shadow thrown by the pup tent and the lilacs with old withered blossoms. An accelerating car in the street labored from gear to gear, the crackle-gulp of a cricket started and stopped, my hand was shaking.

"Only don't look at me," Evelyn said, teasing me with a giggle, but she was looking down, too, concentrating on the lighted earth between her legs.

She sighed and the next sound was a splash, an uncertain spill and a sideways piddle, and my flashlight made the falling droplets flicker like drizzle against a street lamp, not a stream but a leak that came in spurts, in an interrupted spill. Evelyn was squatting, hunched over and marveling like a monkey with nothing else to look at.

Suddenly she stood up, pulling at her panties and hoisting them into place, snapping the elastic and setting the pretty bows on either side of her thighs.

"See ya, Andy."

She walked into the darkness and through the gap in our fence where the pickets were missing.

In the tent my mind was racing. I could not think. I picked up *Weird Tales* but let it drop, and turned off my flashlight. I lay in the dark and reflected that what I had just seen was stranger than anything I had ever read. And that bold and unexpected oddness beckoned to me. I wanted her to come back and do it again; I wanted a better look. I had had no prior notice of it, and only a little glimpse when it happened, yet the sight filled me with thirst and eagerness: I wanted more.

Entering the house that night, I squinted in the glare of the kitchen, my eyes dazzled and half blinded after the darkness outside, and saw in a terrifying blur my mother and father watching me from across the room. My father had just finished shaving and he was fingering his cutthroat razor, easing the blade into the tortoiseshell handle, folding it like a jackknife. Without a word, my mother turned her back on me, saying something sweetly to Louie, who was at the supper table.

My father's eyes were dark and unreadable, he watched me closely, and I was blinking and wiping my eyes as I grew accustomed to the light. The better I saw, the more frightened I felt.

"I've got a bone to pick with you."

Of all my father's repeated phrases, that one held the severest warning.

I braced myself, narrowing my eyes at the brightness.

"What've you been doing?"

"Nothing."

"Shame on you."

My mother's face was hidden in her shoulder as she held Louie; but I also had the feeling she was fearful of my father's anger, and her timidity made me afraid.

"You should be horsewhipped," my father said, "within an inch of your life."

Now I was shaking, nervous, afraid, clutching my dented army flashlight.

"Your body is a temple. You've soiled it with impurity, you've blackened it. God is everywhere, God sees everything — you think that's funny?"

My eyes still hurt from the glare of the kitchen lights, and as I strained to see, it might have seemed that I was smiling. But I was not smiling, I was terrified. I shook my head and knew I looked pitiful, and now I saw that my father had put his razor down but was holding his razor strop in his hand. It lay folded on his palm, the metal clip at one end, the narrow stitched handle at the other.

"You're filthy," he said, and speaking these words his face was like that of an angry yellow-faced brute in a horror comic.

Seeing what was coming, I turned away as he lifted the strop and struck at me with it, using it like a whip, slashing my shins, raising a red welt on the flesh of my skinny legs. The end of the leather strop gripped my knee and tripped me, and as I fell my father lashed at my legs, cut at me again, while my mother screamed.

I was too timid, too guilty, too afraid to cry out: I deserved my thrashing for my dirty mind.

"Get out!"

My mother was saying no, no, but I hurried outside and didn't stop until I got into my pup tent, my heart pounding, and thinking: It doesn't hurt that much now, at least it's over, he won't hit me again. I lay there not caring that I had been thrashed, but feeling that I had been punished fairly; and not hating my father but fearing him and feeling sorry for him, for he was angry that I had disappointed him. He did not know what to do.

I was so sorry — sorriest because I knew I would never

change. I lost Evelyn Frisch. My mother must have said something to her parents. I was alone. That was how I wanted it. I was a sinner, and would stay that way because I wasn't sorry. I didn't care. I only knew that my life would be harder because of my sins and my secrets, but at least I was on my own and in the world.

III. Seeing Truman

OST DAYS in Medford nothing happened — or the same thing happened. But the day Harry Truman's train made a whistle stop at Medford Station, everything happened, and a lot of it to me. I told my mother I was going to see him with my friend John Burkell. She said, "Mind your p's and q's," helplessly, because she couldn't prevent me from going, even though, as she sometimes said, Burkell was a bad influence. Seeing Truman was my excuse to stay out late in the early dark of October. But the event was bigger than she was. The president's visit made me free.

In Miss Bunker's class that afternoon, I passed Burkell a note saying *Meet me outside the gate.* As he tried to sneak a note back to me, Miss Bunker said, "And I'll take that." She picked it open and read it with no expression, which meant she was angry. "Mr. Burkell, you will stay after school."

He didn't look like a bad influence. He was fattish and pale, with spiky sweaty hair cut in a whiffle. He tried to shock the other kids with morbid songs, but he was teased for seeming weak, for looking uncertain, pink-eyed like a rabbit, his lids crusted ("It's conjunctivitis") from his rubbing them. He was always chewing his necktie, or else poking wax out of his ears with the wire of a twisted paper clip. "Stop doing that, Mr. Burkell."

Burkell's mother saw me as John's protector — the Burkells were new to Medford, where I was born. His pretty mother always hugged me, crushing the cones of her bra against my ears, when I went to their house. This pressure and the aroma of cigarette smoke and perfume made my head ring. "You're getting so big, Andy!"

I guessed his note was saying yes to seeing Truman, and so I hung around the schoolyard after the bell. There was so much shouting and pushing — everyone high-spirited because of the president's visit — I did not see Burkell leave. His house was on the way to the trolley line, so I stopped there. I liked seeing his mother, I liked her smell and the way she hugged me.

I thought I was early because he wasn't at home, then I thought I might be late because he wasn't at home. Not knowing whether to stay or go, I just stood there looking at a Hood milk truck parked in front of a Nash Rambler with whitewalls. I was half hiding against Burkell's big hedge. The truck confused me. Milk trucks were never parked in a street but always on the move, stopping and starting, the engine running, the empties clinking, the side doors open for the milkman to jump out with his rack of bottles. This truck was locked and silent.

Creeping past Burkell's hedge, I went up the stoop to the piazza and looked into the front window. Staring at the slanted sunlight and furniture inside, I sensed footsteps — not heard them but felt the tramping movement through my own foot soles on the wooden piazza planks, maybe Burkell's big feet. He seldom heard his own doorbell because of his habit of poking paper clips into his ears.

Feeling conspicuous on the piazza, I drifted down the stairs and wandered around the house, past the side entrance and his rusted ash barrels, to the rear. The back door was open a crack, so I went in, calling out "Burkey!," and stepped hard on the stairs as a way of announcing myself.

Then I threw a door open and saw a big naked man smoking a cigarette in the middle of the room. He had a pale body and a long loose cock and was standing in his white stockings in Burkell's bedroom.

"What are you looking at, kid?"

I had never seen Burkell's father before and this man's nakedness made him seem fierce. A pain shot through my belly and I almost peed. I backed away, struggling to speak.

"You don't see nothing, right?"

The words I tried to utter gagged my mouth. I could not look at him. I saw Burkell's cigar boxes, an orange crate, a peach basket — holders for Burkell's yo-yos and horror comics.

"Run along, kid."

But the white clammy skin with so much black hair on it terrified me. I was too nervous to move fast.

"You heard me. If your old man did his homework I wouldn't be here," the man said. "Beat it."

As soon as I got out of the room, away from his naked body, I moved fast, feeling guilty and afraid, as though I had done something seriously wrong. The door at the side of the house swung open as I passed it and Mrs. Burkell stopped me. She was breathless, a cigarette in one hand and buttoning her flowered housecoat with the other. My mouth was open, trying to say sorry.

"Johnny's down the station seeing the president, Andy," she said, not listening to me. I was amazed that she wasn't angry, and relieved that she was so nice. She didn't hug me, though. She took a pack of Herbert Tareytons out of her housecoat pocket. A dollar bill was tucked inside the cellophane. She pressed the dollar into my hand with damp insistent fingers and held on to me. "But if you tell anyone where you got it, I'll have to call your mother. Want a Hoodsie?"

It was a sundae cup, the plump one, with a wooden spoon in a slip of paper stuck to the underside. I backed away from Mrs. Burkell but she was still explaining.

"I've been ironing," she said, smoothing her housecoat. Her body gave off a sharp cat smell of effort that made me think she was telling the truth. "Aren't you going down to see Harry Truman?"

"Yup."

"Better hurry," she said. "Johnny's probably already at the station." She looked panicky and pushed me gently and said, "You're going to be late, Andy."

When she said that, which I understood as clearly as the man's *Beat it,* I hurried off and tried not to think about what I had seen. But the cold wet Hoodsie cup in my hand reminded me of the naked man, so I stopped at the corner of Salem Street and peeled the lid off. Spooning the ice cream into my mouth so fast made my teeth ache from the coldness, and when I finished it I had an icicle in my stomach that reminded me even more of the man. I wished I had thrown it away.

I walked to the Fellsway and waited for an electric car, staring at the bed of stones and the splintered wooden ties under the shiny, fastened rails. Soon those iron rails rang and a tall tottering orange-paneled trolley car appeared at the Fulton Street curve, its upright rods shaking against the overhead wires.

"Shitface," I heard when I dropped my dime and pushed through the turnstile.

Small worry-eyed Burkell was sitting on a smooth wooden-slatted bench at the front, the end of his necktie in his teeth. He looked glad to see me, but still he seemed lost, a Drake's cake wrapper in his hand, chewing his tie, his jacket on his lap, rubber bands on his upper arms to shorten his shirtsleeves. He took his tie out of his mouth and began biting his fingernails.

"Andy's got a mustache," he said.

His accusation made me afraid. I rubbed my arm across my mouth and tried not to look guilty.

"Bunker kept me after school," he said, before I could think of a reply to his accusation. "She sees my note and goes nuts."

"What did it say?"

"*Harry stepped in the oomlah.* She says it's disrespectful. 'How would you feel if the president saw it?' I goes, 'How would he see it?' She goes, 'I should show your mother.' I goes, 'She's at work.' She goes, 'Impudence.'" He looked pleased with himself, gnawing his fingernail, his fingers sucked white from his nailbiting. I had no idea what *Harry stepped in the oomlah* meant, but I liked Burkell's odd words. "You got chocolate gobs in the corners of your mouth."

I licked them, tasting the sweetness that reminded me again of my fright at his house.

He said, "Let's get off at the car barns and walk."

I looked down at his weak bony knees showing where the texture of his corduroys was worn flat. His tie was a chewed rag. Above his head was a *Learn to Draw at Home* sign. The hanging leather hand-straps swung together as the trolley car made the curve at the car barns.

The folding rear doors of the trolley opened and we got off, stumbling at the long drop from the running board to the gravelly trackside.

Walking up Riverside Avenue to Medford Square, Burkell began chanting slowly, "Who'll dig the grave for the last man that dies?"

Other people on the sidewalk gathered around us and bore us along in their excitement, heading for the station.

"The worms crawl in, the worms crawl out, the worms play pinochle upon your snout."

Burkell winced as he recited in an impish way, to get their attention and defy them, as though expecting someone to say, Quit it, kid. But no one took any notice of his teasing, and Burkell went back to chewing his tie.

The great crowd of people, mostly men, was outside the station, all over the tracks and in the street, for the train had already stopped and someone on it was giving a speech. We were small enough to make our way through pant legs to the front of the crowd. A group of men, too many to fit, were standing on the back platform of the last car, one of them shouting, an angry-faced man in a felt hat, shaking his fist. It was the president.

"Because of these phony Republicans!" he cried out, looking as though he meant it and was very angry.

He was a live version of the pale black-and-white pictures I had seen, so pink and physical I was too fascinated watching him to listen to what he was saying. He was smaller than I had imagined and his anger made him seem fearsome.

Burkell said, "Hey, there's my old man."

His saying that startled me, and I didn't want to see the man, but Burkell called out to him and I glanced up and saw an older rounder man than the one I expected. He wore a snap-brim hat and looked like a fatter version of Burkell, the same plump cheeks, turned from smiling at the president to smiling at us. In a striped vest and shiny suit and smoking a cigarette, he looked overdressed and comical and had the same slack smile as his son. Under his arm was a loaf-sized brown paper bag.

"Johnny," the man said. He was pleased to see him. "Harry's giving them hell!"

But at that moment there was applause and Truman waved and the whistle blew. The train pulled away, leaving a space of light and silence, a void where the president had been. We were still standing on the railway track, but awkwardly now, for the crowd had thinned. I thought: The men are here, the women at home, smoking.

"Who's your friend?"

"Andy, this is my father."

"I shouldn't be here," Burkell's father said. "I'm supposed to be at work. But, hey, it's a special day. Harry Truman in Medford! Too bad your ma's at work."

He palmed something from his vest pocket, a small bottle we called a nip, and swigged from it and smacked his lips. He was not anything like the naked man I had seen in Burkell's room. His friendliness made him seem weak and ridiculous.

"Want an ice cream?" he said, wiping his mouth.

He led the way to Brigham's, lighting a cigarette as he crossed the street. He saw that I was staring sadly at his cigarette pack — Herbert Tareyton.

"You think I'm stoopid," he said. "You should see my brother. He walks like this!"

When we were sitting in the booth he swigged from his nip again — Four Roses. Again he saw me staring.

"Like my weskit?" he said. "Hey, hear about the boy who drank eight Cokes?"

Burkell was poking a paper clip into his ear, his red eyes fixed on something out the window, not listening to the joke. I was still guilt-ridden by what I remembered from the house.

"The funny thing is, he burped Seven-Up," Burkell's father said. "Get it?" I stared at him thinking of the naked man. "Hear about the drunk who fell ten stories down an elevator shaft into a pile of garbage? He wipes the garbage off his face and says, 'I said *up*.'"

I pitied this man for being silly, someone making jokes because he was lost, sitting here hiding a nip of Four Roses and chewing his lips and finishing another joke. "Rectum? Damned near killed 'im!"

"Show Andy your trick with your teeth, Dad."

The man made a face and mouthed his dentures as though trying to swallow them, and then opened his mouth showing the dentures upside down, jammed upright like he was gnawing.

"I should be on the stage. There's one leaving any minute. Harry Truman's giving a speech at an Indian reservation. 'I promise! I promise!' Every time he says that, the Indians go, 'Oomlah!' When it's over the chief takes him across a field, says, 'There's been cows in this field. Don't step in any oomlah.'"

I couldn't think of anything to say. Every time I looked at Burkell's father I saw the naked man.

"What's in the paper bag?" Johnny asked his father.

"Leon K's shoes. I had them resoled."

"My father works for a guy called Kelly," Burkell said.

Burkell's father looked hurt. "I don't work for him, Johnny. We're partners in the franchise."

I was embarrassed for him because I suspected he was lying — lying to two eleven-year-olds, about what? He thought he saw everything, the way jokers did; but he didn't know what I knew.

"Know what? You're a real chatterbox, kid," he said to me, and seemed annoyed. I had the feeling he wanted to hit me, or say *Beat it.* "Didn't even finish your ice cream."

His calling me "kid" also reminded me of the naked man in his house, and now I knew in my heart that something serious was wrong, and that he suspected I was an enemy, which was how I felt, for not laughing at his jokes and not telling him what I knew.

"I don't know what time we're having supper, Johnny." He did a little tap dance as we left Brigham's. "Your mother's working."

"Who'll dig the grave for the last man that dies?" Burkell sang in his low quavering haunted-house voice. We walked up the street.

I was looking at Burkell's knees again and the way the cuffs flapped against his skinny ankles and small feet.

"We could go to my house and look at comic books."

Burkell had a stack of them in that room where the naked man had stood in his white socks.

"No one's home. My mother's at work." His fingertips were in his mouth. "Or we could take the electric car to the rezza. Got any money?"

I showed him the dollar and paid his fare on the trolley to Elm Street. We walked in the woods and threw stones at squirrels' nests in trees and kicked along the bridle path to the reservoir. Then we walked home in the dark and no one asked me where I had been, because it was the day Truman came to Medford. But I felt burdened by what I knew and shocked by the president's pink face and loud voice.

The secret burned inside me and made me afraid. I felt responsible, and partly to blame. But I kept the secret, because if I told someone, I thought they would say it was all my fault. I was afraid of his mother and dreamed of the man, and of his father hurting me.

But I never saw his mother or father again. I knew Burkell's house as well as my own, but I was not invited there, not even on his next birthday. One day Burkell said that his mother had warned him I was a bad influence, because I told lies, as though pretending to tease me. I knew he was telling the truth.

IV. Scouting for Boys

I

THREE FIGURES came single file over a wooded hill of the Fells carrying their rifles one-handed and keeping their heads low. They were duck-walking, hunched like Indian trackers, with the same stealth in their footfalls, toeing the mushy earth of early spring. I was one of them, the last, being careful, watching for the stranger, his black hat, his blue Studebaker. Walter Herkis and Chicky DePalma were the others. When we got to the clearing where the light slanted through the bare trees and into our squinting faces, you could see we were twelve years old.

"Where?" Chicky asked in a harsh disbelieving tone, keeping an irritated grin on his face. He had a brown birthmark like a raisin on his cheek. His hair, greasy from too much Wildroot, and his big nose and his yellowish Sicilian face made him look even more like an Indian brave.

"Wicked far," Walter said. Worry settled on his scrubbed features whenever he was asked anything about the incident. He motioned with the muzzle of his gun. "Up by the pond."

Walter's saying it was far made us slow our pace, though we still kept off the path. When one of us stepped on a dry twig and snapped it, someone else said, "Watch it," because in the movies the snapping of a twig always betrayed a person's position to strangers. We wanted to be silent and invisible. We were not three boys, we were trackers, we were Indians. Certain words, such as "sure-footed" and "hawk-eyed," made us self-conscious.

"Skunk cabbage," I said.

Dark red and black claw-shaped bunches of the glossy plant grew in the muddy patch near a mass of rotten wood and dead grass that was pressed down and combed-looking from the weight of the snow.

"Them others are fiddleheads," Walter said, stopping farther on, where the mud was thicker and wetter. Ragged veils of gnats whirred over its small bubble holes. From the evaporated puddle, a slab of mud as smooth as chocolate, rose a clump of packed-together ferns, in sprays like bouquets, their coiled tops beginning to unroll and spring open. Fiddlehead was the perfect name for them.

"Vinny eats them," Walter said. He lifted his rifle and poked the ferns and gently parted the stalks with the muzzle.

Chicky said, "He'd get sick. Vinny Grasso is a lying guinea wop."

"And you're a pissah."

"Eat me, I'm a jellybean," Chicky said.

"Shut up," I whispered. "Someone will hear."

"Fuckum," Chicky said.

For emphasis, he stepped over to the tight green bouquets of new ferns and scattered some in one kick, then broke the ones that remained and trampled them flat, his boots squelching the mud and burying them.

Looking at the damage, he said, "But my nonna eats dandelions."

Chicky's outbursts alarmed me, because they made him sound crazy, and his threats were sudden and scary, especially when he was trying to be funny. To act tough, he sometimes punted schoolbooks and kicked them along the sidewalk. I had never before seen anyone kick a book. He'd say, "Who cares? I can hardly read anyway," which was true, and as shocking to me as wrecking the books.

"Give me a freakin' weed, Andy."

"Coffin nails," Walter said.

"Who asked you?"

"They're wicked bad for you," Walter said, straightening himself with confidence.

"You're just saying that because they're against your religion," Chicky said.

Walter Herkis was a Seventh-day Adventist. He couldn't be in our Scout troop, because Protestants weren't allowed to be Scouts at St. Ray's. He wanted to join our Beaver Patrol, but he would have been shocked by our Scout meetings in the church hall, the prayers especially, Father Staley — "Scaly" Staley — telling us to kneel on the varnished wood floor of the basketball court, and raising his scaly hands, and folding them, and giving a sermon, or else saying, "Let us pray." Walter went by bus to a special school in Boston, with other Adventists. Walter could not smoke or eat meat, not even hot dogs, or tuna fish, and he was supposed to go to church on Saturday. He was playing hooky from church today, as he often did, though today was special: we were hunting the stranger.

"They stunt your growth," Walter said.

"You eat it raw." Chicky snapped his fingers. "Come on, Andy."

I unbuckled my knapsack and found, among the canvas pouches of bullets and the marshmallows and tonic, the crushed pack of Lucky Strikes Chicky had stolen from his brother. I shook out a cigarette for him and put the rest away.

"Luckies," Chicky said. He tapped the cigarette on his knuckle like an old smoker, and said, "Got a match?"

"Your face and my ass," Walter said.

"Your face and the back of a bus." I handed him a book of matches. "You want a kick in the chest to get it started?"

Chicky lit up and puffed and wagged the match to put it out. He inhaled, sucking air with his teeth clamped shut, making slurping sounds in his cheeks. Then he plucked the cigarette from his mouth and admired it as he blew out a spray of blue smoke.

"You're giving it a wicked lipper," Walter said.

"Stick it, goombah. You don't even smoke." Chicky handed the butt to me.

I puffed without inhaling, snuffled a little from the smoke leaking up my nose, and covered my gagging by saying, "Where was he?"

"Not here," Walter said, and walked ahead. Pale and freckled, taller than either Chicky or me, Walter was skinny and had long legs, his bony knees showing in his dungarees. He was such a fast runner we could not understand how the man had caught him — if he had caught him. Walter had not told us much of the story, only that we had to track the man down and find his blue Studebaker. He was round-shouldered hurrying ahead of us, and his twisted hair, his slender neck, made him look lonely.

"I don't even freakin' believe him," Chicky said.

"Quit it," I said. "Walter doesn't lie."

"He's a Protestant."

"So what?"

"It's not a sin for them to lie," Chicky said.

We followed Walter up the hill, away from the path. We passed Wright's Tower at the top of the hill and climbed the urine-stinky stairs to the lookout: Boston — the Customs House

— in one direction; the dark trees in the other. We descended and went deeper into the woods.

Even on this early-spring day, there were mud-spattered crusts of mostly melted snow, skeletal and icy from softening to slush and refreezing. The woods looked littered and untidy with the snow scraps, with driblets of ice from the recent rain in the grooved bark and boles of trees, ice enameling the sides of rocks, the old poisoned-looking leaves, curled and dead, brittle, black, thicknesses of them like soggy trash, the earth still slowly thawing, with winter lingering on top. Even so, spring was swelling, pushing from beneath, like the claws of skunk cabbage rising from the mud, and small dark buds on bush twigs, the knobs of bulbs and plants like fists thrusting up through softened soil, and the first shoots, white as noodles. The first were the hardiest, the most resistant to frost, not even green, nor tender at all, but dark and fierce, small, tight, just starting to take hold. Between the frozen silence of winter and the green of spring were these clammy weeks of mud and stink and the rags of old snow.

Walter was waiting for us at the bottom of the hill, at a cliffside and a boulder pile we called Panther's Cave.

"Was he here?" Chicky said, glancing at the cave entrance, a damp shadow falling across it, for it was already five and would be dark soon. The portals of the cave were two upright boulders, bigger than we were, scorched and smelling of woodsmoke.

"I already told you, no."

"Tell us the story," Chicky said.

"Shove it up your bucket," Walter said, and peeled the cellophane from a package of Devil Dogs.

"Fungoo," Chicky said. "Hey, Herkis, I had dibs on them."

"I'm hungry," Walter said, poking a Devil Dog into his mouth, chewing hard, his voice sounding dry and cakey when he said, with his mouth full, "Anyway, you got cigarettes."

"Give me one or I'll whack your ass." Chicky swung his rifle by its barrel, like a bat, at Walter.

"Let's go," I said, because Chicky's quarreling made me uneasy and this was all a delay in the darkening woods.

"He's a Jew," Chicky said. "Okay, if he's scoffing the Devil Dogs, I hosey the Twinkies." He looked hard at Walter. "Jelly belly."

"Rotate," Walter said, and raised his middle finger.

With his tongue against his teeth, Chicky chanted, "My friend Walter had a pimple on his belly. His mother cut it off and made it into jelly."

Walter, still chewing, staring at the ground, looked hurt, not for anything that Chicky had said but as though he was thinking about something worse.

"Come on," I said. I had meant "Let's go," but Walter took it to mean the story.

"It wasn't here," he said.

"Where then?"

"I told you, wicked far."

"Near the road?"

"No, past the Sheepfold."

"Spot Pond? The rezza?"

"The other one," Walter said. He was licking fudgy flakes and frosting from his dirty knuckles. "Where you see cars sometimes."

"Where we shot holes in that No Parking sign?" Chicky said. Then shouted, "You had to eat all the Devil Dogs yourself, you fucking Jew bastard."

"Doleful Pond," I said. My father sometimes took me fishing there with my brother Louie. We caught small slimy fish, pick-

erel, hornpout, and kibbies, and removing the hook we sometimes slashed our fingers on the sharp fins.

Doleful Pond was so far, we did not bother tracking or whispering, but started off again, walking together on the bridle
path, our rifles slung by their straps on our shoulders.

Chicky said, "Walter's got a new girlfriend."

"Quit it," Walter said.

"Her name's Mary Palm."

"At least I don't eat fur burgers like some people I know."

"You gobble the hairy clam," Chicky said. "Andy plays pocket
pool."

Chicky let the cigarette die. He lit it again and finished it,
puffing it to a small butt, less than an inch, tweezing it between
his fingertips. "Look," he said, and pinched the ashy tip off and
began tearing at the paper and loose tobacco. He peeled the paper and flaked the tobacco and scattered it.

"That's called fieldstripping. My cousin showed me how. He
was in the navy in Japan. He brought back this wicked nice jacket
with a dragon on the back. I'm going in the navy."

"The navy gets the gravy, but the army gets the beans," Walter
said. "That's true, you know. The food in the navy is really
good."

"I bet you've never seen one, Andy."

"One what?"

"Twot."

It was true, but I shrugged in a worldly way, as though the
question was irrelevant.

"I've seen billions of them," Walter said. "My mother's always
charging around the house bollocky."

"That doesn't count," Chicky said. "She's too old."

"I saw my cousin's," Walter said. Though he sounded as if he
was breathless from the memory, it was really from climbing the

path, beating the twiggy bushes aside, kicking the snow crusts with his wet shoes. "She was bollocky. She didn't even know I was looking at her." He measured with his cold reddened hands. "It was yay big. It even had some hair on it."

"Like you'd know what to do with it."

"I didn't have any Trojans," Walter said.

"As if they make them that small."

"Anyway, I wouldn't bang my cousin without a rubber."

"She must be a nympho."

"She's a virgin."

"So are you," Chicky said.

A silence entrapped us with the truth: we were each of us virgins. We knew nothing except the wild talk.

"You Jew bastard, why did you eat all the Devil Dogs?"

"Hungry," Walter said. "This kid I know at school says to me, 'A girl doesn't have to get pregnant. After she gets banged she can just piss it out — piss out all the sperm.'"

Another silence and the crunching of dead leaves as we walked, each of us considering this, trying to imagine the process.

"What a shit-for-brains," Chicky said. "It's impossible."

Though none of us knew why. In fact, it seemed logical.

"I would have known what to do with your cousin," Chicky said.

"Sure. Every day and twice on Sunday."

"Anyway, what's her name?"

"Cheryl."

"Headlights?"

Walter nodded and said, "She even wears a boulder holder."

Chicky said, "I'd say, 'Hey, Cheryl,' and then do like the four Roman emperors. Seize 'er. Squeeze 'er. Pump 'er. Dump 'er."

"Did you really see her knobs?" I asked, and thought what heaven it would be to behold such a miracle.

"Yeah," Walter said. "We was sitting on the glider, on her pi-azza. I was going to feel her up."

"I would have," Chicky said, "'cause I'm in the Four-F Club. Find 'em, feel 'em, fuck 'em, and forget 'em."

Now the woods ahead were indistinct, though there was still light in the sky. The great thing about being in the woods at this hour was that there was rarely anyone else around: the woods were ours, and we were free in them. We walked on, into the thickening shadows.

Walter said, "Look, a toad."

The thing had been startled from the path and hopped next to a crumbling log. Chicky kicked it, saying, "Bastards give you warts."

The stunned toad looked bug-eyed and feeble as it made a low heavy hop.

"Stand back," Chicky said. He worked the pump on his Win-chester and shot it, the first rifle shot of the day, a startling sound, so loud it was unfamiliar, echoing as though there was a wall at the far end of the woods. "Shoot him between the eyes."

Walter and I started firing, Walter with his single-shot Rem-ington, me with my Mossberg, tearing its body open, its belly ripping like the thin rubber on a small squeeze toy. As it flopped forward, Walter shot its blunt head, and burst it, then Chicky booted the ragged corpse into the leaves.

"Beaver Patrol to the rescue," Chicky said in a singsong voice, making a monkey face.

Farther on, Walter said, "Cheezit."

Two riders on horses trotted down the bridle path toward us as we scampered behind some rocks and flattened ourselves on the ground. They were women, in round riding caps and tweed jackets and tight pants and black boots. Unseen by the mounted women, we watched them go by, moving off in the last light of day.

"Think they heard the guns?" I said. We were nagged by the fear of our guns being taken away.

No one replied. Walter said, "They must be rich."

We watched them rocking and swaying back and forth in their saddles, chucking their boot heels against the horses' bellies.

"Women get horny riding horses," Chicky said.

"That's bull."

"They get hot," Chicky said. "Them two broads are so freakin' horny."

We were still lying on the ground, watching the long swaying tails, the twitching flesh of the horses' high hindquarters, the women's packed buttocks and wide-apart legs.

"I've got a bonah," Walter said.

The women rode off, unaware that three armed boys lay hidden, watching them from the margin of the bridle path, excited by the snorting horses, the stamping of hooves in the cinders.

"Tell us the story again," I said.

2

Walter clawed his damp spiky hair and sighed, having to repeat himself. He said in a mumbling way, "I'm walking along the path near where we found the ripped-up magazines that day."

"Doleful Pond," I said.

"Yeah," Walter said. "Where you see cars sometimes and you wonder how did they get there?"

"They're watching the submarine races," Chicky said. He began to snap a narrow comb through his greasy hair.

But I was thinking about the magazines, how they had been torn to pieces, but even so, they were easy to put together. Each fragment was a part of a naked woman, and some pieces were so big there was a whole naked woman, the white of a smooth body so clear, almost luminous, or pale as sausage casing, breasts like balloons. They had seemed like witches to me, powerful and pretty, smiling sinners, representing all that was forbidden.

As Walter talked I saw everything in black and white, because the past was always black and white, as the television was in black and white; because of right and wrong, no in-between. Also black and white because of the weather, for in early spring the green was blackish, the trees were dark, the stones and big boulders were white, the ground bare except for the patches of snow that lay like torn scraps and muddied sheets, black and white rags all over the woods.

"I'm walking past this blue Studebaker and I didn't know this old guy was in it until he says, 'Hey, kid,' and reaches out the window. I looks over — he's smiling with these yellow teeth, and as I walks away I hear the door open."

"Why didn't you take off?"

Walter could run faster than either Chicky or me, but he was slower-witted, so he did not always know when to run.

"I almost shit a brick because he scared me. I didn't know what to do. I just kept walking, to show I didn't really care."

I knew the pond and the road there, so I could easily see Walter marching stiffly away from the blue Studebaker, his little head, his skinny neck, his spiky uncombed hair, his baggy pants and scuffed shoes; trying so hard not to look scared, he moved like a puppet.

"I thought he was supposed to have a bonah," Chicky said.

"That was later," Walter said.

"When he chased you?" I asked.

"No. I looks back and he's in the car, so I kept going. I knew he wouldn't drive on the path. There's a sign, the one we blasted with our guns. There's a gate. He couldn't get through."

"Which path?"

"To the Sheepfold, like I said. I was going up there to build a fire and get warm."

"What about your gun?"

"I didn't bring it."

"You said you did."

"No sah."

"Yes sah."

"My sister hid it, to be a pain."

Chicky said, "You said you aimed your gun at him and he freaked."

"Knife. I had my hunting knife, so that I could make wood shavings to start the fire. I had it in my belt, in the sheath. I pulled it out as I was walking up the path, in case he chased me."

"You said 'gun' before. Didn't he, Andy?"

"I don't remember," I said. Truly, I didn't. All I could recall was the blue car, the old man, his black golf cap, Walter being pestered.

"You told the story different before," Chicky said. "You said you saw him in the woods."

"You didn't let me get to that part," Walter said in a wronged, pleading voice, his eyes glistening so much I felt sorry for him. More softly he said, "So I'm at the Sheepfold. There's nobody around. I whittle a stick and get some shavings. I try to start a fire, and I'm kneeling down and blowing on the sparks and I hear something."

"What?"

"How do I know? Twigs. But I look around and the old guy is standing right behind me. He followed me somehow. He's saying, 'Hey, kid.' His fly is open. That's when he had the bonah."

"What did it look like?" Chicky said.

"He tries to grab me," Walter said, hurrying his story. "I screams at him but there's no one around, right? So then I starts running."

"What about all your stuff, and the fire?"

"I just left it."

"Anyway, you escaped," I said.

Walter didn't say no. He frowned again and clawed his spiky hair. He said, "Then, when I was out to the road and thought it was all over, this blue Studebaker comes screeching up beside me, and it's the guy again, and he's after me."

When he said that, I got a chill. I could imagine it clearly, for sometimes in my worst dreams people kept showing up, I never knew how, to scare me or accuse me.

"Everywhere I go I sees the stupid guy."

Chicky said, "He's definitely a homo."

Walter was silent, paler than when he had started the story, biting his lips.

"But you told it different the first time," Chicky said.

"You think I'm bullshitting?"

"Sounds like bird turd to me," Chicky said.

"You believe me, Andy," Walter said in a beseeching voice.

"Sure." But he had told the story differently the first time. He had a gun. He had turned and threatened the man, who had fallen back and returned to his car. He had not said anything about the Sheepfold and the fire. Seeing the man again on the road, the car stopping — that was new. He was chased more the second time; he was more scared. The whole story sounded worse, which was why Chicky didn't believe him.

"Wait till you see his car," Walter said. "Then you'll believe me."

"Anyway, what did he want?" Chicky asked.

"He was a homo. You know what those guys want."

But we had absolutely no idea, except that it was wicked and dangerous and we were unwilling. In my imagination, such a man would hold me captive in his car, all the windows rolled up, trapping me and threatening me. What he did was not anything I thought of as sex. These men were friendly at first, so that they could grab me and tie me up. In my imagining, I was gagged and blindfolded. Then he would take some of my clothes off, and something happened, something that hurt. In the end, when I was naked, he would kill me, probably stab me.

"I don't get it," Chicky said. He was still impatient and over-stimulated, flecks of spit in the corners of his mouth, blinking hard, his yellowish Italian face looking damp with confusion. "He was bigger than you, right? So why didn't he just grab you?"

"He did grab me," Walter said. "I was fighting with him."

"You didn't say that before."

"You didn't give me enough time."

Walter was looking breathless and wretched, yanking his hair.

"Did he touch you?" I asked.

"I didn't want him to," Walter said, protesting.

"Where did he touch you?"

"I told you, the Sheepfold."

That was new. I had not seen Walter struggling at the Sheepfold, only fleeing. Now I put him back at the Sheepfold, on the ground, the man grabbing at him.

"I mean, did he touch your nuts?"

Walter said, "I was pushing him as hard as I could," and as he spoke he was fighting tears.

"I thought you ran away."

"I did run away. After."

"What else did he do?"

"I don't know. He was feeling my pants. He was really strong and he had this mustache and was chewing something like a cough drop. He even tried to kiss me. He was snatching my hands."

"Was he saying anything?"

"Yeah. 'Don't be afraid, don't be afraid.'"

"I would have shit a brick."

"I was wicked scared," Walter said.

He was quiet for a moment. His face was blotchy with red

patches, he was remembering, his mouth quivering, trying to start a word.

"How did you get away?"

"Ran. Like I told you."

"You never said he touched you."

"I forgot that part."

"How could you forget that, you freakin' banana man?"

Walter lowered his head and said, "When I screamed out loud he got wicked worried. He tried to put his hand over my mouth. His hand was really smelly. That's when I tried to stab him in the leg with my fork."

"Your fork?"

"I was going to heat up some beans. The fork was lying there."

"That's great," Chicky said.

I said, "I don't get why he showed up later."

Walter kicked at the snow crust. This was painful, an awful story, much worse than the first time. I suspected it was true because it was messier, there was more of it, and the new parts were unpleasant.

"He was trying to tell me he was sorry."

"Pretending to," I said. "He was just trying to trick you. If he had caught you, he would have killed you."

"He said he wanted to give me some money. Ten bucks."

"That's bull for one thing," Chicky said. "Ten bucks!"

Walter reached in his pocket and pulled out a little ball of paper and flattened it and smoothed it: a five-dollar bill.

"Jeez," Chicky said.

Five dollars was more money than we ever saw, and it could only mean that Walter, who never had money, might be telling the truth. But it was five, not ten.

"Where's the rest?" Chicky said.

Walter opened a flap of his knapsack and took out a box of

bullets and slid the paper drawer open, showing us the fifty tightly packed bullets. I had a little envelope of bullets for my rifle, Chicky had the same. But this was ammo.

"Vinny sold them to me for a fin," Walter said. "I want to find this guy and sneak up on him. And scare him like he scared me."

"Like how?"

"I don't know."

"Kill the bastard, maybe," Chicky said.

"Maybe we should tell the cops," I said, because whenever Chicky talked about killing someone it made me nervous. He had never done anything so violent, but it seemed that he was always trying to nerve himself for something that bad, and that one day he would succeed.

"Don't be such an asshole," Chicky said.

His saying that worried me too, because not telling the police meant that you took illegal risks, and were somehow always on the other side, never trusting. Only suckers trusted the police.

"And they'd take our guns away," Chicky said.

"The cops wouldn't even believe me."

What kept us from asking any more questions was that we both knew that Walter was going to cry.

"I would have blubbered," I said, because I could see his tears and embarrassment.

Hearing that must have made Walter feel better, because he sniffed and wiped his nose on the sleeve of his jacket and didn't look so tearful.

"I mean, especially if some old guy put his hands on me," I said.

I thought it would help some more, but it made it worse, because when I mentioned the hands Walter got tearful again.

"I'd like to kill him," he said in a fearful, helpless voice.

"Let's all kill him," Chicky said, smiling wildly.

"I don't even care," Walter said. "If he was standing right here I'd shoot him in the nuts."

Chicky loved that and started to laugh, his face growing yellower at the thought of it. When Walter saw Chicky laugh, his anger left him, and he laughed too, but harder, angrier, his whole face brightening. But there were tears in his eyes and stains of tears on his cheeks — smears of wetness and dust. He wiped his face with his arm, smearing it more, looking miserable.

"I will," he said. "In the nuts!"

But the day had gone cold, and dark had come down on us without our realizing it, a dampness rising with it from the dead leaves and rotten earth, and so we headed home with night pressing on our heads.

3

"There were three boys," Father Staley was saying at the Scout meeting in the overbright church hall of St. Ray's the following Wednesday. He was giving a sermon, one of his stories from the navy, about a captain who was trying to find the smartest boy to do a job. "Three boys" made me think of Walter, Chicky, and me, and as Father Staley spoke I saw each of us in the story.

"The captain gave each boy a keg of nails. 'There are five thousand nails in each keg,' the captain said. 'There is also a gold nail in each keg. The first one to find the gold nail will get the job.'"

Father Staley paused and let us picture this, but the pause was too long, and when we began fidgeting after a little while Arthur Mutch, the scoutmaster, said, "I'm going to be handing out demerits!"

"What would you do if you were in those boys' shoes?" Father Staley said.

"Find the freakin' gold nail," Chicky said, much too loud.

"DePalma — one demerit!"

Father Staley then explained that the first boy picked through the nails in his keg, pushing them aside, looking for the gold nail. While he was doing this, the second boy began removing one nail after another from his keg, trying to see which one was gold.

"The third boy asked the captain for a newspaper," Father Staley said, and paused again to enjoy our puzzlement.

Chicky covered his mouth and muttered, "And he read the freakin' newspaper while the other dinks found the gold nail." When he looked up Arthur Mutch was staring at him.

"The boy spread the newspaper on the floor and dumped the whole keg of nails onto it, all five thousand of them," Father Staley said. "He saw the gold nail at once. He picked it up and then funneled the nails back into the keg. And he got the job. What lesson does that teach us?"

We said nothing. We had no idea, though I saw the story clearly: the wooden kegs, the boys, the glittering gold nail in the pile of iron ones.

"Sometimes you have to take drastic action," Father Staley said. "And sometimes, to save your soul . . ."

As soon as he uttered those words, *save your soul,* I stopped listening, and so did Chicky, because afterward, when we were in our circle of folding chairs, the patrol meeting, Chicky said, "What was the point of that freakin' story?"

Arthur Mutch approached us and glared at Chicky and said, "Beaver Patrol, at ease." Then, to me, "What merit badge are you going up for, Andy?"

"Camping," I said.

"What have you done about it?"

"Took a hike last Saturday."

"Name some of the essentials you had in your pack?"

Mossberg .22, twelve bullets, Hostess cream-filled cupcakes, bottle of tonic, stolen pack of Lucky Strikes, book of matches. But I said, "First aid kit. Flashlight. Canvas tarp. Some rope. Canteen. Pencil and paper. And some apples."

"I think you forgot something."

Since none of what I had told him was true, it was easy to remember the missing item required by the badge for a hike. "Um, compass."

"Good," Mr. Mutch said. "Engage in any activities?"

Killed a toad, chased a squirrel, spied on some women getting horny on horseback, listened to Walter Herkis's story of being molested by a man in a blue Studebaker. But I said, "Knot-tying. Cooking. Tracking."

Tracking was not a lie: we had headed toward Doleful Pond with Walter before it got too dark to go farther.

"What did you cook?"

"Beans and franks. And afterward we doused the fire and made sure the coals were out."

More lies, but once — months before — I had done just that, and I considered that it counted.

"What knots and what did you use them for?"

"Sheepshank for shortening the rope. Half hitch. Square knot. Propped up the tarp with them to make a shelter."

"Know the bowline yet?" Mr. Mutch asked.

"I'm trying."

Behind me, a voice — Father Staley's — said, "I think I can help you with that, Andy."

"Thank you, Father."

Mr. Mutch, satisfied with me, turning to Chicky, said, "De-Palma, what badge are you going out for?"

"Civics." Chicky blinked, and as his yellow face grew pale his brown birthmark got darker.

"Civics? DePalma, tell me, what is a bicameral legislature?"

Chicky twisted his face, to show he was thinking hard, and said nothing. His fists were pressed in panic against his legs.

"You don't know, do you?"

Chicky shook his head, his springy curls glistening with Wildroot. No, he didn't know. Chicky could barely read.

"How many merit badges have you earned, DePalma?"

Chicky muttered something inaudible.

"Louder, please."

"None," Chicky said in a hoarse humiliated voice.

"You're still a Tenderfoot after a year and a half in the Scouts," Arthur Mutch said.

Father Staley said, "Try a little harder, son. Do some homework."

"I could go out for car maintenance, Father, but do they have a badge for it? No."

"Any other ideas?" Father Staley said.

"Maybe Indian Lore." Chicky's eyes were shining with shame and anger. "Maybe Camping."

"What makes you think you can earn them?"

"I went on a hike with Andy."

"And did you cook franks and beans, too?"

"Yes, Father. And capacol'. Guinea sausages."

"Well, that's a start."

Father Staley stepped over to me and smiled and lifted my chin with his hand, saying, "You pick up the lame and the halt, don't you?"

"I don't know, Father."

He looked pleased, having asked me a question I could not answer; and he followed Mr. Mutch to the next patrol group.

Under his breath, Chicky said, "'How many merit badges have you earned?' Mutch is an asshole."

"You'll get millions."

"I'd get one if they had car maintenance, engine repair, some shit like that," Chicky said. He stood, hunched over and discouraged. "I got *gatz*."

As Chicky said *gatz*, Father Staley, at the front of the hall, said, "Let us pray," and blessed himself slowly, using the tips of his scaly fingers, "in the name of the Father and the Son and the Holy Ghost . . ."

Another Saturday, Walter Herkis walking ahead through the woods, his Remington under his arm. He had told his mother that he was going to church but instead sneaked off and met us on South Border Road, and we had entered the woods obliquely, skirting the small reservoir and dashing through the trees. Walter did not want us to see his face, because he felt he had not been brave. But he was brave. Whatever the man had done, Walter had at least fought him. He had lost, but he was stronger and faster than me, which worried me. In the same position, I would have been in deeper trouble.

But Chicky said, "Maybe he's shitting us."

I wanted to say, If that was so, why was Walter looking so sad and angry — why so silent, why was he walking that way, why had he cried at the end of his story?

I said, "I don't know. We'll track the guy down and see."

"It's stupid that there isn't a car maintenance merit badge."

"Boy Scouts don't have cars, Chicky."

"I can start my brother's Ford. He lets me rev it. I know how to change the plugs." He was kicking through the leaves, glancing around. "Look, a chipmunk. Let's kill it."

He chased it, and shot, and missed, and then complained that it was too small to hit.

The woods were full of wonders, full of occurrences that only happened in the woods. Some people parked at the edges, but they didn't walk far from their cars; others used the bridle paths; no one but us wandered the woods — or if they did, we never saw them. We hiked beyond the roar of traffic on the Fellsway. Past Panther's Cave, all we heard were birds chirping, the rustle of squirrels, and the wind in the boughs up top.

There were still snow scraps this second week, but wetter ones; more fiddleheads, redder skunk cabbage, bigger buds. We looked closely at them, as self-conscious Scouts and woodsmen, and we took pains to hide ourselves from anyone on the path. That was why, near Doleful Pond on this next hike, we avoided a fisherman who was fussing with his rod and line on the shore, slashing it like a whip.

"Is that the homo?" Chicky asked.

"No," Walter said.

Nor was there a blue Studebaker parked behind him, but rather an old black Pontiac; still, because we had rifles, we kept to the bushes by the side of the pond.

"Hey, you kids, is there a fire station around here?" As he spoke he was holding his fishing rod.

Somehow the man had seen us. He had asked a pervert's question: perverts often pretended to be in trouble. Once a pervert had said to Chicky, "There's a rock under my car. Help me get it out."

A rock under my car was just a lie to get his hands on Chicky, but Chicky had run away. This question about a fire station made us speed up and shoulder our rifles so that he could see we were armed and dangerous.

"He's waving something at us," Chicky said under his breath.

The fisherman had put his rod down and was waving his spread-apart hand. He said, "Hooked my thumb!"

He showed us his thumb, and it was true — a dark wire stuck out of the meaty part of his thumb muscle, like the loop on a

Christmas ornament. I was thinking: Maybe a man would deliberately stick a hook into his thumb in order to look helpless, so that he could trap a boy.

"What do you kids think you're doing with those guns?" he said. He just glanced at our guns but he went on frowning at the embedded hook.

"Boy Scouts," I said. "We're allowed."

"I was a Boy Scout. I never learned how to use a gun."

"Hey, did you learn how to use a fishing rod?" Chicky said.

"What are you, a wise guy?"

"Because, hey, you hooked your thumb — don't look at me," Chicky said.

"It's not funny, I need to get this fucking thing out." He wiggled the hook and winced and swore again.

I said, "You can't pull it out, because of the barb. You're supposed to push the hook in deeper, and twist it to get the barb through the skin, so it sticks out. Then you snip off the barb and you can just slip the smooth part out. Got any pliers?"

"So you're a wise guy, too. I'm going to tell the cops about your guns. Them are illegal, you know."

What I had told him was in the First Aid merit badge handbook, three stages in removing a hook: push, snip, pull. Snip it with pliers, the handbook said, but he did not want to hear it. The hook in his thumb looked just like the one in the picture illustrating the hook-removal technique.

"Where's the emergency people?" he said angrily. "Where's the fire station?"

"And you need a tetanus shot for tetanus toxoid," I said, to irritate him, because he refused to do what the book told him to do.

"You could get lockjaw."

"Another wise guy," the man said, and stooped and groaned and gathered up his fishing tackle with his left hand — I could see a pair of the right kind of needle-nose pliers in the tackle box. He held up his right hand like a policeman signaling to stop traffic, his fingers spread out, his thumb hooked.

"This hurts like hell — it's throbbing," he said. "As if you give a shit!"

And he threw his tackle box and rod into the back seat and reversed down the narrow road, the car bouncing.

"Getting POed makes your heart beat faster," I said. "The poison spreads."

"He's not even supposed to drive here, the stupid bastard," Chicky said. He mocked the man, saying, "It's thrawbing!"

"This is where the other guy was," Walter said.

"The homo?" Chicky said.

Walter sucked on his lips, probably so they would not quiver and show how upset he was, and we looked at him, feeling sorry for him, standing on the spot where the strange man in the blue Studebaker had — what? — fooled around with him. No one said anything for a while.

"Other people come parking here," Chicky said at last. "Submarine races."

About twenty feet from where the fisherman had parked his car there was a barrier gate, just a horizontal steel pipe, hinged to a post on one side and padlocked to one on the other. Above it, the sign with our bullet holes in it, *No Parking — Police Take Notice*. Chicky unsheathed his hunting knife and shinned up the pole and scraped away at the *t*, so that it said, *Police Take No ice*.

"Bastards," he said.

Farther along the shore of the pond, in the water, beyond a scooped-out embankment, there were scraps of paper curling and bobbing beneath the surface. Making sure the fisherman was gone, we put our guns down and broke off branches from the low bushes. We stood at the edge and used these, dragging the branches, to fish up the fragments of paper. The women in the torn pages were alone, some sitting or lying down, some in bathtubs, half hidden in a froth of bubbles, heavy breasts and dark nipples. We knew these dripping pages were from girlie magazines, ripped squarely in large pieces. On one was a large breast, on another a bare leg, a shoulder, the woman's head: bouffant hair, big lips, black-and-white photographs of naked women. They seemed much wickeder soaking wet.

"I like this one," I said.

"She's wearing socks," Chicky said.

"She looks more naked that way."

"You're nuts."

Chicky found the cover, all in color, *Naturist Monthly,* two women playing tennis, seen from the rear, a nudist magazine. We pieced some pages back together and saw naked people putting golf balls on a miniature-golf course, others playing Ping-Pong, some swimming, and oddest of all, a family eating dinner at an outdoor picnic table, Dad, Mom, and two little flat-chested girls. Mom was smiling: droopy tits and holding a forkful of droopy spaghetti.

"You can't see the guy's wang," Chicky said, "but lookit."

Naked children frolicking in shallow water with naked parents, a whole bare-assed family. And even though one of the teenage girls was being splashed I could see her breasts and a tuft of hair between her legs.

"I bet she's not a virgin," Walter said. And then, grunting, "I've got a raging bonah."

"Give him some saltpeter," I said.

That was the remedy we had heard about, to prevent you from getting a hard-on. People said that in some schools the teachers mixed it with the food, to keep the kids out of trouble.

We trawled with the branches, hoping for more thrown-away pages. There were certain secluded places at the edge of the woods or near the ponds, where cars could park, where we found these torn-up or discarded magazines. They were always damaged; we had no idea where anyone could buy them. Without being able to explain it, we knew that men took them here, as part of a ritual, a private vice, to look at the forbidden pictures and then destroy the evidence.

And we did the same, piecing the wet pages together, and gloating over them, and then, feeling self-conscious, we scattered them and kicked them aside and walked on.

At the far margin of the pond, there was another parking place, another barrier, more litter, broken beer bottles and paper.

"It wasn't here," Walter said.

We knew what he meant. We were more relaxed, kicking the trash, for sometimes there were coins in the cinders.

"Lookit. A Trojan," Chicky said.

A rubber ring, partly unrolled, thin balloon skin protruding, lay lightly on the ground.

"Never been used," Chicky said. He poked it with his gun barrel. "No jism in it. All dry."

"What do you figure he did with it?" Walter said. "Huh, Andy? Tell us the story."

"He goes, 'Open your legs.' She goes, 'Use a rubber.' He takes it out but she's so hot and bothered he doesn't have time to put it on his dong. Her legs are open so wide he can see up her hole and into her tonsils. He throws the rubber out the window and bangs her."

Chicky was giggling as he said, "What else?"

"She's saying, 'Farther in, farther in!' He goes, 'I'm not Father In, I'm Father O'Brien and I'm doing the best I can.' Now she's knocked up."

"I like the way you tell stories," Chicky said, as Walter, holding up his Remington, showed us a rubber dangling, suspended from the nipple on the front sight. "It's used," he said.

The slimy smooth gray-white rubber reminded me of naked bodies, hairless women's skin, and penises.

"Prophylactic," I said, trying out the word that was on the Trojan wrapper.

"You can get a wicked disease from that."

Walter flopped it onto the ground and fired his gun into it, and at the same time the three of us looked around, hearing the gunshot echo, blunted by the pond.

"Let's go," I said, fearing that someone might have heard.

As we walked quickly away, Chicky said, "I know this guy who got a pack of his brother's Trojans and stuck a pin through each one. So that when his brother banged his girlfriend a little bit of sperm leaked through."

We tried to picture it. *A little bit of sperm leaked through* did not seem very risky, not enough to make a baby. You needed a lot of sperm for that, and in my mind some sperm represented arms, and some legs, and more would make the baby's body and head.

We left the bridle path and crouched, ducking through the budded bushes, traversing the hill. No one could see us, and as always when we were sneaking through the woods like this we were careful not to step on any twigs. We trod on the balls of our feet, "sure-footed," as though in moccasins, like the Indians we saw in movies who were indistinguishable from the bushes and the mottled light of the forest.

"Heads up," I said, hearing muffled hoofbeats, a lovely sound, because it was not a gallop but a slow tramping gait, the hooves crushing and grinding the cinders on the bridle path. The sound made us feel more than ever like Indians. "It's a mounted cop."

He rode upright in the saddle like a sheriff in a cowboy movie, wearing a wide-brimmed hat and shiny black boots, a big black holster at his waist on a wide belt. We pressed ourselves against the ground, like Indians in the same movie, watching him, feeling anxious pleasure that he did not see us as he passed, and when he was gone, just the distant sound of hooves, intense excitement.

"We could have told him about the homo."

"He wouldn't have believed us."

"He'd take our guns away," Chicky said. "He'd tell our parents."

Another mile onward, walking along the margin of the bridle path, we came to a clearing, the meadow of the Sheepfold, some scorched stone fireplaces and picnic tables and stumps to sit on. The place was empty this cold afternoon: all ours. We gathered wood and started a fire, warmed our hands, piled on more wood, and I whittled a stick to roast the hot dogs.

Walter said, "Those things have shit in them, real pieces of shit."

"You're just saying that because you don't eat meat," Chicky said. "Because of your religion."

He unpacked some Italian sausages, bright red meat and pepper, speckled white with fat, and held tight with filmy sausage casing that looked like a Trojan. These he penetrated lengthwise with a sharp narrow stick, and held them over the fire, letting them sputter and burst.

"I'm going up for a Cooking merit badge," Chicky said.

Walter ate a chocolate bar while I burned my hot dog and, trying to toast it, burned the roll I had brought. Chicky nibbled the burned end of one of his sausages, and roasted it some more over the fire.

"It looks like a bonah," Walter said.

"Hoss cock," Chicky said.

While we were sitting there, the fire crackling, the smoke blowing around us, three people approached through the meadow, two men and a woman. They were much older than we were, and had the look of being strangers, not just to these woods but maybe to the state.

"What's the name of this place?" one of the men asked — the taller one, in the sort of thick warm sweater I associated with college students.

"Sheepfold," I said. "Where are you from?"

"Tufts," the man said.

Chicky said, "Hey, can I see that pocket book?"

The smaller of the two men, young but balding, wearing a blue windbreaker, was holding a paperback book. On the cover was a crouching woman clutching her head. You couldn't see much of her, but you knew she was naked. The title was *Escape from Fear.*

"It's a psychology book," the man said.

Chicky snatched at it and almost got a grip, but before he could try again the taller man batted Chicky's arm, hitting him hard and knocking him off balance. Chicky, too startled to get to his feet, held his elbow where he had banged it on the ground and began to wail — not cry, but howl.

"Hey, you hurt my friend," Walter said, and I admired him for stepping up to the man who was flanked by two other people.

"I'm sorry," the man said, looking suddenly worried and regretful. He pulled a pack of gum out of his pocket and gave it to Chicky, who had stopped wailing but was still holding tightly to his elbow.

"I'm telling the cops," Chicky said.

The man said to me, perhaps because I had said nothing at all, "I didn't mean to hurt him."

The woman, who was pretty, a college girl — wearing a skirt, thick white socks, a tweed jacket — said to the man, "Let's go. These kids could get us into trouble," and before she finished speaking she screamed.

Walter was pushing the bolt action into his gun, which he had picked up from where he had hidden it, behind the stone fireplace.

"What are you doing with that thing?" the taller man said, trying to be calm.

The woman looked too terrified to speak. The smaller man in the windbreaker said, "You're not supposed to play with guns."

"I'm not playing," Walter said.

Without their having noticed him, Chicky had crept to his feet and found his rifle behind the fireplace. When the three people turned he put a handful of bullets into his mouth and began spitting them into the tube under the muzzle, loading it.

"You crazy? What do you want?" the taller man said, looking panicky and taking the woman's arm, shoving her behind him.

"What do I want? I want you to pound sand up your ass and give your crabs a beach," Chicky said. "Say you're sorry."

"I already said it." The man was angry but he was also afraid. In an abject voice he said, "Okay, kid, I'm sorry. Put that gun down."

"Fungoo to you," Chicky said in defiance. He slid the handle on the pump action of his Winchester, putting a bullet into the chamber.

The three people, perhaps without realizing it, had begun to raise their hands, and held them chest high, as though being robbed. They backed away, the taller man saying, "Look, we're going — we don't want any trouble." And then they were running across the meadow and toward an opening in the trees, where the road led to the parking lot.

"You hear what I said? Pound sand!" Chicky said. He was excited, jabbering crazily. "He hurt my friggin' arm!"

Walter said, "Why didn't you get your gun, Andy?"

"Didn't have time," I said, but the fact was that I was afraid —

fearful of being caught with it, fearful that it might go off, fearful of something awful happening, hating the recklessness of Chicky and Walter, wishing that we had not brought the guns.

"We better get out of here," I said. "They might see that cop and tell him."

That was a danger. We put out the fire by dumping dirt on it, and flung away the burned sausages and hot dogs.

"Let's make sure they didn't tell the cop," I said, because I was still concerned.

We went through the woods to the parking lot, just in time to see the car — three people in it — speeding down the road. We looked at the lot, the space where they had parked, and saw a dollar bill and some change.

"He must have been pulling the keys out of his pocket," I said, "and this fell out."

"So it's mine, because I scared him," Chicky said, and picked it up. "A buck thirty."

Back in the woods, heading home the long way, over the hill, off the path, we saw a squirrel, and chased it, throwing stones at it because a gunshot would be heard clearly so close to the road. And chasing it, the squirrel leaping from bough to bough, pushing the branches down each time he jumped, we came again to the margin of Doleful Pond, without realizing how we had got there, and losing the squirrel in the darkness.

That was when we saw the headlights, so bright the glare of them obscured the shape and color of the car.

"That's him," Walter said.

"Bull," Chicky said, because it was just a pair of yellow lights.

We crouched down and watched the car reverse, moving slowly, and where the road was wider, the car stopped and made a three-point turn, lighting the bushes, illuminating itself, a small blue car sitting high on its wheels, a Studebaker.

4

So Walter Herkis, who sometimes fibbed, was telling the truth after all. He did not gloat about being right — he didn't even seem glad that now he had us as witnesses to the blue Studebaker, the man inside. He even seemed a bit sorry and looked as though he had eaten something bad and wanted to throw up. He looked more worried than ever, even sick, which seemed like more proof that he had not been lying. And maybe the truth was even worse than he had admitted. Certainly he had been very upset and we were not quite sure what had really happened, what the man in the blue Studebaker had done to him at Doleful Pond. We asked again but this time Walter did not want to talk about it, only made the swollen pukey face again. That meant that something serious had happened.

The man had driven past us. He was not a blurry villain anymore, but a real man in a shiny car and looked strong. We had not seen his face — we were on the wrong side of the car, hiding against the pond embankment. He had driven fast, in the decisive way of a person who had finished something and wanted to get away; not on the lookout for anyone, not noticing anything, like a man in a hurry to go home, someone late.

The way the man was leaving fast seemed to make Walter angry, and he watched, growing helpless, like the man was escaping from him. Walter's eyes were glistening. He held his gun in his arms tightly as though he was cold. But he was clutching his stomach and retched, started to spew, a moment later bent over and puked into the bushes, and paused, labored a little, and splashed some more, coating the leaves with yellow slime and mucus and chewed puke.

He wiped his mouth with the back of his hand and said, "I'd like to kill the bastard."

"Yeah," Chicky said. "Let's kill him."

I did not say anything. I was retching myself, my mouth full of saliva from having watched Walter. I was also afraid of the word; and they knew it, they noticed my silence.

"Andy's chickenshit."

"Yah. Let's get him," I said. I could not say the word "kill" without feeling unsafe. "You all right, Herkis?"

Walter nodded. He was not all right. He was pale and pukey-looking. But he was angrier than ever, and his anger excited Chicky and touched me too. The anger gave us a purpose that was better than going out for merit badges but involved the same concentration. We had found the car, we had glimpsed the man, we had to find him again and do something. We were not Scouts, we were soldiers, we were Indians, we were men, defending ourselves.

"Kill him" was just an expression, but one that frightened me. Walter and Chicky were not so frightened of it — Walter was angry, Chicky was excited. We did not explain what killing meant, but I wanted to think it was stalking him, trapping him, not firing bullets into him.

"We'll put him out of commission," I said, so that they would see I was on their side, because they thought of me as the sensible one, the cautious one, the chicken.

"Even if we really do kill him, no one will know," Chicky said.

That was the way we reasoned in the woods — getting away with something made it all right. If we killed a squirrel, or started a fire, or shot bullets into a sign and no one caught us, we felt we had done nothing wrong: nothing to explain. If we found money, we kept it. "What if we discovered a dead body in the woods?" Walter had asked once, and Chicky had said, "What if it was a woman and she was bollocky!" In the woods we were conscienceless creatures, like the other live things that lurked among the trees. Even so, Chicky's excitement disturbed me — he was jabbering to Walter now — because talk of killing, even in a reckless jokey way, made me uneasy. My hesitation was not guilt, not even conscience — I was afraid of getting caught and having to face my parents' fury and shame.

"They'll never catch us. They'll think it's some big murderer. They'll never think it was kids."

"Let's shadow him first, and then see," I said, dreading their conviction.

Walter said, "Chicky's right. Kill him."

"We can track him. We're good at that," I said.

Lurking, hiding, hunting; scouring the earth for footprints, tire tracks, clues; the lore of Scouting was real and useful.

The sky had gone gray, some of the clouds as dense as iron, as black, with streaks of red and pink between them, like hot iron that had begun to cool. And not only that, but more because the evening sky was always a mass of unrelated marvels — above the iron were vast decaying faces, tufts of pink fluff in a soup of yellow. The light in the sky was all the light there was; the woods were dark, and so was the surface of the pond at this low angle, and not even the path was clear.

"We should head back," I said, and started walking.

"I don't even freakin' care," Walter said, but from the way he said it I knew he was glad to go, a bit wobbly and gagged from puking.

Chicky said, "We could wait till he parks his car, then cut a tree down. It falls across the road, he can't drive away, we nail him."

"Or dig one of those big holes and put sticks across it, and leaves and stuff, so that it looks like the ground," I said. "He walks right in. We could say it was an accident."

"Or just shoot him in the nuts," Walter said.

Talking this way in the darkness of the woods seemed unlucky and made me nervous about bumping into a stranger, maybe that very homo. The others might have felt that way too, for although they were talking big, they held tightly to their rifles, bumping shoulders and sometimes stumbling. When we heard some cars and saw the lights of South Border Road, we walked faster and were relieved to be out of the woods.

Chicky started across the Fellsway alone, walking stiffly to conceal his gun. He turned around and took out his comb. "Anyway, don't do anything I wouldn't do," he said, tilting his head, raking his hair with his comb. "Or if you do, name him Chicky."

Walter and I turned toward Foss Street. He was silent, except for his puffing — winded and sick from the experience of having seen the man — a big boy out of breath, his whole body straining as he plodded up the hill.

"We'll get the guy," I said, to reassure him.

"Who cares?" His voice stayed in his mouth and sounded awful, as though he couldn't swallow. When we got to the Fulton Street fire station at the top of the hill he said, "My mother thinks I went to church."

The special Saturday church of a Seventh-day Adventist made it sounded pagan and purposeless, just an empty ritual on the wrong day.

Looking miserable, saying nothing except "See ya," he turned and headed down Ames Street toward his house. I walked off wondering and anxious, for so much had occurred during the day and I was still not sure what it meant; sometimes such events just happened and were never repeated, but other times there were consequences, and those I feared.

Entering my house, leaving my rifle behind the sofa on the piazza to hide later, I went into the kitchen, which was filled with light and warmth and the steamy odor of sweated meat.

"Where have you been?" my mother said. She was standing at the stove, poking at a pot roast in a kettle.

"Nowhere."

"You smell of smoke."

"I went for a hike. For a merit badge."

"Have you been playing with fire?"

"There was a forest fire. I helped put it out."

"Take your shoes off — you're tracking in mud. Wash your hands and face. You're filthy. And set the table."

I did as I was told, but it was hard to do the right thing here at home, hard to know what to say. I felt uncomfortable and out of place in the house, in this world that was parallel to my outdoor life, as though I did not belong indoors, could not reveal anything of my real life. Only in the woods, with my gun, my wool hat pulled over my ears, did I feel free, "sure-footed," "hawk-eyed."

The next Scout meeting was on the following Wednesday. We gathered at St. Ray's hall and were talking and fooling until Arthur Mutch yelled at us to pipe down and to line up in patrols.

"Close interval, dress right — dress!"

Each boy stuck his left elbow out, making a space, and because Chicky was on my right he jabbed me hard and laughed.

"Ten-shun!"

Mr. Mutch led us in the Scout oath while Father Staley stood at the side. After the oath, Scaly led us in a prayer, the same prayer as always: "Let us pray. Dear Lord, help us to be worthy of your love . . ."

"At ease," Mr. Mutch said afterward. He lectured us a little on obedience and how we had a duty to behave with respect. Then he nodded to Father Staley, who held up one finger to get our attention and said, "This, too, is a house of God." Then Mr. Mutch told us to meet in patrols and that he would be coming around to check on us.

The leader of the Beaver Patrol was an Eagle Scout named Corny Kelliher, a redheaded thirteen-year-old with freckles and spaces between his teeth. He hated camping but was good at arithmetic and hobbies: he had a ham radio and knew Morse code and raised tropical fish. He wore a sash stitched with merit badges, twenty or more. He had gone out west to the Jamboree by train and had showed us snapshots he had taken of Pikes Peak and Grand Coulee Dam.

Corny said, "So let's talk about what Scouting activities we've been doing. How about you, Andy?"

"Learning about tracking," I said.

"Can you identify any animal prints?"

"Yup. Bear. Deer. Muskrat."

"How can you tell a muskrat track?"

"Drags its tail between its footprints and leaves a line."

"How do you know if the prints are fresh?"

I didn't know, so I said, "If they're kind of wet?"

Corny said, "No. But if they have snow inside them, then you know that they're not fresh, because it snowed after the animal left them."

"What about in the summer when there's no snow?"

I liked asking him outdoor questions because he was always indoors.

"The prints are soft," he said. "What else did you do?"

Chased a squirrel. Saw a man with a fishhook in his thumb. Got yelled at by him. Found some dirty pictures and rubbers. Quarreled with some people. Found a buck and change. Tracked down a homo's car.

But I said, "Hiked. Identified some plants. Skunk cabbage and stuff."

Saturdays were for tracking. We went back again, we could only go that day, but we went with the same dedication. We were small, we were not strong, so we valued cunning and skill and made being small our asset. If we could not come face to face with the enemy, we would find him, shadow him, then make a move on him. We whispered, we tiptoed, we wore dark clothes, we avoided stepping on things that made noise, stayed off the path, moved from big tree to big tree keeping our rifles pointed down, used hand signals. We were trackers, we were stalkers, we were scarcely visible.

Our stakeout spot was a grassy overlook near the big smooth boulder above Doleful Pond, in a natural trench like a foxhole, sluiced by a gully wash. There we lay in the speckled leaf shadow and watched the bridle path where cars — lovers, fishermen, crazies with girlie magazines — sometimes parked. We got to know them, the ones who cuddled in the back seat and tossed rubbers out the window, the fishermen who stayed until dark, the loners who tore up the magazines.

"I'm cold. Let's start a fire," Chicky said one Saturday.

"No. They'll see the smoke."

"Who made you the chief?" Chicky said, and lit a cigarette, and warmed his hands with it. He was becoming an expert smoker and boasted of the nicotine stains on his fingers.

Walter said, "Cigarettes are stupid. You're going to be a shrimp."

Chicky blew smoke into Walter's face and said, "Know what? Dwyer got bare tit off a seventh-grader at Helen Slupski's birthday party."

Walter was listening closely, a Seventh-day Adventist envying us our wild life and our parties. He said, "Is she pretty?"

"She's a dog, but she's a tramp," Chicky said. "Probably a nympho."

We watched the road, the parking space, side by side, prostrate, like braves. A car pulled in: lovers, the green Chevy.

While we watched them, I said in a low voice, "This guy was banging his girlfriend up the Mystic Lakes and she clamped his dong so hard in her twot he couldn't pull it out. It was stuck wicked shut, like in a vise. The cops found them. 'Let's see your license and registration.' Then they saw what happened and took them to the hospital. My brother told me."

"That's a pissah," Chicky said. "So they're in the ambulance together and his dong is stuck inside her."

"Sometimes your finger gets stuck in a Coke bottle," Walter said, thinking of how it might have happened.

After a while the Chevy backed out, and with its lights on we realized that the day had gone dark, time to go home. We descended the hill, rounded the pond, and lingered where the car had been, in the tracks of all the other cars, the fishermen, the crazies, the lovers, about fifty feet from the post where the sign we had vandalized said, *No Parking — Police Take No ice.*

I said, "They all see that sign and stop."

"Let's lose it," Chicky said. "Then they might park over there."

"So what?"

"Easier to kill the homo," Chicky said, and a moment later was climbing the pole and hanging on the sign, tearing it from its rusted fastenings.

"Your fingerprints are on it now," I said.

"As if I give a shit." Chicky walked to the edge of the pond and winged it into the water, where it skipped twice and then sank. He went back and kicked the iron pipe from its supports, shouting crazy, "I'm leaving my footprints!" He was strong and he had gotten bolder, and even his reckless talk was a worry.

The next time we went was milder, mid-April now, some lilacs and forsythia in blossom at the edge of the reservoir, and purple azaleas already starting to show. I knew their names from the flower book that Mr. Mutch had loaned me. We waited for Walter, who was later than usual. His mother had found out that he was skipping church, and forced him to go. But he was loping along with his gun when he caught up with us at the stone pillars at the entrance to the Fells.

"I took it to church," he said. "No one even saw me."

"That's wicked great," Chicky said. "I'm going to do that."

I tried to picture it, sitting in a pew at St. Ray's with my rifle lying under the kneeler.

"I still don't get why you have to go to church on Saturday," Chicky said as we walked into the woods, making our usual detour through the trees.

"Because it's the Sabbath."

"Bullshit," Chicky said. "Sunday is."

"Saturday," Walter said. "Jews go then, too."

"That's why they're Jews. You're not a Jew, except when you're hogging the Devil Dogs."

"Cut it out," I said, seeing that under Chicky's scolding Walter was getting pink-faced and a little breathless, as he did when he was upset.

But Chicky was annoyed because we had waited most of the day for Walter, and he was so late there were only a few more hours of sunlight. Chicky had said, "Let's go without him," but I argued that we needed Walter — to be a team, to act together, and so that Walter would see the man's face.

"Yeah, we don't want to kill the wrong guy," Chicky said.

Walter trudged ahead of us, as though compensating for being late. From the way he was silent and thoughtful, his shoes flapping, I knew that he envied us being Boy Scouts. But Scouts were forbidden by his church, like coffee and tuna fish.

"We're supposed to be tracking," Chicky said. "Get down low."

"I'm a tracker," Walter said. "No one can see me."

We glided through the woods like wisps, like shadows, alert to all the sounds. Blue jays were chasing a squirrel, harrying the creature from tree to tree the way we might have done ourselves if we had not been so determined to conceal ourselves. We were off the path, and the dead leaves were flatter and wetter these days, not like the brittle crackling leaves of winter. We moved hunched over in silence.

More buds made the trees look denser, and the tiny bright leaves on some bushes gave the woods a newer, greener feel, hid us better and helped us feel freer. The sky was not so explicit, the boughs had begun to fill out with leaves as delicate as feathers. And a different smell, too, the crumbly brown decaying smell of warmer earth and tufts of low tiny wildflowers.

Once again, Walter pointed out some fiddleheads, the only wild plant he knew, though most of them had fanned out into ferns. The skunk cabbage was fuller and redder. Nor were the woods so silent. There were insects and some far-off frogs. We wanted to be like these dull-colored creatures and wet plants, camouflaged like the wildest things in the woods.

Because it was so late there were no horseback riders on the bridle paths, no other hikers, no dog walkers. They must have all left the woods as we had entered: the wilderness belonged to us now.

We cut around Panther's Cave, climbed the hill behind it, and kept just below the ridgeline, parallel to the trail, listening hard. The light was dimming and the sun was behind us, below the level of the treetops.

"I can't see squat," Chicky said. "It's all Herkis's fault. Fucking banana man."

"My mother made me go," Walter said in an urgent tearful whisper.

"Let's hurry," I said, hoping to calm them.

"How can we track anyone in the dark?"

"We'll learn how," Walter said. "Indians track people in the dark. Indians stay out all night. No one expects to be followed in the dark. We'll get good at it. Then we'll be invisible."

"I have to be home for supper," I said.

But we kept on, and the gathering darkness did not deter us, it was a challenge and a kind of cloak, a cover for us in our tracking as we crept unseen below the ridgeline.

And walking this way we made a discovery, for cresting the last hill behind Doleful Pond, in our foxhole, we saw that the water still held some daylight, the smooth surface of the pond reflecting the creamy gray of the sky.

The shore was dark, the woods were black, we saw nothing on the road. Instead of lying there whispering in the shallow trench, we made our way down the hill, as slowly and silently as we could, as though moving downstairs through many large darkened rooms of a strange house. Even so, I could hear Chicky breathing through his fat nose, and Walter's big feet in the leaves, clumsy human sounds that made me feel friendly toward them.

Before we got to the road, Chicky said, "Look," and swung his arm to keep us back, liking the drama of it.

At the very end of the road, the place where we had removed the No Parking sign and the iron pipe, there was a car, but so deep in the trees we could not see the color or the make.

I put my finger to my lips — no talking — and took the lead, duck-walking to the edge of the pond, where the little trail encircled it. The others followed, keeping low and still watching the car, trying to make it out. Closer, we could see it was small and compact.

"It's the Studebaker," Chicky said, whispering fiercely.

Walter knelt and slid the bolt of his rifle. "Let's kill him."

"Yeah," Chicky said. He too knelt and fumbled with his gun.

"Wait a minute," I said. I could not think of any way of stopping them, nor could I put my worry into words. We had bullets, we had our guns, only mine was not loaded: the other guns were cocked. In the darkness of Doleful Pond, having achieved our objective, there was nothing to stop us. We had made a trap for the man by removing the sign and the barrier, and our work was even more effective than we had planned, for the car was almost hidden in the narrow gullet of the road.

"We'll surround him," Chicky said. "We'll just gang up and shoot from all sides. He won't have a chance."

I felt sickening panic and wanted to vomit. Until that moment it had been unreal, just a game of pursuit, Indian tracking, and I had enjoyed it. But we had succeeded too well and now I dreaded that we would have to go through with it. I saw in this reckless act the end of my useful life.

"Maybe he's not inside."

The car was dark. I hoped it was empty.

"My mother's going to kill me if I'm late," I said.

"Andy's chickening out." Chicky's vicious gloating made him sound psycho.

I was afraid. I thought: If I do this, my life is over. I also thought: I cannot chicken out, I can't retreat.

"We should call the cops."

"They won't do anything," Walter said.

"Just take our guns away!" Chicky said.

The car moved, not visibly but we heard it, the distinct sound of a spring, the squeak of metal under the chassis, as though it was settling slightly into the road, for there was another accompanying sound, the crunch of cinders in the wheel track from the tires. A weight had shifted in the car.

That sound stiffened us and made us listen. The next sound was louder, not from the springs but the crank-creak of a door handle, and with it a light came on inside the car, the overhead bulb.

We saw the man's face briefly as he turned to get out of the car and, as he left the door open, the light stayed on. Another shape barely bulked in the front seat — it could have been a bundle, or a big dog, or a boy's head. There came a spattering sound, like gravel on glass.

"He's taking a leak," Chicky said.

"Shoot him in the nuts," Walter said in a husky sobbing voice. "Shoot the bastard."

"Hold it," Chicky said, and I knew what he was thinking.

The man was not a blurry villain anymore. He was a real person, and that was much worse. He wore a black golf cap and buttoned to his neck a shapeless coat that looked greasy, the way gabardine darkens in winter. Slipping back into the car, he flung out his arm to yank the door and we got another look: big nose, small chin, a pinched mouth, and a face that was so pale his mustache was more visible, a trimmed one. He looked like a salesman in the way he was so neat, like someone who put himself in charge and smiled and tried to sell you something.

When the light went off, Walter raised his rifle, and Chicky pushed it down hard, saying, "Quit it."

I thought the man might hear, but the door was closed, the engine had started, the gearshift was being jiggled and jammed into reverse. The brake lights reddened our faces.

"We can't do it now," I said. I was giggling, but still panicky.

"I'm gonna," Walter said, and tried to snatch his rifle from Chicky's grasp.

"Tell him, Chicky."

"Freakin' Scaly," Chicky said.

The relief I felt for our not having shot him was joyous, a kind of hilarity, a light like a candle flame leaping in my body making me feel like a small boy again. In my guts I knew that if you killed someone, you died yourself.

5

In the woods we were free to do anything we liked. We knew from what we saw — the torn-up pictures, the tossed-away magazines, the used Trojans, the bullet-riddled signs, the women on horseback, even the fisherman with the hook in his thumb — that other people felt that way, too. We could make our own rules. We thought of the woods as a wilderness. It was ours, it was anyone's, it was why we went there, and why Father Staley went there. No one looked for you there, and if they did, they probably wouldn't find you: you could be invisible in the woods.

But we were Scouts, we were trackers, we could find someone if we wanted. We had found the man who had bothered Walter, maybe molested him, though I did not have any clear idea of what "molested" meant, other than probably touched his pecker. "He tried to kiss me" didn't mean much. We talked wildly of sex all the time, but none of us had yet kissed a girl.

Walter would not tell us what the man had done. Whenever he tried he shook and stammered and got blotchy, pink-cheeked and flustered, and sometimes so mad he began talking about killing the man.

But the man was Father Staley. We could not explain how important that man was; how we could not even think about harming him. On the way home that night, walking at the edge of the woods among the low bushes, so that none of the passing cars would see our guns, Walter was upset.

"Stop crying, Herkis," Chicky said.

"I'm not crying."

"What's wrong then?"

"What's wrong is, I saw him. That was the same guy. You thought I was lying. I was telling the truth!"

He was screeching so loud he sounded like his sister Dottie, who was almost his age and had the same pink cheeks and pale skin.

"I don't get what you're saying," Chicky said.

"I saw the freakin' homo!" Walter said.

What he seemed to be saying was that by seeing the man, he remembered everything that had happened. That had upset him all over again.

"We'll get him, don't worry," I said. But I was glad the moment had passed, that none of us had fired our guns at Father Staley. The woods were free but we would have been arrested for killing a Catholic priest, and would have been disgraced and been sent to jail forever. It could have gone horribly wrong, for at that point our pretending had become real — pretending to be Indian trackers, pretending to be hunters and avengers, following the tracks, carrying guns. We had talked about what we would do when we found the man, but I hoped it was just talk, that *We're Indian trackers* was the same as *Let's kill him* and *Shoot him in the nuts* — words we said to ourselves for the thrill of it.

Chicky would have shot if it hadn't been Scaly; Walter had wanted to fire, and was angry we hadn't let him.

"You both chickened out," Walter said. He sang off-key, "Chickenshit — it makes the grass grow green!"

"We'll do something," Chicky said. "Something wicked awful."

"No sah. You're chicken because he's supposed to be a priest. You actually know the guy."

Thinking of a priest as "a guy" was hard for us, because he was a man of God, powerful and holy. Because Chicky and I were Catholics, and Father Staley was a priest, we felt responsible for him. It gave Walter another reason to dislike Catholics. We knew that the Seventh-day Adventists said bad things about Catholics, just as Catholics said, "This is the True Church. Protestants are sinners. They're not going to Heaven," and "Jews are Christ killers."

"He's a homo," Walter said.

That hurt, but it was true.

"He's a Percy, he's a pervert," Walter said. "He was trying to make me into a homo."

"He's still a priest," Chicky said. "He's chaplain to our Boy Scout troop."

"Big deal."

"It is a big deal. We can't shoot him," Chicky said. It sounded strange to hear Chicky being solemn and responsible, his close-set eyes, his yellow skin, his big nose, his picking at his birthmark as he spoke. "But we can do something. Beaver Patrol to the rescue."

"Just don't broadcast it," I said.

They stopped walking and stared at me. We had come to the Forest Street rotary and were standing under a streetlight. Cars were rounding the rotary, going slowly, so we stood holding our rifles upright against our sides, the butt tucked under one arm like a crutch, while keeping the muzzle off the ground. By being silent, they were querying what I had said.

"Because we could get into trouble," I said.

They saw that I was right. It was certain that if we had reported Father Staley to the police, he would win and we would have to answer all the hard questions: What were you doing in the woods? Why did you each have a .22 and a lot of live ammo on you? Were you lying when you said you were going on a cookout? Why were you fooling around near Doleful Pond with those dirty pictures? Staying out after dark, we were up to no good. We had no answers.

Father Staley would say Walter was lying: people would believe him, not us. And no matter what happened, we would be known forever as the boys involved in the Father Staley scandal, wicked little fairies and tattletales. We would never get a girl-friend. Other kids would tease us and pick fights. We would lose.

"We'll figure something out," I said.

We parted that night in the shadows of the street like conspirators, swearing that we would not say anything to anyone.

When I got home and my mother said "Where have you been?" and I said "Nowhere," I did feel I had been nowhere. We had come close to almost killing a man. I would not have fired my gun, but Chicky and Walter would have. I would have been arrested with them. People would have pointed their finger at me and said, *You're just as guilty as they are.*

I took my gun into the basement and stashed it behind a leaning stack of storm windows.

Upstairs, my mother said, "Is there anything wrong, Andy?"

"No," I said, and felt sorry for her, because she didn't know anything of what had happened, and there was so much to know. She did not know me, either. I was just a stranger in the house.

At the next Scout meeting, Chicky and I stuck together, not saying anything, but looking at Father Staley when his back was turned. He wore a black cassock with a hundred black buttons on the front, and the skirtlike lower edge of it touched the toes of his black shoes. Now the thing seemed like a dress to us.

When he looked at me, I felt he knew something — he smiled in a suspicious way, pinching his mustache. Being near him made me quiet and fluttery inside: I couldn't think of anything to say.

But Chicky was more talkative than ever in a bold, mock-serious voice. Looking straight into Father Staley's face, he said, "I'm going up for my First Aid merit badge, but I'm having some problems."

"Maybe I can help," Father Staley said.

"Father, hey, I'm not sure what you do if a snake bites you."

"Get straight to the hospital, son. That's what you should do."

Chicky said, "Um, some people say you're, um, supposed to suck out the poison."

It was the thing we always joked about. What would you do if a snake bit a girl on her tits, or a boy on his pecker or his ass? Suck it out. Even the word "suck" sounded wicked to us.

"You only do that if you're in the woods," Father Staley said.

"But, hey, that's where all the snakes are, Father," Chicky said.

He was trying to get Father Staley to talk about sucking out the poison. Father Staley put his hand on my leg — his hand had never felt scalier — and said, "You've got a First Aid merit badge, Andy. What would you do in a situation like that?"

I hated being asked. "In a situation like that," I said, and hesitated. Then, "You cut the wound with a sharp knife, making an X. And when it bleeds, you kind of, um, suck the poison out. And I forgot to say, maybe put a tourniquet on the person's arm between the snakebite and his heart."

"If he's bitten on the arm," Father Staley said, and his eyes glittered at me.

"Yes, Father."

"Very good. So there's your answer, DePalma," he said, walking away.

I said to Chicky, "You're such a pissah."

Pleased with himself, Chicky said, "I just wanted to see what he'd say. I know Scaly's a homo now. He was trying to feel you up."

"Beaver Patrol," Corny Kelliher said, calling the group together.

We scraped the wooden folding chairs into a circle and sat there, waiting for Corny to lead the patrol meeting.

"Let's talk about tracking. Anyone?"

"We done some tracking the other day," Chicky said. "Me and Andy."

Father Staley crept over to listen.

"Want to tell us about it?"

"Oh, yeah. We were in the woods," Chicky said. "We seen some tracks. We kind of followed them."

Nothing about tracking down the pervert, nothing about our guns, nothing about Walter Herkis, nothing about our spying from the hill, nothing about Father Staley and his blue Studebaker — and who knew he had a Studebaker, since none of the priests even owned a car?

"Do any sketches of the tracks?"

"No. But I could draw a picture." Chicky took a piece of paper and a pencil and sketched some circles and shaded them, while glancing from time to time at Father Staley. When he had finished, Chicky said, "Maybe a wolf."

"Must have been a dog," Corny said. "The prints are similar."

"It was a wolf," Chicky said.

"There are no wolves in Medford," Father Staley said.

"Hey, have a seat," Chicky said. His yellow Italian face made his friendliness seem sly. "Ever been up the Fells, Father?"

Father Staley just smiled at the direct question and said, "My hiking days are over, I'm afraid," and joined our group, sitting himself on a folding chair, plucking his cassock at his knees, like a woman in a gown, except his fingers were scaly.

Sort of bowing to Father Staley, who was at the center of the Beaver Patrol — bowing was his way of treating Scaly as though he was holy — Arthur Mutch handed us each a sheet of paper, saying, "I just mimeographed these. I want each one of you to take it home and study it."

The heading at the top of the smudged sheet was "Elements of Leadership," with twenty numbered topics. The first was "Inspiring respect by setting an example."

As he passed by, Mr. Mutch said to me, "Andy, you should be

asking yourself why you're not a patrol leader. You've got the ability. You just don't use it."

Hearing this, Father Staley said, "Mr. Mutch is right. You pick up the lame and the halt."

I faced him, I couldn't answer, I knew my face was getting red.

"People like that just drag you down."

I wanted to say: *What did you do to Walter Herkis?* But I knew that if I did, I would have to pay a terrible price for talking back to a priest.

"You know what I think?" Father Staley said, because he still wasn't through, and now he was so close I could smell the Sen-Sen on his breath. I knew that smell: we sucked Sen-Sens to take away the stink of cigarettes when we were smoking. "I think you enjoy hiding your light under a bushel. That's just plain lazy. It's also a sin of pride."

I wanted to shoot him in the face. *Shoot him between the eyes,* we always said. I located a spot between his eyebrows and stared at it with a wicked look. The other members of the Beaver Patrol were pretending to read "Elements of Leadership" but were really sneaking glances at the way Father Staley was scolding me. Buzzy Dwyer, John Brodie, Vinny Grasso. And Chicky's yellow face was twisted sideways at me.

"Shall we talk about leadership and taking responsibility?" Father Staley said to the others when he was finished with me.

Homo, I thought.

Corny Kelliher said, "That's a good idea, Father."

"Or we could practice some knots," Chicky said. "I'm trying to learn the bowline. Maybe go out for the Knot Tying merit badge."

"I might be able to help you with that," Father Staley said. "You know, I served in the navy?"

"I want to go into the navy, Father." Chicky was smiling at

him, and I knew he was deliberately choosing things to say to Father Staley, even trying to please him in a way, like a small boy dealing with a big dog.

Picking up a short length of rope and extending his scaly fingers so that we could see his movements, Father Staley slowly tied a bowline knot. With a little flourish, which seemed to me a sin of pride, he presented it, dangling it in our faces. I hated his fingers now.

"Now you do it," he said. He picked the knot apart with his fingertips, then handed the rope to me.

My hands went numb because as soon as I started to tie the bowline, Father Staley lowered his head to peer at my fingers for the way I was tying the knot. His head was sweet from cologne, and I could still smell the Sen-Sen. I made several false starts, then tied the bowline.

"DePalma?" Father Staley handed the rope to Chicky.

Chicky started the knot slowly, his tongue clamped between his teeth. But then he bobbled the rope and tugged on the ends and the knot became a twisted knob.

"That's a granny knot," Father Staley said.

He got up and crouched behind Chicky and put his arms around him, and taking Chicky's hands, which held each end of the rope, he guided Chicky, pressing on his fingers, tying the knot using Chicky's hands.

"See?" His head was in back of Chicky's head, his breath on Chicky's neck.

Squirming free of the priest and looking rattled, Chicky said, "I think I get it, Father."

In the navy you learned many different knots, Father Staley said. He had been stationed in Japan. He tied a knot on Vinny Grasso's wrists and said, "Japanese handcuffs. Go ahead, try taking them off." When Vinny yanked on them, he grunted and his hands went white. Instead of untying Vinny, Father Staley used more pieces of rope to tie Chicky's wrists and mine. I left the rope slack, because I thought from Vinny's reaction that the knot would tighten if I put pressure on it. Instead, I made my right hand small and it was so sweaty I managed to slip it out of one side, and untied the knot.

Father Staley saw I had freed myself, and he smiled and put his scaly fingers out for the rope and said, "Want to try again?"

His friendliness made me so nervous I couldn't speak. I watched him untying Vinny's wrists. Afterward, Arthur Mutch told us to line up and stand at attention. Father Staley made the sign of the cross and said, "Let us pray," and my pressed-together hands got hot, for when he prayed I was more afraid than ever.

"Dear Lord, make us worthy of your love . . ."

On the way home, I thought Chicky would talk about Father Staley hugging him and holding his hands to tie the bowline, but instead he said in a trembly voice, "Scaly thinks I'm dragging you down."

"He's full of shit," I said.

"We should kill him," Chicky said.

"What will we tell Walter?"

"That we'll get the bastard." Kicking the pavement, scuffing his shoe soles, he was thinking hard. "Know what we should do? Wreck his stupid car."

"Like how?"

"There's billions of ways," Chicky said.

I remembered how he got angry because there was no car maintenance merit badge, and he knew everything about cars.

Before we parted that night, he said, "I think you drag me down, because you're such a fucking banana man."

We went to Walter's house after school the next day and hid behind a tree, waiting for him to come home. After a while, a car stopped in front of his house and Walter got out — a car full of kids, more Seventh-day Adventists, more bean eaters, who never danced, who went to church on Saturday. So many of them made the religion seem stranger.

Seeing us lurking near the tree, Walter looked around and then sidled over and whispered, "What're we going to do?"

"Kill his car," Chicky said. He loved the expression. He licked his lips and made his yellow monkey face. "Kill his car."

Chicky put himself in charge, because cars were the one thing he knew about. He said, "Andy's the head tracker. And you're the head lookout, Herkis. But you've got to do what I say."

"No guns," I said.

"Why not?" Walter said.

"Because if we get caught they'll take them away." But my worst fear was that if they had them they would use them and would kill Father Staley.

"How are we going to kill his car, then? I thought we were going to shoot bullets into it."

"That'll just make holes and dents. We're really going to wreck it wicked bad, inside and out."

The next Saturday we spent in the woods, lying on our stomachs in the foxhole on the wooded bluff above Doleful Pond, watching for Father Staley's blue Studebaker. He didn't show up, though others did — fishermen, lovers, dog walkers. We watched them closely but stayed where we were, and we were well hidden by the leafy branches, for spring had advanced. Twice during the week we made a visit: no Scaly. Maybe he had given up?

When we did not see him at Mass, we asked Arthur Mutch, Chicky saying, "Father Staley was supposed to teach us some knots."

"Father Staley is on a retreat."

"What's a retreat?"

"It's what you should do sometime, DePalma," Arthur Mutch

said sternly, because he didn't like Chicky. "Go to New Hampshire, to pray. Lenten devotion."

Whispering to me at the Beaver Patrol, Chicky said, "I bet he's not praying. Five bucks says he's whacking off."

We did not see Father Staley until just before Easter, saying the Mass on Holy Thursday. We reported this to Walter, who sort of blamed us for Father Staley.

"We'll look for him tomorrow," I said.

"You going to church again tomorrow?"

"Good Friday. Holy day of obligation."

"I don't care what you say — that's worse than us."

The Good Friday service lasted almost three hours, and the priests wore elaborate robes and faced the altar, but midway through the incense ceremony, one of the priests turned and swung the thurible at the congregation, waving a cloud of incense at us, and Chicky nudged me, whispering, "Scaly."

Attendance at church was not required on Holy Saturday. We didn't expect to see Father Staley by the pond, but we had the whole day for tracking, and it was a cold sunny day, with some flowers in bloom, and so we were glad to head into the woods. Even if Father Staley didn't show up, we would have more chances, for the following day was Easter, the start of a week's vacation.

Walter was early. He said, "I was in this Bible class. I put up my hand and said, 'Excuse me.' The teacher says, 'Okay.' So I just left. He thought I was going to the john."

Chicky wasn't listening. He said, "If we kill his car, we'll put him out of commission."

We stopped and had a snack at Panther's Cave, sitting out of the wind, in the warm sunlight.

"What have you got?"

"Bottle of tonic. Some Twinkies. You?"

"Cheese in a bulkie. Bireley's Orange."

"I ain't eating, I'm smoking," Chicky said, and lit a cigarette, and with smoke trickling out of his nose, he looked more than ever in charge.

The day was lovely, the woods so much greener than on that first day, when Walter had told us his story. We had been cold then, and the goose bumps of fear in our bodies too. Afterward, frightened by the thought of the man chasing Walter, we had stumbled through the woods, not knowing where to go or what to do. Now we knew. The weather was warm, the ground was dry, the woods smelled sweet.

We were not boys anymore but men with a purpose as we made our way by a zigzag route to the crest of the hill above Doleful Pond, approaching from behind, flattening ourselves on the ground, sliding forward in the leaves until we could see the far shore, then dropping into the foxhole.

"What did you bring?"

Walter had taken off his knapsack. "Couple of bricks."

"I've got the rope," I said. "About fifty feet. Chicky?"

Chicky kept his eyes on the pond. He said, "A potato. A bag of sugar. A couple of tonic bottles. Pair of pliers. Usual stuff."

He had always been talkative before, but now that he was in charge he liked to be mysterious. He wasn't good at schoolwork, but he knew how to fix things, and was even better at breaking them.

"Someone's coming," Walter said.

But it was the Chevy, the lovers. We watched closely.

"They're making out — he's feeling her up. Hey, this guy I know told me the best way to get laid," Chicky said. "You get a girl in a car, huh. 'Cheryl, hey, let's go for a ride.' Then you drive into the middle of the boondocks, like where they are now, and when it gets dark you park the car and shut off the engine and you say, 'Okay, fuck or walk.'"

"What's supposed to happen?" Walter said.

"Listen, banana man. The guy leans over. 'Fuck or walk.' It's dark, it's cold, it's wicked far. So the girl has to take her clothes off and let him bang her, or else she'll have to walk home."

"I'd go with them," Walter said. "I'd get sloppy seconds."

"You'd just jerk off. You'd leave pecker tracks."

I said, "When I was young and in my prime, I used to jerk off all the time. But now that I am old and gray, I only jerk off twice a day."

"Andy plays with the one-eyed worm."

"And you get hind tit."

"You can kiss the snotty end of my fuck stick," Chicky said.

The next time we looked up, the Chevy was reversing down the road.

"She came across," Chicky said. "Didn't have to walk."

By now the sun was low enough to cast long-legged shadows across the pond and the road. The place where the Chevy had been parked lay in darkness.

None of us saw the blue Studebaker appear. All we saw was its rear lights winking as it braked, sliding into the shadows at the end of the road, where we had removed the No Parking sign and the iron pipe barrier. Its rumplike trunk was blue, though just a few minutes after it parked, even while we were staring at it, we could not make out the color.

Each of us had one job to do. Walter's was first — to get Father Staley out of the car and up the road, chasing him, long enough for Chicky and me to do our jobs.

"There's someone with him."

"Probably some kid."

"Maybe someone we know."

"Like they say in Russia, tough shitsky," Chicky said.

"What are you going to do?" Walter said.

Slow-witted and sly, liking the mystery, Chicky said, "I got my ways. Just make sure that bastard is out of the car and up the road for a few minutes to give me time."

"If he sees us, we're screwed," I said.

"He's only going to see Herkis," Chicky said. "Herkis is Protestant!"

"Let's put on bandannas," I said. The word was from the cowboy movies. I took out my handkerchief.

"You mean a snot rag," Chicky said, and shook out his own and tied it around the lower half of his face, as I was doing.

We crouched in the foxhole on the bluff, watching the car. The sun sank some more, the temperature changed, the woods grew cooler, damper, darker, while the pond held the last light of the day.

"What's the bastard doing?" Chicky said.

The end of the road where the car was parked was so shadowy, a person passing by would not have noticed the car. After it had parked, it had seemed to darken and shrink and disappear.

"I can't see him," Walter said.

Chicky said in his conspirator's whisper, "If we wait any longer, he might take off. So let's go. You're dumping the bricks, Herkis. Andy, you're doing the bumper."

"What about you?"

"You'll see. Meet back here, after." Chicky then put his finger to his lips: no more talking.

Keeping low, we descended through the bushes single file to the edge of the pond. We used the thick brush at the shore to hide ourselves. Approaching the car from the rear, we could not see anything of the people inside. We were sure it was Father Staley's car, but where was his head? Now we were kneeling.

Chicky turned and poked Walter's arm, and as he did, Walter snorted air and looked alert. With a brick in each hand, Walter rocked back to a squatting position, sort of sighing as he did so. I could see how angry he was from the way his head was jammed between his shoulders and the sounds of his shoes when he crossed from the dirt path to the cinders.

We heard nothing but his shoes for a moment and then two loud sounds, one of a brick hitting the metal body of the car, the other the crunch of a brick against the windshield. Just after that, a complaining two-part shout that was so long the first part was muffled inside the car, and the second part a very loud protest as it was released by the car door swinging open.

Father Staley stumbled out, pulling at his clothes, and Walter screamed "Homo!" as he ran into the woods, and he was gone, hidden by darkness, before Father Staley had stumbled twenty feet. But Father Staley was still going after him.

My hands trembled as I tied the bowline knot on the front bumper. The other end of the rope, another bowline, I tied to the nearest tree. While I was tying the knots, Chicky rushed from the rear of the car, where he had been doing something, to the side, where he was pulling the flap that covered the gas cap. The last sound I heard was the smash of glass, the tonic bottles under the tires.

Passing the car door, which was still gaping open, I saw someone inside, a boy, huddled in the seat, his head down, his knees up. I was glad I could not see his face. Then I was off.

Chicky kicked the car repeatedly, making it shake, and ran, flinging his feet forward, and crashed into the bushes by the pond. He was right behind me, running hard, feeling the same panic that frightened me, the going-nowhere running of a bad dream, skidding on the soil that was cool and moist from the end of day, like running on fudge. We were racing in darkness, but after all the stakeout time we knew where we were going, and when we got to the lookout boulder on the bluff I knew we were safe, because I saw the car's headlights switch on, blazing against the green leaves.

"He's taking off."

Chicky said, "Did you see me kick the freakin' car? I didn't even give a shit!"

The blue Studebaker was still stationary, its lights dimming each time the engine turned over.

A noise behind us startled us, but before we could react, Walter flopped down and said, "I wrecked his window!"

"Lookit," Chicky said.

The car grunted and roared, the gearshift grinding, the engine strained against the rope I had tied — strained hard, making no progress, trying to reverse. When the rope snapped with a loud twang I expected to see the car shoot backward, but it had not gone ten feet before the engine coughed and died. Chicky was laughing. The engine groaned to life again — Chicky said, "Hubba-hubba, ding-ding" — and then gasped and died again. But seconds later it was stammering, the intervals shorter and shorter, the engine noise briefer, until at last there was only silence.

"Car's freakin' totaled," Chicky said.

And gloating, combing his hair, Chicky explained: my rope had made the engine rev, but he had jammed a potato into the tailpipe, to delay Father Staley in case the rope broke. He had put a pound of sugar into the gas tank, and that was now in the fuel line, gumming up the pistons. The engine was destroyed, the car was a wreck. Father Staley was stranded in the woods with whomever he had brought there.

After we left the darkness of the woods, there was one last thing, and it was I who raised it. I said, "What about confession?"

Chicky said, "Was that a sin?"

"We were helping Walter," I said.

"Maybe it's a sin if you're helping a Protestant," Chicky said.

"Not a mortal sin," I said.

"What's the difference?" Walter asked.

"If it's a mortal sin, you go to Hell."

We detoured past St. Ray's to go to confession, Walter watching our guns in the shadows beside the church, near the statue of Saint Raphael with his wings and his halo. I confessed seeing the pictures of the naked women, and fighting, and having impure thoughts: venial sins.

The next day, Easter, we performed our Easter duty, sitting at Mass, Walter the unbeliever between us in the pew, not knowing when to kneel or pray — skinny, blotchy-faced with embarrassment when he stood up, surveying the priests in their starched white lace-trimmed smocks, and whispering, "Where's Scaly?"

Scaly was not on the altar. The pastor's sermon that day was about the meaning of Easter, Christ slipping out of his tomb, being reborn, pure souls. That was true for me; the holy day reflected exactly how I felt, and made me happy. The smell of the church was the smell of new clothes. When the singing started I shared the *Sing to the Lord* hymnbook with Walter, who mumbled while I sang loudly,

> *Christ is risen from the dead,*
> *Alleluia, alleluia!*
> *Risen as he truly said,*
> *Alleluia, alleluia!*

Father Staley had vanished. All the pastor said was "Reverend Staley has been transferred to a new parish." People said they missed him. At Scouts, Arthur Mutch talked about Father Staley's contribution to the troop. His hard work. "He was a vet." But Mutch wasn't happy. The blue Studebaker we destroyed was his: Scaly had borrowed it. The thing was a writeoff.

"Banana man," Chicky said. That night he said he was quitting the Scouts.

No one knew what happened to Father Staley, and we never found out who the boy was — maybe a Protestant, like Walter; a secret sin. That was also the mystery of the woods. We had discovered that, going there as Scouts. The woods might be dangerous but the woods were free, the trees had hidden us, and had changed me, turned us into Indians, made us friends, so we couldn't be Scouts anymore, because of Walter. When I quit the Scouts, my mother said, "You'll have to get a part-time job, then," and I thought: Great, now I'll be able to buy a better gun.

We had made Staley disappear. We had made ourselves disappear. No one knew us, what we had done, what we could do, how close we had come to killing a man. I was glad — it meant I was alone, I was safe, now no one would ever know me.

An African Story

I

AN UNSPOKEN RULE stipulates that a writer does not appropriate another writer's talk. The one who says, "An odd thing happened to me," and tells you the oddity, is sharing a confidence that must not be betrayed, because he will eventually use it. Telling you is a way of trying it out, and the better he tells it, the more he possesses it, making it untouchable. There is no question of your borrowing it: any use of it is theft.

Lourens Prinsloo told me what happened to him at the age of sixty in similar words, stilted because his mother tongue was Afrikaans: "Quite a curious thing befell me." But now he is dead, killed as a consequence of the events he described to me, so the story is mine to relate. No one else knows.

I could tell this story by inventing a fictional name for Prinsloo, but he is so well known, his work so widely read, that there is no point. And I have been around too long to hide myself in fiction.

I say "well known" and "widely read," but that is in South Africa, of course. Prinsloo does not exist in the United States — untranslated, unpublished, not spoken of. I would never have been aware of him were it not for Etienne Leroux, my near namesake, author of many novels in Afrikaans, some of them translated into English, such as *Seven Days at the Silbersteins* and *The Third Eye*. Leroux, a farmer in Koffiefontein, in the Orange Free State, was introduced to me by Graham Greene. Greene put some aspects of Leroux's farm life into *The Human Factor*, on the basis of several visits.

When Leroux came to London in the 1970s he urged me to visit him in South Africa. I did so, many years later, when I was traveling from Johannesburg to Cape Town after South Africa's political transformation. Lourens Prinsloo was Leroux's houseguest.

"I am homeless at the moment," Prinsloo said, "but I am an optimist."

Leroux called him Louwtjie, pronounced "low-key," a name that suited him, for he had the most placid disposition. Prinsloo spent the day licking his thumb and turning over the typescript pages of his short story collection in the English translation, preparing it for publication. This typescript he shared with me — lucky for me. Because of a legal dispute that arose after his death, his family squabbling over the copyright and the royalties, there was no publication in English.

2

The best introduction to Prinsloo is the collection of stories I was privileged to read. Too long for magazine publication, too short for individual books, the stories — novellas, really — appeared two or three at a time in slim volumes, published in Afrikaans in Cape Town. They were admired by Afrikaners, but not enough of them to allow Prinsloo to write full-time. So, like Leroux, Prinsloo remained a farmer — lucerne and cattle and seed maize — supporting fifty black families.

The farmer-writers of South Africa were like the literary men of old Russia, running country estates and writing at night by lamplight of the rural life they led, servants' quarrels, local gossip, scandals, superstitions, the low comedy of country life with its adulteries and pettiness, its vendettas and pieties. Blacks in South Africa were like the serfs in old Russia — owned, beaten, barefoot hut dwellers, worked to death. The setting was not a country but a twilit world of loneliness and squabbles, with darkness all around it.

Prinsloo's stories were strange. Very long, very detailed, vividly depicted, they were like tales from another age. They had all the elements of Russian stories, but when animals and trees were mentioned they were freakish — two-headed calves, night-blooming bat roosts; and racial oddity abounded — albinos, freckled Bushmen, white men with one Zulu on a remote branch of the family tree. The stories tended to be forty to fifty pages long — what magazine would publish them? But published two or three together in a book, they looked impressive, well printed, on good paper, with tight bindings, old-fashioned handiwork of self-sufficient South Africans. I could not read them but I did have this translation, the pages thickened, physically dented, by the typewritten letters. That in itself reminded me how old typescripts showed the force of the prose, how words were punched into the page, underlinings were slashes and some exclamation marks punctured the paper, and altogether the typewriter gave the pages the raised texture of Braille.

Etienne Leroux, known familiarly as Stephen, didn't mind that I was absorbed in Prinsloo's manuscript rather than one of his. Typically generous, he said, "If you read these stories you will understand this place." I supposed "this place" to mean Africa, though maybe he meant Koffiefontein, OFS.

The stories were the more terrifying for being rural comedies. The element of the grotesque that I associate with farming was in the grain of all of them, for a raw acceptance penetrates the barnyard. The nearer we live to animals, the more naked life is.

Yet while varieties of animals and humans can seem ridiculous and conspiratorial on a big aromatic farm, they are partners deep down, for farm life makes everyone fatalistic. Faulkner at his broadest is a good example of that. Not much is hidden, modernity does not exist though faith is everywhere, life unfolds outdoors, and people's lives come to resemble those of their animals. Existence is a browsing and a fattening, and then comes the harvest and the slaughter.

The first story was the strangest. A white farmer in a remote dorp of the Free State lusted after one of his female servants. He could see that she recognized his desire, but she made no move, merely waited for him to act. He did nothing. He was nearing sixty, his wife a bit older, and "she had shut up shop some years before," which I took to mean had lost interest in sex.

The farmer's wife was approaching a thorn tree one day to photograph a bird (a gray-headed bush shrike) when a snake (a boomslang) wrapped on a bough above her dropped to the earth and bit her. She died soon after. I was later to find that Prinsloo's stories were full of the particularities of South African natural history.

Very soon after his wife's death, the farmer consoled himself with his African servant. But he was so ashamed afterward that he did not repeat the deed. When the African woman appeared at his door she was turned away. Humiliated, she left his employ, but not before putting a curse on the farmer.

The farmer mourned his wife and asked her forgiveness. He took to staring in a mirror to assess his misery. One day he noticed a mole on his face that he had never seen before. Within a few days it grew larger, and soon it was "the size of a Krugerrand," not a mole anymore but a deep brown blotch, an irregular stain that spread to cover his cheek. He could not hide it. Other parts of his body were similarly affected. The lower part of his left leg was brown. Soon his entire body was dark.

At first he dared not show his face in public, and for months — captive to his changing color — he did not leave his house. But when, inevitably, he had to go to town, he hid his dusky face. To his surprise he was not recognized, nor was he singled out — was not noticed at all. He came and went unseen by anyone, and with this new racial coloration became invisible.

He was so unrecognizable that, although he was fully present, a rumor circulated that he had died. To deny the rumor would have meant revealing himself, and so he let the rumor circulate. Hearing of his death, the African woman showed up with her child — the fruit of their brief union. She intended to stake her claim to the property, using their child as proof of what had occurred between them. The child was white. The woman was chased away by the servants, arrested for kidnapping a white child, and given a long sentence. That story was titled "The Curse."

That element of the supernatural seemed to be a trait in Prinsloo's work, and was more believable than the sort of thing you find in, for example, Edward Lucas White's "Lukundoo." In that horror story a white explorer in Africa comes down with a case of apparent measles — boils, anyway — and suffers as they grow, and at last, pricking them, he finds that each boil contains a little black man standing in his flesh, upright on the center of each eruption, looking furious. Prinsloo's stories were subtler than that, but then Prinsloo considered himself an African.

In "Katje and Koelie," the lives of an old woman and her servant are depicted with ironic sympathy. The women, one black, one white, the same age, have been raised together on a remote farm in the eastern Transvaal. At first they are playmates; then the black woman, Koelie, becomes Katje's servant, washing her clothes, shining her boots. Katje teaches Koelie to read and write, and for a while the servant excels in her studies and speaks of leaving; but, hearing this, Katje forbids it, ends the lessons, and Koelie is reduced to servitude again, until Katje falls ill and is nursed by Koelie, who makes all the decisions. In middle life they have become like a married couple. Katje's eyesight fails. Koelie becomes her eyes, and because she is literate she writes checks for Katje, deals with Katje's money, and becomes Katje's protector.

You think that something sinister is about to occur when Prinsloo describes them arm in arm, the black servant steering her white mistress, but it is only a characteristic death scene, one of Prinsloo's signature devices: the white woman, sleepwalking, falls and breaks her hip, and lying an entire night, she is set upon by huge ("mouse-sized") armored crickets (*Acanthoplus discoidalis*), which chew her flesh. Katje is found in the morning by Koelie, dead, part of her face eaten away. Koelie buries her lifelong friend and keeps one of the crickets, not, as the African staff thinks, for *muti* (medicine), but as the embodiment of Katje, now and then — this is the last paragraph — allowing the cricket to chew on her own arm.

"The Justus Family" reminded me of Arthur Schnitzler's play *Reigen:* a series of ten encounters takes place, all of them sexual assignations, and all the characters change partners. In the first scene the soldier is bedding the shopgirl, in the second scene the shopgirl is being wooed by a lawyer, in the third the lawyer is pouncing on the society woman, and so forth until the last pairing, the soldier again, with the woman from the penultimate scene, linking her in this human chain to the first scene. It's about syphilis, some critics have said; but why? *Reigen* is about how the world works. "The Justus Family" had a similar movement — peristaltic almost.

Prinsloo's story, which opens with an obscure funeral, I took to be autobiographical, since there were eight children in it, the same as in Prinsloo's family. Each of the children sought the approval of a domineering mother. Little alliances were formed among the children but none were secure; in fact, no sooner had one sibling confided in another than that one used the confidence to jeer at the sibling and take the secret to a brother or sister, who in turn passed it on, whispering it to another brother or sister, who of course broke the promise of confidence, undermining the teller and becoming the subject of more whispers. Peristalsis.

This story of apparent betrayal — no one is true, no one keeps a secret, everyone is mocked — is the more sinister and unsettling for the figure of the mother, a highly respected Boer matriarch and widow, who in fact keeps the whole process going. Her presence gives "The Justus Family" more density than Schnitzler's play, because it is more than just a round of sordid encounters; it involves complex interaction.

Whenever Mother Justus detects a note of resolution she steps in and stirs, feeding the whispers with whispers of her own, and so the story of the Justus family is really the story of this woman, whose children seem less and less malicious and more and more the victims of a manipulative and insecure mind. The shocked children realize their secrets have been betrayed. Mother Justus laughs and says, "If they were secrets, you wouldn't have told me."

But they love and obey her, and when a black farm hand makes an offhand remark about her tyranny he is set upon by the children and killed. The obscure funeral on the first page is his.

The most ingenious and modern of Prinsloo's long stories was one of his last, written in his period of birthday melancholy — perhaps for that reason it was his funniest, his cruelest, his most unsparing. It is called "The Translator."

The translator of the title is a wealthy farmer of citrus in Nelspruit named Finsch, who on his sixtieth birthday acquires the ability (we don't learn how, but it is so convincing we don't ask) to translate what people say to him into what they really mean. The story — novella, really — is all subtext and no text. In a verbal sense everyone who encounters Finsch is naked: nothing is hidden from him, people's motives are baldly apparent.

I can only approximate the dialogue because I am recounting it from memory. The narrative is almost all dialogue, and the piece would make a superbly wicked play. As I mentioned earlier, I was given a thick typescript of Prinsloo's stories at Etienne Leroux's house. I spent a day and a night with it, and then was told to hand it back. I was not able to make notes. The only photocopier at the time and place was a big inky machine, predating the mimeograph. It was a Gestetner brand Cyclostyle machine which produced cloudy brown representations of text on crinkly curly sheets of flimsy paper that faded and became unreadable if sunlight fell upon them.

One of the aspects of the story that is lost in translation, Prinsloo told me, is the elaborate courtesy of the man Finsch, faced by people who plainly dislike him and want something from him. The moral, if such a cynical tale can be said to contain a moral, is that no one means what he says; everyone is out to get something they don't deserve. But as soon as you conclude that in these encounters there is not an ounce of generosity, you realize that Finsch — for his amazing gift of translation — is the soul of kindness.

The narrative occupies an entire day in the life of Farmer Finsch, a day in which he sees an old friend, interviews some men for the job of driver, has lunch with his son-in-law, and later, walking in the graveyard outside Nelspruit (all Prinsloo's stories seemed to take place in deeply rural South African settings), meets and talks with a pretty young woman.

In the opening paragraph, the early morning of that day, the old friend stops by for coffee. Finsch greets the man amiably and the friend says, "You look terrible — much worse than me. Your face is fat and blotchy, probably from drinking."

The reader thinks: What's going on here? But Prinsloo knows what he is doing; gives no warnings or preliminaries, just plunges into these heartless dialogues. Finsch the translator is implacable.

"And how are you?"

"As if you care, you egotist. Your money has blinded you to the misery of the rest of us poor souls."

"I haven't seen you for ages," Finsch says.

"I never liked you! Once a year would be too often! God, what a scraggy neck you have. Watery eyes, too. The blood blotches are stamped on your face."

Antagonistic people are scrupulous noticers of faults, Prinsloo seems to be saying. And Finsch, although burdened by this prescience, does not reveal what he is hearing.

"One of these days we should have dinner," he says.

"I don't think I could stand a whole evening. And now I want to go. I want to find a way of ending this conversation. It must be those cigars that make your skin like parchment."

"Would you like a cigar? Here, take one."

"You think that offering me a cigar means I'm your friend? On the contrary, it makes me despise you more, because it reminds me of how little you've given me in all the years I've known you."

More of this and then the friend goes away, and Finsch is not insulted but calmed by the encounter. And though we have not been told explicitly what Finsch's gift is, we know what is happening when the men show up for the driver interviews.

"A bit more than a driver," as Finsch explains, for he also needs a handyman and mechanic, someone to keep the car in good repair.

"What experience do you have?" Finsch asks the first man, who is a big blond ex–army sergeant.

"How much experience do I need? I can drive well, as if you'd know the difference. Put me behind the wheel and I will dazzle you."

"Are you knowledgeable about engines?"

"The usual. I can change the oil, I can fuss and fool. Anything serious would go to a real mechanic — you can afford it. You can't expect me to know everything."

"I need someone who's handy," Finsch says.

"People like you always say that without having the slightest idea of what you mean. You'd never guess how little I know. But I know more than you."

Other interviews follow, all the men just as harsh as this; and then a new note is struck, one of timidity, the man revealing himself as fearful of Finsch.

"I'll bet you're always snooping," this man says. "You'll be watching everything I do."

Finsch says, "You'll be expected to look after the car as well as drive it."

"And it will never be enough for you. You'll do nothing but complain and make my life hell."

After more exchanges, the man cringing, terrified of Finsch, he is offered the job, which, almost mute with fear — little to translate — the man accepts.

Lunch with the son-in-law was painful to read for all the obvious reasons, the young man mocking Finsch and reflecting on what a close resemblance he has to his selfish pig of a daughter and saying, "I am going to get something from you, or else. I am just deciding what it is I want." Finsch remains serene. We see that he is content with his seemingly diabolical gift.

Later in the afternoon, in Nelspruit's white graveyard, Finsch meets a young woman. He realizes, as soon as she begins telling him she is there "to mourn a dear friend," that her boyfriend has just left for a job in Durban. While she talks to Finsch she is pondering a scheme to ensnare him — get some money out of him — so that she can join her boyfriend.

"I see you glancing at my breasts. I know you want to play with them. You are so simple. But it is going to cost you. I know I can make you pay."

"My wife is buried here," Finsch says.

"That is wonderful news. You will be all the more willing to do as I say. You're pathetic, but what a lovely ring on your finger. That will be mine."

"I miss her greatly," Finsch says.

"One glimpse of my naked body and you'll stop missing her. You're weak, but I won't hurt you. After a little while I'll take what I deserve and go on my way."

"We might meet for a cup of tea one day," Finsch says.

"I'll wear my red dress. I'll hold my nose. Sometimes men your age can really perform. That's my only worry — your demands."

Of course, Finsch avoids the woman — he has been warned. But he loses his serenity when he realizes that his knack for knowing what people are saying, what is in their heart, makes him lonely. He becomes isolated to the point where he won't see anyone, so disgusted is he by people's meanness and cynicism, their insincerity and greed. But in a redemptive moment with his daughter he understands that she genuinely loves him — or at least seems to. Dining with her, he reads her thoughts, as he has those of the others. Her kindness is sincere — or is it? Overwhelmed by a feeling of love, has he lost the ability to translate what she is saying into what she really thinks? The reader must decide.

There were about six other stories, the shortest of them about a farmer — another farmer — who finds a young abandoned monkey on his land. In his loneliness the farmer raises the monkey, names it, and trains it to become a helpful companion whom he comes to regard as a partner. At the end of the story the farmer is visited by a man who says, "Your monkey is staring at me." The farmer loses his temper. "That is no monkey!"

A similar story about a gray parrot with a vast vocabulary and the same name as the main character: at the end you are not sure whether you are reading about the farmer or the parrot.

In "Drongo," a bird appears on a veranda, pecking at the railing. The bird will not be deterred by the farmer, who is at first friendly — offering it food; and then hostile — plinking at it with a rifle. This simple bird visitation takes place against a backdrop of the wedding of the farmer's son, the appearance of the farmer's first grandchild, the promise of continuity. But without any warning the house collapses. "Eaten away." Had he looked more closely the farmer would have understood that the drongo he killed was picking at termites and keeping the house whole. Now there is nothing of the house left.

Strange stories — but Prinsloo's life, the last years of it, were stranger than anything he wrote.

3

"Quite a curious thing befell me," Lourens Prinsloo said to me — and as a writer I was keenly aware that he was trying this story out on me, as he had probably tried it out on other people. Because I was a writer myself I would not be able to use the story, though I would be allowed to repeat it, and when this master of the bizarre story finally wrote it, I could compare the version he wrote with the one he had told me in confidence.

I was listening hard, with the exaggerated attention a younger writer gives to an older one, an intense alertness that is both respect and curiosity. I was not taking notes — it would have been rude, would have seemed too businesslike — so I can only approximate what he told me as I have approximated his translated stories. But Prinsloo had a knack for dialogue, and speaking it, he made it easy for me to remember.

"It's an African story," he said. And then he told me that he had been married to Marianne, a pleasant, helpful, loving woman who had borne him two sons, Wimpie and Hansie. The marriage had flourished for more than thirty years. Farming life had bonded them — she too was from a farming family, cattle ranchers from the wilderness of Kuruman. Prinsloo and Marianne were both descendants of the oldest families to arrive in South Africa, represented centuries of settlement and work, but also of a changelessness that is known only on a farm in the African bush. Her parents had traveled by ox cart; his had had motor vehicles, but even so, they lived the isolated lives of their ancestors, side by side with Africans and speaking their language and feeling that they knew them well.

As Prinsloo told me this, I was reminded that in his long stories all of his protagonists were either widowers or spinsters. He did not write of the satisfactions of married life — a significant omission, given the fact that he was smiling as he told me how happily married he had been.

I was on the point of mentioning this when he said, "Happiness is not a fit subject. Happiness is banal. People who read are not happy, or else why would they be alone in a room with a book in their hands? I am a farmer, and on a farm you are neither happy nor sad. You work too hard ever to consider such things. You have no set hours. You are part of a much bigger process of life and death. You tend your animals, you watch the weather, you hope for rain — the right kind at the right time. You try not to think too much, or else you'll go mad with worry. Farming is the opposite of writing stories."

It was easy for me to recall his saying that, because it was a general statement of farming life. His next statement was memorable, too, for its succinctness.

"Nothing happened to me for sixty years. Then I had my birthday, and everything happened."

His saying that made me especially attentive. I let him proceed at his own pace — first a long pause, a silence, as though to allow him to find something equally dramatic as a follow-up. And really, nothing could have been better than what he said next.

"Do you remember the African woman who appears toward the end of *Heart of Darkness* — probably Kurtz's lover, 'wild, animal-like . . . flamboyant . . . all in feathers . . . a magnificent creature,' all of that?"

He had some of it right. Conrad describes the African woman in the most vivid terms: "a wild and gorgeous apparition of a woman . . . treading the earth proudly, with a slight jingle and flash of barbarous ornaments . . . She must have had the value of several elephant tusks upon her. She was savage and superb, wild-eyed and magnificent . . ." And so forth.

When I said I remembered her well, Prinsloo smiled one of his ironical smiles and said, "This woman, my woman Noloyiso, was nothing like her."

If Nolo had been the educated eldest daughter of one of his farm laborers, there would have been no obstacle to his having a casual affair with her — though he had never touched an African woman in his life. Yet, because Africans had worked for his father, their children would work for his children, it was impossible not to regard them in a profound sense as his property: they all belonged to him. Many of the girls in the fields were pretty, but in time they lost their looks, they bore children, their lives were short. He saw them not as they were but as they would become.

Nolo he saw first at the store in town and was struck by her beauty, her youth, a sense of vitality — and it was only afterward that he found she was unmarried, thirty-four years old — late middle age for an African woman. She was not dressed in the African style. She wore a gray pleated skirt, a blue blazer over a white blouse. She could have been a dining car attendant on a minor branch of the Spoorweg. Her full name was Noloyiso Vilikazi.

Her head was small, round, close-cropped hair, with a child's face, a child's ears, large dark eyes, and her figure was slight yet sturdy. Prinsloo was a good judge of an African's strength. He could tell who would last in the fields, and the women were far superior to the men.

This woman was not in the least interested in him, but for the first time in his life Prinsloo's head was turned — and by an African. She was a schoolteacher in town, so he learned. She lived alone in a simple house in the staff compound. She had been educated at a training college. She was very pretty, but her beauty was not remarkable. He was fascinated by something else, a trait he had never noticed in anyone, man or woman. What struck him was that he, a great imaginer, could not imagine Noloyiso old. He was certain that she would always look as she looked today, as lovely, as young, with the same glow of health.

He needed that assurance. He was desperate to have her. And her seriousness, her indifference, her aloofness, even her posture, all these aspects like the aspects of a watchful impala — she had the same eyes — only made his impatience worse. The second time he saw her, he noticed that her left arm was missing. Had she just lost it? No, for her left side had been hidden from him the first time. The missing arm made her more attractive to him — not pity but the opposite, an admiration for her strength.

Something within him responded, an inner voice, which was not speech but knowledge. Yet if it were put into words, it would have said: With this woman you will be young again, you will be happy, you will be strong, you will sire children, you will love the land again, you will enjoy your food, you will know passion and desire, you will be loved, you will be admired, people will smile with satisfaction when they see you, you will live longer, you will discover new subjects to write about.

A sexual awakening, perhaps, but more than that, for sex was just hydraulics, a frenzy of muscle and fluid. A new life was what he saw. The beauty of it was that he knew this woman was able to transform him, to re-create him as though fictionalizing him, making him into the other, better person he had been as a youth, hopeful, happy, energetic, fascinated, innocent — someone who slumbered within him, the pure-hearted being who, to be animated and given life again, needed only to be woken with a kiss by this one unexpected woman.

What he saw and felt was like a definition of love. It was deeper than desire. It was the awakening of a whole being, and the need was powerful because only this one woman could do it. Without her, he was only his incomplete self, half asleep; with her, he was the better person — forgiving, strong, generous, imaginative — because of her love. Sex was part of it, sex was the magic; but the bond was love.

4

Mingled in his mind were sex and creation — his writing. He believed that he was an imaginative and prolific writer because of his powerful sexual instinct, that he owed the extravagance of his imagination to his persistent sexual desire, a sort of engine that drove his writing. He hardly distinguished between the two, his desire for sex, his desire to write, and steaming in all his writing was this rosy-hued lechery — even the sober-seeming people in his strange excursions, such as Finsch and Katje and the Justus family, were running a temperature. Sex was exploration and conquest, so he reasoned. And the fever of sexual desire gave the imagination its wild and sometimes blinding fulguration. Sex was also the hot velvety darkness behind the dazzle of his creation. He would have been lost without it, he would have been lost if he had been wholly fulfilled: repressing it was a way of harnessing it and using it. "Thwarted desire was the steam contained under pressure in the boiler of his body" was a line from one of his stories, I forget which.

No man in South Africa ever found it difficult to locate a like-minded woman, a willing partner. Prinsloo knew by the look alone whether a woman was willing. Farmers' wives, farmers' daughters, Rhodesians, Mozambicans; but commonest of all were the women known as "coloreds" — ambiguous mixed-race beauties who were welcome nowhere and everywhere, looking for security. The slightest hint that he was interested animated them, and he loved watching them and seeing how clever they could be in devising ways to meet him covertly, in a nearby dorp or in remote parts of his own land, for his farm was so extensive an estate as to have hidden corners and places for assignations.

With sex he was rejuvenated. He was granted new ideas, new confidence. He did not distinguish between his literary notions and the ingenuity in these sexual affairs.

Sex was a disease, sex was also a cure. He would feel the desire to make love to a particular woman — like a rooster spotting a hen. The seduction preoccupied him, made him impatient, drove his imagination, helped his writing. At last, when the day of assignation came, the act might be clumsy the first time, better the second time, a great deal smoother the third time, but after a while, gaining skill, it lost passion. Sex was the cure for sex, like medicine three times the first day, two the second, dwindling in dosage as the condition improved, until no more was needed; and then he looked for a new woman. His wife knew nothing, for — such was his sexual charge — he did not neglect her.

At the outset he believed that with Nolo the repetition would rid him of his desire — odd, too, for she was the first full-blooded African he had ever slept with, one of the plainest, and — since she was missing one arm — incomplete.

It was her strangest feature, something like an asset, for in the dark she seemed to possess not one arm but three. His whole body was gripped. She used her mouth. She clamped him between her agile legs and wrapped herself around him and, snakelike, squeezed him until he gasped for air. This small creature in the dark became an immense boomslang, and he the soft yielding thing being devoured.

He felt small, even vulnerable, caressed and embraced by this woman who had seemed like a child. He felt young when he was with her — the first time youthful, the subsequent times like a child, with a child's physical vitality and optimism, as though at the beginning of a long life. That he had only fleetingly felt with other women. Now it was a condition of being with Nolo: he was not an older man but a youth.

Everything contributed to this feeling — the time of day, the secrecy of the place, the passion of the act, the mysteriousness of the woman. It was all new to him. Being new, it took the place of his most original writing. He had not written anything since the day, weeks before, when he first saw Nolo in her blue blazer and pleated skirt in the shop. But sex with her much resembled his best days at his desk, writing brilliantly — was in some respects superior to those days — the desire he felt like the joyous drug that lay behind his most enigmatic fiction.

Here was the woman at first glance: dependable, serious-seeming, soberly dressed as only an African schoolteacher would be, rather tense with the self-conscious piety of the educated African — and a bit defensive, too: incomplete — that missing arm. She hardly smiled.

In the bedroom, in his *bakkie* (pickup truck, he explained to me), she was a cat — wild, reckless, full of surprises — and seemed to know what was in his mind at every moment.

Just like a cat, facing away, she crouched and raised her buttocks and said, "Do it to me" — she had no word for the act, did not want to know the word, only wanted the struggle and satisfaction.

That different woman in the dark helped him discover a different man in himself; and over the course of a month he discovered much else — all revealed to him when he was with Nolo, much as in the writing of a paragraph or a page he discovered with pleasure the thought or incident that lurked there, that proved he was uncovering something new.

So instead of burning itself out, the flame grew fiercer, hotter, and brighter.

He loved the idea that only he knew that she was two people, and neither of them was African in any sense he had known or seen before. And he a man, a *baas*, who had been born in the country!

He was enough of a man of the world, had lived long enough, to understand the lover's illusion of the beloved as someone unique — and, more than that, someone known only to the lover. The lover's conceit that no one else may intrude, no one else has the capacity to see or understand. Desire was this special way of seeing the lover as irreplaceable. Smitten meant hit on the head, he knew that, and he still felt that he was in sole possession of the truth.

Desire, need, urgency, made him reckless. He could hardly believe how much. Loving a black was breaking the law. What he felt was the nearest thing to love he had ever known — yet to call it that was unnatural and illegal, and while it was normal for him to feel affection and even desire, love was absurd.

Nevertheless, she gave him something powerful without speaking a word — bewitched him. She made him whole, made him strong, restored youth to him, gave him power. She inspired him. Seeing him the first time, she had seemed to understand him and silently to respond with promises. In their lovemaking she kept her promises. So she was true.

Without telling his wife why, he found a house for her, asked her to live in it, and said that he needed to be alone, to think.

She knew what was wrong. Many times in the past, working on one of his long stories, he had absented himself, vanished somewhere on his vast estate, so that he could understand the story better.

Nolo was like a character in one of his strangest stories. So was he. Exactly. The sense of living inside one of his own stories roused and compelled him to look deeper. The feeling did not pass away, nor even diminish. He wanted more of it.

5

Distracted, almost demented by this fever of passion and attachment, feeling unwell, he had no doubt that there was only one cure for his ailment, ridiculous as it might seem to the whites he knew — a sickening desire for the half-educated schoolteacher with one arm, just a kaffir and, outside the bedroom, a deeply moralistic munt. All he wanted, now that he was separated from his wife, was for the African to move into his house with him, something any African woman would have been eager to do, to share his life, to be waited on by servants, to know a degree of luxury that was way beyond the imagining of most of them, like winning the lottery.

She said no.

Prinsloo almost laughed. This was a ruse, surely. He demanded to know why.

"Because we are not married," she said.

He stared at her.

"In the eyes of God," she added.

"In the eyes of God we are!"

"Not married," she said stubbornly, frowning, defying him.

This from a woman whose people hardly used the word, who stuck a spear upright, twangling in the ground, before the door of a rondavel, which meant, *I am a man. I am here. This is my woman.*

Prinsloo still smiled. He said, "We have done nothing but sneak around and make love for almost a month."

"I regret that."

He reminded her of certain acts she had performed, words she had said, noises she had made.

"I should not have," she said, looking demure, pressing her prim lips together. "Because of my Christian vows."

Prinsloo wanted to hit her. He had spanked his children, and one drunken night he had smacked his wife; he had never struck an African, though such beatings were common enough in his stories — thrashings with sjamboks that cut flesh and drew blood. Having rehearsed them in his work, he was able to imagine snatching a whip and slashing her with it and belaboring her on the floor until she agreed with everything he said, until she submitted.

He wondered whether she was deliberately provoking him, wishing to be thrashed and dominated. He was reaching for her wrist, on the point of grabbing it, when she pulled away, looking shocked, and said that he would have to think seriously about marrying her before he touched her again.

"You have no right," she said.

That fascinated him, as though she were making a kind of promise: if they were legally together he would have a perfect right to make her submit.

She said no more, she just withdrew, she vanished into her schoolroom. He turned to his work, which had lain untouched, stopped cold, since he had initiated the affair with Noloyiso and left it as he had left his wife. But he was stumped. He could not make a sentence. Work that had taken the place of sex, that had inspired sex, that was inspired by sex, that had been his life, was inert. His pen was small and loose in his hand, just a dry stick he used to make crosshatches in the margins of his sheet of paper. He wanted to stab himself with the thing.

Or stab her with it, injecting her with ink. The one-armed Bantu schoolteacher had rebuffed him. Apparently her life was complete: she turned her back on him and went on teaching. Was it possible that she felt nothing?

At least he knew where she was. At certain times of the day, unable to work, the times when he would have worked, he crossed the dorp in his *bakkie*, bumped over the railway tracks that divided the town into black and white, and, parking on the road, he walked the last hundred yards on stony ground to the hencoop of a school.

Black children in the playground stared at him. It was not unusual for a white school super or inspector to appear, but this man went to the window and looked in, standing and staring like a reproachful ghost.

Nolo continued to teach her class, with him at the window. But when the bell sounded she hurried outside looking stern, her face immobile.

"If you don't leave the premises I'll have to call the police."

"Premises" — this scrubby acre! "Police" — those lazy villains! Prinsloo said, "I am not committing a crime."

"You are trespassing."

He thought: Imagine being accused by a Bantu!

But he said, "I want you to come with me."

"You know my position on that. You know my terms."

"Position"! "Terms"! He wanted to laugh. He hoped that her speaking to him in this way would fill him with self-disgust and act as a signal for him to reject her. Yet the opposite happened. He was humiliated and humbled. Her speaking sharply to him clarified his feelings. He realized that he could not live without her.

He divorced Marianne. The poor woman's face crumpled with grief, as though she had just gotten news of the death of a loved one. In a sense, that was just what had happened, for he was lost to her for good.

She begged him to change his mind. He pitied her, but he also wanted her to wish him well. He said so.

She said, "I don't wish you ill," and then, considering the words she had spoken, added, "No, I do wish you ill. You deserve to suffer."

He said, "I haven't written a single word for six months!" — meaning that he had already suffered.

"You're divorcing me and all you think about is your writing."

"Because that's all I ever think about."

Why had he said this? Was it true? He did not think about his unwritten stories, only about Noloyiso the Bantu schoolteacher, who had one arm, who possessed him, body and soul.

He told Nolo in a letter what he had done.

She agreed to see him. She allowed his advances, they made love again, but it was understood that she would not move in with him.

"My people would call me a harlot."

"Your people are always living together. That's the usual arrangement!"

"With each other. In the same age group. Not with a white man. And you are old."

She had him there.

What made Prinsloo think it would be a reasonable idea for him to introduce Nolo to Hansie? Wimpie was in Cape Town, or else he would have included him, too, at the lunch in the hotel dining room in the dorp. It was bad enough with Hansie; Wimpie would have made it worse. Prinsloo saw at once it was a mistake. Nolo and Hansie were the same age.

Hansie's eyes were cold, his lips were tight with fury, his voice quietly mocking, asking questions that were accusations, not expecting answers.

"Doesn't it seem a bit strange to be eating in here, sitting at a table rather than standing outside at the window?"

Africans just seven years before had been forbidden to enter the restaurant and had used the take-away window at the side of the building.

Nolo said, "Not really. I always thought it was strange to use the window, and so I never did it."

Prinsloo admired Nolo's composure. Her strength gave him strength.

"What's your opinion of Dad's books?"

That threw her. It was clear from her expression that Nolo did not know Prinsloo was a writer. What had his writing to do with their love affair? Nolo simply stared at him.

"She will read them when they are translated," Prinsloo said.

"*Praat u Afrikaans?*" Hansie nagged.

"*Ek verstaan net 'n bietjie Afrikaans. Ek praat Engels,*" Nolo said.

Saying that was the nearest she had ever come to expressing a political opinion.

"Into English, of course," Prinsloo said.

Prinsloo sat in a sorry slumped posture, as Hansie looked at his father with contempt for his foolishness.

The meal was awful. Before it was over he knew he had lost his son; that Hansie saw this unique woman and thought, Kaffir.

More alone afterward, Prinsloo saw that he had only one choice. He proposed marriage. Nolo accepted. The little ceremony took place in the town hall — Nolo's elderly father, some of her cousins, an auntie, all of them dressed in stiff, ill-fitting clothes, newly made by a man working a Singer sewing machine on a veranda in the dorp. Nolo wore a long yellow dress. And another awkward lunch in the hotel dining room, the old man smiling with worry and saying, "I have never been in here before in my whole life."

Later that day she moved into his house, bringing one suitcase, the size she would have used for travel of a week's duration, containing everything she owned, including a clock, a Bible, some pictures, some books — serious self-improving ones; and she submitted to him.

She became his slave, but a happy one, joyous in their lovemaking — imaginative, too, for she allowed Prinsloo to dominate her utterly, to treat her like a servant, a whore, a sex object, a stranger, living out passionate fantasies of master and slave. She allowed it, then she encouraged it, finally she demanded it. Prinsloo tied her one arm and used her body; she did not object, she said she enjoyed it. She suggested more degrading episodes of submission in which she sat handcuffed to a chair or secured to the bedposts. She willingly got onto her knees, her one arm making a tripod of her posture. She urged him to thrash her buttocks, and while he did so, she raised them so that he could enter her. Still she asked for more, begging to eat him, drink him, swallow him.

When Prinsloo ran out of ideas for abusing her, it was Nolo who supplied him with variations, acts he had not imagined in his wildest fictions. How did she know what was in his head? Where had she heard of such things? Perhaps only an African knew how to please such a man, since sex is about power, and the African story was about power. What a mind she had! She was so willing to take any form of abuse she became his partner; she invited him to enslave her.

Her submitting in this way proved to Prinsloo that she was stronger than he was, that she enjoyed these games even more than he did, that the manipulation was hers: she was using him.

So he was absolved of any sense of guilt. Sex filled his life. These were the first weeks, the first months, of a passionate marriage. He loved her seriousness, he adored her recklessness. She was wilder than he was, she was impossible to know. His life was complete, like a finished story, but the marriage was both a satisfaction and a blurring, for now he had no idea who she was.

She had kept her promise. That was worth a lot. She belonged to him. His nonwriting life was as full as his writing life had ever been, as rich, as unexpected.

But one day, drawing her arm behind her, she hesitated before he twisted it, preparing to restrain her.

"Not too rough today. I don't want to hurt the baby."

He backed off, raising his hands, as though she had shown him a weapon, and when he tried to resume, his efforts were enfeebled by what she had told him. He could not proceed.

6

The news of a baby surprised and preoccupied him in a way he had never known. He had hardly been aware of the births of his two other children. This was different. He monitored the progress of Nolo's pregnancy. He had the time. He was not writing. Anyway, this was better than writing and yet similar — something new every day, a discovery, growth, wonder, he was humbled. She was the pen, bringing forth something new. Nolo became inward, compact, budlike, concentrating on her body. She swelled, she lost her girl's body, she became fruit-shaped; he studied her tightened flesh, he pondered the loss of her sexuality.

When the day came and she signaled that she was ready, the doctor arrived and Nolo gave birth in their own bedroom, a wonderful thing, a celebration, a boy, a gift.

The infant was gray at birth, then pink, darkening, with thick hair. He was not black or white, but maculate, pinkish patched gray, more a reflection of Prinsloo than either of his other children, intelligent, responsive, alert.

Nolo called him Nelson. Prinsloo called him Zulu, to represent his people: and "Zulu Prinsloo" had the right sound, a haughty assonance.

Children in Africa seldom cry, seldom fuss, don't clamor for attention, don't have to, since a cloth binds them to the mother's back, a bundle she carries everywhere, and suckles whenever the child is hungry. Nolo kept the boy close, took him to bed with them, suckled him there, Prinsloo looking on, the child always lying between them.

Nolo was a new woman, fulfilled and fattish, beautiful in her bulk. The skinny young woman had become rounder, with pale clear skin and serene eyes and great heavy breasts.

"No," she said when Prinsloo reached as though to weigh one in his lifting hand.

She would not allow his fingers the slightest touch, and she shrank when he approached.

The African custom stipulated that a woman could not engage in sex while she was breastfeeding. Nolo, who had never shown any curiosity for her culture, reverted to her traditional customs.

Months passed. Prinsloo played with the baby and, though rebuffed by the mother, was consoled by the child's response — a bright child, golden-skinned, his own, more him than his others. He endured the no-sex stricture, and eight months later the child was still seeking his mother's nipples.

Prinsloo, though indulgent and proud of the child, was eager to change places with him, to nestle between those breasts, where he had once spent whole nights.

Sometimes he took his small son to town, binding him into the baby seat in his Land Rover, the child contentedly gurgling. On such occasions, the entire day devoted to one trip to the dorp — no writing, no reading, only hours of proximity to the child — Prinsloo reflected that for over a year now he had not written a word; he had been silent. Had anyone noticed?

That day of writing would come, he was sure, though this was the longest he had gone without writing, for his creative life had been spent writing stories end to end, finishing one, starting another, linking them in his head; and this was a break, an emptiness.

What made him confident was the knowledge that this too was a story, his love affair, the marriage, the child. Not that any of this compensated for setting words down on a page, yet he was living an African story.

The most African of African stories, for he was a farmer, descended from Boers who had trekked to the Transvaal two hundred years before; he was a white man who had made a whole life and abandoned it upon falling in love at a feed store with a black woman who had one arm; he had embarked on a new life, a new family, with a mixed-race child — an amazing story, and living it was almost as satisfying as writing it.

He wanted more. The fullest expression of her fantasies was fresh in his mind, the slave business, the submission, the play with silken ropes and restraints, the leather mask, the gag.

The child was asleep in the next room one hot afternoon. Prinsloo approached Nolo from behind. They were alone in the dark humid shadows of the house, he was impatient and eager, wishing to hold her and subdue her and use her as she had allowed him a little over a year ago. Not just allowed; she had encouraged him, pleaded to be dominated, begged him to tie her to the bedposts, her eyes glistening with anticipation as he knotted the ropes, and when she was immobilized and he was sitting astride her, her sighs of satisfaction. The ritual had been central to their love affair and had been a marriage rite, too.

Prinsloo snatched her arm, held her, and before she had time to struggle or shout encouragement he gagged her with a scarf and drag-shuffled her to the bedroom. Now she fought him — that feeble pretense, wagging the stump of her arm, had always been part of the ritual — but her opposition only excited him the more. He turned her over, his hand jamming her head down, her face into the pillow, and he mounted her from behind. He took her muffled howling for the eagerness she had shown before, and he covered her with his body, one hand holding her skull, using his other hand as though thrusting hard with a dagger until he was done.

He had possessed her, she was his captive, as in the oldest days of the colony.

But when he was exhausted and lay beside her, loosening the scarves, she swiped at him with her good arm, and dragged off her gag, and accused him of abusing her. In the past she had flattened herself against him in gratitude and obedience, like a cat warming herself against her owner.

Drowsing, stuporous after sex, he was rattled by what she was saying.

"You're joking."

"You raped me."

"You want me to. It's a game."

"Your game."

"Our game. You're my wife."

"I'm afraid of you," she said, and she touched herself where he had held her roughly, smoothing the pinch marks on her skin.

"No," he said, and looked closely at her, expecting her to laugh.

"I want a divorce," she said.

Prinsloo had no reply. What she had just said knocked the wind out of him, and all he could think of was his first wife's anguish, a suffering he understood now, how she was shattered when he said he wanted to leave her, looking at him with horrified eyes, hoping it was not true.

Nolo, never much of a talker, said there was nothing to discuss. She regarded him as an intruder — kept away from him, did not argue, watched him coldly.

"I want you to leave."

Minutes after sex, this rejection.

Prinsloo was smiling at her schoolteacher's tone, the shrill authority.

"This is my house," he said.

"How can you force me to leave with a small child?"

7

Prinsloo's estate had been vast, not just fruit trees and lucerne, tobacco and seed maize, but animals — sheep, cattle, poultry, an experimental ostrich farm, a game ranch with herds of eland and waterbuck, zebra and buffalo; crocs and hippos in his river. A settlement of workers, too, that amounted to an African village. Underneath it all, below a ridge that ran like a protective berm at the southern limit of his land, were seams of platinum. A mining company's survey promised a great haul of ore, and though what was under the ground was the government's, not Prinsloo's, the mining company would have to lease many hectares for buildings and equipment.

Half of this Prinsloo lost in his first divorce; half of what remained he lost in the second, the sudden split from a woman he hardly knew. What appalled him was that he had been looking at people just like her his whole life and believed he knew them, and how could Nolo be any different? Some of them, Africans like her, had appeared in many of his stories. He wrote about the intimacies of their lives, he approximated the way they spoke, he described their heartaches and tribulations.

He knew nothing, this proved it: he was a man of sixty-one, rendered imbecilic by his rashness. "I'm stupid," he said to people, startling old friends and perfect strangers, shoeshine boys and parking lot attendants and the men in skullcaps who pumped gas for him. "I'm stupid. Look at me. I'm not joking — I'm an idiot."

Like a man making a mockery of himself after losing a large wager, seeing his money swept off the table, and laughing horribly, a fool who seems dangerous because he has nothing more to lose.

"Stupid!" And, saying so, cranking his finger at his ear to mean "out of my mind."

He had lost the dairy, the game ranch, the cattle, the sheep, the orchards, the farm, the ridge of ore, even the workers' settlement. The lovely farmhouse, roomy and white-plastered, from which he had sent his first wife, was now Nolo's. He kept the chicken operation and hired a colored man, Petrus, as a farm manager, and he moved away.

The day he left, giving his last instructions to Petrus, he caught a glimpse of Petrus's wife, Myra, who looked patient and winsome, with a small child, and thought: Why didn't I marry her or someone like her? I would still be here, in my study, at my desk, writing my story, a good story, about the farmer who marries a submissive black woman with one arm.

He did not say, "They're all the same." He said, "I made the worst possible choice, not an informed decision but a reckless throw of the dice, and I lost."

You would have done, he thought whenever he saw an attractive woman, white or black, usually black, and he reproached himself for having been such a fool. I'm stupid!

He did not mind that he was a laughingstock — he deserved to be hooted at. He minded that he had no life — that he had forfeited all his effort, his inherited property, the work he had done. He kept a few things, the clock, his grandfather's saddle, the photographs, his manuscripts, a rotting collection of assegais and knobkerries, baskets, neck rests, spears.

The fact of the child Zulu — he could not bear to think of him as Nelson — was the worst of all. The mixed-race child he loved belonged to a devious black woman he now hated. But was devious the word? He told himself yes, but in his heart he knew the choice to leave his wife and marry her was his alone. He could have said no, even as Nolo made noises about her Christian vows.

I wanted to write, I had no subject, I was stuck, I thought this would help, I loved her.

He could barely recall the sequence of events that had led to his being almost homeless. He winced, remembering sex with Nolo, how she had pretended to be his slave, how her being his slave had made him stupid.

Writing this African story might redeem him. The story might be perfect, but even if it was not, it was true, and the truth was always prophetic. He imagined all being well if he wrote his story unembellished, a narrative of a white farmer and his submissive black lover, keeping all the details: the sjambok, the slave chapel, the barred windows, and the fields of lucerne glowing in the moonlight. The story was about sexual desire — how it was mute and ignorant magic that cast a spell, making the lovers dumb.

But he did not write it. He missed his son and he devised ways of seeing him.

Nolo seemed to welcome his visits. She encouraged his taking the boy out, but she could be unsentimental and rigid — her schoolteacher's severity adding to her enigma — and one day Prinsloo showed up without warning, aching to see his son, and she called the police, who arrested him for trespassing. His own house! Black police.

Prinsloo appeared in court, sitting in a dock that was a steel cage, packed with farm invaders, all of them Venda, who badgered him for cigarettes.

The country was upside down, the government black now, though the judge was white. Prinsloo got off with a warning and a fine, just like the farm invaders. And the day after he paid the fine Nolo sent him a letter through her lawyers saying she wanted more money.

8

The harsh syllable *ach* gargled at his back teeth and made his jaw sore with incredulity. *Ach!* The woman he saw as simple and submissive had become his tormentor — ingenious, wicked, venal. She allowed him to see the child but at the same time demanded more money. When he delayed paying she found ways of obstructing his access to the boy, and so he paid up, hating the unfair tax on him for seeing his own child. He told himself that a woman of his own race would never have subjected him to this humiliation.

He drove to the house in the morning, early. The child was already in the road, the servant holding him by the hand. Prinsloo drove the child to school — not the school where Nolo had taught but a private preschool outside the dorp. Prinsloo waited, killing time in the dorp, then fetched him in the afternoon, hoping the boy would be hungry, so that he would have the pleasure of feeding him.

He loved him, it was agony, he sorrowed for the child and himself, saw his own frailty in the small frail figure walking away from him later on, up the path toward the house — the old white-plastered Prinsloo farmhouse, the model for so many of the farmhouses in Prinsloo's stories. What pathos in that little head and those narrow shoulders, the skinny legs and small trotting feet.

The child was like a little old man, like Prinsloo himself, and Prinsloo feared for them both and hated the one-armed woman who was the cause of this whole horrible affair. But how could Prinsloo blame her when he himself was the cause, first as an intruder, then a terror, finally a weakling. Nolo was looking old, too — as old as he felt. She had aged quickly, as African women do, losing their looks in their thirties, in their forties becoming crones.

Once, he saw Marianne. She did not recognize him. Had he grown so ugly and so different? She was first startled by him and then, recovering, hardened against him. She spoke of emigrating to Australia with Hansie. Wimpie was in Cape Town.

He forgave Marianne for her coldness. Nolo was crueler than she was, and with what reason? Was she demented? Was she simply ambitious and material-minded? He reflected that a woman who had married so late had to have something wrong with her. The missing arm did not explain much. She seemed to take pleasure in his suffering. She bled him. Her money demands were like whippings. Was she a sadist? Africans could be cruel, and some were jubilant in their cruelty, finding power in violence and feeling joy. Used to pain, their most merciful judgment was *Let him die,* not because they lacked a common bond of humanity but because they felt it and despised it. Revenge made them happy. He was amazed to see that they were just like everyone else on earth.

Prinsloo heard she had a lover, but could not prove it. Anyway, what if she did? She had no sentiment. The lover would be swindled — good riddance; or she would — ditto.

What tipped him off was her saying, "I want to work."

What work could a one-armed woman do, apart from the teaching she had done before? What need was there? She was wealthy. She owned a farm bigger than a township, and a settlement of black workers within the farm, humans and animals and all their food, too. So what she was saying in wishing to work was that she wanted to circulate, have some freedom, be social.

This business with Nolo made him think of his first marriage, and always with regret. Marianne had never been manipulative. He reproached himself for having been so hard on that patient woman. And he played along with Nolo, encouraging her to work. She became a committee member in the dorp's local government, not much money, but an office, some status, and offering occasions to dress up, ceremonials, welcoming foreign visitors, formal teas, lawn parties. Nolo left the child in the care of an old servant.

Prinsloo easily persuaded the servant to release the child, so that he could take him for a drive. Prinsloo brought biltong and bread, and they sat at the margin of the game ranch Prinsloo had built and lost, and they watched the eland browsing in the bush. Prinsloo returned to find the police waiting for him — black police. They arrested him.

"Attempted kidnapping, *baas*."

"That's my child!"

Nolo would not return his calls, she worked through a lawyer, took out a restraining order, demanded more money to pay her legal expenses, and this time there was nothing in return, only the promise that if he paid promptly she might not ask for more.

Prinsloo had lost everything, even his own freedom. He had nothing left, nowhere to go.

9

He said to me, sounding like a character in one of his stories: "I imagined a new life. This was a new life. But not the one I imagined."

What he called his exile was not exile in a conventional sense. He was not driven out of South Africa. He found a place to live in, just a bolthole in Johannesburg, and made visits to his friends. Most of them dreaded his arrival because of the failure and hopelessness he dragged with him. But Prinsloo made it impossible for them to refuse. "I want to come and sleep on your floor for a few days." How could they turn him away? Etienne Leroux in Koffiefontein, one of his staunchest friends, encouraged him to visit. Prinsloo said that his condition could perhaps best be described as "internal exile."

He had lost his estate, his first family, his second family, his writing life — the life that he wanted, that he had never believed anyone could take from him. But no, he had handed it over.

"Exiled!" He joked about his homelessness. Not bitterly but lightly, because he had no hope, and the facetious humor of the truly hopeless sustained him. He knew that no one could tut-tut and remark upon how things would improve. Nothing would improve.

"It's a tragedy," Etienne said to me.

All I had heard in South Africa were stories about massacres, political scheming, torture and imprisonment, different sorts of violent crime — nothing about a domestic tragedy such as Prinsloo's. And with all the extravagant stories of terror circulating, no one wanted to hear Prinsloo's story. He tried telling it; no one would listen, the country was changing too fast for anyone to have the patience for pettiness.

It was about this time that I met Prinsloo, a white-haired man, prematurely feeble, making each complaint into a joke, seeming to ask for reassurance, then jeering when I tried to reassure him.

"But he will write it," Etienne said.

A writer needs to take pleasure in solitude. Prinsloo could not bear to be alone now. He loved the fact that I was a visitor to South Africa, that I was eager to read his typescript of stories, that I was such a stranger to him, so willing to listen. And over the course of the week or so that I stayed in Koffiefontein he told me his story.

I listened closely, excited at the thought that this man, such a fabulist in his own work, had material of this kind for a new story, perhaps his greatest. It would be the equal of André Brink, or J. M. Coetzee, or Leroux himself. It was an African story but a peculiarly white man's story, one of Prinsloo's weirdest, as though everything he had written had prepared him for it.

Even before he finished telling me the story, I sort of understood it: at the point in his life when Prinsloo loses the imagination to write his extravagant stories, he decides to embark upon a narrative of his own. Leaving the security of his marriage and family and ancestral farm, he makes love to and marries a one-armed African woman schoolteacher whom he has met in a feed store. He proves his point, acts out a story he could live, but loses the ability to write. What he hoped would be greater inspiration almost destroyed him.

His eyes were lively as he told me his story, and with a strange glee and no self-pity he answered every question I had, smiling even as I asked for more details about the wooing, the lovemaking, the bondage and submission, the slavery reenactments.

Then he said, "That episode is the story I should have written.

But I couldn't both live it and write it. So now I know how the rest of the world suffers."

He was never more animated than when I tried to tell him that his story was unique.

"No! No!" He got to his feet and, unsteady, his laughter revealing his decaying teeth, the rattle of his bad lungs, he said, "Not just my story. That's why it is useless to write. Many men have lived this. The woman that arouses our sexual passion — weak, pretty, submissive, childlike — is nearly always the opposite of the woman we want to live with, who is strong, undemanding, motherly, and trustworthy. In my case there is no moral to be drawn. It's just an African story."

He died alone, unknown, unmourned. His farm was not improved, yet the momentum of its operation had never been interrupted and it continued to prosper. Nolo did not remarry. She became fiercely respectable, sometimes lending her name to good causes. She had not changed her name from Prinsloo. When foreign visitors toured the province her estate was one of the stops, the foreigners marveling at the fruitful fields and the animals, and clucking at Nolo's son, praising his looks and saying, "Where did you get those lovely eyes?"

Disheveled Nymphs

I

LELAND WEVILL told me he was a lawyer. Instead of
walking away, I asked him what kind of lawyer he was.
He said, "I bite people on the neck for a living. That
kind." So I decided to get to know him. He didn't do much law-
yering now. "I've got plenty of money." Early on, he said to me,
"I beg you to believe that the things I don't have are things I don't
want." Even after I found out that he was quoting the French
aphorist Chamfort, I believed him. That it was plagiarized didn't
make it less interesting or, in Wevill's case, less true. Wevill had
everything he wanted.

He was devoted to living in Hawaii and to perfecting his beautiful house. He said, "I want a house that I never have to leave."
He meant an estate, his own world with a wall around it. I had
seen it and I had been invited back. I had passed the test. We had
another bond — our mutual friend the kindly lawyer Lionberg,
who had killed himself. "Long story short, Royce overreached
himself," he said. "Bad decisions have a long tail. Create a lot to
untangle."

Wevill was not the simple cruel man he seemed. He was one
of those wealthy men who had made his house into a shrine — a
secular shrine, representing his mind and his taste, filled with fe-
tishes and trophies peculiar to his own passions. The house was

like an extension of his own body, as his Jaguar was, as was everything he owned: no buffalo heads or zebra skins but many Japanese prints, a rack of samurai swords, and the carved throne — it looked like a spindly leather-seated chair — of a Chokwe chief. "Your Chokwe live in eastern Angola." The house was off limits to everyone except his family — that is, his mother and his two children. They were on the mainland, so he hardly saw them. He disliked all visitors, for their intrusion and their envy and resentment, for the way they coveted what he had. He loved Rita and Nina, the two women who cleaned his house, the young mother and her attractive daughter who could have been sisters, who were not covetous at all; in fact, the house was richer with them in it.

Like many such men who lived in lovely houses they had furnished themselves — anyway, men I knew, never women — Leland Wevill regarded his unwelcome visitors as subjects and his house as the test. He judged people by how they behaved among his possessions. You went there and he watched you react and sometimes he gave you the third degree. He seldom entertained, but because he was a retired lawyer from the mainland, his former associates sent people to him, other lawyers mostly, who happened to be passing through the islands. He resented being on these travelers' itineraries, a stopping place on their tour, and so out of hostility he put them to the test, judged them by the objects they touched and how they handled them, the details they noticed, the items they ignored — obvious treasures in some cases — what questions they asked, how they responded to his answers, how they reacted when he lied, as he often did.

"It's just something I picked up in India," he said of a rare Japanese inro.

"It's one of Hiroshige's classic images," he said of a Hokusai print.

Of his favorite piece, an original Watteau, bought at an auction in New York for a fabulous sum — but he would have paid anything for the large detailed drawing of two disheveled nymphs, their tumbled hair and rumpled low-cut blouses — he said, "I'm told it's a shoddy reproduction. It's kind of fun."

And, "I don't know much about it. Just a chair, I guess. Shaker, maybe?" of the Chokwe chief's throne.

Then he waited for the guest to speak. Tribal art so often looked indeterminate, ageless, generic even — a Masai rongo club like a Fijian head-basher, a Papuan highlander's spear like a Kikuyu's, Ethiopian icons could pass for crude Byzantine altarpieces.

To the trained eye, to anyone who visited museums, Wevill's estate was a treasure house.

"Maybe some kind of kitchen implement," he said of a whalebone slasher, called a *patu,* used by nineteenth-century Maoris in close-combat battle. "Maybe a false nose," he said of a highlander's phallocrypt.

Most people failed his house test — wanted the thing they were most ignorant about, took him at his word when he lied, admired the ordinary picture in the priceless frame or the fake stones in the jade dagger handle, accepted his saying that the beautiful thick-petaled blossom in the painting was by Mary Cassatt when it was an early Mondrian.

Just the way visitors handled objects told him everything he needed to know. Some people would pick up the dagger handle and not want to let go. There was a stare people had that meant they were taking possession of the painting and would have no hesitation in stealing it.

The visitors' envy exhausted him because it gave him no rest, and he was suspicious — he saw them as potential thieves. They wanted what he had. One visit to his house revealed everything about them.

But here was the paradox. Rita and Nina, the cleaning

women, asked no questions. They were as careful with the Tibetan silver-rimmed skullcup as they were with the plastic soap dish in the bathroom — and were careful without being covetous. He was impressed by the lightness of their touch without their having the least idea of what they were handling. Because of this, he knew almost nothing about these two women. He could not test them.

They talked intimately with each other, conversations he could not enter, on subjects that bewildered him, information they got from television programs he'd never heard of. He just listened.

"The Psychic Hot Line is a rip-off. Plus, they keep calling you up after, saying they got something else to tell you."

"Psychics give you good news, like, 'A big change is coming.' But anyone can say that."

"I actually visited one. I was pregnant with you and I says to the psychic, 'When am I going to have a baby?' and she says, 'Not for a few years.' I was like sticking out and she didn't even notice."

"I want numbers from psychics. Like, if they can see the future, why aren't they rich?"

"Maybe they can only see the past, but what's so great about that?"

"I'd like to go to Vegas with a psychic. Just to see."

"Or one of those cruises where you just play slots and eat."

They often mentioned gambling, which seemed odd to Wevill, because they were two of the unlikeliest gamblers — just pretty island women, all smiles, easygoing, in old clothes, with none of the obsessive behavior and tasteless outfits he associated with gamblers, no superstitious rituals, no strange jackets.

They threw him, everything about them foxed him.

Most people walk a certain way in their own house, with a confident nakedness — efficient, unselfconscious, with an economy of gesture, not noticing anything, fixed on the one thing they happen to be doing, undistractible. "I'm in here," while stretching out a hand in the darkness to flick a switch, taking the shortest route among the sharp corners of furniture without looking, all the flourishes of ownership. Wevill was like that six days a week.

On Saturdays you would not have believed Wevill to be in his own home, this shrine to his life and taste, his enlarged being, for his distraction and his impatience were obvious. That was the day the cleaning women were at work in his rooms, and in his head Wevill was bereft, he never felt weaker or more superfluous.

Wevill, who told me "I bite people on the neck for a living," watched helplessly as the cleaners possessed the house, possessed him, the pretty witch, the skinny ballerina, mother and daughter.

The day the cleaning women came was usually the day you went out or made yourself scarce — "The check is on the kitchen counter" — but that was the one day Wevill made a point of staying home, looking like a brain-sick potentate, big and ineffectual, bumping into his own chairs, too numb with desire to do anything but gape at their ungainly grace.

The women cleaned as though mimicking dancers, the same approximations of bending and stretching, sometimes on tiptoe, reaching straight-armed, darting forward and back, bowing to the lowest shelves, often kneeling, crouched like spaniels, showing Wevill their dusty footpads and their pretty buttocks. They wore no makeup, their hair was loose, they favored baggy sweatsuits. They might have just crept from bed, that was their look as they worked, disheveled nymphs.

Wevill — pretending to be busy, shifting vases, squaring-up papers — watched them, the twenty-year-old, her mother not yet forty; young, husbandless, no partners — he had obliquely asked, they had answered directly. "Let's say you had a boyfriend." "No thanks!" Knowing he could have been father to one and grandfather to the other, he desired both of them.

Mopping, scrubbing on all fours, lying on their backs to beat a feather duster at cobwebs under the sofa, straining on tiptoe to brush at geckos, they hiked up their shirts and showed smooth honey-colored down on their lower backs. All the demanding postures of housework, which represented the most passionate postures of lovemaking. And still they talked.

"Dwarfs marry each other sometimes, but sometimes they get normal big-sized kids and sometimes they get more dwarfs."

"Britney and Christina used to be Mouseketeers, and so did Justin. That's why Britney and Justin are dating."

"What makes a guy lolo is living with his mother."

This is just a miscellaneous anecdote in the life of Leland Wevill, someone universally acknowledged to be a powerful man — who died a few years ago and has been written about endlessly for his contributions to charities, his shrewd investments, his vast holdings, his career as a lawyer, his role on the boards of several large corporations, his successful innovations, his superb art collection. In almost everything he did he acted from a position of strength — bought weak companies and built them up and sold them, found an inexpensive but ingenious product and represented it for a share of the proceeds, acquired paintings and sculptures years before the artists' reputations grew and the prices shot up. Even in the case of the Watteau he had been bottom-feeding.

Everything he accomplished was a species of transformation. Even himself, his own life. He was born into an ordinary family in Massachusetts, the city of Cambridge, the unfashionable side. But he was bright. He got into Harvard as a townie, lived at home to save money, earned a scholarship to Harvard Law School and afterward seemed like someone special: Bostonian,

Harvard graduate, with a distinguished-sounding name — "Leland" was his own idea, he hated being Fred Junior. In the active part of his life he made a fortune, the sort of lawyer who owns a portion of every case he represents, not taking risks but studying the client's odds, and winning big when he won. He had moved to Hawaii in his fifties, on the suggestion of Royce Lionberg. He was sixty-one now, just under six feet, a healthy man, and until answering the ad in the *Star-Bulletin* for the two cleaners, he had believed he was very happy.

Apart from Lionberg — the former personal-injury lawyer who had fallen in love with a woman of twenty-three, was rebuffed, fell into a depression, and died by hanging himself from the door handle of his Lexus with his Hermès tie — Leland Wevill was the most powerful man I knew.

He was a highly intelligent man, which made it all the more interesting to me that he had the capacity to behave foolishly.

Ever since coming to Hawaii, Wevill had been keenly aware of his aging body — he was a big soft man with white hairless legs and a potbelly. He didn't mind being conspicuous, he hated being a fool. He didn't swim much, he didn't play golf at all. A good golf swing would have won him playmates in Hawaii. He did not understand the social scene at all. Now and then when he went to a strip club he was horrified to recognize that many of the other patrons were men who looked exactly like him — bored, sixtyish, desperate, no friends, just rattling around, more lonely than horny.

He would not have come to Hawaii at all except that Lionberg had come. Lionberg's suicide had nothing to do with living in Hawaii — it was the failed love affair. He had been a friend to Wevill. Wevill felt the loss.

Now and then, Wevill saw a tidy old man in new sandals, carrying his lunch in a bag to the beach, and the man sat on the sand at the center of his own neatness — the beach towel, sunblock, water bottle, the newspaper folded into quarters to show the day's crossword. The man pretended to be busy, pretended not to notice the loose breasts of girls in bathing suits, the way they pinched and snapped their bikini bottoms — pretended to be content while he was dying of loneliness. At the beach, not swimming. Wevill feared being that man.

Such a man was killing himself with his routines. Having come to Hawaii to live, to escape a routine, he suffered an even more punishing routine and felt his age more sharply. He had no pleasures — he was just conspicuously growing old, a dying man among the living. It alarmed him to think that he would do anything to make things different.

The mother and daughter, Rita and Nina, murmured and giggled together like sisters, usually about gambling or psychics or both, while Wevill watched with the complacent horror of a man surrendering to being sucked into a vacuum. He could not be still, he felt like a stranger in his own house, he dropped things, and defying the logic of the house owner at home, he bumped against his own furniture. The two women seemed more at home to him than he was. That also fueled his ardor. They did not talk to him, though now and then they had a laugh with Ramon, the gardener.

Wevill lusted for them both, he did not differentiate, they were so similar, Rita and her fine flesh, Nina and her slender solemnity. Both were divorced, Nina had a small child — Rita a grandmother! — they worked hard, they were strong. Their strength was part of their beauty, their alluring untidiness. They had no idea how lovely they looked or how Wevill desired them, which made it possible for him merely to gape at them while they unselfconsciously cleaned his house.

He had made his life by resisting fantasy, yet, captivated by the women, he found himself one day on the verge of making a wild suggestion to them: paying them to work naked. Knowing the penalty, he was able to resist. He was well versed in sexual harassment settlements, the vindictive juries, the severe punishments, the awarding of costs; he knew how much he would claim were he their lawyer and this fantasist employer their stalker. The knowledge made him circumspect, almost passive. The women were so innocent of his desire he went on watching them mop and dust, the multimillionaire in his fabulous house reduced to an unsatisfied voyeur.

Life had once been so simple. Long ago, a touch told him a woman was willing, a smile said the answer was yes. "We could share a taxi," he might say to a woman he had just met. The merest hug in the back seat, his hand on her leg, or hers on his. At her house, if she said, "Want to come in?" it meant yes to everything.

Rita and Nina sometimes looked so at home there he pictured himself approaching them and delivering lines he had carefully rehearsed. The lines were ambiguous enough to dissolve in any possible lawsuit.

"I've been studying massage with a practitioner," he imagined himself saying. He would discuss the details of his progress, stressing the health benefits. And then, casually: "Want one?"

You did not mention sex. A massage was a respectable medical procedure, but of course a woman willing to be massaged — to be touched — was open to other suggestions. But you could say, "Don't worry — strictly an R-rated massage," to emphasize the point that there were other kinds. Hyperbole helped. Such a proposition was impossible without innuendo.

Wevill said nothing. He was judicious, but his caution was not all that restrained him. "Seduction" was the inaccurate word for what he planned, "invitation" was better, but whatever it was called he could not initiate it in his own house. He told himself that it was not really his fear of a lawsuit, or even snobbery on his part, but just bad timing — a sunny morning in his huge house on the North Shore was wrong for what he had in mind. He could imagine meeting either of them after dark in a bar or one of the cheaper tourist hotels in Waikiki and taking her upstairs. But something told him that it was wrong in his house, while they were cleaning, making the beds, dusting the sofas. He could not imagine them sleeping on those beds or sitting on those sofas. It seemed a kind of defilement.

He stared at them like a big hungry boy looking at hunks of homemade cake, his fingers damp, and he talked to them, stupid questions about the weather, or holidays, or their jobs in town, how they worked in Housekeeping in one of the hotels in the Ohana chain. He was only making plausible noises to detain them, so that he could rest his eyes on their bodies as they worked.

A woman in repose did not interest him. He loved to see women being active, engaged in something strenuous, stretching, bending, carrying heavy loads, dealing with an impediment — anything that made their bodies contort with effort and their hair shake loose. Tight tensed knees, clenched buttock muscles, elbows working, the neck stiffened with concentration, the tongue clamped between the teeth — he watched with his own tongue clamped that way.

Rita was the pretty witch, Nina the skinny ballerina, and Wevill imagined that he had his pick.

His neat, dusted house irritated him, for it represented a job done, no reason for these women to deal with it. He preferred a room that needed attention. He had been a very messy husband with a pretty housekeeper and an impatient wife. "Someone to pick up after you!" his second wife had scolded. Yes, that was just it. He had slyly watched the exertions of the young dark woman. When his first wife had been alive, her sitting had bored him; her perfect hair and her way of picking at lint had killed his desire.

Nina the ballerina cleaned his car, she got dirtier as the car got cleaner, got sweatier and wetter with suds on her bare toes as she squeegeed the windows and dried the door handles, got damper and duller as the car got shiny and dry; and finally she was dirty and the car was clean, and he desired her that way and hated the car for being done.

Ramon came every two weeks — weed-whacking, mowing, watering the potted trees. The simple fellow easily talked to the women, usually in pidgin. That made Wevill bolder.

He was trying to talk with Nina one day, not hold a conversation, just mouthing meaningless pleasantries to attract her attention.

"Great weather."

"Ya."

"All that rain yesterday."

"Ya."

Getting nowhere, he said, "Maybe you could do the rugs next month."

Anticipating it gave him a foretaste of pleasure, mother and daughter swinging the old beaters like wire tennis rackets, their clothes flying as they spanked dust from the rug.

"Sorry," Nina said. "Next month we going to Vegas, Rita and me."

He was thrown. He said, "You were there just recently."

"Five months ago, ya," Nina said with a precision that startled him, for he expected her not to know, at any rate not to remember.

He was at first deeply disappointed, feeling abandoned, and he imagined she was gloating — enjoying turning him down. But that was irrational. Then he grew curious. Where exactly? How long for? What to do?

Nina reminded him of their routine, that they went twice a year on a gambling tour — two weeks in Las Vegas.

In his sixty-one years Wevill had never been to Nevada, and

when this young woman answered his questions with a casual unintentional rebuff, he was impressed and humbled.

"Leave the kid with Auntie, stay at the California, play the slots, come back broke. The Vegas package."

This lovely young woman talking such nonsense appalled him, and he was sad for her, almost sorrowful for her loving this ignorant pleasure, grieving for her wasted beauty. Her mother was no better.

"And party a little." The older woman laughed.

"Vegas," he said, and wondered if any of this information would kill his desire.

On one of his working weeks, Ramon didn't show up. Rita said he was sick with a backache, that he had seen a doctor and was taking medicine. The next week Rita said she had seen Ramon's sister at Foodland; Ramon was dead, the muscle relaxer he had been prescribed had shut down his liver.

At the end of a twisting road in the middle of the island Wevill found the chapel and Ramon's grieving relatives. A clergyman read from the Bible, delivered a homily, quoted Kahlil Gibran. Wevill sat at the back, a stranger, wondering if Ramon's family had a lawyer for this personal-injury suit, and where were Rita and Nina? They must have gone to Las Vegas. When the time came for Wevill to pay his respects, he stood before the closed casket and a color photograph of Ramon in an aloha shirt, smiling broadly, youthful, the picture of health, confident and vital.

2

The moment Wevill arrived in Las Vegas and tasted bitterness in the hot dust of the air, he felt he was in a corrupted desert city built on sand, one he imagined he might find described in the Bible, the damned rejoicing, worshiping a gilded animal while a godly prophet lamented somewhere on the perimeter. Wevill was out of his depth — humbled was no exaggeration. Since he had never been to Las Vegas, he could not think of it familiarly as "Vegas." It bewildered him as much as any Third World capital. He was dismayed to be among people who were delighted to be there, so many of them from Hawaii. He learned late what everyone already knew: because Hawaii was heavily taxed, and gambling illegal, tax-free Nevada was full of people from the islands, many settled there, many visiting, he recognized the faces. Two he looked for but did not see.

He did not mind feeling helpless. It was a more accurate reflection of his condition, the big brooding man enthroned in his mansion, for he was now lost in his house.

To understand the women's lives better, he had asked for the one-week package that included the airfare, the room, and coupons. But: "Been sold out for months!" Was the clerk rubbing it in? The first-class ticket he bought was absurdly more expensive than the package, but at least he had his anonymity. He had no plan other than to be away from his house and near these women, to be here, in this place. But the place was more bizarre than the bizarrest pictures of it.

In his desperation he realized that he seemed more like a stalker than a mere admirer. He excused his obsession by reminding himself that he was helpless, he had time and money, he could have anything he wanted. Where were they?

I just want to look at Las Vegas, he told himself, have a drink, see what all the fuss is about. A place I have never visited. It was a plus that he happened to be near Rita and Nina. What next he did not know. Being close to them would clear his mind and make him happier. But he knew he was kidding himself.

As a lawyer he was able to hold two different, opposite ideas in his head at the same time, the prosecution's argument and the defense. Happiness was his defense, but he was well aware that he was driven by physical desire, a sort of hunger he had known very few times in his life, most of them as a boy, for he was captive to the feeling and unsatisfied, and what in his life had he craved that he had not enjoyed? He always knew the answers to the questions he asked.

He felt the insecurity and frustration of his early youth, for he had no idea what would happen next. His needing to be near them, not thinking of them as his cleaning women, yearning to satisfy himself, made his mouth dry. The desert heat of this big blighted place didn't help. In Las Vegas, where money was everything, he could have anything he wanted, because he had money. But his first day showed him the falseness of that proposition, for he was still alone.

He chose not to stay at the California Hotel, because they were there and he had no clear plan. His only pleasure in his room at the MGM Grand lay in his remembering how he had desired the two women in Hawaii — washing his car, mopping the floor, disheveled nymphs. Las Vegas itself he found appalling for its lights and its carnival atmosphere, the mindlessness of its advertised pleasures. The frenzy, built on sand.

With a stranger in the elevator, tapping the poster for the casino, he found himself saying that it was silly to think that anyone actually believed you could get rich by gambling.

"Then what are you doing here?" the stranger said.

The stranger, a white-haired blotchy-faced man, was wearing a cheap shirt and sneakers, but Wevill found it an intimidating question, for his coming here to see the women was a greater gamble than throwing down money.

Still, that first day he located the California Hotel and Casino, where they were both staying. He watched it from across the street but went no closer. He longed to see the mother and daughter, but just to gape, for he was not yet prepared to confront them. His sneaking satisfied him, gave him a way to pass the time — stalker time.

The frenzy evident everywhere in the city was something he could not share. His mood was opposite — the only watchful, cautious person in Las Vegas. He was passionate but he was particular, and there was only one way out. Apart from buying tasteless meals — there were no other kinds for him here — he hardly spent money. Steeling himself, he went into the California's casino and scanned the faces and saw islanders pushing money into slot machines, others plopping chips onto numbers on the roulette felt, turning over cards at the blackjack tables, always losing. It was a place for children, big old idiot children, a terrible place, and he began to feel the rage of the prophet at his first Las Vegas sighting.

He knew that he was in this defiled and pagan desert just as obsessively, but that his desire was pure.

Bumping into the women would be best — just let it happen. But his wandering in the casino turned to methodical pursuit as he stalked the rows of gaming tables and banks of slot machines, like an anxious father looking for his missing children.

They were nowhere in that crowd, or any crowd he searched on his second day of being in Las Vegas. He was embarrassed to seem so serious and sad as he walked among the shouting, laughing people on the sidewalks and in hotel lobbies. He looked everywhere, the hunt made him sadder. His only satisfaction was that he saw no one who even remotely resembled them in the whole riotous city. The trouble was, by lingering as he did, and looking uncertain, he was pestered by hookers, who seemed to understand that here was a lonely man with a hole in his life.

Am in town for some meetings — just thought I'd stop by, he practiced to himself, trying to strike the most casual tone in the note he eventually wrote and left at the front desk of the California Hotel. Then he went and hid in his room.

Rita called that night.

In the lobby of the California he was approached by a dark woman in a green dress. Her tight pulled-back hair gave her foreign face a gleaming largeness and a fierce beetling confidence. She said, "How's it?" and he stepped back. Even after he sized her up he did not recognize her. Then another, smaller woman appeared, with the same hair, the same peering face, and tapped the first one on the shoulder. Now both women were smiling, so Wevill smiled uncertainly back at them — he did not have a clue — and his anxious suspicion was that they were both hookers, not soliciting sex but working a scam whereby one bimbo would hold his attention while the other picked his pocket.

"So how long you been here?"

The first woman was still smiling in the familiar way of a con artist.

"He don't get it," the other said.

And he almost objected — Excuse me, I'm here to meet some people — when he realized it was them.

They were much taller in their stiletto heels, and they were darker but in the same towering and stylish way — almost as tall as him. Their new dresses gave them bosoms and cleavage. Their legs were long and in flesh-toned tights seemed bare. He had never seen their legs, for they had always worn sweatpants and slippers. No baggy clothes here, not disheveled at all. Their hair was perfect, they wore makeup, mascara, red lips, nail polish. He was still stepping backward when he saw who they were.

"Sorry!"

He was dreadfully embarrassed and off balance, with an odd toppling sense of being in the wrong.

The Hawaiian housecleaners looked poised and prosperous in the lobby of their Las Vegas hotel. They looked prettier and better dressed than the other women there, more self-possessed.

"For a minute there, I didn't . . ."

Didn't know what to say, for though he now knew they were Rita and Nina, now that the two women were the same height, he was not sure which was which.

He was still backing up, gabbling, trying to cover his embarrassment. He said, "I made a dinner reservation at my hotel."

"You're staying which place?"

"MGM Grand. It's very nice. Excellent kitchen."

One of the women laughed and the other said, "She wants ribs."

He was lost again. Hadn't she heard "I made a dinner reservation"? It was the height of bad manners, he was thinking, and then realized how glad he was to see them. But he was thrown by the awkwardness of the meeting, and put off by the way they were dressed — intimidated as much by their stylishness as their sense of being so at home here.

"There's this place — Tony Roma's. Famous for ribs."

He had no idea; but this woman's voice was Rita's. He glanced at the other woman and recognized Nina by her eyes and her smile.

"Three for dinner," Rita was saying into her cell phone. "Ten, fifteen minutes. Under 'Nelson.'"

This Filipino-Chinese haole's name was Nelson?

The restaurant was a block away. Wevill felt small and conspicuous as they walked, some passersby staring at them, seeing the gray-haired man with the two young dressed-up women. But in the restaurant he felt like King Farouk — other diners glanced as they made their way among the tables, following the waiter.

"Mom's bummed 'cause I'm wearing her dress."

They wore each other's clothes. That he found sexy, as though they were sisters and equals, not mother and daughter.

"You look like sisters."

"Now Rita's bummed, you saying that."

"Nina is so bummed!"

But their calling each other by first names also proved what he meant. Wevill was holding the menu. He said, speaking carefully, "Is it baby-back ribs or baby back-ribs?"

They stared at him and Nina seemed to mouth the word "whatever" as the waiter appeared.

"Offer you cocktails before dinner?"

Rita said, "Vodka tonic. Straight up. You got Absolut?"

"Bailey's Irish Cream," Nina said.

Wevill was startled by their promptness. He said, "Beer for me."

Stumped for something to say, Wevill studied his menu until the drinks came.

"We're ready to order," Nina said to the waiter.

"The ribs here, like, melt in your mouth," Rita said to Wevill, as though hurrying him. He took the hint and ordered ribs, as the women did.

The food was brought within minutes. Everything happened quickly here, speed was a feature of the place, even the way people gambled seemed speedy, jamming coins into the machines, plopping chips on the grid of the roulette felt, dealing and snapping cards, the whole loud overbright town like the lurid midway of a carnival.

The women were chewing the meat — Wevill took pleasure in the way they gnawed the bones; but he could not eat, he was too nervous, he felt like a child, a sick patient with two inattentive nurses. He was in their hands. He was astonished at their confidence.

"Like Ma says, they melt in your mouth," Nina said.

"I don't know why I just thought of this," Wevill said, "but back in the days when I was seeing a shrink — my wife suggested it, first wife — I saw him four times a week. One day I was at a movie. It was *The Godfather.* I saw my shrink at the counter buying popcorn. It was very awkward. I mean, seeing my doctor at this movie. He pretended not to recognize me — and he looked different, too. He just walked past me."

"Al Pacino looked like a little kid in that movie," Rita said.

"I always put mochi crunch in my popcorn," Nina said.

"It just came to me, that thought," Wevill said. His mouth was dry with throat strain from a sorrow that ached like unslaked thirst. "Not important."

Meat flecks on their glistening lips, chew marks on the animal ribs in their hands, the two women ate, smiling as they swallowed, their breasts brushing their plates of meat and bones.

"So how's the gambling?" Wevill asked.

"It ain't real gambling," Rita said. "It's just gaming, like a game, mostly just slots. Just feed the slots."

She wiped her mouth with the back of her hand. Wevill loved the juicy way she said the word "slots," then he muttered the word himself and was slightly disgusted by it.

"You win, though?"

"My machines are junk. Not coming across," Rita said.

Nina said, "One wahine from Waipahu won big in slots."

She seemed to imply that this woman's win made their chances slimmer.

"You got special machines?"

Nina had finished her ribs and picked up the small dessert menu on the table. "They got this pie with Oreo cookie cruss that is so *ono.*"

Meanwhile, Rita was answering Wevill's question, explaining

to him, as perhaps she had once explained to her daughter, that you first played a lot of machines, then narrowed your choice to the luckier ones that paid out, and played those, feeding quarters, two machines at a time.

"To tell you the truth, I came here after I saw Ramon in his coffin. I was moved."

The women half glanced at each other, then checked their glances, reacting like jurors, maintaining poker-faced court etiquette. But he knew he had made his point.

"How do you spend the day?"

Rita was at first evasive. Then she said, "Big breakfast buffet, then do some shopping on the Strip, play the slots, bite of lunch at the casino, then play the slots again. Free beer if you keep playing. At night we take in a show, or maybe get a few drinks and ribs, or play the slots."

Shtrip and *djrinks* set his teeth on edge and reminded him of where they were from, where Strip, drinks, slots, ribs, Vegas, and party were their code words for pleasure.

"We saw that guy that's on TV. George Carlin. Funny comedian."

"In a show?" Wevill asked.

"No. He was eating one ice cream," Nina said. "On the Strip."

"We went to Le Cirque with a group. Kind of a group from home."

What he had anticipated as vicious turned out to be like camp for adults — organized, devoted to games and friends, with regular meals and even the circumscribed campsite of the Strip — the sort of vacation he had never taken himself, pure mindless fun, spending every penny you had, drinking yourself silly, gorging on rich food, then going home to your ordinary life after this harmless binge.

They knew their way around, they were familiar and unafraid — quite different from the two diligent women who sweated at his house every Saturday. And now, after the meal, they were a bit tipsy, too, a condition he had never seen them in.

Rita said, "I'm going to check out the slots."

Was she more than tipsy — drunk, maybe? She simply got up, gave her daughter a kiss, and waved goodbye, murmuring.

Adding to Wevill's bafflement was the fact that neither of them, so far, had used his name. With Rita gone, there was a silence, Nina gnawing at a fingernail until she became self-conscious.

"I broke it — on a machine. Stud poker. Gotta glue it," she said, picking at the nail. "So how's business?"

"Fine," Wevill said, thinking, What business? Then he remembered his lie. He said, "To tell the truth, I'm kind of lonely."

"You'll be okay once you get back home," Nina said, and reached for the dessert menu.

He winced, not at being patronized by a twenty-year-old but at the thought that he would not be okay back home; he would be miserable.

Summoning all his psychic strength, he leaped into the darkness, saying, "I could use a massage."

Nina laughed and said promptly, "You sure came to the right place. Vegas has billions of ladies for that." She smiled fondly at the dessert menu, as though she had just recognized an old friend. "I am such a chocoholic."

Wevill persisted, saying, "You wouldn't be interested?"

With the dessert menu in her hand she was confused by the question at first. She squinted as his proposition sank in, but she didn't look up. Her finger rested on *Oreo cookie crust,* and she said, "You serious?"

Her tone told him she took the question to be preposterous, and he was embarrassed, not so much because he had exposed his yearning to her but because she was so strong. The mother, too; they were powerful here. He had suspected it from the beginning. They even had money — they didn't need him. Nina was young, he had been rash, but if he hadn't asked the question, he would have cursed himself for his hesitation.

"Sorry," he said, though he didn't regret it: he had needed to know.

"You don't have to apologize," Nina said.

But her saying that infuriated him — his housecleaner patronizing him again. He called for the check.

"I'd like to see your slot machines," he said after he signed the credit card slip.

"Be my guest."

Her casual way of saying that, with such confidence, aroused him, and all he regretted was that she was uninterested in him. Walking out of the restaurant behind the young woman, being stared at, he thought, This is my housecleaner and she has just turned me down.

The casino in the California Hotel was just off the Strip — bright lights on the marquee advertising the music and magic shows, a red carpet at the entrance, and mirrors on the walls framed by glitter and more lights. But for all the sparkle, the place was filled with shabby older people, heavy smokers, shufflers in windbreakers and baseball caps, old men in big white sneakers, a drabness that depressed him.

"There's Ma."

Rita was feeding dollar tokens into two machines, side by side, not paying much attention but being conscientious, even laborious, as though priming a pump, which in a sense was exactly what she was doing. While Wevill watched, Rita lost thirty-two dollars.

Nina smiled at him and, as though late for duty, went to the cashier and got a bucket, took her place on a stool, and began to press coins into the slots. She made it seem strangely like work, just as joyless. Even when they won, got a payout in a clatter of coins, they didn't count them but instead scooped them out of the metal dish and, without looking, dumped them into the buckets of tokens they were feeding into the machines.

Wevill was fascinated for ten or fifteen minutes, and then utterly bored to the point of annoyance and wanted to leave. Between them in that time the women had lost a couple of hundred dollars, not a lot to him, but to them a day's pay. Pure folly.

Rita saw him looking agitated. She said, "Try your luck. Them ones and them ones are pretty good payers."

Each of these flashing goggling money-gobblers held for her a distinct personality.

Wevill said, "I think I'll have an early night."

"In Vegas?" There was contempt in her incredulity.

Wevill said, "Unless you want to do something later? Catch a show?"

"Nina and I are seeing someone."

Another rejection. Their indifference back in Hawaii had been bad enough, but this rebuff was terrible. They were still like Watteau nymphs, just as selfish, hovering, teasing, forever slipping out of his grasp, so self-contained, so independent, but tidy and strangely efficient. They did not see his interest, or if they did, they took no interest themselves in him, in his feelings, in anything he owned. They laughed and agreed with anything he said, which was their way of not listening, not agreeing, hardly caring.

Standing there in the casino among the slots, he saw them turned away from him, dressed up, even stylish, and he desired them and wanted to possess them. As a wealthy man, a successful lawyer, he was not used to being rebuffed and, unused to it, had trouble dealing with it. Crushed and wounded, his desire was raw and on his mind. He had not imagined rejection to be so painful.

So, what could have been something trivial, a lack of interest, a pair of unresponsive women, was a goad, and they obsessed him.

He was used to being needed. They didn't need him. That made him want to possess them, either one, or both.

Wevill could never have admitted that he envied them, yet he did envy them in the worst and most shameful way. He was hungry and helpless, and they defeated him with half-smiles and evasions — as he had done so often with envious visitors in his house. That was what shamed him. That he recognized the feeling, the experience of envy and defeat, seeing someone more powerful than he was.

In his room, he fell asleep watching a made-for-TV movie about a schoolgirl persecuted for being new to the school and friendless, and he was moved by it, saddened by its pathos, the weak and isolated girl, her insensitive parents ("You have to face up to them!"), the beasts who teased her until she was in despair, the one teacher who understood and defended the girl. His eyes dampened and he was further moved by his own almost-tears. He woke sorrowing that he had not seen the ending, but hating the thought that lonely people found meaning in such movies. He had been susceptible. It had to be crap.

The following day he made plans to leave Las Vegas. He was humiliated, the worst possible outcome, for now he had to fire Rita and Nina — how could he face them? — and would have to find other housecleaners.

"All our flights today are full," the airline clerk said on the phone.

"I'm holding a first-class ticket."

"I'm looking at first class. I'm not seeing any seats. You want me to wait-list you?"

"What about tomorrow?"

"Nothing in first class. I have a coach seat on the seven-ten."

A coach seat among half-wits returning to the islands, having flung all their money into slot machines. But he took it, because the indignity of the seat wasn't as hurtful as the humiliation of staying in Las Vegas. He resolved to kill the day in his room. He found the city excruciating for its crass appetites and confidence tricks, and he suspected a greater, hidden debauchery. He went without breakfast, he sat glowering, cursing the place, mumbling denunciations, feeling lightheaded and virtuous because of his hunger.

Around noon the phone rang, startling him. Who knew he was here?

"It's me."

Who? Then he knew, it was one or the other, slightly drunk, making no sense, like the grubby gamblers bingeing here in this carnival freak show.

"Gotta talk."

"Maybe we could arrange to meet somewhere — go out for coffee."

"I'm downstairs," she said, and sounded to him like a cop.

He hurried to the lobby and saw Rita. He easily recognized her because she was wearing slacks and sneakers and a T-shirt lettered *Vegas*. Her hair had come loose. She looked as she had some Saturdays when she arrived with Nina to clean, and that pleased him and gave him hope and put an edge on his desire.

The hotel coffee shop was called the Cactus Flower Terrace, a sign at the entrance saying, *Please Wait to Be Seated*. Rita muttered something and walked past the sign and seated herself at a booth. Wevill followed, feeling he was trespassing and wondering if the waitress who appeared with menus would reprimand him.

"Just coffee," Rita said without glancing up.

She looked darkly assertive, with her head down and her

elbows out, not looking at Wevill, even when the coffee was poured and she was holding her cup in two hands and blowsucking at the steamy surface.

"Shoulda had some of this before. As a rule, I don't normally drink nothing at lunchtime." Now she looked up, her red eyes on him. "But I was stressed."

"That's understandable," he started to say, thinking, *Shtressed?* But she cut him off. "My money's *pau,* and plus all that other stuff too, besides."

He had no idea what she was saying, but he was aware of another creeping sensation that was binding him to his seat, making him wait, holding him captive. It was not for him to negotiate. She was proceeding at her own speed. He recalled being in his room, at the window, denouncing Las Vegas, and the phone ringing, and *I'm downstairs.* He had been summoned to this meeting. Something unsaid disturbed him.

"Give me a minute," she said.

"I was just wondering," he said.

"Try wait. I'm drinking my coffee."

He leaned back as though she had scooped him with an uppercut.

"So what's this I been hearing about one massage?" she finally said.

His dry mouth would not allow him to lie, yet he tried, saying, "I don't know what you mean. I was just upstairs getting ready to leave. I've got a flight back to Honolulu first thing tomorrow."

"Nina said you hitting on her about one massage."

"I was not hitting on her," Wevill said. Some of the time he was just a civilian, but certain words, actionable language he heard with his attorney ears, set his attorney mind in motion.

"She say you was."

Why, he wondered, was bad grammar so much more threatening than proper English?

"I mentioned that I was thinking of getting one, not that I expected her to give me one personally. I mean, my asking her there and then — that would be ridiculous."

Saying this, denying what he had done, and trying to laugh, he understood his guilt and saw how foolish he had been.

The waitress returned and said, "Would you like me to tell you what's on special today?"

Rita said "No!" with such ferocity the waitress stepped back and hurried away.

Wevill said, "Why did you react when I mentioned Ramon? Were you impressed?"

"I was trying not to laugh," she said. "Ramon didn't like you. One day he says, 'I dig holes for a living. I could dig one big enough for that bugger to fit in.'"

And still she was not through with him. Alert, despite her drunkenness, she said, "So when you go, 'Are you interested?,' you don't mean Nina, you mean someone else?"

It was diabolical how her drunken alertness made her more intimidating than a trial lawyer, for her pounce and probity were unexpected. She was a deadly combination of gruffness and barely articulate intelligence.

"Try give me some kine answer."

He felt old and weak and breathless and whatever was the opposite of desire — fear more than repulsion — and all this had destroyed his will. He was trapped like a felon on a plastic cushion in the Cactus Flower Terrace. He could now understand a mumbling and terrified man being cross-examined on a witness stand. He was defeated. He was dreadfully embarrassed by what he had attempted, and the attempt was an act. The words she had quoted were almost verbatim. He could not deny saying them.

"I'm sorry. I made a mistake. An inexcusable error of judgment."

"She just a kid, Nina."

Rita was right. He had taken advantage of the girl, yet everything he had experienced in this loud hellish-hot city proved that he was weak. Sitting here he felt powerless, his head bowed under the scolding.

"You coulda asked me first," she said, swallowing coffee.

This was ambiguous to him. She might have been saying, "You could have asked me instead of Nina," or, seeking permission, "You could have asked me if you wanted Nina."

"What would you have said if I had asked?"

"I woulda said," she murmured, drinking from the cup, "I woulda said, 'Try explain.'"

"I admit it was a mistake," he said.

"So you don't want nothing?"

Her staring, her scolding, forced him to be particular, and to endure the final humiliation in order to clear himself, he said, "Yes. I wanted a massage."

She would not accept this. She said, "You don't mean massage when you say massage."

He just closed his eyes and prayed for someone to yell "Fire!" or for a fight to start or an earthquake to hit and topple the whole miserable city.

Rita said, "Okay, pay the bill. Let's go."

He left money on the table — too much, so that they could leave swiftly — and in the lobby he said, "Where?"

She said in a gummy way, phlegm clotted in her throat, "You know where."

He did not desire this unstable, unfamiliar woman, not even in the irrational way of lust. He was never at his best in the afternoon in any case. He would have preferred a meal or a drink at dusk, a prologue, a beginning, a middle. This was all end, not simply abrupt but cold captivity. In the elevator she stood apart but confident, less like a jailer than a kidnapper, and in his room he felt like a hostage. No, not at all like a hooker and a john.

"Okay, get naked."

Wevill said, "I've changed my mind."

"No," she said loudly, as she had in the restaurant, sounding crazy, but here her voice had the gnawing ferocity of a big cat. Her irrationality made her confident, and she watched without interest while Wevill undressed, pulling off his shirt, stepping out of his pants and folding them.

"You try tell Nina I come here and I cut your balls off."

That did it. He had been having trouble locating desire within himself, but hearing those words he felt giddy terror and used his hands to cover himself.

"Look at you," Rita said in a mocking way, flicking her fingers.

He said, "How much do you want?"

"Coupla hundred."

"Done." He gave her the money gladly, paying her to go, which she did, seeming to swagger, slamming the door.

When it came time for him to leave Las Vegas, Wevill did not feel he was fleeing a scene of failure to one of greater failure. Did they know they had a case against him? Stalking. Harassment. Mental and emotional distress. He did not even consider firing them, though he wanted to. He told himself he was not afraid of them, but in his own house he was. He should never have left his house in the first place.

The women returned, not so much disheveled nymphs as slatterns, but no less attractive. Wevill was disgusted and afraid. He was on the point of saying, "The check's on the counter," when Nina left the room and Rita looked straight at him and smiled.

"We was in Vegas."

Wevill began to back away.

"It was a blast."

Wevill smiled insincerely.

"I met a great guy."

Wevill was surprised, then confused, finally sad.

"The check's on the counter," he said, and left his house.

How was he to know the woman was capable of such subtlety? It was weeks before they spoke again, months before she told him what was on her mind, that the man she had met in Vegas was him; that she was going back alone; that there was still time for him to get the Vegas package.

They flew separately. They met discreetly. While Rita played the slots, he read on the terrace. Together, in the room, they were passionate. She was the stronger here, the more confident; he delighted in her teasing him with demands. The week of delirium and exhaustion was over before he was ready. He returned reluctantly to Hawaii, where he was, just as reluctantly, the boss and she the good mother and grandmother. The arrangement continued for several years — six trips to Vegas altogether — until Wevill died, only sixty-four. As his executor, I had the pleasure of telling Rita of her substantial share of his estate. But she hardly seemed to care about the money, and was devastated, unlike his ex-wife, who by the way got a lot less.

IF YOU HAVE TO CRY, GO OUTSIDE

IF YOU HAVE TO CRY, GO OUTSIDE

AND OTHER THINGS YOUR MOTHER NEVER TOLD YOU

KELLY CUTRONE

with MEREDITH BRYAN

HarperOne
An Imprint of HarperCollinsPublishers

HarperOne

HarperCollins books may be purchased for educational, business, or sales promo-
tional use. For information please write: Special Markets Department, HarperCollins
Publishers, 10 East 53rd Street, New York, NY 10022.

HarperCollins website: http://www.harpercollins.com

HarperCollins®, 🏛®, and HarperOne™ are trademarks of
HarperCollins Publishers

FIRST HARPERCOLLINS PAPERBACK EDITION PUBLISHED IN 2011
Interior design by Laura Lind Design

Library of Congress Cataloging-in-Publication Data
Cutrone, Kelly.
If you have to cry, go outside : and other things your mother never told you /
by Kelly Cutrone with Meredith Bryan. — 1st ed.
p. cm.
ISBN 978-0-06-193094-2
1. Women—Life skills guides. 2. Self-actualization (Psychology).
I. Bryan, Meredith. II. Title.
HQ1221.C995   2010
646.70082—dc22   2010003773

11 12 13 14 15 RRD(H) 10 9 8 7

For Ava,
my mother,
and the
Universal Mother

CONTENTS

ARE YOU THERE, BABE?
IT'S ME, YOUR SOUL

This is how you've been imprinted to use your relationship to power—to use it against yourself. Every day we create reality based on what we've been programmed to believe. So we spend most of our lives not really thinking clearly and coherently —not initiated thought. We spend a great deal of our lives not really living, but existing in programmed, reactive belief that we call thought.

We can blame the oppressor, the predatory mindset, we can blame it forever and it doesn't mind. It doesn't care.

We need to use our energy, our intelligence in an alternative way to the way we have been using it.

—John Trudell

I was a sophomore in high school when MTV debuted in 1981. I remember it clearly because Joe Morris, a college football player who ended up going pro, was our cable guy at the time, and it was he who brought *Video Killed the Radio Star*, MTV's first video, into our conservative Catholic home in upstate New York. My world would never be the same. I was riveted by the VJs, and in fact, I can still name them all: Martha Quinn, Mark Goodman, JJ Jackson, Alan Hunter, and Nina Blackwood (the blond girl who looked like an ostrich). They were raw and edgy and cool, and I loved the stuff they were talking about. They were like portals into a world I didn't know existed, and I immediately thought, *Oh my God, that's where I want to go. I wanna be* there. I miraculously convinced my overprotective ex-marine father to buy me a trip to New York City for my sixteenth birthday on the condition that it be chaperoned by my twenty-two-year-old half-sister, and the two of us set off on a weekend of pretending we fit in, even as we ate in tourist restaurants in Little Italy and, ultimately, fell asleep during *A Chorus Line*.

I will never forget how, in that very first visit, the energy of New York captivated my every sense. It was like I had stepped out of a boring silent film and into the greatest musical of all time, with Radio City Rockettes kicking to the tune of Frank Sinatra's "New York, New York," while seven thousand angels cried: "*Kelly! You are home!*" I was hearing the sound of my inner voice, and it was *not* subtle. On midtown's crowded streets, I felt electric, vibrant, and alive. I'd never seen a place where people from all over the world spoke different languages, where gay people walked down the street holding hands, and where acceptance was king. I sensed a purpose and vitality in people's lives, not only because of how they looked and how they dressed, but by the way they walked and where they were going and how they were getting there. They were doing real things; they weren't just circling the town in their station wagons, slowly growing old. Here the game was on, and if anyone didn't like it, they could just fuck off. I loved that. I had no idea what I'd actually *do* in New York—I had never heard of a "publicist"—but once I stepped out of my first cab in Manhattan, I knew my days in Syracuse were numbered.

More than twenty years later, I live in a downtown loft (to be honest, I still get a kick out of the fact that the elevator opens into my apartment—how chic!); run my own PR company with offices in New York, L.A., and Paris; produce runway shows in London, Paris, Moscow, Los Angeles, New York, and Miami; and pay my seven-year-old daughter's private school tuition on my own. But this isn't a book about how to be a smart businesswoman, because I'm *not* a smart businesswoman. Frankly, I'm not even that smart. What I am is fearless and intuitive. I'm attuned to the sound of my inner voice, and I've been following it blindly for most of my life, without any clear goals. It doesn't speak out loud; it's more like impressions beaming into my brain from my soul. (Only when I visited New York did it suddenly grow its own horn section.) I believe it has known where I was going from birth. I grew up in Syracuse, after all, a town known as the number-one blue-collar testing market for brands like Tide and Nabisco, whose marketing reps flocked to our grocery stores hoping to determine how their products would fare with the most average consumers in America. Girls from my town didn't move to New York and start their own companies; they met their husband at a nearby state university and worked at the mall or as teachers until the birth of their second child, at which point they left the snowbelt for a warmer life in an average town further south. I may have been organizing elaborate neighborhood barbecue fund-raisers by the age of eight and even landing myself on the local news, but no one around me took this to mean I should consider moving to New York to pursue a career in publicity.* Instead, I was encouraged to study nursing. But I knew from a young age that I was special and that something magical would happen to me. It was my journey inwards—the process of learning to listen to and trust myself— that electrified and transformed my outer journey, helping me conceive and achieve things beyond my wildest dreams.

* In fact, most people I know in Syracuse still think I work in *publishing*.

I'm not here to tell you how to get the perfect Margiela wardrobe or the perfect man or the perfect job in fashion. I've had all these things (though not all at once), and trust me, there's a bigger prize to be had. I want to help you awaken to *your* inner voice—the voice of your soul—and I want you to use it to chase your destiny, which I define as the greatest possible outcome for your life. (Your destiny might involve fashion, but it might also involve teaching rehabilitated sex workers in Cambodia.) *Inner voice?* you may be thinking. *Soul? Destiny? I thought this was a fashion book!* Well, fashion's full of trickery, darling. But if you're going to believe this season's Prada boots will make you sexy and powerful, you should at least be as open to the concept that you have a soul and that that soul has a purpose as unique as your fingerprint and eye scan. If you aren't hearing your inner voice, it could mean you're overburdened or not stimulated enough, or that you've learned to shut it off because the people around you have refused to engage it. Perhaps you've had a hardening of the arteries around your soul. I believe the choices we make in our lives and the people and places surrounding us increase the volume of our inner voice, decrease it, or annihilate it entirely.

This book is a call to awaken and celebrate the magic inside yourself. Here's what you need to do.

1. Ask yourself: Is it possible the voices you've been listening to from birth may not have been your own? Can you separate the voices of your parents, your teachers, your friends, the media, and Hollywood from the voice of yourself—your own inner voice?

2. Believe that your inner voice is the voice of your soul—your own unique spark of the Divine (I would like to point out the similarity between the words "diva" and "divine")—and that it knows and wants what's best for you and will lead you to your individual purpose and destiny. (If you're like me, where you're headed may have *no* connection to where you started.)

3. Gather up your courage like an armful of free clothes at a McQueen sample sale and follow your inner voice wherever it takes you.

If this book inspires you to do one thing, I hope it's to take the years when you're young—say, between the ages of fifteen and thirty-five, before you have a mortgage or kids or anything else that needs to be fed—and go balls out on intuition and follow your dreams. Dreams won't always take you on a straight path to destiny, but they're usually related to what your soul wants for you. They'll force you to ask yourself the hard questions, they'll kick your ass, and most importantly, they'll turn you on. Do you want to go live in Spain and ride motorcycles through the mountains? Awesome. Do you want to become the world's most famous clothing designer? Do it. Actress? Model? Go for it. Do you want to become a CIA agent, a rocket scientist, a Playboy bunny, or a lawyer? Please, be my guest. Maybe when you get there you'll really hate it, at which point you'll know you're *not* a Playboy bunny and can cross that off your list and move on to the next thing. Sometimes, if not most of the time, you find out who you are by figuring out who and what you are not.

The only dream I ever had was the dream of New York itself, and for me, from the minute I touched down in this city, that was enough. It became the best teacher I ever had. If your mother is anything like mine, after all, there are a lot of important things she probably didn't teach you: how to use a vibrator; how to go to a loan shark and pull a loan at 17 percent that's due in thirty days; how to hire your first divorce attorney; what to look for in a doula (a birth coach) should you find yourself alone and pregnant. My mother never taught me how to date three people at the same time or how to interview a nanny or what to wear in an ashram in India or how to meditate. She also failed to mention crotchless underwear, how to make my first down payment on an apartment, the benefits of renting versus owning, and the difference between a slant-6 engine and a V-8 (in case I wanted to get a muscle car), not to mention how to employ a team of people to help me with my life, from trainers to hair colorists to nutritionists to shrinks. (Luckily, New York became one of many other moms I am to have in my lifetime.) So many mothers say they want their daughters to be independent, but what they *really* hope is that they'll find a well-compensated banker or lawyer and settle down between the ages of twenty-five and twenty-eight in Greenwich, Darien, or That Town, U.S.A., to raise babies, do the grocery shopping, and work out in relative comfort for the rest of their lives. I know this because I employ their daughters. They raise us to think they want us to have careers, and they send us to college, but even *they* don't really believe women can be autonomous and take care of themselves.

I named my company People's Revolution not because I'm a Communist—a popular misconception—but because I happen to believe the world will change only when we change ourselves. And that starts with finding ourselves. And *that* starts with listening to ourselves: learning to quiet the clamor in our minds and the voices of everyone around us and move toward what feels right—toward the things we know, for reasons we can't explain, that we're meant to do, the things that make us feel alive. It means taking a journey like the spectacular and terrifying and ultimately mind-blowing adventure I've been on for twenty years. I hope that you too will choose to have a journey instead of just a life. Actually, I hope it's a full-on *expedition*. We live in an intense place, and it will never be transformed unless we as women are encouraged to dream and to find and manifest our highest selves. The planet is here for our delight, but it is also here for us to change, to make it the best it can be. It's not just about sleeping and fucking and getting the right dress. Let's *hope* not.

ONE

FIND YOUR TRIBE:
Your Dreams Are Ballbusters,
Not the Yellow Brick Road

AUNTIE EM: Find yourself a place
where there isn't any trouble!

DOROTHY: Some place where there isn't
any trouble. Do you suppose there is
such a place, Toto? There must be. It's
not a place you can get to by a boat
or a train. It's far, far away. Behind the
moon, beyond the rain.

—from *The Wizard of Oz*

It's the Village Girl who will
change the world.

—Kelly Cutrone

grew up fourteen miles from the Yellow Brick Road. No, really, I did: quaint Chittenango, New York (pop. 4,883), has yellow brick sidewalks in homage to L. Frank Baum, author of *The Wizard of Oz*, who was born there. But my journey to Oz was nothing like Dorothy's, except that I too met gloriously eclectic comrades along the way. When you leave home to follow your dreams, your road will probably be riddled with potholes, not always paved in happy Technicolor bricks. You'll probably be kicked to the ground 150 million times and told you're nuts by friends and strangers alike. As you progress you may feel lonely or terrified for your physical and emotional safety. You may overestimate your own capabilities or fail to live up to them, and you'll surely fall flat on your face once in a while. In breaking away from the familiar and the expected, you'll be forced and privileged to face greater challenges, learn harder lessons, and really get to know yourself. But like Dorothy's, your journey will be much easier with a tribe of mentors, advisers,

[13]

and trusted friends to help you chart your course and to support you when you stumble. There's power in numbers. It takes a village. Say it however you want to, but the truth is that we cannot go through this life alone. Some of us are lucky enough to be born in the vicinity of our tribe; others will have to travel far and wide to find it, as I did. But I truly believe that whoever you are—whether you're a lesbian who wants to make maple syrup in Vermont, a gay Muslim man in the Middle East, or a fashion-following trend-bitch who wants to get her groove on in New York—there's a place for you to fit in. There are towns and cities where groups of people who reflect you and your own inner beliefs and interests live, and there are communities in which you will thrive. There are people we're related to physically, and then there are people we're related to spiritually, emotionally, and socially. The road to your dreams is sometimes dark, and it's sometimes magical, but *The Wizard of Oz* had one thing right: it's ultimately about the journey and the characters who accompany you on it, *not* about the destination.*

Growing up in Syracuse, while I loved my parents, I never saw myself reflected in the world around me, *ever*. I was like a hovercraft, floating from field hockey to pot-smoking to honor society, seeking a place to land or connect, earnestly trying on identities but finding none that stuck. While I had assorted friends, I never had a *group*. I was a promising figure skater for a while, but even that was a lonely preoccupation because, as you can imagine, I had a hard time connecting with blond girls who

---

* My spiritual guru, a woman known as the Mother, said that true joy is in progress.

wore headbands. My destiny was briefly foreshadowed in an electrifying romance at fifteen with a boy named Eric Klein, who had just moved to town from New York City, where his dad had played in a band with Debbie Harry. Eric was tall and skinny and Jewish and wore a Mohawk and safety pins all over his clothes—which, trust me, was super-hot at the time. He was so irreverently and swashbucklingly pirate-handsome that I couldn't believe my good luck—to be stranded in this fish-fry and Friday-night-sports kind of place and have somebody like *him* appear. I soon found myself engulfed in an exhilarating education in hard-core punk, from the Dead Kennedys to the Circle Jerks. Eric's house was full of curious things like Oriental rugs (we had wall-to-wall carpeting), a futon bed (we had Ethan Allen), and granola and tofu (we had Hi-C and Twinkies). The signs that he was free to express himself included an upside-down crucifix on his wall and the e. e. cummings books stacked on his bookshelves. In hindsight, Eric—he insisted people call him by his punk name, Belvy K—was an early member of the tribe of creative renegades in which I'd always feel most comfortable. He and his family were also my first exposure to a type I'd come to know intimately in the future: New Yorkers. It was no wonder I felt drawn to their house as if by a magnetic force field. Belvy was proof that finding your tribe, like following your dreams, isn't always about what makes sense; it's about what your soul needs. As much as we're looking for experiences that turn us on, we're looking for *people* who do the same, whether creatively, emotionally, spiritually, or intellectually. So if you don't have a well-thought-out dream, you can start by figuring out where you want to *go*. If you cannot see yourself fairly or accurately represented in the community where you live—from restaurants to department stores to clothing choices to conversations at the dinner table—and nothing there makes you feel awake or alive, I suggest you start doing some research on some other communities.

When my dad picked me up from the airport after my first trip to New York at age sixteen, I informed him that I was moving to New York City someday. This didn't go over well; it had been a stretch to get him to agree to let me go there for two days. He pulled the car over to the side of the highway and made me get out. "No way in hell is one of my kids going to live in that hellhole of a city!" he bellowed before literally leaving me on the side of the road (where I remained for a good ten or fifteen minutes; today we would call that reckless endangerment of a minor). But I wasn't dissuaded. I graduated from high school and then college, even majoring in nursing like my parents wanted me to, but I tucked my dream safely away until five years later, when I walked into my dad's study and told him again that now I was really moving to New York. "You must be very rich," he said. "It takes a lot of money to live in New York City." Then he called my mother into his office. "Bev, Bev, come in here! Did you know your daughter wants to move to New York?" Of course my mother knew; she knew everything before my father. In fact, she was a protocol thermometer indicating the best way to approach him with difficult matters. (Sometimes her advice would be, "We're not approaching him at all.") In this instance, she had instructed me to be soft, to explain to my dad how important moving to New York was to me, to ask for his blessing, and to demand nothing. This strategy didn't immediately work: "She can't even handle herself, Beverly!" my father shouted. "You've done her laundry her whole life!" He mocked my meager life savings of $484. ("I can't believe that's all you've saved in four summers of working! You have a closet full of clothes!") Then, finally and somewhat astonishingly, he got out his checkbook and wrote me a check for $2,000. This was an incredible amount of money for him at the time. I knew this, and I started crying. "I love you dearly. You're my daughter, and I would do anything for you," he said, tears forming in his eyes too. "However, as long as you choose to live in that city, I will never give you another dime. If you want to come home, all you have to do is call me, and I will come pick you up and bring you back, no matter what." And that was it. I understood the beauty of his gesture and how hard it was for him to look me in the eye and see me off to a city that fundamentally terrified him. Both my parents seemed convinced I'd come back raped or murdered; it was bad enough that I was already clearly becoming a liberal. But I'd tried things their way, and I was *done, done, done.* Like many parents, mine really thought they had my best interests in mind; they had no idea they were attempting to squash my destiny. You'll find as you set out after your dreams that most people don't really want you to transcend the situation you were born into. Perhaps they're scared for you, perhaps they don't believe in you, or perhaps they're just nasty, negative naysayers. Whichever it is, I advise you to stop sharing your dreams with people who try to hold you back, even if they're your parents. Because, if you're the kind of person who senses there's something out there for you beyond whatever it is you're expected to do—if you want to be *extra*-ordinary—you will not get there by hanging around a bunch of people who tell you you're not extraordinary. Instead, you will probably become as ordinary as they expect you to be. We have a saying in New York: when you're the most happening person at the party, it's time to leave.

It was 1987 when I packed my wardrobe in black Hefty bags, stuffed them into my red Toyota Corolla, scribbled directions on the back of an envelope, and set off on Highway 81. I sincerely believed I was equipped for life in the big city, which was, on the one hand, a nod to the confidence my parents had instilled in me and, on the other hand, total and utter delusion. The place I was headed toward bore no resemblance to the groovy urban utopia I'd been picturing all those years. I'd taken an apartment unseen on Avenue C in the East Village, which in the late eighties was *not* boutiques and noodle shops; actually, it was a Puerto Rican ghetto.* I often felt that the only thing protecting me in my early days there was my black hair, which made me imagine I could maybe pass for a girl from the neighborhood. I soon learned that many of the things my parents insisted on could get me killed: saying "please" and "thank you," for example, only held up the subway token line and caused the people behind me to yell. And none of the transit workers wanted to hear it. They'd just roll their eyes, as in, *Where the fuck are you from, honey?* I also learned

---

* A year after I moved to the neighborhood an infamous pothead named Daniel Rakowitz would kill his ballerina girlfriend and serve her to Tompkins Square Park's homeless population in a soup.

that no one wanted to hear my chatty comments on *anything*: "Hey, how are you?" or "Nice shoes!" or "Do you know what time it is?" No one wanted to help, and nobody cared. That was when I first observed a phenomenon I now call the "New York Slide": you offer your words to try to communicate and connect with someone, but your words just hit a brick wall the person has erected to ward off human contact—the words slide down it and roll away.

But I was a cute girl with a taste for adventure, so I soon managed to befriend the bartenders, punk-rockers, artists, and down-and-outs I encountered in the dive bars I'd stop into for shots of tequila on my way home. (Yes, my neighborhood was so scary that I needed shots to get home.) It wasn't long before I found my way out of the East Village most evenings and into the best nightclubs of the day. It was the late eighties, right before AIDS and crack got out of control and changed New York night-life forever, and an infamous club called the World was still so packed every night with people on coke gyrating and jumping up and down that it always felt like the upper level was about to collapse onto the spiky-haired models and glam-rockers below. It was clear that clubs like this were where the people I'd seen on MTV got their inspiration; *this* was the source, the real deal. I felt immediately like a long-lost cousin of this world. Night-trawlers, party girls, poets, club owners, actors, and riffraff: *these* were the people whose New York lives appealed to me, not the bankers or socialite women stepping out of town cars on the Upper East Side. The people in the clubs worked at night, they had creative jobs, they wore wild clothes; they were like no one I'd ever met at West Gennesee Senior High, except possibly Belvy. I was in awe of them; I desperately wanted them to like me. Still, it was kind of like wanting to be a trapeze artist when the circus comes to town; you're not sure you can swing from those bars.

Luckily, I soon met a woman named Diane Brill, a famed glamazon of the nightlife scene who you'd think wouldn't have time for a skinny little girl straight off the boat from Syracuse. She took me under her wing, spiriting me to places like the East Village boutique stuffed with drag queens and club kids and owned by Pat Field, the now-famous *Sex and the City* costume designer who was not just the first lesbian I'd ever met but a doyenne of the scene herself. It was Pat who gave me the black Unitard with a push-up bra that would become the staple of my PR wardrobe for years to come. (Later I would wear it uptown with a Chanel jacket and English riding boots and downtown with motorcycle jacket or stilettos, all in the same day.) As I formed my tribe, my tribe shaped me. My new friends weren't encouraging me to climb the corporate ladder and make a lot of money, but they were teaching me once-in-a-lifetime lessons about creativity, music, expression, and freedom of speech (and, ultimately, the price of debauchery). Among them I felt energized, alive, and myself for the first time in my life. And so I went towards them (and still do).

My raging social life had its costs: it cost me my job, for one. I was training nurses for NutriSystem and viewed working for this diet company as more of a stamp on my ticket than an actual career plan. It required me, unglamorously, to make my way to far-flung areas of Brooklyn, Queens, and Westchester to meet with nurses in various NutriSystem offices. Manhattan was hard enough, but in the late eighties the boroughs were a completely different story: grim, desolate, poorly marked, their bridges falling apart. Even Brooklyn was many years from becoming the maze of strollers and brownstone renovations it is today. I'd find myself in the strangest places—GPS and cell phones were not yet invented—with my bag full of rolls of quarters, too scared to ask for help. But that wasn't the only problem. My strict upbringing had failed to provide me with any self-management skills, and my late nights on the scene repeatedly sabotaged my 7:00 a.m. wake-up time. (Let's face it, that was far too early for a future entrepreneur.) One morning, lost and sweating in a subway tunnel, hungover, late to work again and certain I'd be fired, I called my supervisor from a pay phone to say I was quitting.

Rather than look for a new job, I began going out to better clubs and staying there until later hours. I learned that corralling a bunch of cool people I'd met to come with me could get me free drink tickets, drugs, *and* cash in my pocket! In New York parlance, I became a party promoter. And since I was an entrepreneur in my soul, I soon eliminated my overhead, though not on purpose. One Sunday afternoon when an older artist I was dating dropped me off after a weekend jaunt to the Hamptons, I climbed my six flights of stairs to find an eviction notice on my door and all my stuff locked up inside. *Oops*. Party promoting was less lucrative than my former day job, and I was behind on my rent. I never got my stuff back; my possessions were now limited to the contents of my hastily packed weekend bag and my red Toyota Corolla . . . which was my next loss. Not really knowing my way around, I'd forget where I parked it, and I was racking up parking tickets.

When the car was towed, I owed more in parking tickets than it was worth, so I never bothered to claim it.[*]

So there I was, homeless, unemployed, and without a vehicle mere months into my life in the city. I'd been bouncing from one experience to the next, a naive ball of energy and intuition, filled with good intentions (and a dash of the devil), applying myself to everything, focusing on nothing, and making no attempts to curb my appetite for the edge. I lacked mentors, or anyone to call me out on the excesses that were preventing me from charting a course for myself beyond staying out till 6:00 a.m. at nightclubs. Luckily, I did at least have my new tribe of fabulous friends, and though they weren't helping me find gainful employment, they kept me off the streets. I crashed for a few weeks on the floor of the Times Square apartment of an artist named Bernd Naber, a sort of industrialist Andy Warhol who drove a silver Checker cab. Unfortunately, Times Square in the eighties was no less frightening than Avenue C; in fact, it was a human wasteland, littered with crack addicts, hookers, and everyone else who had come to New York with a crime in their head or a dream in their heart and made a few wrong decisions. Every day across the street in the Times Square Hotel a crazy woman would come out in a bathrobe and curlers and walk through the rotating door screaming *"Help me!"* It was a cautionary refrain that echoed my own mounting distress. But I never considered calling my dad. For one, it would have killed him to learn that his oldest daughter

---

[*] The sad thing about my car was that my dad had saved a lot of money to buy it for me as a Christmas present. Only three years after seeing it parked in my driveway with a big red bow on it, I couldn't even be bothered to get it out of impoundment.

was homeless in Times Square. And to leave New York would have been to give up on the only dream I'd ever had, and the only place I'd ever felt at home, mortal danger or not. Besides, I was naive enough to believe my life was slowly getting better, since I'd now moved *uptown*.

When you're following your inner voice, doors tend to eventually open for you, even if they mostly slam at first. I hadn't lived with Bernd two weeks when the universe sent me an angel. Anthony Haden-Guest, the art critic for *Vanity Fair*, was a celebrated and controversial writer twenty-eight years my senior who was known to have inspired the character of Peter Fallow in Tom Wolfe's *Bonfire of the Vanities* (played by Bruce Willis in the movie). I met him at a backyard cocktail party when he suddenly, out of nowhere, slapped my date—a dashing young advertising executive—across the face, knocking him off his chair, and screamed: "What are you doing with my wife?" It's odd, but we became instant friends. Despite his violence, I found his charisma charming. He offered me the couch in his elegant townhouse on East Eightieth Street, a leafy stretch of the swank Upper East Side. I call him my Colonel Pickering, after the benevolent character in *My Fair Lady*, because despite his status as an irrepressible icon of New York nightlife, he was always generous and gentlemanly to me.* He became my confidant, professor, attentive if infrequent late-night booty call, and one-man crash course in New York in the twilight of its party decade, introducing me to an entirely

---

* Our arrangement was hard for my mother to understand from afar. So she told my father, preposterously, that Anthony—one of the city's most notorious womanizers, who had once photocopied his penis at a party and distributed it to all the female guests—was gay.

different tribe of people and things that made the city go *BOOM*. It was through Anthony that I eventually met my first husband, and it was also Anthony who finally pointed out the obvious— that I needed an income—and arranged the interview for my first PR job. You could say he was one of the first members of my "tribal council"—a group of wise elders I've assembled over the years to advise me on everything from money to spirituality to how to raise a child alone. My parents never had the answers I needed to navigate my life in New York because they never lived there; they had no idea how things worked. Anthony, on the other hand, had conquered the place and was willing to be my benevolent tour guide. Without him, it might have taken me many more years to get a job, an apartment, and a life.

I advise you to seek out your own Anthonys *before* you are homeless in Times Square. There's a reason human beings once lived in tribes: it's useful. (In fact, I believe the breakdown of the tribal system is responsible for much of the sickness in the world today.) Start by identifying people in your community you look up to and then, graciously and with their blessing, use their hard work and experience to your advantage. Pick their brains. I can't imagine anyone refusing to be a mentor if they're asked in a spirit of sincerity and humility. And if you don't see any of these people around you, do as much travel and research as you can to figure out where they might be waiting for you.

But beware: tribal relationships are a two-way street. As you forge your own tribe, you'll become a member of other tribes and, ultimately, if you're lucky, a tribal elder yourself. This means you'll be compelled to give and give, even when nothing's really in it for you. Now that my days as an ingenue couch-surfer are behind me (I hope), I maintain several floors of live/work space in a large building in Manhattan, and my home has become a temple for an international cast of souls and tribal members needing advice or just a warm meal as they traverse the bumpy roads of their dreams. Lately, these include an Argentinean male supermodel and aspiring actor I met producing a fashion show in Mexico; a friend from an ashram in India who is trying to sell her jewelry line in New York; an employee who is between apartments; my nanny's granddaughters; and even my ex-husbands and current lovers. I cosign leases when my assistants are transitioning from their parents' place to their own apartment; I invite interns to my country house for the weekend; I rush to the bedside of friends' ailing children in the middle of fashion week. I even buy my girls the right lingerie, just as Pat Field did years ago for me. You never know who will end up being your family or where you'll find them. All that matters is that you do find them. After all, your tribe members, whether people gifted to you by the universe or people you seek out and pay, will not only add something unique and essential to your journey but make it much more colorful and fun. These days, my artist ex-husband, now a good friend, may come in off my elevator unannounced to crash for the night while I'm trying to watch a romantic movie on the couch with my current lover and the Argentinean supermodel types away on his computer in the kitchen, and then later all three men may teach my seven-year-old daughter how to play poker. This scene might seem hellishly complicated to an average girl like Dorothy. But not for a tribal priestess in her own temple.

TWO

FAKE IT TO MAKE IT

Faith without works is dead.

—King James Bible

It was Susan Blond, my first boss in the PR business, who predicted I'd be a famous publicist. We were at a record release party at the iconic nightclub the Palladium in 1988, and I was ushering her and Michael Jackson through a packed crowd when she turned to Michael, then her client, and said: "This girl's going to be huge. I've never seen anybody who can get through a room like this." I'd already mastered the indelicate art of using my extended arm as a dowsing rod to part sweaty, intractable seas of people, thereby facilitating safe passage for VIPs. Self-assurance was 90 percent of the game, it turned out; if you act *as if* you know what you're doing, and *as if* you're in charge, you'll be surprised how many people will let you be in charge. This was why, a year and a half after arriving in the city armed only with buckets of enthusiasm and a car full of out-of-date mall clothing, I was leading Susan Blond and Michael Jackson through a crowd of people in New York City. I couldn't believe I was getting paid for this.

Being from the middle of nowhere, I had learned to fake it long before I got into PR, when I was still a club promoter. Homeless and living on Anthony Haden-Guest's couch, I found myself seated at elaborate tables set with several forks and spoons, reading menus offering dishes I'd never heard of, and surrounded by people who were raised in London, Paris, New York, Beverly Hills, Palm Beach, Miami, and Milan. "Where did you go to school?" they would ask one another. "Boarding or college?" another would inquire. "Harvard," "Columbia," "Penn," "Yale," "Switzerland," came the inevitable replies. Meanwhile, there I was, from Syracuse—well, not even Syracuse, but a small town about seven miles *outside* of Syracuse called Camillus, where I'd spent my summers hostessing at Bob's Big Boy. I was beginning to feel as if my past was a curse keeping me from being included. I held my breath during these conversations, not wanting to talk about things I didn't under-stand or ask questions that might embarrass my date.* I made mental lists of questions to ask Anthony later, such as, "What do people do in Geneva?" or, "What's a venture capitalist?"

My knowledge and pedigree weren't the only things lack-ing. I'd been raised on Jordache, not Chanel, and my wardrobe mostly consisted of tank tops and the cowboy ankle boots that were popular in the eighties. One night Anthony bought me tickets for a charity raffle at Mortimer's—the infamous and now-defunct Upper East Side eatery then frequented by an inter-national who's who list, including Dominick Dunne, Carolina and Renaldo Herrera, Donald Fagan from Steely Dan, Henry

* Sometimes the best way to fake it is to shut up.

Kissinger, and Richard Nixon—and there I was named the winner of an almost unimaginable prize: a $3,000 shopping spree at the atelier of Bill Blass (translation: two gowns). I couldn't believe it. I knew this was a ticket out of my perpetual outsider status and a chance to make my horse and saddle match up to everyone else's. But while the two stunning Bill Blass gowns I chose may have told the world that I was an urban sophisticate and I'd *arrived*, it became obvious on one fateful evening that they were lying.

It was a crisp fall night in New York when I wore one of my new gowns, an astonishing black velvet and cream satin number with Swarovski crystals striping it, to a black-tie dinner with Anthony on the Upper East Side. Seated with an Italian count on my right and a countess on my left, and engaged in a serious eye-lock with the famous film director Taylor Hackford across the table, I felt more beautiful than I ever had in my life. I'd only been in New York eight months, yet here I was, wearing a gown worth more than the red Corolla I'd lost to parking tickets, my hair cut pixie-short, my body superthin, seated among people I couldn't have dreamed up only a short time ago. Standing in front of the three-way mirror at Bill Blass's headquarters only days earlier, I'd known I was doing the same thing I'd done since age three, whether with princess costumes or, later, punk-rock T-shirts—I was trying on a new identity. The power of clothing as a communicative medium—a way of drawing things toward

---

* Of course, his check bounced. Anthony was notorious at the time for bouncing checks, which earned him extra points in his four-year run as the winner of *Spy* magazine editor-in-chief Graydon Carter's annual Ironman Nightlife Decathlon, a competition that also rewarded lewdness and stealing other men's girlfriends.

us or pushing them away—wasn't lost on me even then. Being at the atelier had provided a glimpse of what it might be like to be *that* woman and to have attendants in ateliers waiting on me hand and foot. It felt good.*

Unfortunately, I lacked the experience and self-control to actually behave like the worldly creature I was impersonating, and I soon scored drugs off the Italian count after his wife let it slip during the appetizer course that he was just out of rehab. The count was more than happy to oblige. I assumed he'd given me coke, which people snorted openly from the Bowery to the East Eighties and still do; instead, the bastard slipped me heroin. It was my first and last experience with that terrifying drug, and let's just say it wasn't pretty: after a night spent traipsing to nightclubs and apartment parties and everything in between, I woke up in the morning fully encased in my gorgeous gown with a strange man above me wearing only tube socks, brandishing a whip, and telling me he'd been "a very bad boy." I managed to escape into the bathroom with a piece of the pervert's mail to call Anthony, who arrived promptly to haul me back home—I was somewhere off Lexington Avenue in the Seventies. He wrapped me in his Burberry raincoat and screamed at my captor, in his charming British lilt: *"Don't you evah fuck with her again! I'll have you killed by the Lebanese army!"* We trudged slowly together up Park Avenue, my patient Colonel Pickering and me, my head tousled but my gown perfectly intact. Anthony had saved my life

---

* If finding one's fate is a matter of experimentation, like playing the "hot or cold" game you played as a kid, then this was *hot!* (whereas waking up at 6:00 a.m. to discuss diet plans had been *cold, cold,* very *cold*).

yet again. I felt disgraced, beyond exposed; I'd gone from doing the walk of fame to the walk of shame in a matter of hours. It was becoming obvious that I needed more than witty small talk and the right look to survive in this town. In other words, you can fake your way to the table, but ultimately you have to learn how to eat. Clothes do not make the woman (even if they do make her look *good*).

Anthony said to me soon after, "Darling, you can't do this anymore, you need to get a job." He was understandably weary of me rolling off the couch just as he prepared to draw his bath and go out for the evening. But I still had no idea what to do with my life. It was obvious to me by then that New York was not exactly the meritocracy it's cracked up to be and that, while there were no guarantees for anyone in life, if you were born into a wealthy family there was a network and you'd be fast-tracked. Many of the women I encountered in Anthony's world had attended the same Manhattan private schools, which have names like Spence and Chapin and churn out fashion editors, PR directors, and Lincoln Center board members. (Growing up in Syracuse long before socialites and fashion ruled TV, I'd had no idea these places even existed.) I noticed that these women were not suffering indignities like working at NutriSystem or promoting clubs until 5:00 a.m. I'd have bet that very few of them were washing up on Lexington Avenue in strange men's apartments in their Bill Blass gowns. Their paths seemed straighter, easier— paved. But though I may not have been born on the power-girl starting line—in a hospital on the Upper East Side, with a grandmother on the board at Brearley—I did have one distinct advantage: a very benevolent tribal elder in my corner. When I told Anthony I wanted to be an MTV VJ—I was unable to think of any other profession that really spoke to me—he was unimpressed. "You're far too smart for that," he said. "You should be a publicist." "What's that?" I asked. "It's what you do anyway," he said. "You just talk all day and put people together." He called his friend Susan Blond, who presided over her own firm (and still does), and arranged an interview for me.

I took the subway to Susan's offices on Fifty-seventh Street, and sitting in her anteroom, I was terrified. As I looked through the glass at a well-dressed army of people who arrived at 9:00 a.m., coffee in hand, to do important things all day, I had the same feelings of inadequacy I'd had many months before when I gazed at the excess of silverware at Anthony's friends' dinner parties. I had never known any powerful women, let alone any publicists, and Susan was a revelation; she had long skinny arms and an elegant office with shag carpeting where she sat behind her glass desk with her hands folded, one on top of the other, delivering instructions in a distinctive voice that sounded like a nasal high-pitched bird. In hindsight, she was Popeye's Olive Oyl, as imagined by Karl Lagerfeld. Everything about her oozed chic and power, including the two assistants who manned her office door. And then there was her client list: she represented musicians like the Fine Young Cannibals, Tammy Wynette, the Pet Shop Boys, and Michael Jackson. I was totally out of my league, and I knew it. There was no way to fake it here. But in this case, it was actually my ignorance, not my posturing, that saved me. Susan gave me a quiz, mostly about the music writers at various glossy magazines like *Rolling Stone*, and I got every question wrong but one: what is porthenol? I happened to know the answer to this random inquiry, probably from some extended conversation with my grandmother: porthenol is a kind of lace. (Italian Americans *love* lace.) She was impressed. "Oh, my God," she squawked. "You're the only person who *ever* answered that right. Would you like to be my assistant?"

And just like that, I went from drunk young indigent to salaried PR girl. Granted, I hadn't exactly made it yet. I'd still feel like I was faking it for years. But a road map to the life I'd been intuitively chasing was beginning to reveal itself. I signed on for a scant $150 a week toiling pretty much from 9:00 a.m. to 3:00 a.m., plus Saturdays. My glamorous responsibilities included having organic macrobiotic noodles delivered for the Fine Young Cannibals for lunch—not an easy thing to find in the 1980s anywhere outside Berkeley—picking up dry cleaning, making reservations at the Russian Tea Room, and footing it downtown to Chinatown to see Susan's "doctor," Xu Zhiang, a homeopathic tea maker who didn't speak a word of English and accepted only cash for the remedies he'd prepare for one of Susan's real or imagined ailments.* I threw myself into these menial tasks, never once thinking that I was too good for them or that they were beneath me. I was from Syracuse, after all, and I suddenly *wanted* to be that girl who could walk into a florist and know that long-stem roses were completely un-chic and baby's breath was the enemy, who had a great Rolodex of self-help people at her disposal and knew

---

* Woody Allen would later mimic this man in the film *Alice*.

exactly where to have lunch with her important industry colleagues. I recognized in Susan the kind of woman whose power I'd tried on briefly at the Bill Blass atelier (before one of the sales associates asked me if I'd brought shoes and I was forced to admit I only owned Doc Martens). Finally, I had a *female* tribal elder, and a woman whose path could inform my own.

Susan taught me that I didn't want to be just sexy and fun; I wanted to be powerful. And that just because you're not getting fast-tracked doesn't mean you can't get on the ride. It's a bit like Disneyland: if you don't know about the fast-pass lane, you just have to wait in line for two and a half hours. Is the ride any less fun? *No!* By the time you get there, it might even be better. The great thing about coming from nowhere is that you're able to experience a series of victories on your way to what some people would consider just a normal job.

Of course, deciding I wanted to be in charge didn't mean I had any idea of how to be a publicist. When I was finally given actual PR responsibilities, it was in the form of a record no one else wanted to work on by a musician named Dan Hartman, who had years before penned a huge disco hit called "Instant Replay." His new release was therefore even sadder: he'd had a spiritual awakening and was aiming to pioneer a new sound called "new age" music. The record sounded like something you'd hear in a dentist's office in Scottsdale, and it was suddenly my job to get the most influential music magazines in New York to write about it. I knew I'd been given a rare chance to prove myself by succeeding where virtually no one expected me to; the senior publicists had tossed me this record with a smirk: *Oh, you think you're so*

THE ULTIMATE POWER-GIRL MOVIE LIST

All About Eve
Baby Boom
Belle Époque
Carrie
Cleopatra
The Devil Wears Prada
Elizabeth
Erin Brockovich
Fatal Attraction
Flashdance
Heathers
Idol-Maker
National Velvet
Nine to Five
Species
A Star Is Born
The First Wives Club
Thelma and Louise
Truth or Dare
Two or Three Things I Know About Her
What Ever Happened to Baby Jane?
Working Girl

smart, you wanna be a PR girl? Well, here — good luck! Not wanting to waste time figuring out what to do, I just *did*. I cold-called David Thigpen, a well-known music writer and critic for *Time* magazine, and said something like: "Hi, um, my name's Kelly, I'm Susan Blond's assistant, and no one wants to work on this record, and

I don't think it's very good, but there are some things that are interesting about it, would you please come to the reception for the artist, it's my job to get people there?" David and I became friends instantly, and my unorthodox and brutally honest pitching style was born. I realized that writers, who are used to hearing rote speeches all day, thought I was hysterical, and the turnout for the event was fantastic. (The same cannot be said for the album's sales.) Susan was sufficiently impressed to promote me from fetching her dry cleaning to helping promote such records as *She Drives Me Crazy* by the Fine Young Cannibals. Soon I was flying all over the world, staying in hotels with rock stars, and, yes, ushering Susan and Michael Jackson through the Palladium. It eventually occurred to me that I wasn't faking it anymore, at least not as much as I had been. I was being paid to deliver a message for my clients by talking on the phone and attending concerts and parties, which, let's face it, I had a real knack for.

Still, my leap into entrepreneurship was reactionary more than visionary. When I started my own company, I again had *no* idea what I was doing. It all began when I left Susan's to become director of PR at *Spin* magazine for Bob Guccione, who more than doubled my salary to $400 a week. Unfortunately, Bob was sexist and domineering, and after putting up with him for less than a year, I decided impulsively to strike out on my own. I hated that someone like Bob could fire me on a whim. (*That*, to me, felt like true powerlessness.) This way, I figured, if I died, at least I would die at my own hand. But while my inner voice was clearly telling me I was at my core an entrepreneur, it's inconvenient to decide at twenty-three that you can't really work for other people.

Being direct, funny, social, and cute—the traits that had often helped me get by—were simply not enough when I was running the show.* At one of my first red-carpet events for a nightclub, my main area of expertise at the time, I stepped out of my town car to find a horde of photographers waiting for me, demanding to know where the tip sheet was. Huh? *Tip sheet?* I stood there with a confused expression, paralyzed and humiliated, as they unleashed their chuckles and sneers on me. "*Booooooooo!!*" Yes, I was being booed by the paparazzi! I had somehow yet to learn that a tip sheet is the who, what, where, and when of any publicity event: it provides basic information about the event and its sponsors and the proper spelling of famous attendees' names for the newspaper coverage the next morning (and nowadays the blog posts twenty minutes after the event ends). How had I missed this? I refused to be discouraged; instead, I labored to fill the gaping holes in my knowledge. Much as I had done with Anthony many months before, I sought out older industry veterans and drilled them on mysterious terms like "tip sheets" and "B-roll." And I belatedly picked up a handy doorstop volume known as the *Book of New York Publicity Outlets*, which listed all the writers in the city whose contact information I'd been trying to dig up for months.

Soon all the extra work I put in paid off, and it became obvious that I was on the right track and that publicity was what I was born to do. Mere months into starting my own business, I organized one of the most successful PR events of my career to this day. If

---

* I now suggest working for at least five years in an industry before striking out on your own.

you don't let what you don't know stop you from doing your best in every situation, you will surprise yourself over and over in life, as I have. It started one quiet evening as I stood in my kitchen on Christopher Street making beef stew for my first husband, Ronnie Cutrone, a well-known artist and Warhol protégé seventeen years my senior whom I'd met and married after a whirlwind court-ship while still working at Susan's. An idea popped into my head for a provocative performance art exhibit protesting censorship in the arts. This wasn't totally out of the blue: everyone was talking about censorship in those days. It was a moment when Senator Jesse Helms was taking on the National Endowment for the Arts (NEA) for providing grants for "obscene" and "indecent" art, and Tipper Gore was busy trying to enforce ratings systems on rock music with her Parents Music Resource Center (PMRC). And there *I* was, married to a pop artist who had been a whip-dancer in the Velvet Underground, living on a famous drag queen–clogged stretch of Christopher Street, and moving in a tribe that included people like brash Velvet front man Lou Reed, the aforementioned Pat Field and Diana Brill, Blondie front woman Debbie Harry, and painters like Julian Schnabel and Kenny Scharf. It hadn't really occurred to me before meeting these people that censorship was a problem, since everything in my entire life had been censored. (As a child, I wasn't even allowed to watch *Laverne and Shirley* — too "racy.") But from Greenwich Village the whole world seemed uptight. Who was Jesse Helms to tell people like my husband what was art and what wasn't? According to the senator's standards, anything society might consider controversial—gay issues, sex, porn—was automatically suspect and marginalized. He needed to be answered, challenged, but liberals and bohemians weren't very good organizers. They clearly needed a good PR girl.

My idea was an art exhibit called "Love. Spit. Love." In it we would announce that "*we* [Ronnie and I] are white, straight, married, monogamous, and angry that people claiming to represent us are creating a dangerously false morality." I pictured three couples of varying ages, races, religions, and sexual orientations kissing, caressing, and even having sex in the middle of an art gallery to a soundtrack of love songs from the fifties through the nineties. An American flag would, of course, be prominently displayed on the wall. The idea was fully formed—a direct missive from my inner voice, all but tied in a bow. When I told Ronnie, he agreed that the idea was brilliant and immediately brought a gallery on Lafayette on board to host the show.

Once we enlisted our couples, we set a date—May 1, 1991*—and I went to work publicizing the event. The only tools I had at my disposal were a fax machine, my *Book of New York Publicity Outlets*, and myself. My one-woman company, KBC Public Relations, had never produced an event anywhere near this ambitious before. But rather than worry about the size of what I was taking on, I just busted my ass. I wrote an honest and heartfelt letter explaining why we were doing the exhibit and spent days faxing it all over town. I handwrote a fresh cover sheet for each fax. On the day of the exhibit, there was not one working writer in New York who had not heard from me. I also pleaded with a few low-ranking friends I'd made in television. One, an assistant producer on the

* This must be my lucky day: I later gave birth to my daughter on May 1, 2002.

Joan Rivers show, prevailed upon her bosses, and on the morning of the opening Ronnie and I went on Joan's show and shocked her and her audience with news of what we had planned for the evening. Our appearance was the highest-rated episode in the show's history. Censorship was a hot-button issue, and we were basically pounding on that button with a hammer; naked couples having sex in an art gallery drove a certain segment of the population berserk. But we *were* getting our message heard. In fact, no sooner did we leave Joan Rivers's studio than it seemed like every TV show in America was calling us, from the local news to *Access Hollywood*. "Art or pornography?" was the question, and every writer, talk-show host, and cultural critic was dying to answer it. (I happen to think my genius husband had the best answer: "It's art," he said. "Because I'm an artist, and I say it's art.")

The apotheosis of the media blitz came the day after the opening, when, with our pictures splashed across all the morning papers alongside pieces by writers like Guy Trebay in the *Village Voice*, we appeared on *Phil Donahue*—understand, this man was the Oprah of his time—with the naked couples themselves. I'd gone out on a limb and faxed Donahue's producer, who, to his credit, read a handwritten missive from a relative unknown and actually called me. Sometimes you don't even have to fake it— you just have to ask nicely. (The day we appeared Donahue also got the highest ratings in the history of his show.)

The opening itself was the largest art opening in the history of America at the time. The line to get in stretched from NoLita to the Lower East Side, winding through all the corridors of downtown Manhattan; over five thousand people streamed through the gallery that night. I wore a short black wig and pink leather chaps, and Ronnie wore an American flag bomber jacket and sunglasses. In one photo, with our arms draped over each other's shoulders, we look proud and happy. Indeed, the night was an example to me of the magical things that can be accomplished in a true romantic partnership. (I wish I could say there have been many more examples in my life of this phenomenon, but sadly, there have not.) I also learned that you can't fake hard work, and that when you believe in something and truly go after it with all you have, amazing things will happen.

These days, I continue to call members of the media myself rather than outsourcing the work to my staffers, because you can never be too good for the things that first made you successful. I will always remember that at twenty-three years old, as an untrained and unknown publicity newbie from Syracuse, I tried my best to get the whole country talking about my message with *no* staff, *no* office, *no* assistant, *no* BlackBerry, and *no* know-how— just with conviction, truth, and balls. And it worked.

THREE

IT'S NOT A BREAKDOWN, IT'S A BREAKTHROUGH

Lucy: You can't drift along forever...
you have to direct your thinking.
For instance you have to decide
whether you're going to be a liberal or
conservative. You have to take some
sort of stand. You have to associate
with some sort of cause.

Linus: Are there any openings in
the lunatic fringe?

—*Peanuts*

Ego was the helper; ego is the bar.

—Sri Aurobindo

One of my favorite memories from my early years in New York was a New Year's Eve party I threw in the early nineties on the roof of One Times Square, the building from which the ball drops. My then-business partner Jason Weinberg and I invited an exclusive group of editors and celebrity friends to dine al fresco under heat lamps atop the building so as to observe the ball up close before it plunged. When I arrived, the police officers manning the barricades outside at first refused to admit me to the building and couldn't believe that this shockingly young woman in a gorgeous double-breasted silver raincoat from Barney's was in fact the publicist for one of the city's biggest events of the year. But I managed to talk my way past this obstacle, as I had done many times before, and soon I was hosting a dinner party in the sky in an amazing raincoat, my famous artist husband keeping me warm as thousands of people crammed into Times Square below like ants. Several feet away from us on the roof, I was shocked to see eight guys with wires in their hands shouting, "Move to the left!" The sparkling dropping ball, this hyped yearly event that the whole world looks to as the epitome of glamour and celebration and ritual, was really, when you got close enough, just a flagpole surrounded by union workers with cables. It was an apt metaphor for my life at the time, though I may not have known it. Three months later, Ronnie and I were headed for a divorce that left me clutching a bottle of Jack Daniels in one hand and a Marlboro in the other, sobbing and jumping up and down in my underwear on the bed repeatedly singing "Nothing Compares to You" by Sinead O'Connor. But the death of my first love was just one of many deaths I've survived so far in my life. I tell my employees I've died several times while in the same body, each time paving the way for an amazing rebirth (talk about multitasking). After all, you can't truly be happy if you've never known pain. You can't truly feel joy if you've never felt heartbreak. You can't really know what it's like to be filled unless you've been empty. And here's the other thing: sometimes in life seasons don't come in order; instead of fall, winter, spring, summer, we get three winters in a row. (By *my* second winter I tend to feel like a cavewoman frozen in a glacier.) But that doesn't mean spring won't come eventually.

I met Ronnie Cutrone in 1989 at an art opening. It wasn't love at first sight; actually, I found him to be an arrogant asshole. When I asked Anthony Haden-Guest who he was, Anthony said that he was one of those "crazy pop artists." I ran into Ronnie again several weeks later at a club called Carmelita's, but this time he turned on the charm, offering me his coat when I became cold. It was an eight-ball of coke I left in his pocket that finally brought us together. When Ronnie dropped it off the next day with a pint of ice cream, we couldn't keep our hands off each other. (We had sex on the roof of the building.) After that, I immediately began auditioning for the role of his wife by offering to make him breakfast. We moved in together in a matter of days. (By that I mean I moved my stuff from Anthony's to Ronnie's apartment in the West Village.) Several months later, Ronnie said, "I want to marry you." "Great!" I exclaimed. Like most other women, I had been waiting most of my life to hear these words. I was living with a well-known artist in a spacious apartment facing the Hudson River, and he made me laugh. Of *course* I wanted this to go on forever!*

That's how I found myself standing at the altar in a church in Virginia—where my parents had moved after I left Syracuse—in a hideous sparkly sequined dress purchased at my mother's insistence for $300 at an Orthodox Jewish store on the Lower East Side after she'd vetoed the Commes des Garçons wrap-jacket and wide-legged cream chiffon pants I wanted to wear. As a matter of fact, when I woke up that morning in my parents' guest bedroom, "Going to the Chapel" was playing on the radio. It was a perfect opening for the David Lynch movie my marriage would

---

* The fact that Ronnie was seventeen years older than me seemed totally irrelevant. The fact that he'd popped the question while we were having sex also failed to raise any red flags. Certainly no one ever sat me down and said, "Honey, a young publicist and a much older painter? You don't have a chance in hell!" In fact, my mother, who didn't even know I was dating anyone when I called to share the news, quickly recovered from her shock and took to planning our traditional Catholic wedding like she'd been waiting for it her whole life. (She did suggest we lie to my father about Ronnie's age, but I refused.)

soon become. My hair was curled, and my face caked in makeup. My mother couldn't stop telling me how beautiful I looked.* It was obvious that she'd been programmed to get me married as much as I'd been programmed to get myself married; nothing about my wedding had anything to do with *me* or *my* desires or *my* vision. There I was, agreeing to things like "till death do you part" and "in the name of God" and other things I had no business uttering. What the fuck did *I* know? I was young and impulsive, basically a windup toy charging in the direction I'd been pointed—toward Happily Ever After. I had no idea that there's a difference between being in love and actually being life partners. I hadn't been told that you can make great food together and have all the same interests, but that if you're not working toward a common goal—if you're not actively building something together—there's no reason to get married. In fact, my parents were so pleased with my decision that they proudly staged their own PR stunt, issuing their congratulations on the marquee outside the local Holiday Inn. (Seeing it as I drove into town with my chic New York friends was one of the more embarrassing moments of my life.)

The co-opting of my wedding was the first clue that my fairy-tale marriage, despite the fact that I *did* love Ronnie, was exactly that: a story I'd been told, and someone else's script I was following, *not* something that had anything to do with who I really was or what I really needed at that point in my life. Let's face it:

---

* My mother is a proper 1950s housewife who curls her hair every morning and will not go to the mailbox without her makeup on, so she has never understood why I refuse to dress up and insist on looking "like I live in the Third World."

I didn't even know who I was! I'd made ballsy and intuitive choices in my life, sure, but when it came to love, even I wasn't impervious to the cultural messages thrusting us toward marriage, security, and babies. Only when my marriage crumbled after three years did it occur to me that in buying into all the magical things I'd been told about love and marriage and how to go about building happiness in this life—and I swallowed these notions hook, line, and sinker—I'd built my house on a set of beliefs that were not my own. And a house built on matchsticks will ultimately fall down (though in my case it was more like arson). This was when I learned that you have to give up your life as you know it to get a new one: that sometimes you need to let go of everything you're clinging to and start over, whether because you've outgrown it or because it's not working anymore or because it was wrong for you in the first place. I'd done this before, at twenty-one, when I drove to New York from Syracuse with all my belongings packed in trash bags. This time I wasn't pursuing a dream so much as retreating from one, or several. I'm not saying you shouldn't chase the things I chased—in fact, I still want many of them, minus the Chanel jackets and the husband— but I am saying they are ultimately worthless, regardless of their price, without a knowledge and love of yourself and a firm belief in something greater than yourself.

At the beginning, Ronnie and I were happy. As a glamorous young art wife, I attended dinner parties and art openings and partied late into the night with my husband at Canal Bar, where I'd meet people like Tim Leary and famed Warhol cinematographer Paul Morrissey. But our differences quickly became apparent. I was a young, indefatigable optimist at the top of my game, and Ronnie was a jaded artist who was obsessed with the Yankees and had been inhaling toxic paint fumes for years. As I became more successful at work and more confident and independent, Ronnie began treating me like a naughty little dog that needed training, refusing to let me in when I forgot my keys and at one point forcing me to hire a locksmith and pay $600 of my own money to break into our apartment while he sat on the couch in his pajamas watching the game. He wasn't making me laugh anymore; instead, he seemed depressed and controlling. I didn't know then that if someone's depressed, it's not your fault and there's nothing you can do about it, so I blamed myself for our problems, as many women do. Maybe I wasn't smart enough or pretty enough, or maybe I needed to be more nurturing. I tore through my whole bag of tricks trying to reengage him. But nothing worked. At twenty-four, when I found out I was pregnant, I was thrilled; maybe *this* was the spark we needed. I expected tears, gratitude, and excitement, a loving marital moment—I'd seen this exact scene on TV and in the movies many times—but what I got from Ronnie was paranoia. He said we didn't have enough money saved for a baby (this despite the fact that the man owned Warhols) and that he wanted me to terminate the pregnancy. His reaction broke my heart, and I had an abortion. It was the beginning of the end of our marriage; when I looked at my husband from then on, I just saw a baby-killer. Don't get me wrong: I believe in a woman's right to choose, and I don't regret my abortion—I now know I needed to give birth to myself before giving birth to a child—but it was depressing to end my pregnancy while married and in love. My fairy tale had veered fatally off-script.

Rather than ask myself the important questions in the face of this failure, I threw myself into work even more. I'd taken on a business partner, a former Susan Blond intern named Jason Weinberg, and we started one of the first boutique PR firms in New York, called Cutrone, Weinberg & Associates. I'd been craving a partner who could lend professional support and kvetch with me over the insane people and situations that filled my day. Jason was Jewish, gay, charming, and dashing, and what we lacked in knowledge we more than made up for in attitude. We were soon signing clients like the legendary singer Eartha Kitt, the film director Abel Ferrara, DJ Mark Ronson, Sean Lennon's first band, and every nightclub in New York that mattered, from the Roxy and the Limelight to the Palladium and the Tunnel. This made us *the* kids to know in New York. Actors, rock stars, and hangers-on who wanted to sit at VIP tables and get free booze all night had to go through us, so they all soon had our number. My rising profile on the scene came with exciting privileges like being able to *borrow* clothes from designers rather than actually buy them. I even started appearing regularly in the city's most notorious gossip column, "Page Six," with friends like Naomi Campbell and Justine Bateman. I was a New York girl du jour: I weighed 112 pounds, I owned my own company—for God's sake, I was even in *Vogue*!

And mama, I was miserable. When shit hit the fan, I realized I had few friends I could actually depend on. I knew hundreds of people, but while my tribe was rich and skinny and pretty, we were also shallow; there was no real investment in what was happening in people's hearts and minds and lives. It was as if we'd all made a pact to have short conversations about nothing important. I'd air-kiss these "friends" upon arriving at a club after a long day of work and hear about their fantastic trip to Capri, nod at the appropriate moments, ask the right questions, relay the latest gossip. (I probably couldn't have sat still long enough to have an intimate conversation at the time if I'd tried.) Even my job seemed like a joke and a facade. The truth is that the more zeros you add to your paycheck, the more zeros you add to your expenses, until you're running around like a maniac just trying to keep it all going and you have no idea why you're doing it in the first place. I'd been duped. No one had prepared me for the other side of this pretty picture. What happens when you do meet the man of your dreams—and then you get divorced? What happens when you do get your dream job? Then what? You just get a $100-a-day coke habit and work like a fucking dog all the time? Where was *that* book?

My marriage ended with an explosion, not a slow fade. When I told Ronnie I was leaving him, he didn't take it well: he grabbed a German ceremonial dagger out of his closet and put it to my throat. I managed to escape, which is when he called my father and said, "Lee, I'm going to kill your daughter, and then I'm going to kill myself." He subsequently pushed me down the stairs at the office I shared with Jason, who called the police.* I

---

* Ronnie spent several days in jail and we didn't speak for two years, but we're now good friends and I'm the executor of his estate. His last name stuck, even through my second ill-fated marriage, and I now share it with my daughter.

read about this episode in "Page Six" under the headline "Love Slit Love."

At twenty-six, I had the sense that I had already done all there is to do in life: I'd traveled and toured with kings and partied with paupers, I'd seen babies born, I'd seen friends and relatives die, I'd had a career, I'd been deeply, desperately in love, and now I was getting divorced. My only thought was: *Now what?* Am I just supposed to do this on repeat for the rest of my life? I was reminded of the Peggy Lee song "Is That All There Is?" Was life just a mating game where we're out there looking for a partner and then we have 2.5 kids and, if we're lucky, save over $250,000 for retirement and grow older and either get taken care of by our kids or end up in a nursing home and die? It seemed like we were all just chasing our tails: waking up, going to work, fucking, fighting, loving, saying we're sorry over and over and over again. *What* are we doing here? And who am I? What is important to me, and who and what am I serving? These questions consumed me, but lacking any answers, I did my best to escape them.

I left New York for Topanga Canyon, an amazing vortex of a mind-tripping town in between Santa Monica and Malibu, for the ostensible purpose of opening a West Coast branch of Cutrone, Weinberg & Associates. Really, though, Manhattan had become a very small island where too many people knew my business and I couldn't stop haunting the places where Ronnie and I had hung out, hoping masochistically to run into him. One day Jason called me in L.A. and said, "We just signed Tina Louise," referring to the movie star from *Gilligan's Island.* "But she refuses to talk about *Gilligan's Island.*" This was when I really snapped. *I* *don't want to represent Tina Louise, all she's ever* done *is* Gilligan's Island, *I hate* all *these people, I can't fucking take this, I am* gone! I sold Jason my half of the company and sent my assistant Nancy to break up with the guy I'd been dating in New York, a drummer for Rod Stewart, instructing her to retrieve my couch.* And I got high, releasing myself into the grips of a meth addiction. Soon I was staring at the ceiling pondering a compilation record called *Songs to Commit Suicide By.* (My marketing background told me that the day after Thanksgiving would be the perfect time to release this album.)

It was my second husband, a man named Jeff Kober, who would later put this all into perspective: "Baby, you're not having a breakdown," he said, as I wailed about something or other in the back of our car as he drove down the highway. "You're having a break*through.*" And he was right. The accoutrements of my life in New York had distracted me from really knowing myself, and as I plucked them away one by one—the job, the money, the clothes, even my wigs—I didn't know I was being prepared by a force greater than myself for a major spiritual awakening. The truth was that I'd invested years of my life in a series of beliefs that weren't my own, only to be left with nothing—no tribe, no sense of connectedness or fulfillment—when life dealt me a hit. It turns out there can be a fine line between being courageous in following your dreams and being self-destructive in the service of ego, greed, and approval. But then, my mother never told me

---

* When Nancy arrived at his door with her clipboard, he told her he'd always had a thing for "ginger-haired girls" and seduced her. I see that encounter as one final fuck-off postcard from New York—or at least the universe telling me I'd made the right decision.

that if I did everything I was programmed to do and chased all the things I was supposed to chase—and wear, and *be*—without ever developing a true and unshakeable sense of self, I'd crash into a million pieces one day when something went wrong.

The good news is that while Ronnie may not have been my last great love in life, he was my last true romantic apocalypse: the flaming shards of our love ultimately constructed a bridge I used to walk over into the future. This is an important lesson to remember when you're having a bad day, a bad month, or a shitty year. Things will change: you won't feel this way forever. And anyway, sometimes the hardest lessons to learn are the ones your soul needs most. I believe you can't feel real joy unless you've felt heartache. You can't have a sense of victory unless you know what it means to fail. You can't know what it's like to feel holy until you know what it's like to feel really fucking evil. And you can't be birthed again until you've died.

FOUR

THE TRUTH HURTS:
When Did Spiritual Become
Equated with Nice?

> For those who are afraid of a word,
> this is what we mean by "Divine": all
> the knowledge we have to acquire,
> all the power we have to obtain,
> all the love we have to become, all
> the perfection we have to achieve,
> all the harmonious and progressive
> poise we have to manifest in light
> and joy, all the new and unknown
> splendors that have to be realized.
>
> —Mirra Alfasa (the Mother)

Early in 2009 I met with Ashley Dupre, the former high-end prostitute at the center of New York governor Eliot Spitzer's resignation scandal, as a favor to a friend. Ashley was earnest and sweet, and she was looking for advice on how to redirect the Spitzer media storm toward a music career. I advised her on where to get her hair done and what designers to wear. I also told her she'd been horribly advised for her Diane Sawyer interview: she never should have apologized to Spitzer's wife, because *she* didn't make a vow to her. (An apology for breaking the law and humiliating her mother would have sufficed.) And I invited her to attend New York's upcoming Fashion Week. Little did I know when she arrived at Yigal Azrouel's show several days later that she'd incite a new media storm with *me* at its center. Her appearance in the front row was uneventful; few people even noticed or recognized her, including Yigal himself, who unwittingly took a photo with her backstage. I was preoccupied with plenty of other "delicate" seating issues: a friend who didn't want to sit near her father's former mistress; another friend who showed up with a lover instead of her husband; Katie Lee Joel, then-wife of Billy and rumored lover of Yigal himself; and an army of editors from rival magazines like *Vogue* and *Harper's Bazaar*. Ashley's seating assignment was not the first thing on my mind. After the show, Yigal and I rushed off to greet one of his sponsors, and he thanked me profusely and told me I'd done more for his career than anyone.* But less than an hour later, when he realized Ashley had been at his show, he and two of his associates viciously beheaded me on the telephone. (I like to call myself Mama Wolf; well, this was Mama Wolf being attacked by a pack of hungry hyenas.) He told me he was going to send out a press release immediately announcing my firing. I gave him one last bit of free advice: that that would be a huge mistake. I was on the number-one-rated cable TV show at the time, and my new friend Ashley, well, she'd been involved in the biggest media scandal to hit New York in years. The news would inevitably eclipse any positive reactions to the actual clothes. But Yigal ignored me, blasting a press release to the entire industry that announced he had fired me for "mismanagement." Everyone knew what that meant. By nightfall it had become the scandal of the week.

I cried in my office that night, not because I'd been fired, but because I was devastated by the state of humanity. I knew that the blogs would eventually move on to fresher gossip. I also knew I'd recover from the personal embarrassment of having my name

---

* And I had: I gave him $25,000 worth of free services and pulled in sponsorships that essentially allowed him to show at the Tents for free.

dragged through the mud by one of my own clients at a moment when the whole industry was watching. What upset me most, however, was the hysteria over this young girl who made some bad decisions and ended up in the oldest profession in the world. Could it really be that, in 2009, the fashion industry—which creates images of girls who look like they've been gangbanged on *Alice in Wonderland* adventures and calls them ad campaigns—was turning on me because I gave a front-row seat at Fashion Week to some girl who, like many of the women who attend fashion shows and go to Chanel, had sex for money with a man thirty years older than her? *Fuck that*. When Ashley called to apologize and to tell me I could pretend I didn't know her, I gathered my resolve. "I'm not going to pretend I don't know you," I said. "In fact, tomorrow's Valentine's Day. Do you have any plans?" I brought her along to my client Andrew Buckler's event, where I told a reporter from *Women's Wear Daily*, "We're all hookers in one way or another."* The quote was featured as the 'Quote of the Day' on *WWD's* inside cover, and as a result, it tore around the Internet. My mother soon called to tell me she'd seen the scandal on three different morning shows. It dragged on for almost the entire week, which was one of the longest of my professional life.

Fashion is an industry built on illusion, and publicity is a profession built on spinning the truth. But I'm a person who has become well known for being honest at any cost, whether that means stoking the fires of my own Fashion Week scandal or

---

* And I meant it: we all do things we don't want to do for money. If you're paying me $20,000 a month to be your publicist and you call me to talk about whether aubergine or celadon is going to be psychically on-trend for the season, nine times out of ten I don't really care. But I'm being paid to do a job, so I give good phone.

telling models that they're too thin. I don't regret speaking out against my industry's hypocrisy, though in this instance and in many others over the years it wasn't exactly the easy road to take. Society wants you to participate in its lies, but I've seen this produce terrifying consequences in fashion, from drugs to anorexia to abusive relationships. We tend to spend our lives building a stable of partners in our crimes against ourselves: people to tell us we look thin when we're overeating, people to tell us we look gorgeous when we're spent, and people to tell us we're making sense when we're not. With friends like these, we're almost put off when people decide to be honest. But *true* friends love us no matter what and are willing to call us out.

That's why, at People's Revolution, when someone comes in on Monday morning and says, "Did I gain weight over the weekend?" her colleagues will probably look up and say, "Yes." And if I grab a studded T-shirt off one of the clothing racks that perpetually clutter our office and ask, "Does this look bad?" the answer will also likely be "Yes." I've had to tell my daughter that there is no way her father and I will ever be married, and I've had to tell clients that their collection is not welcome at *Vogue*; sometimes the truth just hurts. You can either let someone be protected from reality or let them be sculpted and birthed by it. I firmly believe the latter option is best. We're constantly getting these messages to mind our own business and look the other way if we want to be well liked, to not tell the truth or speak our mind or say anything too intense. Well, I'm telling you here that this approach not only makes you party to other people's crimes against themselves but is a prescription for mediocrity and delusion.

Many people are surprised to discover that I'm a very spiritual person. After all, I run a business, I say what I think, and I wear all black; we have words for these things in this country: witch, bitch, and cunt. But the truth is that it's *faith* that gives me the power to speak my truth, and faith that makes me fierce. Being "spiritual" and being "nice" have absolutely nothing to do with each other, contrary to the popular notion that "spiritual" refers only to vegans in Whole Foods whispering to each other. Kindness is important, and the heart plays an important role in the progression of humanity, but I don't believe we should all just get naked and skip in the sun. Ultimately, we need to be able to battle our demons within and without to get where we want to go. Jesus turned over tables and defended hookers, and the Hindu goddesses were *not* messing around. Hanging in my office is a large image of the Hindu goddess Durga, who taught me a lot about spirituality. In her eight arms she bears swords, conch shells, tridents, thunderbolts, bows, and discuses: a weapon for every possible occasion. In the Gita, an Indian sacred text, she annihilates demons, rides lions, *and* makes divine love to her husband. (This sounds to me like the perfect day.)

I'm devoted to my job not because I love it, but because I look at it as my spiritual practice. There is a word for this in India: *karmayoga*. I am a karmayogi—someone who becomes conscious of herself and the Divine through work, not through meditation in some ashram or saying Hail Marys. On any given day I'm not just dressing naked male models or negotiating an appearance by a celebrity at one of my client's events, but figuring out who I am by doing what I do. You can do this in any field, of course, but there's nothing like a superficial industry to really make you want to know God and force you to be constantly rejecting false belief systems and defending the truth. New York, Los Angeles, Paris, London—these are places where lower human energies like greed, violence, and lust are always in play. (In fact, "luxury" is derived from *luxuria*; the first of the seven deadly sins, it literally means "lust.") If you work in this industry and have any clue as to what's going on, there will be moments when you think, *This can't be real—we have not just spent twelve hours trying to get a coconut-shell bikini through the agriculture inspectors at customs when there are sixteen thousand homeless kids in New York City!* If I weren't a spiritual person, I would have shot myself in the head a long time ago.

This circus of materialism and superficiality, however, has forced me to learn to trust and love myself and really know that I'm not what I do for a living. It's liberating to be forty-four years old, standing next to a six-foot model, and feeling no anger, resentment, or jealousy—to be able to appreciate her beauty while also loving myself. And it's liberating to be able to make a true, if incendiary, comment to *Women's Wear Daily* and stand by it rather than feeling embarrassed or ashamed. (I felt bad for my other clients and for the state of my industry, but I didn't feel one iota of remorse for knowing or owning up to knowing Ashley.) In a way, fashion is the karmayogi's ultimate ashram.

Of course, before fashion became my ashram, I was just a girl chasing a husband and a great wardrobe like everyone else I knew. The story of how I became a seeker is as unlikely to some people as the fact that I *am* one. I never really belonged to any religion before I moved to New York, least of all the Catholicism of my youth, but by the time I married Ronnie Cutrone I was a devout member of America's number-one denomination: capitalism and ego. (I'm sure most American households give more money to MasterCard than to their church.) My particular sect was the "Don't you know who I am" club, and we subscribed to several mantras: "I am who I know," "I am what I do," and "I am what I have." I never really considered that I was connected to something greater than Hermes—admittedly, a great thing to be connected to—or that there was something more to me than the numbers in my bank account or the solidity of my marriage.

Often the Goddess starts challenging this kind of complacency with gentle taps on your shoulder, asking quietly, "Do you want some help?" At which point, if you're like I was, you'll say, "No thanks, I'm having a really good time!" Eventually she hits you in the back of the head, and perhaps you again refuse help: "No, get out of here. I'm having a really good time!" Finally she sticks her stiletto in your heart chakra like a pre-op transvestite while putting cigarettes out on your body and demands, "Okay, are you ready to change *now*?" Basically, when destiny calls, we don't always go willingly. I certainly didn't. But after losing everything in the aftermath of my divorce, I had a profound spiritual awakening that changed everything I thought I knew about myself. My life would never be the same.

It happened in the fall of 1992. I was living in the decidedly un-chic Beverly Laurel Motel after being evicted from my house in Topanga Canyon for nonpayment of rent. The demands of my drug habit precluded any sort of real employment, so I'd taken to taping my old press clippings to the wall of my room and folding my clothes in alphabetical order by color to pass the time (amber, blue, cinnamon, dusty rose, evergreen). After selling off my Chanel jackets and other remnants of my life as a top PR girl to used-clothing stores like the Wasteland (one reason it's good to buy designer: if you bottom out, the resale value's much higher!), my days dissolved into a cycle of illusion, disillusion, hallucinations, sleep deprivation, isolation, loneliness, and all the other consorts of addiction. I had joined the underworld of people who are alive but not living.

One morning I awoke to a voice telling me there would be a miracle or I'd kill myself at midnight. *Thank God*, I thought. Then I went about my day, which eventually led me to my regular pit stop, the Bodhi Tree, a spiritual bookstore where I'd go to read about astrology and the cult of Mary Magdalene and where I'd sold books to pay for my motel room. I was sitting on a bench outside the store waiting for my cash when I saw him: a middle-aged man with white hair and a belly, walking toward me. "You better watch out, the moon is going to get you," he said, gesturing toward the full moon in the sky. Something in his tone pierced my pharmaceutical trance, and I started to cry. "Pal, can I get your number?" he asked. For reasons I can't explain, I told this man where I was staying and my room number.

It was past 11:00 p.m. when my phone rang. "Listen, pal," the man said. "I'm outside your hotel, and I have something for you." "I have an appointment at midnight," I snapped. "You'd better make it quick." I was already running the bathtub and beginning to undress, admiring my speed-freak body in the mirror. After several bouts with self-diagnosed anorexia, I had decided I was indeed thin enough for suicide in the bathtub naked.

When the man appeared at my door, he asked me if I was willing to go to any lengths to be in the light. "As long as I don't have to sleep with you," I replied matter-of-factly. I let him in to my room. He was wearing a sweatshirt and looked more like a Vietnam vet than a holy person. He told me to lie down on the bed; then, holding his hands about three inches over my body, he moved them through the air from my head to the tips of my toes. When he was finished, I felt my soul sit up into an erect position while my physical body lay supine, and I started to cry. Suspended in the air above the bed, as clear as day, floated the face of a woman I'd never seen before. She was Western yet also looked vaguely Indian; I thought she kind of looked like me. Her presence was, in that moment, the most real thing I had ever experienced. She was silent, beaming divine power and love with piercing eyes, and her gaze beckoned to a part of me I didn't know existed. I described her to the man, whose name was John, and he nodded. "You're one of the Mother's children," he said. He explained that the Mother had been a French-born guru living in India. Then he wrote down a mantra for me. *Om Anandamayi Chaitanyamayi Satyamayi Paramei.* "Say this in repetitions of three, and grow it like a garden inside yourself," he said. Then he left.

For the next six months, I would suffer nerve damage that left me forgetting how to spell words and occasionally having trouble writing, but that night marked the last time in my life I ever touched drugs. The morning after my vision, I woke up completely sober, left the hotel, and, aware that I had tested my parents to the breaking point, called my grandmother from a pay phone and pleaded with her to send me $500 via Western Union. I used the money to book another hotel room on the corner of Beverly and Spaulding.* The man at the front desk practically sneered at the ghastly sight of me. "This is not a cathouse," he said. I didn't even know what a cathouse was. (Evidently, it's a brothel.) "I'm having a very hard time, and I just want to pay," I told him. He let me check in, and for five days I endured the ravages of a truly horrifying detox. When I went in to the shower— which happened often because I was sweating profusely most of the time—it would appear to be filled with cockroaches. I barely ate. I did a lot of sitting on the floor and crying. Though both were pretty strong, my will to live was slowly beating out my will to die.

I soon ran into a girl I knew from New York who told me there was a club opening on La Cienega Boulevard called the Gate. She arranged for me to do PR for the opening, and with the $3,000 fee I was able to get a one-bedroom apartment for $625 a month. Once settled, I dedicated myself to a life of meditation and chanting the mantra John had written down for me. By this time I had lost or pushed away everything that had mattered to me, yet all I could see when I woke up each day was the sheer amount of beauty flooding my life and the world. There was so much I'd missed by indulging the lower energies of my mind: greed, ambition, insecurity, self-doubt, guilt. As I became conscious of something greater at my core—I couldn't prove

---

* I'd been told I was no longer welcome at the Beverly Laurel, owing to nonpayment and the constant presence of my drug dealer.

it, and still can't, but I *know* it—a huge weight lifted off me; I experienced the wonders of the world with something akin to childlike awe.

One day as I sat outside of Erewhon, a health food store in L.A., eating a snack I'd bought with whatever scant money I had, my eyes settled on a flock of pigeons. I was totally overwhelmed, transfixed even. When you really look at them, pigeons have all these amazing shades of purple and blue in their feathers. How had I never noticed? I had lived a fast life in New York and soared to the highest highs on drugs, and now here I was, a yogi having a profound experience with pigeon feathers! And all it had taken was giving up everything I had and washing up penniless and near death on Beverly Boulevard! I sincerely hope you don't have to take such a self-destructive path to get to the same place. But for me, it was through this demolition that my new world was built. I realized I didn't need any of the things I'd depended on. I had the whole tool kit already inside me. That day in front of Erewhon I felt true happiness and peace for the first time in my life. And, sister, I promise you that it was better than any drug I've ever taken.

I began wholeheartedly studying this woman known as the Mother who had appeared to me at the Beverly Laurel, reading everything about her I could get my hands on.* From the beginning, her teachings struck me as real and correct and totally relevant to my life. She became my *guru*, which simply means

* I learned that she was a Parisian-born Egyptian Turkish Jew whose life journey led her to Pondicherry, in the south of India, where she met and partnered with the Indian philosopher and guru Sri Aurobindo (who named her the Mother) in 1920. Something of a spiritual power-girl herself, she played tennis and drove a Bentley!

"teacher" in Sanskrit, initiating me into teachings and belief systems from Eastern mysticism and Hinduism to Kaballah and Tantra. I discovered goddesses like Durga, who challenged every perception I'd ever had of the feminine in religion; I began to understand that the Catholicism of my youth is not the only way to know "God." There are notions of the Divine that don't include the man with the thorns and the blood and a congregation of submissive, veiled, silent nuns. In fact, in ancient schools, women had power too and were worshiped equally. Native Americans refer to Mother Earth and Father Sky, and the Hindu gods Shiva and Kali are partners and draw their powers from each other—Kali can't dance without Shiva, and Shiva can't sleep without Kali. These feminine forces weren't just the weaker half of lopsided pairings, quietly riding on the donkey while Joseph figured everything out. I realized that all over the world women are taken to places of worship where they have no voice. Somehow it's even more ironic that we accept this second-class status in the United States, even as we fight for equality at home and in the workplace. This is why I'd instinctively flipped off religion growing up, and why I've refused to raise my daughter in any one religion.

As I set about assembling a set of beliefs that better represented me, my first thought was, *Why shouldn't He be a She?* So I appointed a She as head of my church and temple: the Goddess. (Of course, this Goddess is partnered with a God, her lover, collaborator and equal. We must not eliminate the male; we must embrace each other and transform.) I choose to believe that my soul is a unique and individual part of the divine feminine force in the universe, as is yours. If I had to describe my DIY religion, I'd say that I'm a Hindu-esque Tantric Toltec Priestess, which you've never heard of because I made it up. My religion is not about worshiping the divine at noon on Sundays, nor is my God locked away in a church to be visited once a week. My religion is about manifesting the Divine in myself and in everything I do. For me, the Goddess embodies compassion, perception, ruthlessness, and a total commitment to the destruction of falsity and ignorance; I aspire to embody and be all these things. The Mother remains my guru to this day, and I continue to consult her teachings for guidance. But ultimately my religion is deeply personal. I've used ancient belief systems as a way to dig through modern nonsense and really get at my core: to discover who I truly am and to understand what I'm meant to do here.

I'm not trying to convert you to my religion, or my concept of the Divine. I'm not the Mother's publicist, nor does she need one, and I don't think Eastern meditation is the answer for everyone. In fact, the Mother's spiritual partner, Sri Aurobindo, estimated that there are 64,000 paths to the Divine. What I am encouraging you to do is to think and to question. Too many people believe BMWs are great cars because everyone says they are, not because they've ever driven one. Too many people get married in Catholic churches because their parents want them to, not because that institution provides them with any spiritual meaning. I'm suggesting that you don't have to go to churches that don't honor you, and you don't have to tithe your money to institutions that don't believe in birth control. You can instead appoint yourself High Priestess of your *own* religion, and you can

TWELVE STEPS TO STARTING YOUR OWN RELIGION

To start your own religion, you must be open to the idea that there is no one religion unifying the whole world and that we must step away from strict religious affiliations and envision and embrace a new world where people are allowed to have their own concept of God and the Goddess, where each person is entitled to worship, embrace, and know the Divine without conflict, war, or persecution.

Although starting your own religion may seem like a lofty endeavor, the time is now and you are indeed a pioneer. As a love-bringer who will help transform the earth, human beings, and, yes, even yourself, you are a part of a new truth. Following these suggestions will help you manifest that truth.

[1]   Uncover, discover, or recover *your true self*.

[2]   Accept the fact that you have been programmed by society, your family, religions, Hollywood, and other influences. Become fully conscious of this programming so that you can deprogram yourself and resist what society has been demanding of you.

[3]   Forge an unprecedented alliance with yourself. Most people don't have an intimate relationship with the caring voice of knowingness that is actually a part of each one of us. *The Divine lives in you. You are divine.*

start by examining what it is you're already worshiping. If you're in a store spending all your rent money on a single article of clothing, awaken to the idea that there might be a better church for you than Gucci. Book a trip to Oaxaca, Mexico, or Machu Picchu or Stonehenge or Paris or the Grand Canyon or any number

[4] Study as many spiritual texts as you can, including philosophers from Plato to Tolle, Sri Aurobindo, Amma, Castaneda, and beyond.

[5] Attend different churches, temples, and synagogues and worship with everyone from Sufis to Muslims to Catholics to Jews.

[6] Take what you like from each religious tradition you encounter—in other words, *what resonates with you*—and leave the rest.

[7] Weave all of your truths together, then piece together one big quilt of your true beliefs.

[8] Ask yourself why anyone would place God in a building to be visited at their leisure. Promise yourself that you will never do this with your religion. *Incorporate conscious contact with the Divine into your daily life.*

[9] Be open to new lessons.

[10] Tell the truth no matter what.

[11] Let the truth be expressed in your life at this moment with abundant and balanced energy.

[12] Celebrate and cultivate the health, strength, beauty, and ease of your physical body. Be happy in your body.

of other sacred places around the world. Study as many religions and teachings as possible; take what you like from each and leave the rest. Visit a mosque, a chapel, a temple, an ashram, and while you're there read the great texts. Women should spend as much time looking for a religion of their own as they do trying to find a hot guy to have sex with. Because let's be honest: there are too many examples of magic and miracles in this world to say with any certainty that there isn't something fantastically wonderful going on here. The searing emptiness I felt after my divorce taught me one thing, and it was one more thing my mother never told me: if you don't have faith in yourself and in something larger than yourself, and if you want to take this world at face value, you're going to have a fucking nasty ride.

Perhaps you're wondering how I went from blissed-out yogi in L.A. to overtaxed—I mean this in more ways than one—fashion publicist in New York. As the days of my detox churned into a spiritual awakening, I received what I can only describe as a cosmic installation giving me the ability to read tarot cards. Luckily my entrepreneurial spirit was still intact, so I took my new gift to Venice Beach, where I gave readings to tourists, Angelenos, and freaks on the boardwalk every weekend. Whatever compelled me to take the hour-long bus ride from West Hollywood to Venice Beach that first day, I can't really explain; it *must* have been a force greater than myself. But as my readings got better and I turned up the charm, my business grew, and soon I had private clients. The business that started out with $10 donations on the boardwalk grew to $120-an-hour consultations in my apartment in West Hollywood. I even supplemented my income by chatting on the phone for $3.99 a minute on the Psychic Friends Network.

Meanwhile, I took my first tentative steps into the fashion business. I started going out to thrift stores in the Valley to buy interesting pieces of clothing priced at $4.25 that I could flip for $15 at the Wasteland, the same vintage and resale store where I'd desperately pawned my Chanel jackets for $50 not so long before. I was just trying to eat, but as a natural kar-mayogi, I couldn't help but pour my heart into my work, and my side businesses were soon flourishing. Totally by coincidence, I received a call one day from one of the owners of the Wasteland. He was looking for someone to do his PR, he said, and he'd heard that I was a publicist from New York. Was I interested? I found it mildly devastating to consider represent-ing a used-clothing store on Melrose when I'd formerly worked with people like Frank Sinatra, but the Wasteland was offering me $3,000 a month, which I couldn't refuse. It was certainly a lot more than my fledgling resale operation would ever bring in. I turned again to the teachings of the Mother, who advo-cated getting off the ashram, so to speak, and taking not just your knowledge and peace and joy but your character defects as well—in other words, your whole self—out into the streets. *Then* we'll see what you're made of, she said; *then* we'll see who's spiritual. (Her teachings echoed the exhortations of my actual mother, for whom watching me make my living on the Venice Beach boardwalk had been almost as terrifying as wit-nessing my descent into drugs. "You can't keep living like this!" she'd blurt out when we spoke.)

From the Wasteland job, my career took off quickly. No sooner had I begun working out of an office in the back of the store than a friend called me up saying that she knew a woman who wanted to sell her vast collection of vintage Pucci and did I know anybody who might want to buy it? In fact, I *did*. I arranged for my clients at the Wasteland to purchase the collection, branded it "The world's largest collection of vintage Pucci" and arranged a party, a fashion show and a sale, which tripled the store's revenue in under one month. I also secured a feature story on the front page of the *Los Angeles Times*. Encouraged by my success, I went on to snag the store a three-page feature in *Vogue* that focused on its celebrity clientele. The Wasteland was a local L.A. phenomenon no longer—and I was officially a publicist again.

Next, I signed the Sunset Marquis Hotel, and soon after that Deepak Chopra came calling. "Shut up," I told my assistant when she came in to tell me he was on the phone. "Take a message." I certainly did not believe that Deepak Chopra was calling me—but I was wrong. He'd gotten my name through a mutual acquaintance, and he and Rasa Records owner Donna D'Cruz wanted me to do PR for his new record, which featured people like Demi Moore, Madonna, and Goldie Hawn reading the poems of Rumi. Just like that, I went from reading tarot cards on the boardwalk to counting one of the most famous spiritual figures in the country among my clients. The flower was in bloom; I was an up-and-coming power-girl entrepreneur yet again.

This time, however, I was determined to do things differently. My business pursuits weren't exempt from my divine aspirations to show compassion and destroy falsity (even though, as with any yoga practice, I would have to keep making these efforts for years before they really came naturally). I wasn't just accumulating status and possessions, as I'd done in my early twenties. I now knew that I am ultimately here to take in the adventure of life and to know and express my highest self and best qualities, thereby doing my part to transform the earth. This knowledge almost always makes my course of action clear.

For instance, when I saw a man violently hit his child at an airport in Mexico recently, I walked right up to him and told him he was a monster while fifty other adults stood around thinking, *Gee, I'm kind of uncomfortable about this* (I'd like to stress that I was in an international terminal full of people from all over the world). Guess what? You're also implicated. All of us are taught to sit back and just watch this sort of thing when it happens. But ask yourself: Why do you act, or not act? Who are you defending? What are you doing here on this earth? My odyssey in the years since my vision has repeatedly tested everything I learned about myself in my days as a yogi, forcing me to slay demons again and again, but I look at every challenge and mistake as an opportunity to progress. And most of the time my beliefs steel me with the power to speak my truth and take responsibility for it. *This*, to me, is true freedom.

At first I thought young women would be afraid of me because of how harshly I'm portrayed on television, but when I meet them walking around my neighborhood or traveling to L.A. or flying to London for London Fashion Week, they all want to know how they can be power-bitches too. They want to own their own companies and be truth warriors and achieve the same freedom I've fought so hard for. I believe all women know in their heart of hearts that they truly are divine and magical, even if they've temporarily forgotten. Speaking the truth has made me some enemies. But it has also gotten me much further than I would have otherwise progressed in life. Let's face it: being nice does not always remove obstacles, and in fact sometimes it creates them. That's why, the next time you hug someone you secretly despise and say, "It's great to see you," I want you to bite your lip. You don't have to say anything you do not mean, and I urge you not to. The night I was fired by Yigal Azrouel, while I was still reeling from my industry's prudish and hysterical reaction to Ashley Dupre—I mean, let's face it, this girl would've been on her way to being a huge star by now in Europe!—I called another of my clients, Jeremy Scott, and told him to make me a T-shirt that said, WHAT WOULD MADONNA DO? "Oh please, I don't need to make you a T-shirt," Jeremy replied. "Madonna would've grabbed that girl by her ponytail, made out with her, and said, 'Why are you talking about my girlfriend like that?'" Suddenly I realized that I hadn't maximized my moment.

FIVE

WORRIER TO WARRIOR

> The spirit of a warrior is not geared to indulging and complaining, nor is it geared to winning or losing. The spirit of a warrior is geared only to struggle, and every struggle is a warrior's last battle on earth. Thus the outcome matters very little to him. In his last battle on earth a warrior lets his spirit flow free and clear. And as he wages his battle, knowing that his intent is impeccable, a warrior laughs and laughs.
>
> —Carlos Castaneda

If anyone really wanted to change the world, they'd bring in the fashion bitches, because nobody gets things done faster. If we went about saving the world like we go about producing fashion shows, well, let's just say New Orleans after Katrina would've been fucking *sorted*. (We'd all have been wearing Paul Smith wellies and barking, "What do you mean your head's bleeding? Get up, let's go, *move!*") My experience in the fashion industry has taught me to act confidently and decisively, without regret or self-doubt—in other words, with detachment from the outcome, which is the end goal of any good yogi. At this point I've experienced most of the possible frightening outcomes, and I'm still alive, as is my business. This is why, while I may be intense during the day, when people ask me how I sleep at night, I tell them I sleep like a fucking baby. Detachment doesn't mean I'm trying less hard. It just means that fears and emotions that used to torment and paralyze me no longer have the same power over me. Getting to this point hasn't always been easy; it took me years to really learn to silence my mind. But as you move through your career and your life, you will have to learn that if you're not what you do, then what you do has no business keeping you entertained at night.

When I first started People's Revolution in Los Angeles in the midnineties, it had one employee: me. I did all my own FedExing, answered my own phone, and crafted all my own pitches to the press. I even got my own coffee. Not that this held me back. After the Wasteland's feature in *Vogue*, I set my sights on *People*, which soon ran a huge spread highlighting the store's crocheted shrugs, worn by celebrities like Erykah Badu and Fiona Apple at the time. When I signed the Sunset Marquis Hotel, I was suddenly a fashion and lifestyle publicist making $7,000 a month with virtually no overhead. (*This*, I still believe, is a genius way to do PR.) As People's Revolution grew, I hired an assistant, incorporated my business, took on a partner, rented a cute little house in West Hollywood as my office, and took on even *more* clients to be able to afford all this. But the Mother was right when she said that taking your spirituality to the streets and actually putting it to work is much harder than living in an ashram and meditating all day (or reading tarot cards in the beach, as the case may be). I soon found myself victimized by familiar thought patterns— most persistently fear—despite my newfound spiritual perspective. I had more to lose materially than I'd had in a while, so some fear was inevitable, even productive. But when a prestigious client like Bulgari or Valentino left, as PR clients eventually do, I became convinced that my whole business would collapse. I worried constantly about clients leaving me or staff members quitting. I couldn't shake the notion that *they* were somehow responsible for my success—not me.

My fears got so out of hand that I didn't even need an actual event to trigger them. A single thought would creep uninvited into my mind at the grocery store, at my desk, or even when I was having sex, and suddenly I'd be barreling down this freeway of fear, and it would be packed, with no off-ramps or exit signs. *Something really bad is going to happen to you, you'd better work harder, something really bad is going to happen to you, he's going to fire you, you're going to lose everything, you're going to be all by yourself, you'll be HOMELESS. And by the way, that guy you're dating is cheating on you!* These thoughts would have their way with me, wracking me with self-doubt and paranoia, then leave me by the side of the road, spent. I'd have another three or four days of freedom before they came back again. *You're a faker, you're going to lose everything; you know it's true.*

How did I get to this place? And why was I so attached to the things I had anyway? I called Mikael, my longtime spiritual adviser in India and a prominent member of my tribal council; I'd met Mikael through a friend years earlier and had been consulting with him on matters such as these ever since.* He suggested that I fight my incessant internal chatter: "Your problem is that your name means 'Warrior,' but all you are is a Worrier," he said. "Why don't you drop the 'O' and put in an 'A'?" Once I started thinking of myself as a spiritual warrior, my life started making a lot more sense. I turned to the controversial anthropologist and

---

* Mikael is the one constant in my life who doesn't live in the United States, work in the fashion business, or want any of my money.

philosopher Carlos Castaneda. He described the warrior in *The Wheel of Time: The Shamans of Mexico, Their Thoughts About Life, Death, and the Universe*:

> We talk to ourselves incessantly about our world. In fact we maintain our world with our internal talk. And whenever we finish talking to ourselves about ourselves and our world, the world is always as it should be. We renew it, we rekindle it with life, we uphold it with our internal talk. Not only that, but we also choose our paths as we talk to ourselves. Thus we repeat the same choices over and over until the day we die, because we keep on repeating the same internal talk over and over until the day we die. A warrior is aware of this and strives to stop his internal talk.

My "internal talk" was not just a nuisance: it was trapping me in repetitive action and paralyzing me into *in*action. I had become a deer in the headlights of my own life. And I wasn't alone: many people spend large portions of their lives in this state. Fear is big business, and companies from Hollywood studios to insurance giants spend millions of dollars a year to keep our freeways of fear packed and our "internal talk" on high volume: *Wow, your child was just admitted to the hospital with a life-threatening illness, too bad you didn't switch to Geico!* Or: *New York City is going to be demolished by a giant tidal wave!* Or: *If you don't buy this product, you'll look wrinkled and old and no man will ever want you!* Our minds—inclined toward repetition, not progress—absorb and play all this back to us in difficult times, parroting society's negative views on women in power, dwelling on past failures, or repeating nasty things our clients have said to us. The mind uses fear throughout our lives as one of many blunt objects with which to clock our soul over the head before gagging it, binding it with black electrical tape, and throwing it out of the driver's seat and into the trunk. This is what sends us off the path of our destiny and onto the packed freeway of fear—or worse, into a traffic circle (and we all know how dangerous those are). For all my supposed spirituality, I had to get out of my own way. I was so caught up in doomsday visions of the future that I'd entirely lost sight of any joy in the present.

So I started to play ball with my fears. "Bring it!" I'd say when seized by that familiar pit in my stomach. Or: "Party on, motherfucker, tell me more." I asked my fear exactly what it had to say to me. *You're going to lose everything and you'll be out on the street.* "Okay," I'd reply. "I can stay with friends." *Well, you can only do that for three days, since they're going to get tired of you.* "All right, well, then, I can go to Virginia and stay with my parents. And I'll totally lose my mind there, but I'll only be there for six months, because in six months I will have thought of something that will get me back on my feet. Or, plan B, if I go out of business, I'll move to southern India, where I'll teach in a school and have no money to ever travel back to the U.S." I followed my fears to their worst possible conclusions, becoming penniless and alone (these are most people's worst fears), and what I realized each time was that no matter what happened, I was going to be *fine*. I remembered that family and tribe members are key, but also that ultimately I have everything I need to survive inside of me.

There are a million other yogic tricks a warrior can use to quiet his or her mind and banish it to the backseat (or better yet, the trunk). Some people suggest watching your fears like a movie in your head until you become desensitized to them. I also like writing them down over and over again, hundreds of times—*I'm going to lose everything, I'm going to lose everything, I'm going to lose everything, I'm going to lose everything*—until the words lose their power. Then I can burn the paper in the kitchen sink and literally watch them turn to smoke. (If you're really feeling adventurous, you could try this in your backyard or in one of those holy places I told you to visit!) There is also the garden metaphor: your negative thoughts are weeds strangling the progress of your soul; you must find a way to kill them. Killing the weeds won't keep them from growing back, but it's like waxing: eventually, if you keep waxing, your hair growth just becomes less and less.

The problem with "internal talk" is that it masquerades as intuition. Sometimes your fears really are conveying a message from your inner voice, whether it's telling you to work harder or pointing out that you're dating a domineering asshole who will never change. This is why a warrior needs a highly developed sense of discernment. Fear of losing everything becomes less irrational in a worldwide recession, after all. My company had been on a huge streak when the economy began its long plunge in 2008, and suddenly certain clients couldn't pay their bills and I found myself having to be their psychotherapist in addition to their accountant and publicist. I had thoughts like, *Did I really work my ass off to build this business for the last twelve years only to have it all come crashing down on top of me?* I was seriously considering closing my Paris office and wondering whom I'd have to sue for payment. Rather than banish my fear, or think *That's preposterous, that'll never happen to me, I'm protected by the Goddess*, I knew it made sense to ask, *Am I being wasteful somewhere? Are my results less than they have been? How do I receive my clients when they call me? How do I decrease my overhead and increase my revenue?* I like to think of fear as a messenger that doesn't always make sense: you have to figure out who sent fear before you can dismiss it outright.

I learned to do this in the long, arduous days after my drug detox, when I'd moved out of the run-down Beverly Laurel Motel and into a tiny apartment on Spaulding, where I formed a habit of scrounging together sixty-eight cents every afternoon to run down the street to the gas station to buy a doughnut. I followed this routine like clockwork. Four o'clock would roll around, and I *had* to have a doughnut. After all, I was off other substances, and I really loved these doughnuts. One day John asked me why I was always running out for a doughnut. "Close your eyes and ask yourself what would happen if you did not get that doughnut," he said. "I really need a doughnut," I said. I knew by that time that spirituality is often about doing away with things we've become attached to, and frankly, I wasn't in the mood. Still, I closed my eyes and asked myself what would happen if I didn't go out for a doughnut. That's when a thunderous voice inside me shrieked, *"You will die!!!"* "Well, then," said John, satisfied, "do you really think that is the voice of God?" I've used this so-called doughnut barometer over the years in moments when I am gripped by worries over anything from my daughter's safety to my ability to make my payroll. If you ask yourself often enough, *Is this the voice of God?* the answer usually becomes obvious. A voice telling you that you suck, that you're not important, that you're heading toward impending doom of some kind or another, is probably not the voice of your soul, or the Divine, or the Goddess. But if there *is* an important message to be found in your thought, you must take positive action immediately in order to glean it. For me, during the recession, that meant calling my clients more often to check in, cutting costs, more actively managing certain accounts, and laying off staff members who weren't pulling their weight. Once you've acted positively on a legitimate fear to the best of your ability, then, if it persists, it's time to banish that fear to the backseat too.

If you allow fear to live inside of you after you've already put it to any possible good use—if you allow your mind, instead of your soul, to drive your car—you risk more than just finding yourself on a hamster wheel. You also increase the possibility that you'll manifest that fear and negative thinking outwardly. One of my best friends—a totally hot, sexy woman and one of the coolest women I've ever met—once fell madly in love with an actor twenty-five years younger than she was. The age difference gave her pause, but she decided to marry him anyway. They were very happy together, except for one thing: she was terrified on a daily basis that he was going to leave her for a younger woman. *Every. Day.* She'd say things like, "Oh my God, he's in an acting class, those girls are so pretty, I feel so old, oh my God!" Soon enough she got pregnant, at which point her fears only intensified: "Oh my God, I'm so fat, he's going to leave me, *Oh. My. God!*" What do you think happened? After four years of marriage, her husband came home one day and said, "I'm leaving you." He left her for someone his own age. I don't think he would have left her had that not already been her reality. Thoughts have power. Fear of being left was so much a part of her world and her thinking that she manifested her own divorce.

I believe that the universe constantly rearranges itself to support your idea of reality. If you're always thinking, *Life sucks, and I suck*, you're definitely going to see a lot of dismal shit out there. On the other hand, if your idea of reality is that you're a privileged, elegant human being and every day you think, *I am a privileged, elegant human being, I am a privileged, elegant human being*, then eventually you will become a privileged and elegant human being. It may take five minutes or it may take five years, but that will become your experience of yourself.

Fighting the tyranny of your mind and freeing yourself to enjoy the journey, stumbles and all, is a lifelong process. There will be plenty of days in your life and career when you feel like you literally do not have air left in your lungs. I haven't exactly cured myself of fear and doubt either. Sometimes, while sitting in my office late at night, I'll feel it welling up inside of me and have to say, *"Oh my God, are you still there? How much longer are we going to be in this relationship?"*

In the summer of 2002, with New York still reeling from the job losses and concentrated regional despair of September 11, 2001, the fashion industry held several town hall meetings to discuss how to handle Fashion Week, which would fall on the one-year anniversary of 9/11 (and which had been in progress during the attacks). We wondered: Where is the rule book for this? Are we allowed to do something so frivolous and shallow as a fashion show on the first anniversary of such a tragedy, with so many people to be honored and so many families' feelings to be respected? How will there ever be a place again for something like Fashion Week? As concern among my colleagues grew, I knew *I* didn't want to live in fear and try to be less than celebratory so that everyone could feel okay on a day that I thought should be a celebration of the strength of a people and our ability to *not* be held back by fear. I also thought Fashion Week was a great way to bring beauty back into the world. So while my competitors backed off the fashion show time slots at the Bryant Park tents on September 11, 2002, I made a deal with IMG—the company that produces Fashion Week—to take all three tents for my clients and produce an arduous load of six shows on the same day, among them Asfour, Jeremy Scott, Alexandre Herchcovitz, and Rachel Comey. I was able to wrangle good financial deals for these clients, who were thrilled.

However, even though I haven't exactly made a career for myself by playing it safe, some industry friends were scared for me. They thought my clients would be overshadowed by media attention to the anniversary, and they worried about how the press would react to fashion shows being held on such a day. I had plenty of moments when I wondered what I'd gotten myself into (and whether anyone would come to the shows), but ultimately my fears were mere shadows of what they might have been ten years earlier. The Fashion Week experience that year was kind of like giving birth: I was going to have this baby, and it was going to be fine. That day, as I dashed furiously between tents, presiding over backstage areas in rehearsal while catching snippets of my clients' actual shows on the television monitors set up outside in the park for passersby, I also felt a great sigh of relief from my colleagues. Many had seen their shows canceled the year before, after all, and their businesses had been devastated in the last year. The industry was grateful that business was going on as usual, and I was proud to be a part of that.

We've already established that life is going to kick you in your ass sometimes and that there's no way to avoid that, but if you get up and keep doing what you do, giving your best self each time, you eventually achieve not only success but that great psychic coup of detachment. After years of worrying that banks would close me down, that clients wouldn't pay me, or that I'd get sued for missing articles of clothing that weren't returned to me by editors, I now employ four lawyers and do business through airtight contracts, and when I'm served with court papers, my response is more like: "Oh, hi, how are you?" The fashion industry is excellent yoga for a naturally fearful person like me in part because its fast-paced, apocalyptic energy requires that you feel and act, not think. In fact, for years I'd call Mikael with a problem and say, "What do you think about that?" and he would reply, "I do not think. I feel." There are some things that the Goddess just takes away from us—my addiction, for example—and others that we're supposed to work through step by step in this lifetime so that we can have the power of victory over them. Often you can't achieve this victory without experiencing pain until you have no emotional, physical, or psychic response to it anymore.

Take my old fear of losing my business when a client fired me. A few years ago, a fashion designer client asked me to meet him to discuss his upcoming show. He wanted to review the collection and hear all my ideas about what he should do for the next six months. At the end of our meeting, having gotten the whole thing on tape, he fired me. It was frustrating to give all this freshness and good intent to the relationship with the understanding that it was a continuing collaboration, and then to have my ideas basically stolen. But I didn't flinch. His words didn't penetrate me or send me careening off-course. I'd already spent years asking myself whether I was a good publicist and a hard worker and a valid person, and I knew the answers to those questions. I just told him he was a disgusting human being and that any time I had the opportunity to share that with other people in the industry, it would be my pleasure.

In an industry like fashion, people always behave badly all around you, but if you resolve to become a spiritual warrior, you learn to laugh and laugh, knowing that other people don't define you and that ultimately their behavior is just helping you work out your own shit. For a publicist, being fired can be its very own yoga! I personally have been practicing it for years, and I can now say I'm an expert.

Several years ago, I represented Brad Korzen, a now-prominent hotelier best known for the design-y Viceroy Hotels. We launched his first signature property, the Avalon in Beverly Hills, we helped christen it a fashion-crowd hangout, and we even helped transform his girlfriend (now his wife), Kelly Wearstler, from *Playboy* pet to *Vogue*-sanctioned interior designer. But one

Monday morning not long before Brad was to open the Viceroy in Santa Monica, he called me up and said, "Did you know more people kill themselves on Monday than any other day of the year?" I admitted that this was news to me. "Listen," he continued, "I just want to tell you that you're a really great publicist, but you're the only publicist I've ever had, and I thought it would be good to change the energy up a bit before the Viceroy opens. But I also want to tell you that if I'm not happy, I'll come back to you, and I hope that we can remain friends." Ouch. I was tempted to allow the situation to drag me into familiar thought patterns: *What's wrong with me? Am I a bad publicist? Is my business going to tank? Maybe I need to be smarter, maybe I need to work harder, maybe I need to part my hair differently, maybe I need to wear more makeup, maybe I need to wear* less *makeup, maybe I need to be clearer in my speech? Is my business going to tank?* But I knew that People's Revolution had done an excellent job for Brad and that he'd been written up all over the world. I had also already been fired enough times to know that Brad wouldn't make or break me. Instead of collapsing into sobs, as I might have at twenty-four, I picked up my scepter. "Okay," I told Brad. "But let me tell *you* something. I feel like I've been married to you for seventeen years and you just told me you want to go out and fuck the tennis coach. Fine, go fuck the tennis coach, but don't come back to my house afterwards."

SIX

CHECK YOUR PRECONCEIVED NOTIONS AT THE DOOR

Not even the slickest
wordsmith or spinning
spin master can describe
the delight and dedication
which is motherhood. This
is a secret society which
words cannot touch, but
the heart holds dear.

—Kelly Cutrone

For women, life is set up like a video game. It starts out in childhood with the Disney princesses, followed by the need to become the prettiest girl, the pop star, or the model, and then, in high school, we're told that it's time to become the thinnest girl, then to become successful, find a guy, convince him to move in with us, get married, have a baby, and live happily ever after! (Hell, *yeah*!) We're constantly moving from level to level, trying to collect the promised prizes, without stopping to think about the order *we* want these things to come in, or whether we even really want them at all. From *Cinderella* right on up to *He's Just Not That into You*, we're inundated with programming that influences how and when we think we should experience various life steps and that makes it devastating when we find ourselves in another position altogether. Many of us grew up with our mothers literally serenading us with the words: *First comes love, then comes marriage, then comes a baby in a baby carriage.* Yes, our own mothers! The Life-bringers themselves are in on this conspiracy.

The unavoidable truth is that in the real world things don't always come in the order we're taught to expect them. A lot of women ask me, "How do you have it all?" I tell them that it's not actually that hard to have it all; you just can't always have it all in the same proportion or at the same time. Sometimes your career is winning, sometimes it's your peace of mind, sometimes it's your faith, sometimes it's motherhood, and occasionally, if you're lucky, it's your love life. I didn't set out to become a single mother, but I was not totally surprised when I became one at thirty-five—even though I'd been married twice by then. Long-term relationships are difficult for me. I also have a hard time biting my tongue. If my partner's flirting with a waitress at a diner, I'm going to want to go at it on that topic right then and there, whereas people who live together peacefully are probably able to let some things pass. I was forced to accept at a certain point that I was likely to end up on my own. But as I do with most glorious, challenging, and worthwhile tasks, I not only made the best of my single, unplanned mother-hood but *excelled* at it. And I learned that when things happen out of order in your life, you can choose to take them not as blows but as blessings in disguise.

I found out I was pregnant with my daughter Ava at 11:30 p.m. on September 10, 2001, smack in the middle of New York Fashion Week. I was making my way back to my SoHo loft after a long day of producing runway shows and had stopped at a phar-macy, where I bought a box of Honey Nut Cheerios (something I had a strange new passion for), paper towels, laundry detergent, and a pregnancy test. To be honest, I don't even remember pur-chasing the test, but when I got home, there it was in my bag. I figured that, like the other tests I'd taken over the years, this one would turn out negative, a result I'd always greeted with a burst of relief and a tinge of hidden sadness. But no, not this night. I was soon staring at two pink bars. And, well, I was delighted!

It wasn't exactly the best timing. If someone had told me I'd be separating from my second husband, breaking up with my original partner in People's Revolution, moving from Los Angeles back to New York to run a growing bicoastal company, and draining my savings account to pay a team of lawyers to oversee these changes—all while pregnant by a man who was not my husband but rather an incredibly sophisticated and sexy Italian nine years my junior who I'd met in Paris while producing my first couture show—even *I* would have said they were crazy. I'd finally moved into my spacious new home and office on Grand Street just in time to see my world—and *the* world— utterly change.

I remember running upstairs before I went to bed that night to grab *Savitri*, an epic tome by Sri Aurobindo, the Indian philosopher who was the Mother's spiritual partner. I closed my eyes as I flipped through the pages, thinking, *Is this something I'm meant to do now? Is this the right time? Mother, please tell me: what is this about?* It was my way of asking for a sign that I could handle motherhood on top of a life that was already careening again toward insanity—even if much less destructively than the first time around in my early twenties. My finger landed on a paragraph that talked about new children coming down the amber stairs from the Divine into this world. It read:

I saw the Omnipotent's flaming pioneers
Over the heavenly verge which turns towards life
Come crowding down the amber stairs of birth;
Forerunners of a divine multitude,
Out of the paths of the morning star they came
Into the little room of mortal life.
I saw them cross the twilight of an age,
The sun-eyed children of a marvellous dawn.

I felt like the Goddess was talking to me through the pages of this book, telling me that my unborn daughter was one of "the Omnipotent's flaming pioneers." I'd opened to the only page of the book's 956 pages that even mentioned children. Taking the passage as a clear sign that my pregnancy was indeed meant to be, I called my daughter's father, Ilario. We'd been dating for only two months, but we were in love, and he was very excited to hear the news. Next I called my friend Myra, a fifty-two-year-old power-girl publicist who had never had children. "Kelly," she said, "this is a blessing. We are going to have *so much fun!*"

My parents were a different story. "I know you're in love with Romeo or whatever his name is, but being a mother and being in love are two different things," cautioned my father when I called to share the news. "I *know* you, and this relationship might not last, so you need to ask yourself, do you want to be a mother or do you just want to be a family? Because those are often two different things." He ended our conversation with a vote of confidence in me. "If you were eighteen years old, we'd be having a different conversation," he said. "But you're thirty-five, and if anyone can do this, Kel, it's you." It was good advice, especially coming from a man who had once threatened the life of my prom date.

My mom, who had already taken in several of my dogs, was less supportive. She wanted to make sure I was in a position to actually *watch* this child. At that point I became very upset with her for even raising such a question and told her that if she continued to speak like that she'd never meet her grandchild. I had a lot of unknowns in my life, but I never doubted for one minute that I'd be a good mother. I reminded my mom that I'd been raising young women in my office for years, not to mention devotedly taking care of my clients, and that the only reason I'd shipped my dog off to her anyway was that I was living on Christopher Street at the time and the poor beast happened to be terrified of drag queens. In other words: *how dare she?*

My euphoria was short-lived. The next morning my phone rang. It was Ilario, calling from Paris to tell me he'd just watched a plane crash into one of the World Trade Center towers on TV. I looked out my window and saw the second plane hit, and then the two towers were suddenly engulfed in flames, just blocks from my apartment. This was the moment I became a mother. I ran to the back of my loft, still cluttered with boxes, and began sweetly consoling Ava in my womb. "Do not worry," I told her. "We are going to be just *fine*, baby, just fine."

Weeks passed, and as my father had stopped short of predicting, Ilario and I split up—distance and hormones were not on our side—leaving me single, well on my way to gaining a whopping seventy pounds, and struggling to run a business in a wounded, reeling city that seemed eerily abandoned. I finally had to acknowledge that the modern, very empowered, very *difficult* version of motherhood I was about to undertake would be nothing like the one I'd always envisioned. I had been raised to think that I'd be married at the birth of my child, that a man would be present in the delivery room, and that he would put a cold compress on my forehead and give me ice pops and buy me a birth gift. Instead, I had a stick-thin fashion editor and a lesbian couple vying to see me through to the delivery room. As much as I appreciated their can-do, girl-power camaraderie, I was scared to death. This was not the VIP list at a nightclub; it was the birth of my child, and when it came down to it, I was alone.

I tried to console myself with thoughts like, *How much harder can this be than having a dog?* At the time I had a beloved Boston terrier named Japa. Unfortunately, about a month into my pregnancy, she was eaten by coyotes in L.A., where I'd sent her to stay with my soon-to-be ex-husband while I was busy with Fashion Week. When I heard the news of her death, I began crying hysterically in my office. It sounded like whales mating. All heads in the office turned in my direction as the troops froze in fear: *Leader having breakdown! Leader having breakdown!* I couldn't shake the possible symbolism here. Eaten by coyotes! What did it mean? Was this what became of sentient beings for whom I was responsible? I immediately called Mikael, who tried to console me by explaining that Japa was a guardian and a protector, that her work here was done, and that her death had nothing to do with my pregnancy. That still didn't change the fact that I was single, emotional, and pregnant and my dog was dead.

Luckily, I had little time to sit around thinking, *What's going to happen to me?* I was gaining weight the way only a Mediterranean village girl could, which distracted me from the larger, more terrifying issues at hand and helped me focus on several urban single power-girl pregnancy challenges. First, I could *not* wear maternity clothes—ugh, yuck, no way, no thanks, never! Pea in the Pod made me want to kill myself. What were these fabrics? *Floral prints?* I was sure I'd rather clean toilets than be seen in them. And as for those little tie-back tunics infesting downtown Manhattan's paltry selection of maternity boutiques: maybe useful as a beach umbrella in Tunisia, darling, but they certainly weren't meant to be worn. After all, I was no longer a music publicist—I was in fashion. It was bad enough that I had to carry my groceries in the middle of winter by myself—I could not possibly do it in these outfits. Their bland, vaguely submissive frilliness threatened to drain all of my hard-won strength and ball-busting, soon-to-be single mom courage. In a moment of deep sartorial despair I called a friend at *Vogue* magazine. "What am I going to do?" I complained. "I cannot be seen in these clothes. They'll put me out of business *and* into a mental hospital!" She told me to go to a Hare Krishna temple—this was what she'd done during her pregnancy—to buy a series of Indian Punjabi outfits in muted tones. She warned me that black might not be available.

I have to say, the Krishnas make a lovely vegetarian lunch, and their oversized pure cotton clothes were an oasis in a depressing polyester pregnancy-wear slum.

Burgeoning curves accommodated, I began fretting that I'd

be fired by some of my image-conscious clients for getting fat. (This was long before Nicole Richie and Angelina Jolie started on procreative tears and baby bumps became a hot accessory in *Us Weekly*.) I managed to keep my condition a secret from clients and professional acquaintances for just two months, at which point the legendary designer Paco Rabanne outed me during Paris Fashion Week after I produced his runway show. "Kell-eee, why didn't you tell us you were pregnant?" he screamed. We were eating lunch with a bunch of editors and industry friends at the Costes, the trendy fashion hotel for rich attention-seekers (and certainly one of the last places on earth I'd want to have my secret revealed at deafening volume). Paco, who considers himself something of a psychic, informed the group with certainty that it would be a girl. There were screams of *"What?"* as everyone looked to me for confirmation, which I provided with a tentative nod.

Luckily, Paco didn't fire me; those fears, at least, were unfounded. But I still had others to address, such as: could I really go alone to birthing classes? I didn't think I could stomach the idea of watching yuppie couples *Ooooo* and *Ahhhh* together on yoga mats while I sat huffing and puffing alone. I don't even like group sports. Besides, girls of fifteen and sixteen in some parts of the world just walk into rice fields and pop out babies all on their own. I was thirty-five years old, a woman of the world; surely I could manage this. I decided to skip the birthing classes.

Instead, I turned to a doula, the hottest new concept in childbirthing. I met Amy Brown, a ripped, no-nonsense, very New York birth coach who looked like Linda Hamilton in *Terminator*, through my well-connected gynecologist, Dr. Moritz. Amy's role would be to coach me, to serve as an advocate on my behalf at the hospital, and to prevent me from being overmedicated or—worse in her mind—getting an epidural. She was a cross between a best friend, a mom, an action hero, and a lawyer, and she was definitely more competent than a husband would have been at running my birth experience.

At our first interview, she asked me who my pregnancy role model was. Sad but true, I couldn't think of one woman I looked up to in that way. I'd never been involved in anyone's birth. I didn't know anything *about* birth. The only thing that came to mind was yet another beloved former pet, Cinder, who, after being impregnated by her brother Miles—my other dog at the time—popped out eight puppies on my favorite Jean-Paul Gaultier coat. The thing I loved about Cinder was that, despite getting bigger by the day and eating more than her share (just like me!), she was completely oblivious to the fact that she was pregnant and went on with her life as usual. For dogs, pregnancy is a normal state.

I told Amy that my role model for birth was my dog Cinder. Then she asked me, "How do you envision your birth?" and I told her that I thought I'd be alone in the middle of the night. She asked me if I had any fears about that. "I just don't want any strangers to see me naked," I said.

This especially applied to hot, younger strangers who happened to be models, it turned out. During Fashion Week in February, I was enlisted to produce my first men's show, J. Lindeberg. When I was incredibly large, alone, and five months pregnant, it was just my luck to be subjected to a parade of the world's most beautiful men. I tried to direct them to a bathroom to change, but most would strip down to their underwear right in front of me, as models tend to do. I was sure the Goddess was trying to kill me. The feeling only intensified one day when a young Italian model named Stefano arrived at my office limping: his bicycle had been hit by a cab. I asked him if he was okay, and I calmed him down. But when he rode his bicycle back to my office the next day bearing biscotti (he owned a biscotti company with his brother—I mean, *please*) and admitted to a crush on me, I freaked out. I had a conservative Betty Crocker streak that recoiled at the thought of kissing a man while pregnant with another man's child. But how do you tell a smolderingly hot Italian model fifteen years your junior who is miraculously oblivious to your rotund figure that you're just not interested? Poor Stefano continued to send biscotti for the next several months anyway, but from then on my only suitors were the very forward Haitian bike messengers who showed up at my office every day to pick up or return clothes for photo shoots.

So I embarked on a love affair with Swedish Fish. I would walk down the street working my way through bags and bags of them; with no coffee, cigarettes, or sex, I needed *something*. One day, as I chomped mindlessly, a little voice spoke to me with perfect clarity: "Hi, my name's Ava. It means free like a bird." I went back to my office and looked it up, and indeed, that's what it meant. I'd been mulling names for months, weighing classics like Camilla with my personal favorite, Indira (a possibility squashed by Mikael, who insisted that I could not name my daughter after someone assassinated in my lifetime). I hired women all the time, so I was aware of how a name could set a person up in life. I wanted my daughter to share my last name, Cutrone, but it was also important that the name go well with Ilario's last name, in case she ever wanted to hyphenate. And now it was settled: Ava, perfect on all counts. My daughter was directing her own destiny already.

Two weeks before my due date, at around midnight, I was listening on the phone as my fashion editor friend blabbered about various ill-fated love interests—something so out of the realm of possibility for me at that point that it was difficult to endure that kind of talk—when she asked if I thought I was going to have the baby soon. "I wish I'd go into labor right now!" I exclaimed. No sooner did the words leave my mouth than *pop*—water came pouring out of me. *Oh my God*, I thought. *I've just wished my own labor.*

"Do not move," said my friend breathlessly. "I am on my way!" Oh, *great*. Despite her good intentions, she was high-strung and literally the last person I wanted to see in the delivery room. In fact, her offer of assistance with the birth was what had prompted me to hire Amy in the first place. I called up my assistant to get my team on the phone. "Cancel all my meetings for the week!" I roared. "I'm having a baby!"

Speedy Gonzales arrived at my door and informed me there was a cab waiting downstairs. "No way am I going in a taxi—call a car service!" I cried. I mindlessly grabbed a pair of jeans, thinking I could wear them home from the hospital. *Ha!* I'd be stuck in my shapeless punjabis for months to come.

By that time my pelvis was opening like a pyramid door.

Eeeeeeeeeeeeeeeee, it creaked, as if a secret code were causing it to slowly and painfully rip apart (this was an understatement). By the time Amy arrived, I was vomiting and had taken to swinging my arms to and fro like an ape to distract myself from the pain and she was looking like the best $3,000 I'd ever spent. Surely she could suppress my excitable fashion editor friend, who had turned herself out for my labor in a red turtleneck in the middle of May and was now repeating, like a parrot: "We've got to get out of here! We've got to get out of here!"

We made our way downstairs to pile into the car, a smashing trio. Our driver was a very young Sikh who seemed a bit embarrassed by the howling of these three witches of the night. "Sixty-nine blocks straight up the West Side Highway to St. Luke's!" Amy cried. But at Thirty-second Street, I told the driver to pull over because I had to pee. "Do *not* listen to her!" Amy countered. "She's fully dilated, we need to get her to the hospital!"

"Pull the fuck over or I will fucking jump out of this car!" I screeched. The driver obeyed, startled. I threw off my punjabi pants and was soon naked from the waist down, squatting on the side of the West Side Highway, attempting to pee. "Nothing is coming out," I called in the direction of the car. Amy replied that it was the pressure of the baby and ordered me to get back in. Meanwhile, trucks beeped and passengers cheered as my worst fears about strangers seeing me naked were realized a hundred times over before I even got to the hospital.

I jumped back into the car, situating myself backward on my knees, staring out at the lights of the city through the rear window. My body felt like a pinball machine, every light ignited with pain, blinking and throbbing. I could sense that it knew what to do, and the baby knew what to do, but my mind was still screeching, *Get me out of here!* I fired off a desperate eleventh-hour prayer to the Goddess, offering to remain in a state of pregnancy for the rest of my life if I could just skip what was about to happen.

We stampeded into St. Luke's, Amy massaging my back, me screaming at the frightened nurses: "*I want drugs! I want drugs! I want drugs!*" I sensed them whispering about me, and in short order they were trying to interfere with the beatific and very trendy water birth I'd hoped for. At this point two of my three longtime birth fantasies had already been slashed—the one involving living in Venice while pregnant and delivering at the American Hospital there, and the one involving, you know, a *man*—and I wasn't about to give this last one up that easily.

"She is over thirty-five, we need to get her on a fetal heart monitor," one nurse directed. "*I want a water birth!*" I bellowed. "Well, even if you get in the water, you need to get out of the tub and have your baby on a bed for insurance reasons in New York State," replied another nurse. "*Get the fuck out of here, I do not ever want to speak to or see any of you ever again!*" I screamed, and they left. Finally the bossy nurses had met their match.

Eventually Dr. Moritz appeared. "Kelly Cutrone, of all the fashion girls who are having a natural childbirth in New York City this morning," he said with a laugh. He'd been hearing from me regularly for at least a month. "Moritz!" I'd shriek from my office. "I can't take this anymore! I haven't seen my feet in months, I can't zip my boots, and I'm wearing Amish clogs!"

He'd offered to schedule a C-section, of course, explaining that this was what women like me (translation: nightmare, rich) were doing now, for astrological or work reasons. But my conservative Betty Crocker streak had intervened yet again, prompting me to go natural. Now here I was pleading for pharmaceutical relief. "I want some drugs!" I cried. "Anything!"

He pointed to his left shoulder. "Put your leg up here, baby, and push, and I'll give you something afterward." I fell in love with Dr. Moritz in that moment. He was part care bear, part knight in shining armor, and he more than made up for any masculinity lacking in my birth equation. I forgot all about my water birth and began to push. There is not one writer in the world who can accurately describe the feeling of giving birth (or getting tattooed, for that matter), so I won't waste your time. Suffice it to say that before long there was Ava: head, shoulders, *swoosh*, spilling out of me. It was less *Born Free* than *Species*. Amy held my hand and cheered me on while the fashion editor cowered in the corner, probably in awe of my vagina, which had not been waxed in months.

Since everything I knew about childbirth had been gleaned from birthing shows on TLC, I was convinced I would cry my eyes out when I first saw Ava. Instead, when she emerged, I was speechless for the first time that day. (Surely the nurses were grateful.) They immediately put her on my chest. She wasn't even crying, and she was already cool. Who was this little being, and how did she come through me like that? Oh my God, she wants to breast-feed already? And now I have to deliver something called the placenta? The *what*? Maybe they'd covered this in the birthing classes I skipped, but birthing one's placenta can only be compared to putting a flaming drink from Trader Vic's onto your vagina after a marathon night of banging a football player. When it was over, the nurses showed it to me. It was bigger than a Frisbee and full of membranes and blood. "Would you like to take this home with you?" they inquired. "What planet are you *living* on?" I replied.

A mere twelve hours after this ordeal, the nurses told me I was free to go home. "Are you kidding me?" I protested. "I'm going nowhere!" I had heard that you could order gourmet food delivery in New York hospitals, and it was true: you could. (I recommend giving birth in New York City for this reason alone.) My mother arrived that night, and we holed up in the hospital for the two full days allowed by my insurance, ordering in elaborate meals. It was only Wednesday, after all, and I had no interest in decamping to my home/office until my employees were gone for the weekend.

My full-floor SoHo loft housed People's Revolution in the front and my two-room apartment in the back. (People's Revolution would later expand to fill three floors, and my own apartment one floor.) I had pledged to Amy to continue breast-feeding once I left the hospital, even though it felt like rolling your nipples in broken glass while someone shoots hot oil through every vein of your breast. This confused my mother, who had grown up in a middle-class household in the 1950s and was of the opinion that breast-feeding was for dirty hippies and "Third World people." "I guess that's what you kids are doing these days," she'd say incredulously, shaking her head. By the third day I was a walking zombie. I tried to channel my younger days as a groovy "It" girl who regularly stayed out until four or five a.m. in nightclubs. Why did I now find these hours to be such an inconvenience?

My mother and I had other generational differences on the subject of my breasts. When Ava was four days old, we took her out to dinner in Little Italy, where I proceeded to nurse at the table. My mother was mortified. I patiently explained to her that this was not a porn movie; I was feeding my child. Nonetheless, in insisting that I cover up, she became one of the many women who would balk in knee-jerk fashion at the sight of my breasts being used for their natural purpose. Once she left town, I bared my boobs all over the world—beside catwalks from New York to Paris and in a meeting with twelve Greek shipping magnates who wanted to talk to me about their image. My tits were like the SoHo welcoming committee.

Most of the time, though, I was genuinely relieved to have my mother's company during Ava's first days. I remember looking over at her, exhausted after two days of no sleep, and saying: "I'm so sorry for anything I've ever said or done to you." I suddenly had this deep understanding of what a mother does for a child. It's as if, during labor, Mother Nature implants a computer chip in your brain that makes you want to love this person you don't even know, so that after three days of nonstop breastfeeding, when you leave the baby with your mom and venture out for a quick slice of pizza, there's suddenly this voice in your head shrieking, "You need to go back to the baby *right now!*" And yet you look at your child and you just know from the beginning that she's going to break your heart. You just know it. You know she's going to steal your credit card and your cell phone and lie to you and call you a bitch because she has a crush on some guy you don't like. But you love her and *want* for her anyway, and it's the most beautiful, selfless love; you instinctively know you'd do anything for her, regardless of what she does to you. My mother stayed four days after Ava's birth before returning to my sick father, and when she left I cried like a baby. "I can't believe you're leaving me here alone!" I wailed at the front door.

I soon had plenty of people volunteering to come over and help, but to my great relief, I found that it's a natural thing to be with your child. People in the West make it into such a big thing, this feat that's going to take twenty-five around-the-clock helpers. But my nanny didn't start until Ava was several weeks old, and in that time my daughter and I developed a rhythm we've maintained to this day. We're in sync. We're separate, but she feels almost like a continuation of me. We still sleep in the same bed, like wolves. We got so comfortable together that after two weeks I realized I had to get off the couch or I was going to become addicted to *Judge Judy*. That's a bad sign, when the highlight in your life is *Judge Judy*. I remember sitting crumpled in a naked heap on the floor one day, breast-feeding Ava, staring down at my ravaged body with its uncut toenails and down-ward-pointing breasts, and thinking, *I need a pedicure and a wax*.

I began bringing Ava to the office and breast-feeding her in staff meetings. It was an amazing time during which I discovered some of the benefits of single motherhood. You're not sharing your time, or your decisions, with anyone else. You're not try-ing to put your child to bed to have sex with your husband, and you're not arguing about the child's religion. (I have friends who are married and can't agree on anything.) Of course, there were also experiences I missed out on, like being intimate with someone in the sixth month of my pregnancy and sharing my excitement with my husband over my breast milk letting down. But to be alone with a child and pick out her name and decide when she's going to go to sleep and where she's going to sleep—there was something exciting about the autonomy of these choices. It proved my theory that when life deals you blows, there are blessings to be found in them if you look hard enough.

As Ava grew and reached certain milestones, I would still have to face brutal reminders of how alone I was. For example, when I was looking for a preschool—an overwhelming task for any parent in Manhattan, but especially a single one—I didn't have a partner I could look to and say, "Can you believe we're doing this? She's eighteen months old already, oh my God!" Instead, I toiled alone, answering application questions like "What is your role in your child's homework?" (She was not even two at the time.) "Ava is a self-starter with an excellent attention span," I'd write. Or: "I'm particularly impressed by the Quaker focus on consensus building and contemplative reflection at your school." During the week of admissions interviews, my lip was literally quivering. I'd had a twitching eyelid before, and I'd had hives and plenty of upset stomachs, but never anything like this—*this* was a whole new level of stress.

It was New York Fashion Week yet again, of course (life in Manhattan can sometimes seem like one continuous Fashion Week), and the dry-erase boards in my office were covered with lists of fashion shows my company was producing and lists of the schools Ava had applied to, reminding us all of deadlines and interview dates. I would stumble out of my Lincoln town car at these interviews, hair totally unkempt, knowing I had just forty-five minutes to make a good impression on some former academic geek of an admissions officer who had probably been waiting his or her whole life to reject cool downtown parents, and then I'd jet back to Bryant Park to put on a runway show. Perhaps this torturous process was why I was excited to hear soon after about a great preschool called the Children's Aid Society, which had an enlightened first-come-first-serve policy and didn't require sign-up until December. Of course, in Manhattan first-come-first-serve really means: "You must wait in line all night. Outside." So I rented an SUV and plotted to park it illegally on the sidewalk for heat, safety, and shelter. (It was December, after all.) How quickly my life had changed: once a fearless creature of the night, pushing my way into packed after-hours nightclubs, I was now terrified to be out on the street alone at three in the morning without the sanctuary of a black SUV.

Luckily, I received a phone call from a client who was genuinely scared that I'd be waiting outside alone in New York to get my daughter into preschool; he told me he had hired a security guard to protect me. It was one of the most touching things a client has ever done for me. As I drove up to the school in my SUV, bracing for my all-nighter, there he was, my security detail, six-foot-four and African-American and loaded up with Freihofer's and Entenmann's to hold us over. We were second in line: the first was a law student who'd been paid by an NYU professor to be

EVERYTHING GOOD HAPPENS AFTER THIRTY

People think their twenties are this really great time because that's when they're hot, but the truth is that we don't even become women, I believe, until we're thirty. I specifically remember being married to my second husband about two weeks after my thirtieth birthday and starting to cry hysterically out of the blue. He asked me if something bad happened at work that day. "No," I told him. "I feel like I'm becoming a woman." And I was: later I would learn that I was experiencing my astrological coming-of-age. Astrologers believe that we don't become adults until our first Saturn returns, which happens between ages twenty-seven and thirty.

The twenties are a time to figure out where you came from and where you're going, and if you're lucky, you're getting closer to these answers by the time you're thirty. You've probably already done everything embarrassing in your twenties, from drugs and binge-drinking to paranoid stalker girlfriend behaviors. Let's face it, the humiliation of getting a locksmith to help you break into your ex-boyfriend's house because you think he's cheating on you even though you're not dating anymore can have a lasting deterrent effect on a person's psyche. Here are ten other things to look forward to after you turn thirty:

[1] Salary increases: If you've followed everything I've told you to do in this book, you'll be making some beaucoup dollars by thirty.

a placeholder. A series of dads eventually lined up behind us—unsurprisingly, there were no other moms—and soon the men were all vying to hang out in my SUV to warm up. I may have been the only parent Ava had at that point, but clearly she was at no disadvantage; $18,000 later, my fears about my ability to over-

[2] After having gone through a plethora of designers for clothing, it's time to step it up a notch and charge headlong into the land of overpriced luxury accessories, where I hope you'll encounter some of the same landmarks I did: Globe-trotter, Asprey, Louboutin, Vuitton, Bulgari, Hermes, Roger Vivier.

[3] A baby. If you want one.

[4] The desire and the emotional wherewithal to date three men at the same time without remorse.

[5] Vacations outside the USA *sans* youth hostel.

[6] Self-control. This is the time when we ride the lion; the lion does not ride us. Like Durga, we sit on top of it and enjoy the ride.

[7] Property ownership, or maybe just your own apartment.

[8] The ability to buy your own muscle car, if you want one.

[9] Decrease in overall paranoia and hysteria, which leads to . . .

[10] Better sex. Definitely better sex. (By this I mean the slow fade of the missionary position and a mind-blowing new cornucopia of sex toys and experiences.)

see her education subsided. (Which is not to say writing those checks has gotten any easier.)

So there I was, taking my daughter to preschool at a time when my high school friends were seeing their kids off to college. I did things almost backward by conventional standards: mar-

riage, divorce, *repeat*, career, baby, and eventually a home reno-
vation involving all-white leather furniture, which many couples
do long before a kid makes such a color scheme impractical.
Nowhere in this picture was there anything like what some other
women enjoy: the nice house in Connecticut or somebody to really
count on. Living and working in the same building, however, has
allowed me to oversee offices in New York, L.A., and Paris and
still take my daughter to school in the morning, greet her when
she returns, and put her to bed each night. Ava is surrounded by a
loving extended family that includes her Italian father, Ilario; her
nanny, Maxine; my dear friends Justine Bateman and Ruth Yang;
my business partners Robyn Berkeley and Emily Bungert; my
parents and siblings; eight cousins; and an entire staff of young
publicists. We are part of a new tribe that is awake and marching,
slowly shifting cultural ideas about what constitutes love and par-
enthood and discrediting the outdated notion of *First comes love,
then comes marriage*, or any other preprogrammed, one-size-fits-all
life progression.

Of course, where I live, everything from same-sex parents
to surrogate moms to single moms to Chinese/German grand-
parents happens to be completely normal. I have gay friends
and a famous pop-star girlfriend who have employed surrogate mothers, the latter because she didn't want to jeopardize
her plastic surgery. I even have a straight male friend I met on a
plane who hired a surrogate when he turned sixty because he'd
never met the woman he wanted to be the mother of his child;
instead, he's raising her with the help of a very capable nanny.
I've done school drop-off in the mornings with mothers who love

their husbands and mothers who hate their husbands and mothers who have given up on their husbands altogether and taken a lover. All around us a whole new world is being born, from single mothers who are *not* urban teenagers in a bind to single fathers, to the interracial lesbians who are every Manhattan parent's worst nightmare in the private school admissions process. (Even as a single mom and CEO, I can't compete with *that* kind of diversity.) This is the new normal.

Now is the time to ask yourself: where do *I* fit into all this? After my devastating abortion at twenty-four, I resolved that I would not give birth to a child before giving birth to myself; at thirty-five, I felt ready. But motherhood is a choice, not an obligation. In my life it has been a teaching, a tangible promise of progress, and a chance to experience totally unfaltering love. I had a baby because I have a lot to give and a lot to learn, not because my husband wanted one or because my parents wanted me to have one or because I viewed motherhood, then or now, as in any way essential to the experience of being female. In other words, not because it was the thing that came next.

Which is not to say that the programmers aren't still hard at work on me. My own mother still calls me up and says, "You know, it was so good to see you. *I just wish you would meet someone*, because God forbid something happens, who would take care of you and Ava?" Reminding her that I'm closer to fifty than thirty-five, I tell her that I can't believe we're still having this conversation. "I know," she'll say. "But you just work so hard, and it would be so great if you could meet someone you could rest into."

I agree that that might be really, really nice, but not what my life is about anymore. If I met somebody I wanted to share my life with *and* that person could be an equal partner *and* my life happened to be at a stage when I could make some time for him, then yes, that would be lovely. But at this point I'm certainly not waiting for anyone else to show up and make me happy ever after. I'm busy scouting out my dream house in the country, making the money to afford it, and making my own happily ever after. Which is why it worries me that most of the girls who work in my office are still operating on a timeline and a set of expectations put in place by their parents or their wedding-obsessed friends who just want them to get married and settle down after a few years of trying on the career thing and have 2.5 children and set about decorating the house. That's fine *if* you feel called to be a decorator, or *if* at twenty-five you've met a man who literally blows your mind in every way. Then you should go for it. Otherwise, examine your real reasons for going along with these expectations. Parents don't want their daughters to come home and say, "I'm going to be a single mom—I'm going to have a baby! I found a sperm donor. Do you remember my friend Jack who I met in London? Well, he's going to send his sperm over, and I'm going to get pregnant." That's not what most parents are waiting to hear. They are still hoping their daughters will make the conventional choices.

Through my daughter, I now see all over again what women are up against from a young age. In fact, I outlawed Disney movies in our house because I thought they were shitty messaging for chicks. From Snow White to Belle, every woman is damaged until some guy shows up and makes everything okay. *Every one* of those stories involves a guy making a woman's life magical. And the first person to try to push this on my daughter was my mother! "We're not buying into this," I told her, but there was nothing I could do to stop it. By the time my daughter was two, she knew who all the Disney princesses were. She never had any of the toys or movies in our house, but she knew everything. Disney is all-powerful.

I eventually adopted an "If you can't beat 'em, join 'em" attitude about the whole thing. I'd say things to Ava like, "What do you think would happen if Belle didn't meet the Beast? Would she still be living in the castle?"

"No," Ava would say.

"Why?"

"Because it's the Beast's castle!"

"But don't you think maybe Belle could've bought her own castle too?"

SEVEN

YOU ARE THE BRAND:
Normal Gets You Nowhere

Those born on November 13 are generally
perceptive and insightful when commenting
on their times. Regardless of what walk
of life they inhabit, they often make
statements about what is going on around
them that attract attention ... they tend
to have strong opinions about how things
work or don't work as the case may be.

—Gary Goldschneider and Joost Elffers,
The Secret Language of Birthdays

was a publicist from birth. By age two, I regularly crawled out of my crib and waddled into the living room proclaiming, "Johnny Carson! *Tonight Show!*" and snuggled up on the couch with my parents. Several years later, I attempted to make it into the *Guinness Book of World Records* for swinging. Nobody took me seriously until it was time for lunch and I still wouldn't get off the damn swing; only *then* did I convince my mom to call the local newspaper. By eight, I had moved on to producing actual media-worthy events, specifically block-party fund-raisers for Jerry Lewis's muscular dystrophy telethon each Labor Day. These were no small-time affairs: we staged elaborate talent shows (one year my brother and I performed as Sonny and Cher) and stationed my dad at the barbecue grill to turn out hot dogs for half the neighborhood. I always managed to land myself on the local news for being one of the top fund-raisers for the "Jerry's Kids" telethon. If all this didn't bespeak a talent for producing six fashion shows in a single day, getting my clients featured in the *New York Times*, and even producing my own television shows, I don't know what would have, but no one around me ever connected the dots and said, "Gee, this girl would make an amazing publicist!" In fact, my teachers seemed to think I was just an attention-seeker. "Student's social interests supersede academic interests," wrote one, Mr. Dominy, and my parents responded by grounding me.* In fact, I spent a large portion of my childhood getting grounded for doing things that would later make me a lot of money.

By now it won't shock you to hear that I don't believe the people who raised you will necessarily steer you toward your destiny—or even cheer you on to it. With their own ideas about where your life is going, your parents, relatives, and teachers might not be looking for clues that point to other outcomes for you. What might become, in the right context, an important part of your later success may seem like nothing more than character deficiencies or annoyances to them. This is why you need to appoint yourself manager of your own personal brand.

It's not enough just to listen to your inner voice and ask yourself the hard questions about who you are and what you believe. Eventually you need to get strategic about refining and communicating to others who you are and what you believe if you want to succeed. In other words, now that we've dealt with the inside, you need to get real about the outside. Personal branding

---

* Many years later, after I became a successful publicist, I sent Mr. Dominy a copy of my tax return.

is about figuring out who you are and what turns you on and then *monetizing* it.*

I always laugh when I'm in L.A. and see the huge sign on top of the Beverly Center that reads: DON'T BLEND IN. The truth is that most of us are trying to do exactly that. But if you think about it, the people who are actually making a difference in the world are people who are *not* like everyone else. The best brands stand out. Think about Virgin Atlantic founder and CEO Richard Branson, for example, who is definitely not your typical business guy, or Oprah Winfrey, who is nothing like other talk-show hosts, or the late *Harper's Bazaar* editor Liz Tilberis, a woman famous in the fashion industry for being nothing like most editors-in-chief of major fashion magazines—she had a heart! I believe these people became successful because what they were selling was authentic and consistent. They found jobs that aligned with their skills and passions, and they brought their true selves—idiosyncrasies and all—to work, day after day after day. Take Andre Leon Talley, *Vogue*'s witty, voluble editor-at-large who, despite looking and acting nothing like your average brittle and aloof fashion editor, has been dashing around New York for years in floor-length capes—he is one of the most respected and recognizable faces in the industry. Or look at Grace Coddington, Andre's quirky and opinionated redheaded colleague at the magazine and the breakout star of *The September Issue*, the documentary about *Vogue*. My daughter's pediatrician, Dr. Cohen, is an adorable French doctor who wears Paul Smith suits and makes house calls on his bicycle.

---

* The Mother herself was a big believer in capitalism. She said that money is ruled by darkness and it's our job to claim it in the name of the Divine.

Every cool mom below Twenty-third Street is dying to get her kid into his practice. Why? Because he's a cute French guy in a Paul Smith suit who shows up on a bicycle, and what's not to love about that? Of course, Dr. Cohen also happens to be really good at what he does, which is key. No one would care about Andre Leon Talley's fabulous capes if he weren't an amazing writer. In some ways, being yourself is a luxury: if I was a horrible publicist, perhaps I wouldn't feel so comfortable showing up to the office without makeup or a blow-out.

Everyone is selling something these days, and if you don't have a clear point of differentiation—something that makes you special, unique, effective—you won't get far in fashion or in any other competitive industry, and you certainly won't succeed as an entrepreneur. All celebrated brands have a point of differentiation. Gucci is selling a black, chic, Italian aesthetic, while Dolce & Gabbana is selling lace and rock 'n' roll and Ralph Lauren is selling chic Waspy Americana. It's time to figure out what *you* are selling and how you are going to make people want to buy it.

In thinking about this question, consider your whole self, and don't be afraid to embrace everything that makes you unique. A family member called me one day, upset that one of her daughters had been diagnosed with a mild case of obsessive-compulsive disorder (OCD). "Are you kidding me? That can be an amazing character trait!" I protested. Look at it this way, I told her: Your daughter's shit is intact! She has attention to detail! *That* is a real point of differentiation in today's attention-deficient world! That girl will make a perfect brain surgeon or photo shoot producer;

all she lacks is a good assistant to manage her time and tell her when to move on to the next task.

Your point of differentiation does not need to be edgy or groundbreaking; it just needs to be different, and it just needs to be you. Most people are mimicking others and dressing and behaving as they think they *should*. But people like Dr. Cohen aren't afraid to challenge accepted molds in embracing their own personal style. Why *shouldn't* a pediatrician make house calls in Manhattan in 2010? And why shouldn't he ride a bike? Similarly, why must all female investment bankers wear pencil skirts and pearls and carry Tod's bags? And as long as we're on the subject, why *shouldn't* a publicist tell the truth?

Since I don't like to lie, one of my points of differentiation in an industry full of falsity is total and complete honesty. My pitching style is truthful and nontraditional; some might even say it's a bit unprofessional. But I get results because I'm saying something different than the dozens of other publicists who call a journalist on any given day. I'm not just doing things the way I was trained to do them or the way everyone else does them. Let's face it: as a brand, adequate and normal will get you nowhere.

How do you find your point of differentiation? The first step is to stop trying to convince yourself—and letting others convince you—that you're something you're not. If you don't like sick people, don't become a doctor. If your idea of a horrible day is fetching coffee and picking up dry cleaning, *don't* go into fashion. On the other hand, if you hate whiny, complaining men, think about becoming a dominatrix, because you'll make a fortune!

This all goes back to the absolute necessity of following your dreams. If you don't know exactly what fits into your life and what doesn't, the best way to figure it out is to follow your inner voice away from what feels wrong and toward what feels right, whether that means moving to New York City on a whim at twenty-one, quitting your accounting job at thirty-five to be an actress, or ditching your job in fashion to swim with dolphins in Hawaii. These experiences won't always take you on an express train to your true purpose and calling in life, but they'll teach you lessons you're supposed to learn. Perhaps these experiences will move you closer to your destiny by revealing that you're *not* in fact meant to be an actress and that what you really want is to start your own fashion line. Most of the girls who show up in my office eventually find out that they are *not* in fact indie fashion publicists. Some have learned that they were designers or stylists instead, and for others the New York fashion world may have revived a dream of going back to school to study anthropology.

Once you have set out on this intuitive journey of dream-inspired self-discovery, you must eventually *focus*. When you find something that feels right, concentrate on refining your skills and educating yourself about your chosen field. Commit to it. You don't have to do it forever—some people are meant to pursue several dreams in a lifetime—but doing one thing well will open doors for you. A plant won't grow as high if it's reaching toward five or six suns, just as a great publicist never works on fashion, beauty, pharmaceuticals, and nonprofits all at once, and an internist doesn't try to also be a cardiac surgeon or a gastroenterologist. Successful people, and compelling brands, are usually highly specialized. They do *one thing*, and they do it in a better or more interesting way than everyone else.

I found my professional niche early, thanks to my willingness to uproot from Syracuse and follow my inner voice to New York. Still, after I sold my PR business several years later in the wake of my divorce and found myself reading tarot cards on Venice Beach, I briefly tried to convince myself that maybe I was not a born publicist after all, but a rock star. This detour taught me that even when a career looks perfect to others or seems perfect on paper, it can still be the totally wrong choice for you.

It all began in 1995 when, high on my newfound spirituality, I ran into an old musician friend from New York named Sean Dinsmore. "Oh my God, you seem so different, what happened to you?" he gasped. I had begun to cultivate a great bohemian look that bore no resemblance to my former label whoredom or my future all-black palette. But it was more than just my look that had changed. I explained that I had gotten into meditation and the Universal Mother*. Fascinated, confused, or both, Sean invited me to visit him in the studio in Hollywood where he was recording a demo. I went, and before I knew it I was lyricizing spontaneously over one of his beats. (The only way to explain this sudden surge of musical inspiration is to say I was *very* relaxed in those days.) Sean recorded me and turned it into a song called "Conversations

---

* I really can't explain the Universal Mother in words. If we sat down and held hands together in meditation as women, we might be able to feel her truth, wisdom, and power. But no alphabet will do her justice, though people have tried over time: Mexicans call her Guadeloupe, the Christians call her Mary, the Egyptians call her Cleopatra, the Greeks call her Athena, the Buddhists call her Tara, and the Hindus call her by several names, from Lakshmi to Durga.

with a Groovy Girl." He then started shopping his demo. When he called me a few weeks later, I asked him if he'd gotten a deal. "No, but *you* did," he said. I was incredulous. But it was true: Atlantic Records wanted to offer *me*—a broke, tone-deaf tarot card reader—the chance to work with the renowned producer Richard Perry (who has produced records for Carly Simon, Rick James, John Lennon, Diana Ross, and Tina Turner, among others). I signed a deal for $150,000, and before I could question whether the Goddess was playing a joke on me, I was pulling up at the bank in Beverly Hills in a pair of cut-off Levis and a tank top, my tattoos plainly visible, to cash a check for $60,000, an unimaginable sum of money for me at the time. I remember the bank teller asking me if I wanted a security guard to walk me to my busted Cutlass Supreme in the parking lot. (I refused, certain that no one would look at me and guess that I was suddenly wealthy.)

Despite my spiritually aspirational state, I was down for rock stardom. After all, why shouldn't the Goddess hit the stage? Surely this was a world that needed some transforming, and no one loved music more than me. I knew in my heart of hearts that I couldn't sing, but I was still going to do my best to make the most of this. I'd faked it to make it before. On my first day in the studio, the producer told me to come in on the sixth bar. "What's a bar?" I asked. I could tell he thought it was going to be the longest recording session of his life. But my songs were pretty good despite my obvious lack of singing talent: I chanted seductively over the beats producers brought me, my style part Lou Reed, part Mazzy Star, my trippy lyrics more often than not tied to my recent awakenings:

I was riding through the cosmos,
Deep in outer space,
Trying to get a grip on this thing we call the human race,
Rat race, out of place,
Krishnas calling out, don't you hear your name?
Darkness keeps on dancing, it never stays the same,
Yes the Mother loves you and it's time for you to know,
Heaven is a comin', it's a souled-out show.

When my album was done, I learned that being a recording artist is not just about making the album; it's about touring, and as cool as that might sound, if you're not looking to get laid or get high, it is one hard job. I was in a committed relationship at the time with the actor who would become my second husband, and the tour lifestyle just seemed tedious and repetitive. It quickly became apparent that I'd been trying to squish myself into a box I didn't fit into. Believe it or not, I'm kind of shy, and I didn't like the kind of attention I got up onstage. In my former career, I'd been communicating and had had actual things to say. Now I was just getting on the bus every day to travel to the next middle-of-nowhere town and wait for sound check before crashing in a depressing hotel. Everything about this just felt wrong. Which is why, despite the money and the promises of fame being heaped on me by my slick representatives at the record label, I admitted to myself and everyone else that I was not a rock star.

My friends at the time were shocked. After all, who doesn't want fame and glamour and money? But I already knew that things that seem perfect rarely are (my first marriage and my first life in New York, for example) and that, in fact, these things can destroy you while you're wrapped up in their supposed perfection. It doesn't matter how glamorous or lucrative a career may seem from the outside; if it's not the path you're meant to be on, you will never be happy or fulfilled doing it. I'd gotten many things wrong in New York in my early twenties, but I had one thing right: I *was* a publicist, and a communicator. Which is why, when the Wasteland came calling not long after I ditched my record deal, I jumped back into publicity with both feet. The rest is history. My distaste for routine, my need to communicate with people on a constant basis, my inability to shut up, my love of language and words—these things are the strengths of my brand as a publicist. And in refining that brand over the years, I've managed to incorporate not only my personal traits but my values and spirituality.

I'd describe my brand today as renegade, strategically kooky, ballsy, bohemian, intuitive, ruthless, and loving. An essential quality of my brand is that people who don't know me often just write me off as a crazy bitch. But *am* I? Everything I do is very well thought out. Sometimes I speak in a loose-associative manner, stunning people and entertaining them into giving in to what I want, even if they have no idea what I'm saying. Other times I might spew a stream of words at someone, going on and on and on until the person just surrenders in fatigue and agrees with me. "Hi, I'm just calling because we're going to need an extra $20,000 for the budget, we've been talking about this $20,000 for two weeks now, and you and I have both probably *already* lost $20,000 individually fighting over whether you're going to give me this $20,000, maybe you just give me the $20,000, and if it doesn't go exactly as you expect it to I'll pay back the $20,000 through some other part of my budget, what do you say, can I have the $20,000?"

The look of my brand, which came later, is also more deliberate than it may seem, and it too was established by moving away from what felt wrong for me and toward what felt right. I started wearing black not because I'm purposefully cultivating a hard-edged image, but because I just happen to look terrible in color! After years of honest appraisal, I realized that black jeans and a comfortable black T-shirt with my hair pulled back and shades suits me best. I now own this look, and it's as much a part of my brand as my pitching style.

In defining the look of your brand, whether you work in fashion or not, remember that there is a danger in trying to create your brand from the outside in. How many girls go into salons every day and say, "I want Jennifer Aniston's hair"? Jennifer Aniston's hair has made her stylist, Chris McMillan, a huge star. Instead of creating an internal sketch, we spend half our teenage years cutting pictures out of magazines and pasting them on our bedroom walls, cobbling together a collage of how we want ourselves represented. If you're lucky enough to be reading this book and contemplating these questions, let me ask you: How do you want to present *your*self? Rather than present someone else's self (*How can I look like Reese or Cameron?*), what is *your* idea of sexy?

These are hard questions. It's much easier to just go with the blond bob and the right bag. Most women by the time they're thirty-eight get their hair frosted and wear running sneakers and signify to the world that they're hunkering down for the next forty years of misery. On the other hand, I believe that the people we perceive as having great individual style have found things that represent their unique inner world outwardly. They're in their truth. They've done the work, and they know who they are and what fits on them and what doesn't. This is why my amazing green, turquoise, soft mauve, black, and white Pucci dress, which I absolutely *love*, is something you will never see me wearing.

People like to know what they're getting when they buy something, whether they're consumers, clients, or employers. At this point, my brand is so well articulated that when I *do* dress up, my clients get scared—they don't know what to think! Backstage at the Chado Ralph Rucci fashion show in New York in February 2009, reeling from my firing by Yigal Azrouel over the Ashley Dupre affair, I wore a purposely sedate Margiela black pencil skirt, a cashmere twinset, and a Burberry coat. Ralph, a new client at the time, was shocked when he saw me: "Are you okay?" he asked. He seemed genuinely concerned. It hit me that my clients don't *want* polished and demure; that's not why they hired me.

Every successful brand has a message, and that message must be painstakingly driven home, in both appearance and substance. It would be bizarre to walk into Tiffany's and see the sales associates putting customers' purchases in red shopping bags because the store's creative director decided that red might be more fun for February. Red just isn't Tiffany! At Tiffany's the service is always imperious service and the bags are blue. In the same way, when a company hires you, remember what you sold them to get the job and be consistent in providing it. And I'm not talking about your wardrobe.

I had an intern a few years ago who came into my office one day and put her head on my desk and started crying hysterically. "I'm about to become disinherited and kicked out of my apartment because my parents won't support me anymore," she moaned. "I'll do *anything* for a job. I'll stay all night. It's the most important thing in my life right now." I gave her a chance, but after three months it was obvious that she hadn't been truthful about her level of commitment. She wanted to leave at seven, she was a big eye-roller, she was the office gossip, and she even turned people against each other. In the end, she quit right in the middle of Fashion Week, screwing over her entire team. Do *not* be this girl. If you sell yourself as a hyper-organized, type A go-getter, that's what you should be as an employee. If you sell yourself as a creative wellspring of ideas, well, you'd better believe your boss is going to want to hear them regularly.

Good brands are authentic, focused, and *consistent*. Of course, your brand will always work both for you and against you: Gucci can never be Wal-Mart in a recession just because it's in the mood to discount; Gucci has to stay Gucci. (In fact, this is why many luxury brands balked in 2007 and 2008 when department stores drastically slashed prices on their goods: the cheap prices detracted from the cachet of the brands.) By the same token, I will never be a demure blonde with a bob in a Chanel jacket who keeps quiet when I think someone is making a big mistake. If that's what a prospective client is looking for—even a client I really want to work with—I have to accept that this is one client who just isn't going to hire me.

Ultimately, no matter how fabulous and well articulated a brand you have, it's of little use to you if you can't sell it to others. I'm talking about getting a job. The best thing you can do for your brand early on is to align it with powerful brands that represent your highest aspirations. This is true whether you're in fashion or heart surgery or sculpture. If you think you may want to work in the luxury fashion business, intern at a prestigious luxury brand like Prada, Louis Vuitton, Cartier, or Hermes—*not* Steve Madden. If you're into avant-garde fashion, you might want to work at People's Revolution or Vivienne Westwood or Bernard Wilhelm. If you're into really high-end, cutting-edge fashion, try Dries van Noten. If you're into art, research the top galleries in the world or contact an auction house like Christie's.

It's the same with your choice of college: if you studied economics at UPenn, you'll get more time from the human resources department of a bank than will someone who went to St. Martin's College of Art and Design in London. On the other hand, if you went to St. Martin's, you'll have a much better chance of getting a fashion position than someone who went to UPenn. Too often guidance counselors suggest the same colleges year after year for wildly different types of people, and that makes no sense. (Which is why you need to seek advice from your own tribal council instead!) Think as early as you can about the network you want to join and the classmates and alumni who will enhance the message of your brand and help you achieve your dreams; be methodical about joining this network. And don't forget about geography: if you see yourself working in high fashion, you should be positioned and prepared to live in a city that offers high-paying careers in fashion, and that is a short list: New York, Paris, Antwerp, Tokyo, London, and Milan. If you are married and living in Chicago and you absolutely never want to leave your husband or that city, it's time to accept that you're probably not going to find opportunities in high fashion and to start thinking about what *else* you may be called to do.

Once you have identified the people who do what you want to do at the highest possible level, start contacting them. You'll be surprised by how many powerful, successful strangers, if you write a heartfelt letter full of good intentions, may agree to be part of your tribal council and give you not only direction but even an internship. If your dream is to work for Ralph Lauren, try sending a letter to *Ralph Lauren*. He may not get it, but you'd be surprised how many times his assistant will, and based on what it says, he or she may be inspired to answer your letter or pass it on to the appropriate person in human resources. Or try calling the main number at Ralph Lauren and saying, "Hi, I'd like to speak to the assistant in the PR department." Don't call the director of publicity; call the entry-level person and ask in a humble way how she got there and whether she would be willing to tell you how to get your résumé into the hands of the right person.

Or send flowers. The assistant might or might not like receiving such a gift, but you're still going to have a better chance of getting noticed than those who send dry form letters making it clear that they haven't done any research into what the department they're applying to actually does. When someone writes me a sincere and humble e-mail or letter, nine times out of ten I'll answer them personally—which often terrifies them—or have someone from my office respond with something like, "Kelly read your e-mail, and here's what she thinks." If it's a ridiculous letter—if a twenty-two-year-old kid who's five-foot-five and fat sends me a picture of himself in his underwear and tells me he wants to be a model—I'm not going to answer it. But a lot of my employees are just people who wrote me moving, persuasive letters in their own authentic voice.

The difference lies not so much in what these letters say as what they don't say ("Dear Ms. Cutrone: If you're looking for someone energetic with a passion for fashion, choose me!"). No one is impressed by a form letter that says, "Dear sir: Upon completion of my graduation in May 2012 . . ." I've never said: "Oh, wow, here's a girl who went to the University of Rochester, had a 2.0 average, and wants to move here from Minneapolis but has no internships. Let's hire *her*!" When it comes to job-seekers who write that they have mad style, and they love fashion because it's glamorous, but they've never even worked in retail or taken a class or interned, I tend to think: *How do you know? How do you know anything about fashion?* Successful candidates in my office speak in their own voices—with excellent grammar, of course— but they're not ridiculous in their assumptions about why we'll be so blown away by them.

In creative industries especially, be careful not to let your personal brand overwhelm your expressed desire to learn. The point, after all, is to make people want to work with you. A kid of twenty-two who breezes in acting like Andre Leon Talley is not really going to do it for me.* I'm not a big believer in the Bible, but I do love the phrase "Faith without works is dead." You will be much more appealing to potential employers if you can point to achievements that show how you put your skills and passions to actual use in the world. Instead of spending your summers in the Greek Islands with your family, try spending them at Condé Nast working for *Vanity Fair* or *Lucky*. If I get a letter from a job applicant explaining to me that when she was in high school she saw a fashion show I produced on YouTube and it inspired her to raise $785 for a women's shelter, I'll *definitely* want to meet her. This person is obviously not just someone who is aesthetically inspired by fashion but someone who can connect the dots and think big picture and use her passions to get things done and make a difference in people's lives.

Finally, understand that selling the world—or your industry, or even just your boss—on your brand takes time. As already discussed, you know that the roads of your dreams are not paved with yellow brick; in fact, they may be paved with rejection letters. The people who succeed are often not just the people with the best-articulated brands; they're the people who respond to rejection by brushing themselves off and moving on, again and again. Many college graduates seem to treat paid work as a right,

---

* And as long as we're on the subject, if you come from a really privileged family and your idea of "Oh, that thing?" is a really nice Balenciaga jacket or a pair of last season's Prada shoes, that's probably not the best way to dress for success. Undoubtedly there will be someone in the office who makes more money than you who *still* can't afford to dress like that. The way you express your brand visually can set you up to be liked or to *not* be liked, and it's the first thing people see when you walk into an interview or into your new cubicle after being hired.

not an earned privilege, and expect to be making $125,000 by the time they're twenty-five. I hate to break it to you, but that's not likely to happen these days, no matter how brilliant or authentic you are. If you're trying to get into fashion, you might have to cocktail-waitress at night while you take classes at FIT and send your résumé repeatedly to every designer in town; you'll probably have to settle for a small apartment or, even worse, a roommate; and when you do get a job you'll probably be organizing a closet and coordinating messenger deliveries for twelve hours a day. But these experiences will broaden your empathy, test your courage, and teach you essential lessons about your job and yourself. In fact, if your job still turns you on after these kinds of experiences, then fashion probably *is* the career for you.

I understand that it takes a lot of courage to reach out to somebody who has made it in his or her field. For one thing, we are programmed to be terribly afraid of rejection. Most of us grew up being supported and protected by our parents, and suddenly we're facing a harsher world in which we're overlooked at the bar, our boyfriends break up with us, and we're not getting jobs. Often the problem is not that parents didn't encourage their kids to dream, but that parents were so encouraging that those dreams became their children's expectations.

Ultimately, if you're doing what you're meant to do—if you're in your truth—doors will open for you. I see it in clients like Jeremy Scott, who uses fashion to express his one-of-a-kind pop-art sensibilities, and friends like Mary Ellen Mark, who has revolutionized black-and-white photography. Jeremy and Mary Ellen are great talents, but they're also relentlessly themselves;

they are the best guardians and defenders of their own brands. Like them, I believe that I'm not just receiving teachings and progressing as a human being in my chosen field; in the end, I'm giving the best I have to offer to the world.

One more thing: don't think that creating and promoting your brand is a six-month program. I'm forty-four years old, and I continue to build my brand. The good news, however, is that my brand is much more powerful than it was when I started. I'm now able to use it to help everyone from interns to emerging designers to the charitable causes I care about to flailing large corporations that need an infusion of People's Revolution energy.

There are many temptations along the way—from the allure of star power and elite associations to the temptations that come in the form of sex or money. But even when your wallet or your need to be on a VIP list is calling you, stand strong and remember what your brand is about. As I've said before, the devil always comes looking good. Take Donald Trump. Many years ago, while toiling day and night as one-half of the boutique PR firm Cutrone, Weinberg & Associates, I had the chance to add considerable luster (not to mention financial oomph) to my client roster by signing Trump. It all started when he invited Eartha Kitt, our client, to perform at the Plaza Hotel, which he owned at the time. This being the Plaza, my partner Jason Weinberg and I pulled out all the stops, inviting a bicoastal troupe of glamorous friends like Virginia Madsen, Mary Stuart Masterson, Robert Downey Jr., Alek Keshishian (who directed Madonna's *Truth or Dare*), and the band Dee-Lite, whose hit at the time was "Groove Is in the Heart." As I mingled in my Randolph Duke pantsuit that night,

Trump himself walked right up to me. "I've been watching you work this room, and you're fantastic," he said. "I'd love to have a meeting with you. Here's my card, please call my secretary Norma." I nodded, stunned, but Jason, who was standing next to me, could hardly contain his excitement. The next day when I arrived at the office, he asked me if I'd called Trump yet.

"I'm not calling him," I replied. "I don't want to work with him." Trump had recently taken out an ad in the newspaper defending the innocence of his friend Mike Tyson, who was facing rape charges, and suggesting that Tyson host a fight to benefit battered women. I found the whole thing disgusting, but Jason found my moral outrage expensive. "This is ridiculous. You'll put us out of business!" he argued. And so I gave in.

Trump's penthouse offices on Fifth Avenue had intimidating panoramic views of the city, and Trump himself, then at the height of his powers as a newsmaker, was youngish, handsome, and impeccably groomed in a pink shirt and pinstripe suit. "I've worked with PR people for a long time," he said when we sat down, "and I feel like you're really different. I'd like to ask you a few questions to see how you'd handle certain situations." He told me that he was going to say a few names and that I was to answer "hot," "very hot," or "hot hot." The first name was Ivana, his newly ex-wife. "She's hot," I said honestly. "Why isn't she *very* hot?" he asked. "Well, she hasn't been away from you long enough for us to know how she's going to do on her own," I explained.

Then he asked about Marla Maples, his blond, Georgian, aspiring-actress lover. "She's not *even* hot," I said. "Why not? Why isn't she hot?" he inquired. "Any girl who throws a shoe at you in a hotel lobby is *not* hot," I replied.

Finally, Trump asked me about himself: "Am I hot, *very* hot, or *hot hot*?" I thought about this and then replied, "Barely hot." "Why would you say that?" he said, incredulous. "Anyone who would suggest Mike Tyson stage a benefit boxing match to raise money for battered women is disgusting, and you should be ashamed of yourself," I said. He stared at me and said, "Well, I guess we don't have anything left to talk about today, do we?" I thanked him politely for seeing me, and I left.

Back at the office, Jason was practically buzzing with excitement. "How did it go?" he cried. "Not very well," I admitted. "You *didn't* bring up the Mike Tyson thing?" he gasped. I slowly nodded my head, indicating, guiltily, that I had. I knew what Trump could do for our business, but everything in me intuitively balked. This was not who we were as publicists. If doing PR often requires losing your dignity, I was *not* prepared to also lose my integrity. Trump might have been a godsend for our bottom line, and he himself might also have been one of New York's most recognizable and well developed personal brands, but I still didn't want that brand anywhere near mine.[*]

---

[*] I never saw Trump again after that. That's the genius of New York: it's four miles long, I attend events several nights a week, and I haven't been in the same room as Donald Trump in over twenty years.

EIGHT

IF YOU HAVE TO CRY, GO OUTSIDE

> The details of your incompetence
> do not interest me.
>
> —from *The Devil Wears Prada*

My friends and I joke that I look like a home-wrecker—the person who's going to fuck your husband and eat your cat. Au contraire: I am a woman's woman. One of the things my job has taught me over the years is that I love knowing and working with women. I firmly believe that each woman is a goddess and that deep down inside herself she knows it. I'm known in my industry as an outspoken ballbuster, so my new employees are often shocked to find a certain level of intimacy in the People's Revolution offices. We play music, we laugh, and we dance; we work, we scream, we destroy and rebuild. (These new employees often face a barrage of questions from friends about whether I'm really a bitch and how many people I've fired. "She's a mom!" they reply. "She makes us cupcakes!")

Still, at the end of the day I'm not in the PR business to make friends. No matter how casual I may seem in the office sometimes, I fundamentally believe in grooming the next generation of women to *win*, not in trying to become their friend. My business is a boot camp, baby, for fashion bitches! And as happens in any boot camp, we have plenty of dropouts and plenty who just can't cut it. Get ready for a no-bullshit, to-the-point instruction manual for the real modern workplace that details the unspoken rules you must know to pole-vault forward on your sword of truth, light, and ambition and not get stabbed by it.

MAMA WOLF SPEAKS

By now you know I love the Goddess, but I run my office with the mentality of a more earthbound but still highly mystical creature: the wolf. To my employees, I'm Mama Wolf—I lead the pack. As PR girls in the New York fashion world, we're roaming a brutal wilderness, often fighting for our survival, and I'm here to hunt, teach, and protect, not coddle. Fashion may be beautiful to look at, but the truth is that it's kill or be killed out there, babes.

It's important that everyone understand their place in the pack and contribute accordingly to its success. Like my partners, Robyn and Emily, I am unapologetic about using titles, emphasizing seniority, and acknowledging how much time each person has put in relative to the others. I tell my girls that they should have a sense of entitlement that reflects their title, and I believe this is true regardless of where anyone works. If you're an assistant, you're entitled to *assist*. If you're an associate, you're entitled to *associate*. If you're a director, you're entitled to *direct* and to have all the privileges and responsibilities that go along with that function. It won't surprise you that when we order catering during Fashion Week to sustain us through the long nights we spend in the office seating shows and putting out fires, Robyn, Emily, and I always eat before the midlevel team, which eats before the assistants, who aren't allowed to touch the food until the rest of us have taken what we want. The senior team brings in the clients, after all, and the clients pay for the food. (Like wolves, we share our kill with our children.)

Many young people seem to think they're above the small tasks that make our office—or any office—run efficiently. I've been shocked at how many graduates of expensive, private four-year colleges cannot take phone messages. In my office, for example, if John calls, I need his last name. A phone number with seven digits requires an area code or a country code. I don't want a message that reads: "Pete, 268-7766." Well, which Pete? What city? What country? Who *is* this Pete? "Oh, he said he's a friend of yours." Gee, that narrows it down!

I can usually tell within the first day or two how an intern or entry-level employee was raised based on how they tackle menial jobs. It's often the best-educated young people, the ones who grew up in wealthy towns and have been given every opportunity, who are unable to properly affix labels to five hundred envelopes inviting editors and buyers to a fashion show. No, it isn't glamorous work, but if you treat it like the utterly important task it is—crooked labels reflect poorly on my clients' businesses and my own, and I won't tolerate them—you'll eventually be trusted with larger tasks. If not, you just may be fired at 2:00 a.m. in the middle of Fashion Week—like three particularly daft assistants in my office two years ago. "Thank you very much, that will be all," I said, standing up in disgust after they botched a series of small tasks. "What time should we be here tomorrow?" they asked. "Tomorrow? There is no tomorrow," I said. I cut them checks and asked them never to come back to my office again.

When I open up my office to interns and assistants, I'm not just using them to get my coffee—I'm offering to teach them how to succeed in my business and, if they work hard, give them my stamp of approval. I'm giving them a front-row seat to the workings of my entire industry, helping them to figure out where they might fit into it and giving them the contacts to progress toward their dreams. These are lessons and tools you won't get in a classroom.

If you fail to treat your internships and early work experiences as the amazing learning experiences they are, you sabotage opportunities with the company you're working for *and* you fail to cultivate the friends and mentors who might be resources or might give you recommendations in the future. When I like an intern and I can't hire that person myself, I make phone calls; I go out of my way to help her get the job she wants. And I do this for her not because she has great style or she got my client featured on the *Today Show*; usually I go out of my way to help her because she fetched coffee and affixed labels cheerfully and efficiently and eagerly pitched in wherever she could. In other words, she understood and fulfilled her role in the pack to the best of her ability.

Still, while it's important to be humble and to do even small tasks as carefully as you can, remember that an employer who has invested in you wants your *whole* self at the office, not just your "work" self. When most people are first entering the job market at age twenty-two, they don't yet know how to launch a new product or run front-of-house at a fashion show, and they don't know how to make snap decisions or close the deal at a pitch meeting. What they *do* have is freshness, enthusiasm, questions, creativity, and a point of view. And sometimes it's a pair of fresh eyes that changes the way we do things and alters the course of our business. I would be impressed if an assistant came into my office and said, "I don't know if you know this, but my mom used to own a flower shop, and I'd like to tell you about the way they did their filing, because I think it would really help this office's organization." Knowing your place in the pack doesn't mean restricting your contributions; it just means keeping your entitlement in check.

The assistant or intern who knows her place in the pack also is someone who calls attention to herself, *not* because she's a fun party girl—or because she wears nice shoes, or because she says things like, "I just wanted to let you know that I found some paper towels on the floor and I picked them up and put them back where they should go"—but because of the work she's doing. I'm going to notice if someone's a picker-upper; I don't need to be interrupted and informed that an intern just pinch-hit a janitorial move for me. I'm looking for people who pull their weight in the pack and contribute to its success and vitality without distracting the rest of us from doing the same.

When I say, know your place in the pack, I'm not just telling you to expect fewer privileges than your higher-ups. I'm suggesting that you use the early years of your career, and the cover of the pack, to really learn how to hunt. I am forty-four, and I don't cry

THE *EM*POWERED GIRLS' GUIDE TO DRESSING FOR WORK

[1] No wife-beaters

[2] No cleavage

[3] No belly buttons

[4] No muffin-top

[5] No stilettos or heels over three inches

[6] No flip flops

[7] No gold lamé

[8] *Absolutely* no corduroy

[9] No belly piercings, eyebrow rings, facial piercings, or any other piercings that don't involve an ear

[10] Nothing obviously more expensive than what your boss wears

[11] No Christian Audigier or Ed Hardy, which are forever banned from fashionable workplaces everywhere

[12] No skipping the bra, even if you don't think you need one

[13] No cross-dressing

when a client screams at me. I have enough power and enough experience to tell a screaming client to calm down and get his shit together before he calls me back. But when you're twenty-four and you have a famous designer on the phone threatening to kill you, it can be pretty devastating. Recently, when one of my girls was verbally abused by one of the most powerful talent publicists in the country over a *Gossip Girl* star—the publicist wrongly accused us of alerting the gossip columns that the star had been partying at a nightclub we represented—I stepped in and forcefully (an understatement) put her in her place.

The more successful you become, and the higher your rank in the pack, the more often you have to assume the hunter's role. I'd prefer to spend less time defending my pack and chasing the money we're owed, but I don't always have that luxury. The animal kingdom is ruthless, and when threatened, a female wolf will attack. She's not going to say, "Oh, I'm spiritual, come on in! Do you want to sleep with my mate? Do you want to steal my babies?" She will howl and fight to the fucking end.

Several years ago, we represented a Greek designer who looked like David Hasselhoff and was screwing a married Greek woman from the Upper East Side who was bankrolling his business. Like many clients, he didn't pay his bill. So when the time came for him to pick up his samples—fashion-speak for the clients' clothing we keep in our office to send out to photo shoots—I refused to let them out of my sight. I knew that once the clothes were gone, he'd never pay the bill, and since this had happened more than once in the past, I'd written a clause into our contract stating that I could hold the clothes until I was paid. This angered his lover, a fifty-something former beauty queen, who stormed into my office one day screaming and yelling things like: "*You will not do this! You will not treat him like this! He is a star in Greece!*" She carried on until I told her that if she didn't leave my office I would call 911. "There's someone here trying to remove things that I have the right to keep," I told the operator when she still refused to leave. "I can throw the bitch out the window, or you can come down here and handcuff her and make her leave." When the police arrived, I produced the contract and explained that I had every right to keep the clothes. The beauty queen went ballistic and was escorted out. She soon paid her bill.

Believe it or not, I lose up to $200,000 each year in unpaid bills. That's over $2.6 million in the thirteen years I've been in business. The point is that being Mama Wolf is no joke; that persona is not just about having someone to get me coffee. Sometimes, if you don't eat others, they will eat *you*.

I take great pride in the fact that, despite our hunter's mentality, in our office we do not encourage hurting our own to get ahead, and we do not reward selling other people down the river in the name of competition. If someone is having a nervous breakdown or a panic attack or a drug or alcohol problem, which comes up from time to time, we pull that person aside and say, "We're going to work through this with you." We don't leave an injured wolf in the forest.

Even though I am sometimes perceived as a bitch or a witch, the office atmosphere I cultivate is nothing like the cultural stereotype of striving women clawing each other to death to get the queen bee's job. Women have been taught that, in order to get ahead, we have to be secretive and plotting and manipulative, because a straightforward route to the top hasn't always existed for us, and in many industries it still doesn't. But I don't believe in playing into these stereotypes. We don't *have* to stab each other in the back, we don't *have* to take things personally and break down when we're criticized, and we don't *have* to advance at each other's expense. Being a member of a pack, whether it's a group of males or females or both, is about recognizing each other as assets to the common advancement of the pack and about cooperation as a means of survival. If everyone plays their role to the best of their ability—and if you have a few good hunters on hand—everyone will always have enough to eat. (And ultimately you will also change the makeup of the forest.)

YOUR BOSS

One of the first rules you learn when you start working in my office is that if you have to cry, you go outside. Picture this scene, which has been repeated many times in my office over the years. An intern carrying a $5,000 gown up the steps is so eager to please and be noticed that she doesn't notice that she's dragging it on a hardwood floor that was built in 1898 and has been soaking up dirt and grime ever since. The bottom of the gown is soon black, and rather than being on its way to a shoot with Steven Meisel, it is now headed to the dry cleaners, thus costing my client an opportunity to be shot for Italian *Vogue*. I confess that it is not my priority to convey my displeasure in the sweetest way possible: "Oh, excuse me, honey, if you don't mind, could you please be a little bit more careful?" My response is more like, *"Pick. It. Up. Now!"* I'm concerned about the job our office is being paid to do, not about the feelings of the person who has kept us from doing it.

When my employees make a mistake, I want them to fix the problem as quickly as possible and move on. The last thing I or any other boss wants to hear is, *"Wahhhh,* I was just trying to be helpful, *wahhhh!"* That's why I officially banished crying to the sidewalk outside. You think I'm a bitch? Fine. Go sit on the street and call your friend and talk shit about me all day. Just get out of my office and stop psychically blowing my vibe and that of the others who came here to make money and be serious instead of being jokers. We may cultivate a purposefully casual atmosphere in our offices, but that doesn't mean we have a casual attitude about work. If we as women want equal rights in the workplace, it's time for us to start acting like equals. You call yourself a feminist? You say you want to advance the women's movement? Then acknowledge that you're no different than anyone else and deserve no special treatment. Haul those FedEx boxes and don't give me or anyone else the luxury of seeing you lose control of your emotions in a professional setting. Once you enter a workplace, you're surrounded by grown-ups, not friends. Your boss is not your boyfriend, and she's not your therapist. She is a person who is paying you to do a job. If you (or she, for that matter) think otherwise, you will be burned.

Still, though she's not your friend, your boss *is* a human being—a little empathy never hurts. Take me, for example. I'm a single mom, I live and work in the same building, and every minute of my day is spent answering the demands of somebody else, from my assistant to my clients to my nanny to my daughter. Because of this, I usually have to eat at my desk while many women at my level treat themselves to uber-chic lunches at the Four Seasons or Cipriani. People call me all day with ridiculous questions like, "Can you get a white horse to a photo shoot in the next twenty-five minutes, because the designer is having a heart attack and will cancel the shoot unless we get a white horse!" If I occasionally snap, "Get away from me, I'm on the phone!" it could be because you're the fourteenth person who has interrupted me since my last latte. Or perhaps the business is taking on more debt and I'm stressed out. Maybe my father is sick. From a very young age women are taught by the culture to regard other women in power as witchy or bitchy, but don't ever take it for granted that your boss is being a cunt because she feels like being a cunt. If you're an oncologist and you've repeat-edly had to tell moms with kids that they're going to die, after a while you might seem a little cool when you deliver such news, even if you started out as open-hearted as anyone.

Nobody knows why another person developed his or her individual style. All you can control is how you react to it and how you learn from various situations at work. Even the boss you think of as a tyrant is teaching you how *not* to be a boss, and that's almost as valuable as knowing how to do it. Positive and negative role models are essentially the same: they're both pushing you toward your own voice, your own brand, and your own style. In other words, you can resolve to learn as much as possible from the people around you, and especially those above you, whether they're benevolent leaders or total maniacs.

I am not the kind of boss who micromanages her employees' to-do lists; I was subjected to that early in my career in Susan Blond's office, and I thought it was a huge waste of time. Instead, I hire people who can manage their own time without my help. But working in Susan's office didn't just teach me what not to do. I *am*, for instance, the kind of boss who will not be held hostage for money when my employees get an offer from a competing

PR firm, and that is something I learned from Susan. (If you've been interviewing elsewhere, my view is that you already have one foot out the door and it's not in my best interest to fight to keep you.)

If you work in a close environment and your boss is someone who keeps her door open, don't be afraid to pop in occasionally and say, "Look, I'm going to go out and get a soda, can I get you anything?" Treat your boss like the queen of her castle, but also like a human being with needs who might feel somewhat imprisoned by her life. Instead of thinking, *Why is this person making me go out in ninety-degree weather to get her coffee?* look at it this way: *What must it be like to not have twenty minutes to go outside and walk to get her own coffee on a summer day?* I'm constantly hearing from people, "Oh, what a brutal winter it's been!" and I'm like, "*Really?* I haven't left the office in days!" I was an assistant once too; I know what it's like to struggle to pay your bills and to be at the mercy of someone you occasionally regard as a lunatic. I'm empathetic toward my girls. But I've also gone without paychecks so that they can get paid. Lower-level employees tend to think the boss has made it and has things easy compared to everyone else, but trust me: if she's still working, she hasn't made it.

THE INTER*NOTS*

Recently an intern in my office—I'll call her Anna—decided to entertain readers of her personal blog with stories about her "VERY *Devil Wears Prada*-esque" summer working at People's Revolution. "Interning has taken over my life," she reported breathlessly. "We all work at least 11 hours a day [*lie!*], without a proper lunch break [*lie!*] . . . in fact we are not allowed to eat in the office and we sneak food in the back room." *Lie! Lie! Lie!* She continued: "On a brighter note, I met Kelly today—she was nice but crazy. Last weekend she was hospitalized because her patent leather Prada boots stuck together and she tripped." Okay, that part was true: I'd recently returned to New York in a full leg brace after an afternoon business meeting ended with me flying into the air and smashing down on my hands and knees.[*]

The veracity of Anna's claims mattered little, however, because she had signed a non-disclosure agreement, or NDA, that prohibited her from writing anything about my company, my clients, or me. The offending post was brought to my attention by another intern, and when I read it, I immediately left a message for Anna on her cell phone (she was off that day). "Hi, Anna, it's Kelly Cutrone, how's it going?" I asked casually when she called me back. "Can I ask you what you're majoring in in college? Oh, really. Are you minoring in law, by any chance? No? Well, maybe you should!" I screamed that she had fifteen minutes to take down her post or I would sue her and her family for all the money they had.

The rest of my interns, taking in the scene from a U-shaped table no more than ten feet from my desk, froze in fear. I believe in an occasional public firing (when deserved, of course) for exactly

---

[*] I felt silly sitting in the emergency room waiting with people who needed three hundred stitches or were having heart attacks, but I still thought to ask if I could get some basic bloodwork done for a breast reduction I'd been meaning to have. Hey, I am a busy woman, and since I was at the hospital already. . . . Unfortunately, the emergency room flat-out refused to draw my blood and send it to my plastic surgeon on Park Avenue.

this reason. Usually we hide consequences away, in prisons or in rehab. But telling seventh-graders that crime doesn't pay is probably less effective than taking them to a prison to let them see for themselves what happens if you steal or rape or vandalize—now *that's* going to deter them. I certainly didn't go into business thinking I'd need a lawyer to draw up an NDA to protect me from people I'm trying to help by opening my doors and teaching them how to work in my profession. But among the many young women (and the occasional man) clamoring for jobs in fashion these days are those in whom a compulsive need to share everything online is matched only by a healthy sense of entitlement instilled by overinvolved parents.

When I was growing up in the industry, we didn't have hazards like Facebook.* Social media sites may be an increasingly important tool in public relations and other professions—I regularly use Facebook to promote my clients—but for entry-level job-seekers accustomed to using these sites for purely personal reasons, they are fraught with danger. If you're going to post things online about yourself or other people, you have to be aware of how those messages are being followed—not only by your boss, who probably doesn't have time to personally monitor your Facebook page, but by your coworkers. Assume they are reading whatever you post, whether on Facebook or your blog or Twitter.

Even if you're not doing something outrageously stupid like violating an NDA or bad-mouthing a superior, think hard

---

* I now like to say that my Facebook page is a collection of all the people I've been trying to avoid for the past twenty years.

about whether you want your coworkers to see pictures of you drunk and half-naked at that sorority barbecue senior year, or whether you want them to know that you're trying to have sex with the office's accessories director. You're not in high school or college anymore, and if you set out to re-create your family or college friend relationships, you will regret it. Even someone who seems like your go-to office buddy, the one who's in on all the gossip and pointing you in the right direction, might just be steering you toward a crocodile-infested lake. It's best to assume that everything you say and do can and probably will be used against you, and water-cooler talk is now much easier to trace since it's usually available for everyone to read online. Anna made not one but two mistakes: writing about me, and not having the foresight to guess that one of her peers would find it and tell me. When people get fired, it's often because they let their guard down (*or* because they have highly overrated their own importance in the office).*

There's another lesson to be learned here. The more successful you become, the more people will write lies about you on the Internet, both your own employees and anonymous commenters on websites. Your success is an invitation to others to use you as a blank slate onto which they can project fears, aspirations, and prejudices. This has been a harsh pill for me to swallow at times, but ultimately I'd rather be the one *living* the life than observing and making catty comments about it.

---

* If only lower-level employees knew that my senior staff and I sit around during times of economic peril and console ourselves by discussing how we could still run our company with six people instead of twenty-four. Often we even fantasize about who we'd let go and why.

Maybe what set me off about Anna in particular was her ridiculous suggestion that my interns are expected to "hide food in the back." For the record: I *make* food for my employees. We eat all day long. We order cakes from Dean & DeLuca. Hell, we fly in a chef from India during some Fashion Weeks to cook for the girls! We take food dead seriously. Do not ever suggest that Mama Wolf starves her pack.

GIVE GOOD PHONE

Long before I got my first job in PR, I learned of experiments conducted in the 1950s by a scientist named Harry Harlow. Harlow separated baby rhesus monkeys from their mothers and presented them with replacement "mothers"; some were made of wire, and others were made of terry cloth. The monkeys universally chose to cling to the terry-cloth mothers, even when only the wire mothers had bottles of milk attached to them. In separate social isolation experiments, Harlow's monkeys responded to long periods of solitary confinement by developing lasting psychological trauma, often rocking autistically when presented with scary stimuli. Harlow's results were taken as groundbreaking proof of the basic need for tactile and social contact among higher primates like monkeys and humans.

This study resonated deeply with me at the time, and it informs the way I do my job to this day. I fear our modern loss of human contact. We're addicted to devices and programs that make us feel like we're connecting when in fact we're just becoming more and more isolated and more and more silent. We use Facebook, texting, and e-mail as substitutes for actual human contact; we even call each other's voice mails to avoid actually speaking to each other! And as we get more and more used to electronic means of communication, our senses receive less and less stimulation and our interactions are stripped of their *humanness*. Our tribes dissolve even further. I believe this is what has made us more neurotic and more violent and even more depressed.

My prescription for this dilemma would be to hold one big human square dance, but in the meantime I insist in my business on breaking down the barriers erected by technology and actually talking to other people. I *insist* on giving good phone. As a species, we cannot afford to live on e-mail or to save our intimate communication for only late nights and weekends. Work is where I spend most of my time, as do most people. No two people can establish a high-quality personal *or* business relationship without actually talking to each other. My insistence on calling people on the phone all day has not only helped me form lasting relationships but is now an important part of my brand, and it has played no small part in my success.

It's not that I'm against e-mail—but I do believe that e-mail is a way of documenting things, not *doing* them. It is a great way to reiterate and bullet-point something you discussed with someone, whether in person or on the phone, and it is also a way to reach out to somebody to request a discussion. E-mail was supposed to save us time, but it usually ends up wasting our time. (And we end up sleeping with our BlackBerries under the pillow, as I did for years.) Why do I need to send four e-mails to arrange a dinner? ("Yes." "See you at 8." "Confirmed." "Great.") Why not just tell my assistant to make a fucking phone call?

TOP TEN CAREER DON'TS—OR, HOW *NOT* TO GET A CAREER IN FASHION

[1] Don't send a résumé in May hoping to get hired in the fashion business, as it's the slowest time of year. To increase your chances of securing a top-level job, try January or August.

[2] Do not Facebook the owner of a company or any prospective boss. Or if you do, make sure you have something interesting and out-of-the-box to say that warrants her two minutes; don't just reveal that you went to college and took a résumé-writing class.

[3] Don't roll your eyes. Or if you do, roll with them toward the exit sign and then head out the door.

[4] Don't expect equal rights in the workplace without being willing to do equal work, which includes transporting heavy garment bags, loading and unloading FedEx and UPS shipments, and rolling racks of clothing down New York City's uneven sidewalks. People's Revolution is an equal-opportunity employer.

[5] Don't call in sick when you're not. At People's Revolution, we give employees the dignity of five personal days a year. I instituted this policy so that I would never have to begin my morning listening to sad stories in faux-raspy

In New York, aversion to the human voice has reached epidemic proportions. Recently I called a modeling agent's assistant to make an offer on a supermodel and received a depressingly familiar response. I told the assistant that my client wanted the model to appear at Russian Fashion Week, where they'd pay her $20,000 for one show. "That sounds great," he said. "Can you send me an e-mail?" "What did I just do?" I replied. "I gave you voices about not feeling good enough to make it to the office that day.

[6] If you're going to be a helper around the office and do things you know your boss wants done—for me that means sweeping the floor and taking out the garbage—don't jump up and down and give her a play-by-play each time you finish a task. She knows. Don't underestimate her radar in her own environment.

[7] Do not try to re-create your family at work.

[8] Do not overemphasize your nationality or gender as a way of making a point. You may be a gay man, but you still have no right to wear a skirt and twirl around in the middle of the day proclaiming you're king of the fairies. And if you're from San Francisco and a closet Zappatista, that does not give you the right to play Rage Against the Machine and scream out Che slogans.

[9] Do not think your boss owes you anything other than your paycheck.

[10] And finally, don't cry in the office. Ever. If you have to cry, go outside.

the dates, I gave you the terms, *you're* the assistant, *you* write it up and give it to your boss! *You* fucking write the e-mail!"

The truth is that your communications arsenal is diminished when you're e-mailing instead of speaking: you lose your powers of empathy, tone, charm, and nuance. You also risk failing to communicate entirely. If Paul Revere had sent an e-mail to the colonists alerting them that the British were coming, I would hope he'd also have ridden his horse over to make sure they got it. I hate it when my staffers tell me they pitched a story to a writer when what they mean is that they *e-mailed* the writer and it's quite possible that e-mail is still sitting in that writer's junk box. In fact, there's nothing that scares me more than seeing an office full of people on my payroll, all of whom are communications professionals or aspire to be, sitting there in total silence—i.e., the phone is not ringing and no one is speaking. If we're all being honest, we know that the only reason we text or e-mail each other in the first place is because we're hiding: we don't have time to talk, or we're too shy, or, as in my case, we just don't like the person. (This is a valid use of e-mail: when you really don't want to be intimate with someone and do wish to alienate them.) But when we hide from our fears instead of facing them, we are unlikely to progress as businesspeople or as human beings.

My love for the phone has not only separated me from the hordes of noncommunicating publicists over the years; it has saved my ass repeatedly. One season I had several clients showing their collection at the SoHo Grand, a downtown hotel that I also happened to represent. We realized the Friday before Fashion Week that the hotel's point person had failed to secure the necessary permits from the Building Commission. After a few frantic phone calls, we learned that the commission had put a hold on giving out new permits owing to a few recent building collapses. I reacted the only way I knew how: by making phone calls until I was blue in the face. I figured out the identity of the only man in the city authorized to sign permits, and I set about befriending his assistant, a woman named Veronica. I begged. I prayed. I called Veronica again and again. In my days as a recording artist, I'd written a song called "Veronica Says Hello." I played this for her over the phone (I was desperate). At first Veronica was unmoved; in fact, she kept repeating things like, "No one is *ever* given these things in a day. You're *never* going to get it. These things take months to get." But through some combination of charm and persistence, I wore her down, and she eventually put her boss on the phone.* I told him the truth, speaking from my heart and appealing directly to his. "We have designers who have flown in from all over the world to show at this venue, and because of the negligence of one person they're not going to be able to promote their businesses," I said. "They'll be devastated." He told me he'd see what he could do and hung up. Several hours later, just minutes before 3:00 p.m., when the Building Commission's offices were closing for Labor Day weekend, he called back. "Send somebody down here right now and I'll sign it," he said. I had an intern positioned outside on the street in hopeful anticipation of this very scenario. I hung up the phone and burst into tears of exhaustion and gratitude. (I allow myself a good cry in the office once or twice a year, provided they're tears of happiness.)

Here's another true story. In 2009 two young women from different publishing houses contacted me to offer me book deals. One called me on the phone. I liked her immediately, and we soon agreed to work together. Some months later, after I'd already

---

* This is another important lesson: *always* be nice to other people's assistants.

inked a deal with her imprint, HarperOne, I was going through my junk e-mail folder and found an e-mail from the woman at the other publishing house, offering me a similar deal. I did her the favor of picking up the phone and calling her to tell her never to rely on e-mail as her primary form of communication.

BE THE FIRST ONE IN AND THE LAST ONE TO LEAVE

Most young people who arrive at my office and say they want what I have are not going to get it for one simple reason: they're not willing to do the work. It's mathematics. One plus one equals two. If you consistently show up and do your best, you're going to win the prize. If you do a great job one day and then are kind of tired the next day and don't really feel like working that hard, come in late, and spend the afternoon uploading pictures to Facebook, you're not going to win the prize. Much like building your brand, getting good at something requires consistency and repetition. There is no other way. With few exceptions, you will get out what you put in.

Hard work is a great equalizer. I came from nothing, but from the earliest days of my career in PR I told the truth, I never complained, I was willing to do whatever it took, and I didn't let people kill me in the process. Even as I made plenty of other personal and professional mistakes, my work ethic served me well. To this day, I'm often the first one in the office and the last one to leave, though I make a point of not letting my assistants leave before I do. I don't care if they're done with their work and are sitting there texting their friends. They're going to sit with me. Why? Because I might want a coffee. And if you think that it's my job, at the age of forty-four, to go find a coffee for myself while I'm slaving over a new-business pitch at 10:00 p.m., you're wrong. I'm training my staff to work the hours the job will require. If you want to leave work at six every day, don't work in fashion, and *don't* aspire to be an entrepreneur.

Besides, you'll learn quickly that it's during late nights at the office that the good stuff really happens. Holding a high-pressure job like fashion publicity is like working in an emergency room: maybe you wake up and make a list of the things you're going to get done that day, but then a massive car crash sends in fifty injured people who need treatment immediately, all your planning goes out the window, and by 5:00 p.m. you still haven't crossed a single thing off your list. It's often not until the end of the day that I can stop putting out fires and focus with my partners and senior team on the meat-and-potatoes of the business. It's the time when we argue and brainstorm about where to present a fashion show, who to invite, who should do the makeup and in what color scheme, the music, the seating—all the things that go into creating a show. After-hours in the office is when people drop their guard a little bit; I get to see people like my partners Robyn and Emily, who are more buttoned-up and rigid with their teams, engage in more casual repartee. You can learn a lot during the late hours in an office, from what you want in your marriage to how to put together a great pitch to when you should use a semicolon. When I promote my assistants, I usually take them shopping for a duvet cover and some 800-thread-count sheets because, as a fashion publicist, I joke that their bed will quickly become their favorite place on earth. It's the place where we fuck and where we sleep—two favorite activities we hold close to our hearts, but sadly don't have much time for.

Of course, you also have to learn where to draw the line. Take on as much as you can and soak up as much as you can, but learn to say no when the situation demands it. Don't become the office martyr. I can't tell you how many times my employees have sabotaged projects because they couldn't say, "I need help," or, "I don't understand what's going on here," or, only three hours before deadline, "I'm worried we're not going to meet this deadline." Bosses and owners of companies, who make their living thinking big picture, may not recall how long it takes to execute smaller tasks. Don't be afraid to tell your boss what you need to meet a deadline, whether it's another team member or being removed from another project you're working on. You have to know when to send up an SOS.

No boss wants an employee she's invested in to burn out. Your employer *wants* you to succeed. I don't actually enjoy firing people—well, with the exception of one or two—and most other bosses would probably say the same thing. Think for a moment about what kind of an investment your employer makes in you. You may think the playing field is slanted in the employer's favor since technically the employer can fire you at any time.* It's true that you can be fired if you fuck up or if you just don't work hard or for many other valid or trivial reasons, but as an employee you are also a lot more powerful than you realize.

---

* This fact of life was one of the reasons I became an entrepreneur, as you'll recall: I didn't like having my fate depend on another person. Nowadays I get fired all the time, but each time it involves only one client among many, not my entire livelihood.

If I hire a senior publicist at $100,000 a year, I have another 30 percent in expenses to pay, including taxes, a BlackBerry, a computer, and unemployment insurance. Hiring this employee is a very costly thing to do, so it's in my best interest if it works out. In addition to the expense, there's the training. Hiring someone is almost like adopting them, especially in a field like PR, which can't really be taught in any college course. I'm not like a chief resident at a hospital acquiring a fully trained surgeon; I'm usually getting a twenty-two-year-old who may or may not have taken a few "Communications" classes in college taught by an academic who's never worked in the industry. I'm agreeing to educate and mentor my new employee and put time and energy into helping her develop the skills that will allow her to interact with my clients as a representative of my company. I want a return on this investment; I'm not sitting around waiting for my new employee to screw up so I can get rid of her and start the headache all over again. All employers are vulnerable to this dynamic, even if they don't acknowledge it.

When my partner Robyn was working too much lately, to the detriment of everything else in her life, I ordered her to spend a month in our L.A. office. I knew that she would never give herself such a break, but I also knew that she needed it. When you suddenly find yourself drinking alone every night or looking in the mirror at vacant eyes, it might be time for you to take a time out too. All of us in this industry, and in any intense industry, need to escape from it occasionally in order to survive. (It's why I have a log cabin in the woods where I retreat every weekend to wear Wellies and row my daughter around a lake in our rowboat.)

There will be days when, regardless of what you do and how much you love it, you'll be disgusted and/or exhausted by it. Anyone at the top of any career has survived their share of mistakes and embarrassments and sleepless nights. I instituted rules like "If you have to cry, go outside," because I've cried. In fact, I've *wailed*! As a young publicist who had not yet learned to control her emotions, I chased people out of my showroom all the time when they offended my client or me, whether by returning a sample item of clothing that had been damaged or by refusing to acknowledge its brilliance. Then, alone, I'd lock the door to my office and break down. Detachment is about learning to have faith in your actions and remembering that you're more than what you do for a living. *And* having a good laugh every once in a while.

When People's Revolution launched the line of the British lingerie company Agent Provocateur in the United States in 2001, we planned an exclusive cocktail party for the press at the brand's new L.A. store. Agent Provocateur made it very clear that the pink color and logo of its brand was a very *specific* pink— Pantone 96C Pink. So I proposed serving perfect Pantone-pink petit-fours with AGENT PROVOCATEUR written on them in black icing. We approached a local L.A. bakery like the really intense PR people we are, barking things like: "Do you understand? This Pantone color has to match *perfectly*! We will accept nothing less than 96C Pantone!" The baker managed to pull it off. So there we were in this elegant, brand-new lingerie store, serving up beautiful little cakes to a crowd packed with celebrities like Dita Von Teese and editors from *Vogue* and the *L.A. Times*. Suddenly I saw

Joe Corre, our client and the owner of Agent Provocateur (also the son of Vivienne Westwood and Malcolm McLaren, incidentally), standing in the corner laughing hysterically, nearly pissing himself. He had already seen what I was about to see: Margot Dougherty, the formidable then-fashion editor of *Los Angeles Magazine*, was turning to me to exclaim, "What a great party!" with black icing staining her lips and teeth. I scanned the room in horror, seeing black tongues everywhere I looked. The icing had semipermanently stained everyone's mouths and lips. I spent half the event in a panic, dragging various fashionable editors into the bathroom under the pretense of showing them "our new vintage wallpaper!" The whole thing was very *I Love Lucy*. But hey, I learned an important lesson: never serve black icing at an event. My mistakes have been some of the best teachers of my life.

NINE

BITCH IS NOT A BAD WORD:
A Call to Arms for a
Return to the Ancient Feminine

> The best way of helping others
> is to transform oneself. Be perfect
> and you will be in a position
> to bring perfection to the world.
>
> —Mirra Alfassa (the Mother)

> We aspire for a knowledge truly
> knowing, for a power truly powerful,
> for a love that truly loves.
>
> —Mirra Alfassa (the Mother)

When I was eleven, I be-
came, by sheer force of will, the first female umpire in my small
town in upstate New York. I had no great love for baseball, but
what's not to love about sitting in the park all day surrounded
by cute boys in tight pants and getting the power job of saying
who's out and who's not? (Clearly, I already liked to call it like
I saw it.) I didn't umpire as any sort of feminist protest; in fact,
I was totally unaware that sexism existed! There were no rules
expressly prohibiting girl umpires, I didn't know about Title IX,
and I also didn't know that women weren't paid the same wages
for the same work, that some chose to sleep their way to the top
or to make their money from the sidelines, or that female sports-
casters were unheard of at the time. In other words, I had no
idea that there was anything different about us. But no sooner
did I make my first call than the controversy began. Certain
families seemed convinced that I couldn't possibly understand
the rules of baseball; they booed me, sometimes even shouting

mean things like, "Go back to your princess party!" This was when I first understood that some people really hate women in power. What shocked me then and saddens me still is that many of these people are other women. Back on the baseball diamond, the mothers' derision was even louder than the fathers'.

Throughout this book I've encouraged you to embark on an inner journey. But as you move closer to inhabiting and manifesting your true self in all its compassion as well as all its ruthlessness—which will inevitably bring you success in the world, regardless of your job—be prepared: there are people with Uzis waiting on the other side of the glass ceiling who want to kill you. Over the years the playground taunts leveled at me have only intensified. I've been called a bitch, a witch, and a cunt; I've been called a dyke, a troublemaker, and a man (not that I dislike any of those words or types of people). The more successful you become, the more people will project their fears and hatred onto you. This is true for anyone, but it is particularly true of women who dare to speak their minds or assume leadership. Our culture seems to think that women in power are still something new and shocking and we need to be put in our place. But let's face it: women have not exactly been wallflowers throughout history. Powerful women are not an invention of feminism or the twentieth century. Take Cleopatra, who rose to power in Egypt through some combination of smarts and brutality and sex appeal, or Hatshepsut, also of Egypt, who was one of the most powerful women in the world by 1492 BCE. The ancient world and ancient belief systems are full of examples of women who were both fierce and loving, both power brokers and peacemakers. It was only with the rise of more recent religions like Christianity and Islam that women were veiled and screwed into believing they were inferior and powerless and stuck. ("All these breasts are really distracting us from our important holy work; let's make these women cover up, or better yet, let's get rid of them entirely!")

This book is a call to arms (hopefully, arms that have been toned by a trainer, pilates, or Iyengar yoga!). It isn't about being angry women, or becoming men, or going at it without men. Actually, it's not about men at all, even though it's important to note that men have been programmed by cultural forces too and in fact may have it even worse than women right now. (They don't know what they're supposed to do or how they're supposed to act.) But I'm not here to talk to straight guys. Let them build their own army. I'm here to talk to women and gay men.

We have work to do. We've lost all sense of duality in the world, and we're out of balance. In fact, we're dizzy. Women have ascended to the highest perches in many companies and governments, and a single woman who wants to have a baby can get sperm FedExed to her from anywhere. And yet we still have arranged marriage in half the world, and even in the most progressive countries we're taught that as women we should above all be sexy so we can find a guy who will buy us a big ring. Don't get me wrong: if you want to have a vulnerable and open relationship with somebody you love, and you've thought hard about what marriage means to *you*, I think it's great—awesome—if you want to get married. But there are a lot of things we do, or don't do, for other people's reasons. Destructive messaging for chicks is everywhere. It starts with Disney and continues right on up to *Sex and the City*, which, in my opinion, ruined

New York women; there's nothing more depressing than seeing four supposedly liberated girlfriends tromping down the street in thousands of dollars' worth of clothes looking like they just spent three hours getting ready to go out and meet men. Most girls on TV are just saying things like, "Do you think he's gonna call me?" It's not surprising that some people, not knowing how to react when a woman breaks this mold, regress to taunts and sneers. The fact that a lot of the name-callers—at least the ones I've come across—continue to be other women just proves that we believe the lies we've been told about ourselves, and worse, that we're passing them down to our daughters.

The truth is that we're not more or less powerful than men; we are partners with men and have an equally important role to play in the progression of the universe. I believe in a rebalancing between the masculine and the feminine, both inside and outside ourselves. I'm not asking you to become a man; I'm asking you to become a *woman*. To awaken and embrace your true feminine powers and stop relying on men to support you or blow your mind. For many people, the ancient feminine is a veiled concept; the images of power we see around us are usually masculine, from Italian gangsters to—worse—American CEOs. But in Hinduism, for example, the feminine is represented by four different goddesses: one who brings grace and light (Maheshwari), one who destroys everything that is false (Kali), one who creates beauty out of what is left (Lakshmi), and one who puts everything in its place (Saraswati).* I believe that

* *This* is how to be organized.

all of these abilities are latent in every woman. We just have to find and fearlessly manifest them.

Truth be told, I have never seen "bitch" as a bad word. Instead, I see the word for what it is: a reflection of people's lack of creativity and inability to acknowledge and embrace a powerful woman. It's as if the best some people can do is give me a nod by calling me a bitch—in which case, I'll take what I can get! It's fair to say that the true definition of "bitch" is a woman who won't comply. I hope humanity evolves to a place where the word "bitch" will no longer be needed and a successful and powerful woman can just be called "strategic" and "ambitious." In the meantime, all over Salem, Massachusetts—one of my favorite towns, I take my daughter there each Halloween—there are signs that read: WITCH: Woman In Total Control of Herself. If that's what a witch is, then a BITCH must be a Babe (or Boss) In Total Control of Herself.

Ultimately, though, I'm not asking you to own your own company, or to do things my way, or to be a CEO of anything except your own journey in this world. I'm asking you to start the church of *you*. I want you to refuse to pray or play at places that won't let you speak or where your gender has no power. Or, fine, if you really have to go to these places, go with the intention of transforming them. I want you to fearlessly pursue your dreams and your destiny, conscious that you are *not* what you do, listening to your inner voice, refusing to let superficial things define you, asking yourself the hard questions about what you believe and what you will serve, fighting the fears in your own mind, and finally, loving other women in the process.

When we're young, we're taught to compete with other women for what we need to survive: money, or a husband. But if you're going to be ruthless to another woman, you'd better make sure that your intent is pure and doesn't come from jealousy or bitterness or any of the other problematic feelings and fears we're taught to have about each other ("she's a homewrecker," "she's going to steal your husband," "she's younger than you and wants your job," and so on). We need to be open to the concept that we as women have more in common than not; we need to stop thinking of each other as adversaries. I was devastated early in 2009 when I read about women in Afghanistan protesting a law that demands they submit to sex with their husbands at least every four days: many of the people pelting these brave protesters with stones were other women. The goal of our inward journey is to change the world by changing ourselves, but none of us can change the world alone. We need to help each other, or at least get out of each other's way.

It's easy to think that the problem is outside yourself, that it's all Hollywood's fault, or that it's other people who need to change. As a young party girl in New York, I often ended my nights at a club in the East Village called Save the Robots, which was open from two to eight in the morning. It served screwdrivers in Tropicana cartons and cranberry vodkas in Ocean Spray bottles. On my way home to Avenue C, I stopped regularly at a bodega to buy muffins to distribute to the homeless people in Tompkins Square Park. They began to refer to me as the Muffin Lady. But they were also laughing at me under their breath. I was trying to solve *their* problems when I was obviously loaded and going nowhere fast myself. I'm not saying we shouldn't use charity toward others as a way of learning lessons and doing good in the world, but I am saying that the primary work of our own lives is inside ourselves (it's a macro/micro kind of thing). The wars in the world are outward manifestations of the war that rages inside each of us; charity and change truly begin at home.

I've spent years wrestling with what's important in this life. Is it being the hottest, coolest girl, the one with the best job who's having the most fun, or is it escaping to someplace like India and turning my back on the material world to immerse myself in the metaphysical? The truth is that for me, neither of these lives works. They're both invalid. My journey has been about forming an "X" on the spot where the heights of glorious superficiality meet the depths of spirituality. Worldly success and divine transcendence are *not* mutually exclusive. Fame and success will *not* bring you happiness without a deeper knowledge of yourself and a connection to something greater than yourself.

At the same time, contemplating the meaning of life under a banyan tree in India is of little use to anyone. As my guru the Mother said, money is a force ruled by darkness, and it's our job to claim it in the name of the Divine, appointing ourselves trustees of her money. We do not need to be starving monks in order to be holy people; this is over in my religion, and I hope it's over in yours too. If I could wish anything for you, it would be that you could accomplish in one year what it's taken me forty-four to figure out. The world needs you. It needs you to find and fearlessly manifest your true and powerful and authentic self, and it needs you to enjoy the pleasures that are here for the taking. I hope you'll find inner peace and know the abundance of prostrating yourself in front of the Divine. And I hope you'll know other kinds of abundance too, whether it's climbing to the tops of the Himalayas or buying bracelets at the counter at Hermes. Tell them Kelly Cutrone sent you.

KELLY CUTRONE SPEAKS

These are questions culled from my Facebook page, which has become the place where I meet and interact with friends and strangers (mostly strangers) in cyberspace. On October 19, 2009, I asked my friends and fans what questions they'd like me to answer in my book. I received seventy-four questions and picked my favorites.

Do you comb your hair?

I wake up in the morning at 7:30 a.m., take care of my daughter, shower, comb my hair once, either throw it in a ponytail or don't, and then work in several time zones for the next fifteen to sixteen hours. This is how my Amish psycho killer look came about. I don't have nice hair. I don't have hair extensions, and I never will.

Why don't you wear makeup on TV?

Because unlike other people on TV, I am really working. My look has evolved out of sheer survival. I think America can handle the fact that I don't wear makeup.

How do I get an internship at People's Revolution?

We hire for three different periods during the year: January to May, June through September, and September to December. We request that our interns work a minimum of three days a week, and we prefer interns who work for college credit. That said, before worrying about getting your résumé on my desk, I suggest that you first build something that will prepare you for a high-ranking fashion career: other internships, a knowledge of the industry, a knowledge of the city you're applying to work in, and another way to make money while you seek work. Then write a meaningful letter from the heart. Your pitch letter should be something more than, "I love fashion, please help me manifest my dream." Also, check your punctuation. If you're applying to work in communications and you don't know the difference between a comma and a semicolon, maybe you should invest $50 in having someone who does know the difference proofread your cover letter. Also, do not use rhyming words on your résumé, as in, "My passion is for fashion." This works only if you're applying to work for the estate of Dr. Seuss, Nickelodeon, or the Scholastic Company.

Who are your favorite designers, past and present?

Margiela, Paco Rabanne, Paul Smith (for shades), Commes des Garçons, Yojhi Yamamoto, Couregges, Dries van Noten, Vivienne Westwood, Jeremy Scott, Zandra Rhodes, Anne Demuelemeester.

What are the characteristics that drive success in this industry?

Creativity, truth, and commitment.

Do you ever get bored with it? Like wake up and go OMFG WTF?

Yes, at least nine times a month, and sometimes more if I've been out late the night before.

How hard was it for you to get to this level in your life?

It took every breathing moment of every day I had. But I guess anyone could say that.

How do you balance your family and free time with your career?

By getting rid of the "I" in the equation. I tend to focus on my daughter and my career. I live and work in the same building. I see my daughter every day, and we go away every weekend to the country. My secret "passion for fashion" is Target.

If you could cast a love-spell on someone, who would it be?

Can I pick more than one? Gabriel Byrne, Jeremy Irons, or Leonard Cohen.

What makes for happiness in the fashion industry?

If it's happiness you're looking for, I suggest you try another profession.

What happened to curvy women?

I believe it's the consumers who drive the market, not the market that drives the consumers. I promise you that if 60 percent of society decided that chunky, Rubenesque women were the epitome of fashion chic, the first people to give it to them would be fashion designers. But society is into the concept of thinner, younger, faster, better. Look around; they've taken great American literature and turned it into Twitter.

Who was or is your greatest inspiration?

The Goddess Durga.

Where do you look for creative inspiration?

I tend to look within myself.

Do you like girls?

Once, I was walking down the street and a few canvassers asked me to give them money for an AIDS charity. I declined, because People's Revolution already gives money to several charities. As

I walked away, the two canvassers said, "You're our favorite lesbian on television!" Well, the truth is that I slept with a woman once, and afterward I coined the expression, "When push comes to shove, I prefer shove." I love women, but I have no desire to make out with them, have sex with them, or go find a sperm donor with them for my second child.

Do you believe in life after death?

Yes.

Has the work of Andy Warhol ever influenced your work?

Well, I did marry his protégé, Ronnie Cutrone, who provided a wonderful foundation of pop culture knowledge. And Andy did say that everyone would be famous for fifteen minutes. I just didn't think that would ever include me.

Why does everyone in your office have to wear all black?

Let me dispel this rumor too: the kids who work for me can wear whatever they want, except to events. When we go to events, black is the closest thing to a uniform we have. It's not identifiably any one designer. If we go to a Jeremy Scott show, we can't be wearing Donna Karan. So black keeps everyone easily recognizable and looking chic.

Why do you wear all black?

I wear all black because I don't look good in color and because it transitions easily from day to night, which is what my job requires.

What's the best city in America for fashion PR?

New York.

What will the next step in your career be?

I would love my own talk show.

What is your view on the future of fashion?

Fashion will always be important because we have to wear clothes to protect our bodies from the elements while we search for mates. That said, I think the focus will shift to emphasize the items themselves rather than huge collections. I also think that retail stores will change and that clothes will be delivered on-time instead of pre-season. Who needs wool pants from Ralph Lauren when it's 105 degrees outside? The Internet, which has played a part in the death of music, will also take a chunk out of fashion and television.

Are you into witchcraft?

When you go on television, you basically make a deal to empty yourself of everything and let the people who are watching you project everything onto you that they want, whether that be fears and hatred or hopes and aspirations. And then there are stereotypes. With women, three common stereotypes are summed up in the words "bitch," "witch," and "cunt." At least, these are the ones most commonly used to describe me. I kind of like the word "bitch." I believe I'm here to own it. But am I a witch? Frankly, it takes way too long to do all those spells. Witchcraft is outdated.

I like to think or say things and make them happen immediately. However, I do go to Salem, Massachusetts, every Halloween with my daughter, and some of my closest friends are Wiccans.

What do you like to do when you leave the office?

I cook, and I try never to answer my phone.